thanx for in Me!

A SECRET REVEALED

Tanya M. Zbitnew

Trafford
PUBLISHING

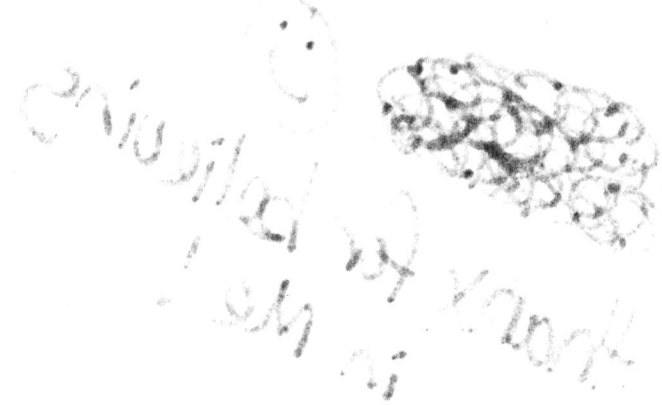

Order this book online at www.trafford.com/07-1392
or email orders@trafford.com

Most Trafford titles are also available at major online book retailers.

© Copyright 2007 Tanya M. Zbitnew.

All rights reserved. No part of this publication may be reproduced, stored in a retrieval system, or transmitted, in any form or by any means, electronic, mechanical, photocopying, recording, or otherwise, without the written prior permission of the author.

Note for Librarians: A cataloguing record for this book is available from Library and Archives Canada at www.collectionscanada.ca/amicus/index-e.html

Printed in Victoria, BC, Canada.

ISBN: 978-1-4251-3566-9

We at Trafford believe that it is the responsibility of us all, as both individuals and corporations, to make choices that are environmentally and socially sound. You, in turn, are supporting this responsible conduct each time you purchase a Trafford book, or make use of our publishing services. To find out how you are helping, please visit www.trafford.com/responsiblepublishing.html

Our mission is to efficiently provide the world's finest, most comprehensive book publishing service, enabling every author to experience success. To find out how to publish your book, your way, and have it available worldwide, visit us online at www.trafford.com/10510

 www.trafford.com

North America & international
toll-free: 1 888 232 4444 (USA & Canada)
phone: 250 383 6864 ♦ fax: 250 383 6804 ♦ email: info@trafford.com

The United Kingdom & Europe
phone: +44 (0)1865 722 113 ♦ local rate: 0845 230 9601
facsimile: +44 (0)1865 722 868 ♦ email: info.uk@trafford.com

10 9 8 7 6 5 4

This book is dedicated to Grannie and Grandad: Irene "Rene" Williams (nee: Craddock) and George Henry "Duke" Williams – together again behind the cloud.

For my mother, Georgina Irene Williams – I love you best of all.

Contents

I	*The Choosing*	1
II	*Let the Games Begin*	12
III	*An Unexpected Detour*	26
IV	*An Amazing Revelation*	42
V	*The Messenger*	61
VI	*Janastari*	80
VII	*Deserts and Dragons*	99
VIII	*A Question of Honor*	122
IX	*The Quest Begins*	142
X	*At Whistlegate Pass*	158
XI	*Separate Ways*	168
XII	*Foreign Affairs*	188
XIII	*Welcome to Shady Haven*	197
XIV	*The Hand is Dealt*	225
XV	*The Cards Fall*	240
XVI	*The Tide Turns*	253
XVII	*The Last Alliance*	271
XVIII	*Death Match*	287
XIX	*Time and Tide*	304
XX	*Epilogue*	319

I

The Choosing

A rich whiff of loam filled his nostrils as he followed the only path leading deep into the bowels of the earth, and as Camber Bloodstone took his next breath, the stench of decay made its presence known, lingering fingers that boldly recalled one sunny afternoon when he and Dane found a rotting rabbit carcass behind the woodshed. *But this was not his backyard.* Wisps of mist shrouded his feet as they stumbled over the cavern's uneven surface. His fingers were now his eyes, brushing across every crevice, every sharp stone. Slabs of rock rose up on either side; a giant hand that curled together forming a prison – *or a crypt* – for it seemed like the ancestral tombs of the ancients, and he resisted an overwhelming urge to flee.

Little hairs prickled his neck, standing up on his arms. *And there it was again.* That awful sense of someone, or something, watching.

"Who's there?" The words floating back to his ears, louder than he had intended; he looked over his shoulder half expecting to see a face, but the watcher did not appear.

Sweat ran freely down his brow, soaking his tunic. He plucked at the hem, drawing it away from his skin. A tingle touched his neck, working its way down his back, and another, a crawling sensation; furry legs creeping underneath his shirt. He ripped it over his head, tossing it across the tunnel.

"Confront your fears." His uncle's voice echoed in his ear; he clung to it, trying to find some comfort to ease his fright. At last he came to the bend. *Here it comes...* and holding his breath, he shuffled around the corner.

Sliding his hand across bare rock he reached out and felt... *nothing?* Green eyes popped open – wild they went; fingers reaching into space, searching for something solid and finding nothing but air. Teetering on his toes, he bent backward, every muscle straining to keep his balance, but at that last possible second, his body the betrayer sent him plunging into blackness.

It was here he would suddenly wake to find himself tangled up in his blankets and his bed sheets soaked with sweat. Not *this* time.

Adrenaline filled his senses, an exhilarating high; his mind, mad with fear sent images to his brain, flashing through a series of events: *his mother holding him in her arms; his father's face reading the note she left; his uncle instructing him how to hold a sword; Camber helping his uncle build the woodshed; Camber waving good-bye to his uncle, watching him leave until he and his horse were just two tiny specks on the horizon.* Past and present came washing back in a flood of memories, some pleasant, some not.

Hours, minutes, seconds – all sense of time gone, dissolving into his nonexistence. *Was he still descending?* He couldn't tell. It seemed his body was inert, destined to spend eternity floating through space. He resigned himself to his fate: forever floating, floating, floating. Camber the floating boy, now a part of that great nothingness that fills the blackness between the stars.

What the? A sudden jolt brought him back, fully aware he had just slammed into something soft, *and... fleshy? Great Savior!* Cold tendrils wrapped his naked chest, pinning his arms; one shot up to his face. With a twist he turned his head. *I don't want to die – not here – not like this. Somebody, anybody... help... me.*

A voice, soothing and soft, spoke ever so gently, stealing across his thoughts, sifting through his memories. *It wanted him.* A wave of revulsion, and he automatically raised a wall.

Whiteness rippled in the dark. A shadow of shadows, and it was just there; an extension of all things, all emotion, expanding until it filled every particle of his being, then blasting outward in a glory of white-hot light. A painful shock split his head in two, hurling him back to the waking world.

Camber's eyes popped open, and he sat bolt upright in bed. Sweat ran down his forehead, big shiny drabs of it. He kicked away his blankets, reached for his tunic, and left his bed for the warmth of the kitchen.

A quiet glow radiated from the woodstove, bathing cream-colored walls in soft orange. Outside, the world slept soundly, wrapped in a blanket of dark; the moon still visible from its lofty position, filtering white light through the tops of the trees and in through the kitchen window, painting Camber's face in silver, making it seem even more youthful than its eighteen years. He sat at the table, head cupped between hands. A sigh accompanied his gaze, following the moon, watching it disappear behind a cloudy curtain. The desire for bed long gone, fleeing the wee hours of night, and all because of a dream.

What the hell just happened? He pinched his arm, then rapped his knuckles hard against the table. Real enough. But the dream too, seemed real.

He dropped his head and the locket he wore slipped over his tunic; a gift from his mother. It twinkled in the dim lighting as he caressed its teardrop shape, running his fingers over the strange rune carved on its shiny surface. More than anything Camber missed his mother.

He sighed softly; she had been the cause of his father's death and she probably didn't even know it. His gaze returned to the window; red and gold tinted treetops, splashing against the kitchen wall as the sun made its morning debut, and he suddenly felt very alone.

A batter at the front door roused him from his reverie, and he tucked the locket under his tunic and wandered into the hallway just as the door flew open.

"I told you he wouldn't be ready." Dane shook his head. "See, he's still in his undergarments." He tossed his pack to the sofa and placed his bow against the wall. The other figure following on his heels barely cleared his shoulders, but could have been made up of three or even four Danes, and his immense bulk glided into the room with the grace of a young bull.

"For the love of... he's forgotten about the tryouts." Jules Sandyman stooped to pick a lump of blue off the floor. He threw it at his friend's head. A hand reached up, snatching the vest in mid-flight, and Dane tossed the garment over to Camber, now sorting through a pile of laundry strewn about the sitting room.

"I haven't forgotten." He pulled the vest over his tunic.

"For once Jules is right." Dane plucked a sock off the sofa, holding it out at arm's length. "Now *that* is ripe."

"You're not exactly helping," and snatching the sock he matched it with another lying on the floor.

The archer pulled his hand back. "Cripes! What's got into you?"

"I didn't sleep well." A half-truth. *Maybe denial would keep that dream away.*

"Any news from Uncle Chance?" Dane plunked himself on the

sofa, sweeping away the mess with one hand and plopping his boots across the padded foot-rest.

"No." Camber fumbled with the buckle on his belt. "Not a word."

"Snakes Alive! What could be keeping him?"

"Don't know. Said he'd be back before spring. Toss me that."

"Doesn't sound like Chance. If he said spring, he meant it." Dane picked up a boot and threw it across the room. "Think something's happened?"

"You know Chance, I'm sure... "

A clatter came from the kitchen, and Jules appeared in the archway holding a loaf of bread and some cheese. "Are you taking this, 'cause if you're not we better eat it now."

Dane uncrossed his boots, leaving Camber to finish up on his own; he dragged a chair to the table and took the bread away. "He'd have more food in this house if you didn't come over all the time to inspect the pantry. You should bring a cartload of stuff just to replace what you ate yesterday."

"You're both a couple of freeloaders." Camber brought a pitcher of water and some mugs over to the table and pulled up another stool. The remnants of the dream flickered away, replacing his unease with the lighthearted humor of his friends. He hoisted a mug. "A drink to the Rangers. And the trials. It's been almost six years since the last one."

"Here! Here!" Dane raised his cup.

"Just think, if we get into the same squad we can all bunk together."

"It doesn't work that way Jules. We'll be lucky to get into the same unit, and if Dane's head doesn't swell, then his marksmanship will probably land him in the top crop."

Dane grinned. "And you, my dear boy, will likely peel potatoes if Dega has his way. Can't wait to see his face when we all show up for tryouts." Dane chuckled, and he tilted his stool until it touched the wall. "Think he's still holding a grudge? It's been years since he left Hartland, 'sides, it wasn't your fault his father was a traitor."

"Tell that to Dega, he's hated me ever since."

Jules liberated a chunk of cheese and stuffed it into his mouth. "Whatever happened to ol' Drake Darkhawk anyway?"

"He fled, or something. Easterlings double-crossed him and that was the end of it."

"Doesn't matter anyway, Dega's the only thing we need to worry about." Dane sat up saluting his cousin. "Camber Bloodstone, scrub the latrines, and when you're done you can scrape the mud from my boots." He slapped his knee. "It'll be like old times. Except he's a Captain now so you'll have to do what he says. I wonder if he's still got that temper."

"Aw c'mon, he ain't that bad." The knife waved to and fro as Jules defended Hartland's favorite son. "Anyway, he's changed, *and* it was Dega who chased the Easterlings out of Wildwood."

Camber raised an eyebrow, and Dane feigned admiration. *"Oh Dega. My hero,"* and clasping his hands he batted his lashes.

"Hey! I was only thinking of my sister."

"Sorry Jules, but I've seen your sister and she's likely to stay a spinster for a long long time," and Dane did his impression of Hartland's citizens: "Our Dega Darkhawk has become quite a leader 'mongst his peers, he has no time for song, women, and wine when there's a world to save." He stood, stretching his legs. "And speaking of which, let's get a move on or we'll be late for tryouts and I wouldn't want to deprive the world of young Master Sandyman."

Camber left the table, and Dane rolled his eyes as he watched his cousin stuffing his bundle. "You mean to tell me you haven't even packed?"

"No, pass the rope."

The archer shook his head. "You're as bad as Jules. It would be a shame if the whole of Hartland depended on the two of you to save the day and neither of you showed up because one was stuffing his face and the other still sorting his clothes!" He frowned at his portly friend sitting at the table polishing off the last of the bread and cheese and licking the tips of his fingers.

"Lucky for Hartland you'll be there to coordinate the battle; you can run around like a mother hen making sure everyone has shirttails tucked and cloaks fastened snugly."

"And if that doesn't work, he can talk the enemy to death." Camber stood in the archway, pack on his back and his father's sword fastened to his side. Dane and Jules grabbed their belongings and followed him out the door, eager to be off at last.

Soft daylight filtered across the sky chasing away the last whispers of darkness. Dane took a deep breath, fresh pine filled the air with the promise of a warm spring, and he hoisted his pack so that it landed with a whump across his shoulders. "Finally! I've waited too long for this day. Time to show the world what we're made of," and poking Jules in the stomach, a grin came fast. "On second thought, you might want to hide some of what you're made of."

Camber laughed, and Jules wrinkled his brow. "And you might want to stick a sack over your ugly self and hide the whole nasty thing." He started down the road and the other two fell in beside him, their spirits uplifted by the excellent weather and the prospect of joining Hartland's cavalry.

Lush fields dotted with white stone farmsteads lay on either side of the road. Farmers trudged behind oxen, grinding rich brown earth into long even furrows. Horses and cattle grazed peacefully over dewy pastures, and windpuffers sailed expertly through the air, darting right, then suddenly banking left.

The trio passed rapidly across farmland and into the highlands. The scenery shifted; tall evergreens crowded the roadside, and tanglebrush and broomweed replaced green rolling fields. Spotted deer moved silently between trees, keeping a wary eye whilst they gleaned bark.

At last they came to the Whitewash; the river flowed down from Wildwood and beyond, and the only crossing was a wooden bridge that had been there longer than anyone could remember. But the bridge had its place as a landmark, and not a square inch of unmarred space could be found on its knotted and worn surface (save the underside, and even that had names vying for space). Scratching one's initials into that soft gray wood was practically a rite of passage, and names belonging to persons far older than even the town's central district were immortalized forever as proof that another son of Hartland had stood on this very spot. Jules stopped his companions and pointed to three such initials inscribed along the railing.

"Hey!" Dane laughed, his grin spreading across his face. "It's still there. How many years ago did we carve that?" The familiar scratches read: CB, DS, JS, and he traced the contours of each letter as he spoke. "Must have been at least ten."

Camber touched his CB. "It was ten. And I still have a scar from your stupid knife." He held up the arm where Dane had drawn his blade for a few drops of blood, mixing it with both his and Jules, and coloring their initials red. "You said a part of us will always be here in Hartland no matter where we end up."

"And I meant it." Dane held up his knife. "Shall we refresh our vows?"

Camber and Jules pulled up their sleeves, offering their bare arms to Dane, and he colored the letters with blood, adding a little of his own. "Looks good as new." He stood back to admire his handiwork. Camber frowned at his arm, dabbing the cut with his sleeve. "Thanks for the scar."

The day was as it had been ten years before, and he couldn't resist the boy within, he turned suddenly and shouted at his friends. "Last one up to Eagle Reach has to carry everything!" Away he raced, pack bouncing across his shoulders as he sped up the narrow trail that led to the summit. Dane gave Jules a smack on the back of his head, then sprinted after his cousin.

Camber was the first to reach the top. But Dane was not far behind, and as they waited for Jules the two friends surveyed the endless region below.

Eagle Reach had a commanding view of all four quadrants: North, South, East, and West. It was a favorite spot, not because of the view, but because of what Eagle Reach had once been. Long ago, before there was ever a Hartland, or even a Cambert, a grim people from beyond the Western Seas had crossed the Dragonspine and set up a colony in the forested plains. *The Janastari:* a warrior race who disappeared long before men settled the Northlands. Some folk said they simply died out, others believed they still dwelt in Astaria's wilderness, shunning everyone, including their distant kin. Camber's uncle had told him that they went back over the Dragonspine. Whatever the reason for their disappearance, they had left behind part of their culture for men to ponder; the crumbling remains of a watchtower stood there still; a stark reminder of this ancient and powerful race.

Eagle Reach was also a pleasant place just to sit and think. The higher elevation created a haven under the shadow of the blackened tower. Tall pines covered the valley like a dark green blanket; brown patches of wild grass could be seen where the trees had thinned, exposing slabs of gray stone – the remains of a rock wall. Further East, a great distance past the edge of the treeline, a slice of deep blue flecked with white caught and reflected sunlight into sparkling miniature diamonds: *the Great Barrier Ocean,* a natural boundary between the Northlands and the Eastern Kingdom. Watchtowers were spaced along the Barrier's shores, and warships from Thayneland patrolled her turbulent waters, though they could see neither from the hilltop. The snow-capped teeth of the Dragonspine barred their view of the West, but to the South they could see the Whitewash; a bright white ribbon cutting across the deep brown ridges of the plains.

As Camber basked in the beauty that was Eagle Reach, something drew his eye. A shadow moving below in the forest instantly raised his hackles. "Down!" he called.

Dane knew his cousin well enough to trust his instincts, and he dropped obediently beside Camber. A rustle of grass announced the arrival of Jules. Two hands shot up, pulling him to ground. "Afffff!" A hand quickly covered his mouth.

"Shhh!" Dane let his hand slip as soon as he saw the younger boy had understood. All three scanned the area near the edge of the forest; it wasn't long before they saw a dark shape move away from the shelter of pines.

A warhorse stepped into the open. It pawed the ground, and threw its big black head up and down, fighting to gain control of its reins. But the rider held his charger with a firm hand. Plated steel glinted from beneath the folds of his cloak, and when the horse danced sideways the hilt of a sword became visible. Both rider and steed appeared to be waiting for something; two black specters in the midmorning sun.

"Is that a Ranger?" Jules lay between Camber and Dane, and was inching closer for a better view.

"No. Can't be, that's not the uniform," whispered Dane, "he must be an – "

"– *Easterling*." Camber finished.

A long mournful howl rose high on the wind. Far away a second wail answered the first. And as they exchanged a fearful look, a third cry took up the call.

A shadow burst out of the trees. Broad it was, and barrel-shaped, and covered in coarse gray hair. Its large round head swiveled right, then left, snuffling the morning air. Black and leathery were its lips, curling back and exposing long sharp teeth. But it was the brow, smooth and flat, and where there should have been eyes – *this creature had none!*

The world, now devoid of sound, held its breath, only a gentle breeze dared to violate the stillness, ruffling the hair on their heads. The wind shifted, and the creature twitched its ears, lifting its great head in the direction of the summit. Jules shut his eyes, trembling uncontrollably and clenching the ground. "What is that thing?" he whispered.

"A *Bounder*." Camber's voice was scarcely louder than the breeze.

"Uncle Chance used to mention them in his stories. I didn't think they were real."

"Neither did I," said Dane, and he popped his head above the grass for a better view.

The Bounder let out another wail, then dove back into cover, followed closely by the horseman, who glanced briefly up at Eagle Reach before slipping back into shadow.

The boys stayed pressed to the ground for several minutes making sure neither beast nor master would be reappearing from the trees any time soon.

"I'll lay odds that Easterling was looking for someone." Dane dusted off his clothes.

"Yeah, but who?" said Jules. He sat up, still visibly shaken.

The archer shook his head, staring at the spot where horse, rider, and eyeless beast had disappeared. "Who knows, but I don't think I want to stick around and find out."

Camber helped his friend to his feet. "It might be a good idea to keep this to ourselves. A story like this will only bring us trouble, especially from Dega. He'll be looking for any excuse to keep us from joining up. I'm sure he'll turn it around so that nobody believes it."

Jules bit his lip. "We better say something." The other two looked at him. "What if there's more of them out there?"

"Now listen, Jules." Dane put his arm around the young man's shoulders and steered him to the footpath leading down from the summit. "If we say anything to the Rangers about this, then you know that overbearing lout Dega will be stickin' his snout where it don't belong, and somehow we'll all end up on the wrong end of things. Fat chance we'll have at getting into the cavalry then." Looking his friend directly in the eye, he asked, "Is that what you want? This has been your dream. Yours, mine, Camber's. Think what your parents will say when you return. And that's if they let you return. More likely they'll lock you up, throw away the key. Do you want to be the one to tell your father you were sent home before you even had a chance to try out?"

Jules shook his head. Once again, Dane made perfect sense, or at least he thought it sounded like good sense; trouble was, Dane had a way of making even the most outrageous situations sound sane.

Dane winked at Camber. "Okay that settles it, let's get back to the main road. We've wasted enough time up here already."

They walked the rest of the way in silence, barely saying

anything upon reaching the rusted iron gates of the former Ranger stronghold.

The old fortress was a favorite haunt. Whispers of yesteryear echoed down long forgotten corridors; a treasure of secrets laid bare for present-day hunters seeking the past, leaving Camber ill-prepared for the stronghold's sudden transformation from abandoned fort to full-fledged academy.

The floors had been swept free of debris, and walls patched with rock and mortar; new timber shanks replaced rotting supports, scenting the air with sweet-smelling cedar. Torches flickered brightly, casting shadows around the entrance hall, dancing across tapestries depicting the history of Hartland's cavalry. Banners representing each branch of the Northern League hung from the barrack's vaulted ceilings, adding a splash of color to its dull gray interior, and as Camber surveyed the receiving area he saw an impressive array of shields painted with Hartland's coat of arms, including the Bloodstone family's own emblem (two crossed swords behind a lunging unicorn). And yes, he was not mistaken, the Darkhawk crest with its blood-red bird-of-prey hung right beside it.

A voice instructed all to form a line in front of the only desk in the hall. Two men in uniform were seated at the desk; one was handing out colored strips of cloth while the other had his head down, bringing it up now and again to call over the next person in line.

Captain Dega Darkhawk stared at the list of names; a frown creased his handsome face. He sighed. Poor turnout. They'd be lucky to fill half a company with today's showing. Jotting down the name of the boy standing in front of his desk, he passed him on to Gareth. His second-in-command was handing out the colored bands meant to keep the recruits in groups.

"Next," he motioned over another youth, eyes glancing briefly at the registry. "Your name?" he said, still counting. His lip curled up at one corner, knowing his careful list of names would undoubtedly be added to an even longer list of names kept in the bowels of the Ranger's record-keeping sanctum, never again to be seen by anyone, nor enjoy a mere moment of sunshine; parchment ultimately doomed to wither away like so many yellowed leaves covered in dust and darkness under the stronghold where he now sat collecting names. The thought struck him funny, and he smiled.

"Camber Bloodstone," said a familiar voice.

The smile disappeared, and he lifted his head. A hardened gaze, honed to perfection, came face-to-face with a pair of ridiculously large green eyes.

The world seemed to shrink, leaving Camber small and insignificant; a dull rhythmic thudding filled the space between his ears; a lump wedged inside his throat, now suddenly dry. To his amazement, a smile spread quickly across Dega's face, evaporating the look of surprise that had been there only a moment ago. He stood and shook Camber's hand.

"Well Camber, good to see you." He gave him a friendly clap on the shoulder. "I'm extremely pleased you've decided to follow in the footsteps of your famous father. I'm sure you'll be an asset to our regiment." And Camber slowly exhaled as Dega wrote his name on the paper.

Dane watched the exchange closely; he had no love for Dega and stepped forward to intervene on his cousin's behalf. But the officer seemed unimpressed as he looked up at the tall figure that had suddenly stepped out from the line.

"Ahh, Dane Strongbow. I thought that was you behind Camber. Guess I can't really say I'm surprised; after all, where one goes so does the other." Searching the line once more he waved to Jules, who started to wave back, but Dane turned with a scowl and the sandy-haired youth stopped waving and dropped his head. Dega added Jules Sandyman to his list.

"There, that's all three of you." He signaled for Jules to step forward, then passed the trio over to Gareth, who handed them each a colored swatch.

"Tie the cloth around your waist, then step off to the side." The Lieutenant pointed to where the young hopefuls stood in groups.

Dega bent his head to Gareth, lowering his voice till it was barely audible. "I don't care how you do it or what the outcome of the trials determine, just make sure those three end up in my personal squad."

II

Let the Games Begin

Camber put his hand up, shading his face from the sun's glare while he scanned the area for Dane or Jules, but the expanse of open field was swarming with activity and it was hard to follow a single body through the melee of multi-colored scarves. He dropped his hand as the corporal in charge made his speech.

"After you finish at this venue you will rotate counter-clockwise to the next, and so forth, until each of you has completed the circuit. You will then reconvene inside for further instruction. If anyone feels he should not be here then let him speak now." The corporal paused, waiting for a reply. "Anyone? No one? Fine. Pair up with the person on your right."

Long hours under his uncle's tutelage paid off as Camber dispatched several cadets from the contest, flipping practice swords right out of the hands that held them. As he faced the last remaining recruit he caught a glimpse of Dega standing off to the side with Gareth, but his attempt to gain an earful was painfully thwarted by a smack across his arm.

The slim redhead grinned as his wooden blade found its target a second time. "Better wake up," he said; he waved his sword with ease, and this time the stroke fell from above, but Camber was more than ready, dancing sideways and avoiding the blow. Swords clacked across and down. At last an opening, and he lunged, but the redhead brought a foot up, hooking an ankle and flipping him onto his backside. Hansil introduced himself as he helped Camber to his feet.

A cool breeze filled the once bright blue sky with a dark dusting of clouds, signaling the concluding stages of the waning day. Camber's group had just finished the dispatch relay when he became aware of a large crowd near the archery venue.

Hansil tapped him on the shoulder. "We're done here. C'mon, let's go watch the action." He nodded toward the gathering and they fell in behind a group walking across the field. "I heard they'd be making the picks tomorrow, but someone said the Captain was selecting his squad today." A frown creased his freckled face. "I hope I get in. Pa wants me to follow in his footsteps."

"You want to be an officer?"

"Well yeah, doesn't everybody?" He raised his hand and saluted to no one as they crossed the field. "You seem to handle yourself well enough, how'd you learn to spar?"

"My uncle taught me."

"Wait a minute." Hansil stopped. "What's your last name?"

"Bloodstone."

"Ha! That explains it. You're pretty good with a sword. Last name's Edgewater."

Camber smiled, his uncle had spoken highly of Lt. Edgewater and he mentioned this to Hansil. They shared their history while they walked.

"Sorry about your father." Hansil lowered his voice. "Was it really Easterlings?"

"Not sure. But I'd give anything to have him back."

"Oh, I didn't mean to... it's just that your father's practically a legend. I don't think anyone actually believes he froze to death."

"Yeah. My uncle doesn't think so either."

"Is that his sword? Can I see it?" He pointed at the glint of polished metal peeking from a well-worn harness.

Camber slid the sword free. Sunlight blazed across a cold surface, razor-sharp and decorated with delicate runes.

"May I?" Hansil curled his fingers around the haft. "It's beautiful." He took a few practice swings. "And light. I've never seen anything like it."

"It's elvish."

"Then it's true what they say." He handed the sword back. "You really are related to the Elves."

"My mother's side."

"Good to know."

"It is?"

"Yeah." Hansil grinned. "If I'm ever in need of a little magic I know just who to call." He stuck his hand out in friendship, and it was eagerly accepted.

The two cadets pushed their way toward the unmistakable shape of Jules, who beamed as he spotted his friend, then parted the crowd, allowing Camber and Hansil to slip through and take a place near the front.

"Have you seen Dane?" It was not like his cousin to miss something like this.

Jules pointed to the archer leaning against a barrel waiting for his turn to shoot. Dane and two other recruits were about to take their final round during the marksmanship event. "So far Dane hasn't missed one target."

Dane took his place, and the crowd roared its approval; he turned and saluted, instigating an even louder cheer. Camber smirked; it was just like Dane to play the showman. He held his breath as his cousin drew the bowstring tight across his cheek. The arrow flew true, plunging deep into the bulls-eye. A cheer went up, then all fell silent as the second shooter took his place. He loosed an arrow but it went wide of the mark and he was ousted from the tournament. To the delight of the fans, he walked over to Dane and shook his hand.

Only two remained. The second cadet took his mark and the crowd grew quiet once more. Arrow nocked, he drew his bow, sending the dart home. It landed next to Dane's arrow. The audience booed loudly, then fell to a hush when the corporal in charge strode out to the bulls-eye. He called over a private and together they peered at the arrows, then signaling another private, he had the two men move the target back fifteen paces.

The crowd had doubled since Camber's arrival, and they applauded loudly as Dane took his place. He loosed his arrow and it sailed effortlessly into the center. And being Dane, he winked at his fans before giving his spot to his rival. Silence now as the other boy took careful aim. The barb ripped home to the sound of a long groan.

Dane took his place, stretched his bow, marking the first arrow and splitting it all the way down the shaft. He released another. It ran the shaft of his opponent's dart and stuck deep into the bulls-eye, thwipping to a stop.

The crowd went wild, and Dane's opponent signaled he was dropping out, knowing he could not possibly top that remarkable shooting. He strode over to his talented rival and shook his hand. As a final showing of good sportsmanship he lifted Dane's arm high in the air and the two of them basked in the admiration of the spectators.

Dane spotted Camber making his way through the throng and a wide grin split his boyish face. "Hey! I was just about to start looking for you." He introduced his new friend Sal and the other two archers. "Looks like the trials are all but over. I guess now we play the waiting game."

"Well you won't have to wait long."

"Why do you say that?" Dane played with an arrow, twirling it across his fingers.

"Dega's making his picks today and from what I've seen of your shooting you'll probably end up in his elite squad."

Dane looked over to where Hartland's favorite son was conferring with his lieutenant. "Guess I'll just have to liven things up a bit. Pity you won't be there."

The sound of a horn signaled it was time to head back to the hall. Camber said good-bye, and he and Hansil went off to find the rest of the red-scarves.

The musty smell of cold stone returned to his nostrils. He stood with Hansil straining to hear what was being said as the corporal's monotone voice reverberated around the hall, mixing with the voices of the other officers.

"Form a single row facing the front," the corporal commanded, and waited for his recruits to fall into place. "Most of you will find out tomorrow where you belong. However, Captain Darkhawk has decided to choose his squad today. Arrangements have been made for the rest of you to use the north end of the barracks as your sleeping quarters. You will be assigned your bunks tomorrow once selections have been made. These barracks will be used only for training; once you've passed all the requirements you will be stationed at Wildwood. Because these barracks are in need of repair, all recruits will have a hand in restorations when not on duty or participating in activities." He continued his speech about what was expected until he was finally interrupted by the announcement for the selection of the Captain's squad.

"Step forward when your name is called," Lieutenant Gareth Comstock commanded, and an immediate wave of silence followed. "Bon Silverman, Dane Strongbow, Camber Bloodstone, Sal Cartwright, Hansil Edgewater, Jules Sandyman, Caleb Whitmore…." he listed off nine more names, bringing the number to sixteen.

Captain Darkhawk watched closely as his recruits fell into place, searching the line for any signs of weakness: slumped shoulders, darting eyes, bowed heads, any type of behavior that might indicate a flaw. His superiors had given him this opportunity to establish a proper training camp at the old barracks; they were expecting him to organize an effective company with raw recruits, and he would not disappoint.

Dega Darkhawk was a man of his word. He took his commissions seriously, fighting tooth and nail to climb the Ranger's ranks to Captain. He had to. It wasn't easy escaping his father's shadow. But Dega had proved himself time and again, rising above Drake Darkhawk's infamous deed, taking dispatches nobody wanted down forgotten and forbidden roads where no Ranger had dared journey in almost a hundred years. He, Dega Darkhawk, had crossed the fell borders of the Easterling King's own empire! By his own blood and guts he had earned his hard-won Captaincy and all the respect that went with it. He would not tolerate anything short of excellence in his newly formed company.

"You men have been hand-picked for your remarkable display of unmatched skill during the trials." He stopped in front of Camber. "You are now part of my personal squad. You will become leaders to your peers. You will work harder than any of the other recruits. You will rise earlier, stand your watch longer, go to bed later. You will display obedience and respect for your superiors and undertake your duties with due diligence at all times. You will not show any signs of weakness." He moved a few steps, stopping in front of Jules. "Nor will you shy away from any task handed to you. I do not tolerate drunk and disorderly men, swearing, or gambling. Nor do I tolerate hijinks of any sort," and he directed his look at Dane. "You are now officers in training and you will conduct yourselves in a manner that befits gentlemen of rank. I will give you one hundred percent of myself and I expect you to do the same." Turning sharply on his boot heel, he motioned for the group to follow.

Dega gave his squad a tour of the barracks, the officer's wing, sleeping quarters, study rooms, and kitchen. And made a point of marching them to his office. "My door is always open," one hand waved his group inside, and they crowded into a corner. "If any of you ever feel the need to come and talk I'm always here." Camber smirked as he caught Dane rolling his eyes.

They followed the Captain outside, passing the stables, the supply hut, and one of two watchtowers. Dega stopped on the parade square and asked if they had any questions. Not one hand was raised, and so he dismissed them; his gaze followed Camber and Dane as they disappeared into the barracks.

The stars were making their twilight appearance, and exhaustion came fast, replacing the day's enthusiasm with fatigue. Camber, Dane, and Jules now lounged in the room they shared with Hansil, sitting on their cots and talking about the day's events, and of Dega.

"Do you think the Cap has it in for you?" asked Hansil. Camber had filled him in on his pre-history with Dega, and the redhead agreed that it could become an issue later on.

"Hard to say. He's like a completely different person," said Camber, reflecting on his initial encounter with the former bully.

"No he's not. He hasn't changed a bit," Dane argued, and Camber raised an eyebrow. "Remember the time we stole his family's only milk cow and he had to retrieve it from the top of the bell tower?" It had taken nearly half the night to coax, push, and pull the stubborn animal up the winding staircase, but it was certainly worth every bump and bruise watching Dega drag the frightened bovine down the next morning. You could hear the cussing all the way from Craddock's orchard.

"Well," Dane prodded, "how long did Dega wait until he ambushed us with his friends at the Whitewash?" He nodded his head like a school marm educating a room full of children. "It was almost a year later. And so, gentlemen, my point is, that he's playing cat and mouse, and when the time is right he's gonna pounce."

"That's just speculation. Maybe he won't do anything. It's no use getting all worked up over nothing." Hansil selected an apple from the fruit bowl, tossed it in the air, and caught it with his other hand. "But if he does have it in for you I'm willing to put my neck on the line for your cause." He placed his hand over his heart. "Camber Bloodstone, there's an invisible bond unwritten and unspoken among heroes, I am proud to continue that bond."

"Idiot." Dane threw a pillow at his head.

A knock at the door announced the arrival of the two archers from earlier, and Sal. "Mind if we join you?" he asked. The three were greeted with laughter as the newly formed Captain's squad imagined future military assignments.

Over the next several days uniforms were handed out, duties received, and simple exercises carried out. The Captain's squad had just finished a two hour drill on the parade square and now they waited for the stable sergeant to finish his introduction.

If there was ever a bigger man than Sergeant Weyland, then Camber did not know of him. Arms the size of tree trunks and a chest broader than an apple barrel threatened to burst the buttons off a uniform already stretched past its limit, and when he instructed the cadets on *his* expectations on the proper care of *his* horses every pair of ears paid close attention. But for all his imposing size, the sergeant was soft-spoken and gentle with his four-legged charges.

"These horses are your best friends. They might even be the best friend you'll ever have," he eyed the group suspiciously, "and if I hear of anyone mistreating my animals I will personally see he's tossed out on his ear and sent home." He took a deep breath, pausing just long enough to scan the faces of the cadets. "Have I made myself clear?" Sixteen heads nodded in unison.

Weyland led them past several rows of horses to the rear of the stables. "These are where I house the officer's horses. You may select your mounts from any that do not have a mark above the door."

Camber started at the back instead of where the sergeant stood with arms folded. He was admiring a magnificent black in the last stall when Dane came up beside him.

"Panther," he read the name on the polished metal plaque.

"Dega's horse," Dane pointed to the mark above the stall.

"Guess I won't be choosing that one then." He moved to the next stall and a curious head poked over the door; ears flicked forward watching with interest. "Now here's a horse that knows a human of quality when he sees one." He stroked its black velvety nose and scratched the bay's soft ears. "I think I just found my friend," and he smiled as the horse tried to taste the buttons on the sleeve of his uniform.

Dane had already moved down a few stalls, inspecting a feisty gray. He tried to touch it, but it snorted and shied to the other side of the pen. He smiled. *Flashy and spirited.*

After each cadet selected his mount Sergeant Weyland instructed them on the importance of inspecting their horses before adding tack. He used Camber's horse as an example, running his large hands gently down the slender legs of the animal, checking for tender spots, bruises, or cuts. He lifted each hoof and showed the cadets how to examine the inner pad. As a final check the stable sergeant tested the iron shoe, making sure it was tightly in place.

"Taking care of your horse will be your first priority," he lectured his pupils as they led their mounts outside. "You will tend to their needs even before you've had a chance to look after your own affairs. At the day's end you will see that your horse is properly fed, watered, and groomed before returning to the barracks."

They followed the sergeant to the largest of the three rings where he promptly turned them over to another officer. Corporal Hollybrook lined them up in pairs, instructing the squad to ride the ring's perimeter, crisscrossing the center on command. He shook his head as pupils fell out of sync, fell off mounts, or lost complete control, allowing horses to wander away at whim. And *this* was the Captain's elite! After an hour of watching every equestrian blunder under the sun, his patience growing shorter than the attention span of his students, he deemed it a day and sent the young men back to Weyland.

"Ow, my back hurts." Jules limped along, favoring his right side as they walked back to the barracks. "I don't think I'll ever get used to sitting up so straight. And then he tells us to look relaxed! Which is it? Straight or relaxed? Bloody hell! I can't do both!"

"Don't be so glum, Jules. You should have seen the look on your pony's face when he saw who his rider was going to be." Sal laughed, slapping the cadet across his shoulders.

They stood by the stairs, debating on whether to eat in the mess hall or the kitchen, but Dane wasn't hungry, he was eager to start pitching in with repairs. He patted the dice in his pocket. "On second thought, I'll catch up with you folks later. C'mon Jules, let's head on over to the wall," and he pushed the cadet away from the group.

"But I haven't had lunch yet."

"Then I'm doing you a favor, you need to lose a couple of pounds anyway."

Camber returned to his room just as the bell tolled two, having spent half the night moving supplies from the old warehouse to the new one; he collapsed onto his bunk still dressed in uniform. Jules was snoring deep and loud, a strange contrast to Hansil's light rhythmic breathing.

Dane was still awake. "What's been gnawing at you lately?" he whispered.

"What do you mean?" Camber unbuttoned his shirt and tossed it to the chair.

"You know what I mean. That morning we left for trials you were white as a sheet. And then the Bounder incident. Jules was right, we should've reported it. But I could tell you didn't want to. Why? What are you afraid of? And don't give me that crap that you're worried about Chance. There's something else going on in that head of yours, so fess up."

"Look Dane, it's something I have to deal with, all right." Then lowering his voice until it was scarcely louder than Hansil's breathing "and it's probably just a coincidence, nothing more."

"What's a coincidence?" Dane turned over on his side and stared at his cousin. "What the blue blazes are you on about?"

"It's nothing. I shouldn't have said anything. Now go to sleep."

"Don't be stupid. I know this is big, I can see it all over your face. 'Sides, you should know by now you can trust me – haven't we always been there for each other?"

Dane was right. But this was different. This was something even he couldn't comprehend.

"Does this have anything to do with what happened on *the Reach?*"

"Don't know," he stared at the ceiling. "It might have something to do with a dream."

"What dream?"

"That morning of the tryouts, you said I wasn't myself. Well I wasn't. Something really weird happened," he paused, not sure whether he should continue. Then taking a deep breath he told Dane about his nightmare. "It's the same every time. I'm in a cave, and it's dark. The ground is covered in mist; just like the time Jules dared us to cross the cemetery at Farthing. So I start walking, feeling my way in the dark. Then the wall disappears and I fall into Blackness!"

"Snakes Alive!"

"But *this* time it was different."

"How so?"

"This time something was waiting for me when I fell through the wall."

"How'd you get away?"

"I don't know. Magic I think."

"What!?"

"I think I'm going crazy." He waited to see if Dane was going to grin and chide him for being silly. But Dane only stared back, mouth open.

Dane cleared his throat. "You're not going to believe this, but that same morning I dreamt you were walking down a tunnel like the one you just described!" His voice barely contained his amazement at the discovery of a possible connection with Camber's dream.

"What!? Why didn't you tell me!"

"Why didn't you tell me about your dream."

"Good point." Camber lowered his voice.

"Look, it's just a dream, right? It might be nothing, maybe bad eggs or something." Dane frowned as he thought of Eagle Reach. "But then again, it could be tied in with that Easterling and his Bounder. Seems like they were looking for something," he lowered his voice, "or someone." The archer thought for a second. "Better keep this between ourselves, but let me know if you have any more of those dreams."

"And Camber,"

"Yes?"

"Don't worry. I'm sure it's nothing serious, 'sides, as long as I'm here they'll have to come through me first." He gave his cousin a reassuring smile. "Now get some sleep."

Sleep. If only he could. A sudden chill made his flesh go all goosebumpy. *Seems like they were looking for someone.* Maybe they were looking for him. He lay in bed thinking about the Bounder. And why hadn't the dream come back? What would he do if it did?

Several weeks had passed and there was much improvement in all areas of Dega's outfit. He was extremely pleased at having accomplished so much with so little to work with, and he sat at his desk drafting a letter to Colonel Ravenhill highlighting his achievements to date. He had just finished sealing the parchment with hot wax and his own personal stamp (two letter D's back to back) when Gareth walked in.

"You wanted to see me, Sir?"

Dega nodded. "Yes, it seems the training has been going quite well. I was thinking it might be time to start guard duty." He shuffled through a stack of papers and pulled several sheets from the pile. "I've taken the liberty of forming a schedule from the cadets in my personal squad." He handed the roster to his lieutenant.

Gareth read the list. "I see you gave most of the graveyard shifts to cadet Bloodstone. Wouldn't it be better to distribute the late-watch among all sixteen?"

Dega raised an eyebrow.

"I meant to say, Sir, that the cadets have their studies on top of basic training and the reconstruction of the barracks. It makes sense to share the shift so none fall behind." Gareth was careful not to raise Dega's ire; he and the Captain had graduated basic training together and though he was usually collected, his temper was legendary once wakened.

"Just implement that particular schedule; if we have any problems we can change it later." He stood, handing his lieutenant the sealed parchment. "Send Corporal Bonner and one of the cadets to deliver this to Wildwood." His second-in-command nodded as Dega strode out the door. "If you need me I'll be on the field observing the recruits." And before his lieutenant could say anything else he was already more than half way down the hall, spurs jingling lightly as he disappeared around the corner.

The Captain found his squad practicing low jumps under the watchful eye of Corporal Hollybrook. At the first sign of Dega the corporal called his cadets to attention and saluted.

"Carry on," Dega called, and Hollybrook gave the order to continue. He walked over to the fence and gave a full report on the strengths and weaknesses of each cadet, but Dega could see with his trained eye which riders were skilled and which were not. He pointed to Jules. "Can't keep a seat – bad form. See, he struggles against the movement of his horse."

"Ahh, yes, cadet Sandyman is not what I would call a natural, Sir." Hollybrook watched his pupil moving awkwardly out of beat with his mount's easy gait. "We gave him Swishtail, but for all the patience that horse could possibly offer I daresay young Jules will ever be barely capable in the saddle."

Dega thought for a moment. "Double his work time. I want him in the saddle four hours a day. Change his mounts as often as you like to accommodate the extra practice time."

Hollybrook raised his brows. "Sir?"

"Believe me Hollybrook, with enough practice anyone can become an accomplished rider," and he turned on his heel leaving the corporal to finish his lesson.

"Snakes Alive!" Dane swore as he read the schedule. "Cripes, Camber they've got you down for just about every late night shift. When are you supposed to get any sleep?" They had all just returned from restoration work, and as was now the custom, were lounging in the room belonging to Camber, Dane, Jules, and Hansil. Caleb had just brought in the roster to show the others. "It must be a mistake," he said when he had handed it to the archer.

Bon and Sal were sitting on chairs, and Camber was looking over his cousin's shoulder. "I guess I'll just have to make the best of it. No one said this would be easy."

Bon shook his head. "It's not just the schedule," he argued. "It's like he's trying to break us. Even though we're expected to work harder than anyone else the workloads are ridiculous. Sal and I had extra time after painting fences and instead of being sent back to the barracks we were sent to muck out stalls." He snorted. "How are we supposed to get any studying done? We have an exam next week."

Jules rolled over on his cot and propped himself up with one arm. "At least you don't have to spend *your* dinner breaks in the saddle." He had not been pleased when Hollybrook informed him about his extended practice sessions in the ring. He took the schedule from Dane's hands. "When do we start guard duty anyway?"

Heavy winds buffeted the watch-tower causing it to sway. Camber folded his arms tightly around his chest and stamped his feet to ward off the sleep he badly needed. He stared out into blackness. *At least the rain is letting up.*

The sky was still very dark except to the east where the sun was slowly rising, tinting the clouds in soft pink. Stifling a yawn, he could think only of his relief and a nice warm bed.

A faint glow of orange against the early morning sky appeared strangely surreal. There it was again, only a little brighter this time. He squinted as he stared at the glow. Then blinked, not quite believing his eyes. *The stables!* On fire! Both hands went for the knotted rope hanging from the tower's bell.

Dane should have been in bed but he wasn't. Dega's latest list of demands now included surprise inspections at night followed by a five mile hike. He ripped the notice from the wall, wadded it into a ball, and threw it across the room.

Dega looked up as Dane marched into his office. He was just about to say something along the lines of knocking first, when the jarring peel of the watchtower bell shattered the early morning silence. He shot out of his chair, shoving Dane out of the way. The archer sprinted after his Captain, followed by Gareth and almost all the officers and cadets in the south wing. The barracks exploded into chaos as enlistees everywhere scrambled to pull on boots, grabbing whatever clothing they could find. Officers and privates joined forces with recruits, already several bucket brigades had started, and anyone who was not collecting water became part of the human transport system, moving the precious resource toward the burning stables.

Dane was already on the scene when Camber showed up, his face black with soot and dark eyes watering from a thick blanket of smoke billowing out from the blaze. "We're trying to get the horses out," he coughed, "there's still some at the back. Dega's gone in for another try." He doubled over as another coughing fit racked his wiry body. "He's been in there too long. Should've been out by now."

Two silhouettes appeared against a wall of red and orange; Gareth raced his horse out of the inferno. But Dega was still unaccounted for, and the fire now raged out of control, there seemed little hope for any more rescue attempts.

Camber dowsed himself with water, wrapped his cloak around his head, then bolted headlong into the fiery furnace. Dega must have gone to the very back to rescue his horse. The heat from the fire fanned his face; his wet clothes drying up fast. The sound of horses kicking and calling horrified his ears; he wanted to rescue them all, but time was not on his side. He made his way to the last row of stalls; Dega lay face down in the paddock.

The Captain's horse had gone mad, rearing up and plunging back to ground in absolute terror. Eyes rolled white with fear, it trumpeted a long high-pitched scream. He scrambled over to Dega's lifeless body, pulling it away from those dangerous hooves.

Fire swept up to the rafters, spreading rapidly across the top of the building. With a splintering snap, a beam gave way, blocking the exit. The stallion renewed its frenzy at the sight of the collapsing roof, and Camber was hit with a wave of panic as he crouched with the Captain's motionless form. The pound of his heart pulsed in his ears; he was inhaling way too much smoke and having a difficult time keeping his wits sharp. "Think Camber," he said, mostly just to hear his own voice above the crackle and snap. "What would Chance do?" He tried to picture his uncle, not a big strapping man like his father, but someone who relied on wits more often than brawn. He clung to his uncle's image as though it were his salvation.

His eyes grew heavy; he fought to keep his body from lapsing into darkness, but blackness closed in, shutting out horses, smoke, and flame. His heart slowed to a dull thudding, its rhythmic beat throbbing in his ears. The ground fell away, stripped out from underneath his feet; he was now outside his body looking down at the ghastly scene unfolding below. An idea formed, taking wing like the flutter of a butterfly; he rode its colorful hum. It told him what to do. It was so simple! He almost laughed out loud as he surrendered himself to the pureness of power.

Crackling white light ten times brighter than the sun exploded outward, forming a protective barrier around the Captain. A second bolt shot from his fingertips, cutting through flame and creating its own spectral glow. Pure energy became one with fire, drawing away heat, feasting on red-hot spark. Walls glowed white; the hum of power climbed to a pitch beyond his ken. Wind rushed his ears, as if a deep breath had suddenly drawn away all sound.

The ground buckled beneath Dane's feet. Jules and Hansil had stopped him from chasing after Camber; they held him tight, but when they felt the explosion he burst free from his friends and raced to the other side of the building. Gareth joined him, and the others were not far behind. All pulled up in surprise to see the whole side of the building completely gone and Camber dragging Dega's body out from the blaze. They ran to help as he pulled the Captain to safety. Camber stopped, his face went white, his eyes rolled up, and he fell limply over the Captain's body.

III

An Unexpected Detour

"Snakes Alive, Camber. Lie still." A familiar voice echoed inside his pounding skull, and a grinning face slowly came into focus; soft daylight replaced the sleepy haze from his bloodshot eyes, and the fuzzy aura framing Dane's head sharpened into clarity, then disappeared.

"Whaah...?" Camber sat up, then fell limply into soft pillows.

"Wait." Dane poured a glass of water and propped him up.

The water was refreshing and he tilted the glass so it could be refilled. He licked his lips. "What happened?"

"I was just about to ask you the same thing," Dane said, pouring more water into Camber's glass. "You've been out for days. We were worried about whether you were going to pull through or not, but here you are, ugly mug and all." Camber touched his face, half convinced it was disfigured, and Dane laughed. The archer filled him in on the events surrounding the fire. "Then we heard a huge explosion! We ran to the other side just in time to see you pulling Dega's body out of the fire."

"Dega!" his eyes went wide. "I forgot about him. Is he... "

"Alive," Dane answered. "It was his idea to move you to this room while you recover."

He hadn't noticed it wasn't his room until just now. The bed was larger and far more comfortable than his cot, and this room even had a window. He looked out at the view, following the black and gray lines of recruits marching on the parade square.

"You said days." He turned his gaze back to Dane. "How long have I been asleep?" He started to drag himself out of bed.

"Whoa." Dane pushed him back. "You're supposed to stay in bed until you've been given clearance. Doctor's orders." He tucked another pillow under Camber's head and leaned back in his chair. "If you must know, you've been asleep for three whole days. But that's not counting the night of the fire, so I suppose you could say four." Dane reached for a bowl of fruit on the nightstand; he held it out. "Hungry?"

Camber selected a pear. "Everything's so foggy, like it never really happened." The headache faded as his body regained its vitality. "All I remember is the roof collapsing, everything else is a blank." He stared at the ceiling, not sure how much Dane had guessed, but he wasn't ready to tell the truth just yet; it just seemed so preposterous.

Dane nodded. "There was an investigation into the cause of the fire." He had a feeling Camber was holding something back. "It turns out two privates were playing a little drinking game in the hayloft." No one could figure out how the men had managed to get their hands on the potent beverage since the Captain long ago outlawed any form of alcohol on the premises. "Apparently one of them knocked over a lantern and before they had time to react the fire was already out of control. That's when you sounded the bell in the tower. Only three horses died, the rest escaped when the side of the building was blown away." He knew Camber had something to do with the explosion. "And I don't even want to think what would have happened had you not been able to get out." Dane lowered his face. The strain over the past few days showed as dark circles under his eyes. Most of his time had been spent sitting beside his cousin waiting anxiously for him to wake.

"Anyway," Dane continued. "Sergeant Weyland stripped the two privates of their uniforms and sent them packing. I'm sure he would have done more but the Lieutenant was there and had orders to restrain the Serge if things got out of hand."

A soft knock interrupted, and the door slowly opened. Two heads peered around the doorway. "There he is!" Jules bounded clumsily into the room, followed by Hansil. He knocked over the pitcher of water as he danced about.

"Careful Jules," Dane's grin returned, and he chided his friend. "If you land on Camber he might never recover." They all laughed, and congratulated Camber on his daring rescue.

Camber was finally given the go ahead to move back to his room and resume his duties. One of the first things he did, to the delight of Sergeant Weyland, was visit his horse. The Sergeant was glad to see him, and clapped him proudly on the shoulder, thanking him for his heroics. "I wish we had more men like you."

Weyland wasn't the only person grateful for Camber's heroism. Dega sat at his desk contemplating every detail about the fire. He folded his arms across his chest, leaned back in his chair, and rested his boot heels across smoothly polished mahogany. *Something wasn't right.* So many inexplicable actions. Like how did Camber escape smoke and flame when even Gareth was forced to abandon his rescue attempts. Dega rubbed the stubble on his chin. He didn't buy Camber's story that his wet clothes had protected him. And if by some strange miracle they did, that excuse did not explain his escape. The next day he had surveyed the damage and was surprised to see one side of the building completely gone. Gareth had filled him in with his version of the events, and Dega had also questioned as many men as he could, but no one could give him a proper explanation for the explosion that had caused over half the stables to vanish. And not one board could be found. It was as if that entire side had never existed.

Dega frowned, remembering Gareth's face as he informed him of the rescue. His lieutenant had simply glowed with admiration for the cadet, and it seemed everywhere he went, inside and out, talk of the daring deed had grown to enormous, almost ridiculous proportions. He bit his lip. Of all people to drag him from the fire – why did it have to be Camber Bloodstone. He chewed on the irony of it, remembering a time when he had made Camber wish he hadn't run into him. Now what? *Let it go,* said a voice. But he shoved the voice to the back of his thoughts. He would just have to keep a close eye on Camber until he uncovered whatever secret the cadet was hiding.

A month had passed since the fire, and the garrison had all but returned to normal. Talk of the rescue was replaced with excitement surrounding the upcoming graduation. Summer arrived, bringing a flurry of activities around the barracks, and all recruits were busy putting the final touches on the fortress.

The Captain's elite had the day off to help with special preparations for the ceremonies, now only a week away. Bon drove the team of horses while Camber, Dane, and Hansil made themselves not so comfortable on the buckboard's hard wooden seats. Jules rode alongside on Swishtail, leading a packhorse; thanks to the extra lessons, he was now the best horseman in the squad.

"I guess we should be grateful the Cap' decided to let us go without an escort," said Bon. Fortunately, almost all the officers had been busy with organizing the grand event, and Dega (after much intervention by Gareth) reluctantly allowed his cadets to run the errand on their own.

"He didn't have much of a choice." Hansil chewed thoughtfully on a long stick of straw. "If he can't trust us to fetch a wagonload of supplies then how's he supposed to trust us on the battlefield?"

Dane agreed, and was quick to point out that by not letting them go Dega would be admitting that his recruiting had failed. "And trust me, he'd rather be thrown into a pit full of snakes than admit that he, Captain Darkhawk, made a mistake."

The wagon jarred to a bumpy halt outside a produce market. *Galey's Market:* the largest open-air market in Hartland. Hundreds of people jostled down aisles, milling about merchant stalls under brightly striped awnings; each row designated to a particular category of goods marked by small colorful flags. Merchants hawking their wares called to prospective customers, singsong voices rising above the din, mingling with the laughter of children and the lowing of livestock. The air was thick with fresh baked bread, pickling brine, ale and chestnuts; an energetic buzz electrified the atmosphere, and Dane was in high spirits as they strolled through the throng. "Ahhh... smell that. That's the scent of civilization," he grinned, dark eyes drinking in the glorious hustle and bustle of the market.

"Don't get sidetracked Dane," Jules warned. "We're supposed to collect supplies and head straight back to the barracks."

"Now Jules," Dane put his arm around his portly friend. "Don't go getting yourself all uptight about nothing. You sound like Dega. Did I say we weren't collecting supplies? Why, that's just what we're doing now, isn't it? And who's to mind if we get done faster than expected, that we can't take some time to enjoy ourselves?" He read the list aloud. "Fifty sacks of potatoes, twelve sacks of flour, eight sacks of sugar, corn, carrots... I think we can handle that. Everything we need seems to be in these two aisles. Shouldn't take us more than a couple of hours if we split into groups. And I bet this is normally an all-day chore. If we get done early we can have some time to ourselves and be back at the barracks before dusk, just like we planned, and no one will be the wiser. Right?"

The cadet gave Camber a pleading look, but all he got was a shrug and a "Sorry Jules, but I'm with Dane on this one." With a sigh he resigned his fate to the hands of his companions.

"Excellent." The archer pointed at Bon and Hansil. "You two get these," he tore the list in half, handing a piece to Bon. "We'll get the rest." He spun Jules toward an aisle. "Let's get this over with."

Crowds of onlookers stopped and stared; it wasn't often that Rangers were seen in town, uniforms and swords creating quite a stir. Children ran behind laughing with glee until their mothers caught them up, towing them away by their tiny hands. Fresh-faced maids peered out from behind the safety of the merchant stalls, and a brave young lass on a dare from her friends, threw back her hood and blew them each a kiss. Dane offered a wink, Camber grinned, and Jules blushed three shades of red.

Bon and Hansil were already loading supplies onto the buckboard when the trio returned. "Good timing," Hansil greeted his friends as they came into view. "We're all done here and it's only mid-afternoon." He and Bon threw the last pack atop the wagon, then gave the other three a hand with their sacks and pulled the tarp across.

"I know a little tavern just down the road." Bon winked at Dane. "We have plenty of time for food and drink before heading back to the barracks."

"Shouldn't we head back now? I don't think we're supposed to stop off anywhere else."

"Jules," this time it was Camber who spoke. "If we head back now we'll arrive way earlier than what's expected and the next time we go for supplies we'll have to work twice as hard just to make it back by the same time."

The cadet swung into the saddle and scowled at the other four. "Fine. But we only stay for an hour." He nudged Swishtail, and Bon made a clicking noise moving the buckboard onto the road. The chatter of his friends drifted back to his ears. "One hour," he repeated, but only a snort from Swishtail indicated anyone was listening.

They stopped in front of *the Duke and Smithy* and Jules tied the horses to a hitching post. The lighting inside was dim at best, and smoke from too many pipes wafted heavy in the air. Loud music played in the background, and even louder conversation rose above the clamor as the pub's patrons all tried to outdo each other, raising their voices above the racket. As soon as the five cadets entered all noise ceased abruptly and every head turned to stare at the newcomers.

"I think we made a mistake," said Jules, he turned for the door, but Dane held him fast and pushed him toward a table. Once the boys had seated themselves all heads turned back to the business at hand and the ruckus resumed at its former level.

A serving girl appeared at their table and took their order, returning promptly with a pitcher of ale and five mugs. Dane poured them all a round of drinks and leaned back in his chair. "A toast to Captain Darkhawk for allowing us this afternoon of pleasure."

Everyone answered with a "Here! Here!" except Jules; he sat with his head between his hands staring at the floor.

After the second pitcher was replaced with a third, and the food had arrived, Jules had long since tossed aside his fears, refusing to listen to the little voice of doom nagging in his ear. The door of the tavern opened and a shock of sunlight spilled into the common room. He turned his head slowly and blinked away the bright glare. Sal and Caleb stood in front of their table.

"What are you two doing here?" he asked, but even as he said it he had already guessed the answer. Sal stood with arms folded, looking down in mock disgust. "My dear Jules," he said, "we've been sent on an errand by our most esteemed Captain to find out what *has* been keeping our trusted companions." Sal burst out laughing when his friend dropped his head. "Actually, it was our idea to go find you. The LT was worried the Cap' might go hunting for your heads so he asked us if we would locate your whereabouts and escort you home."

Caleb nodded. "Fortunately, Sal knows all the taverns in town and figured *the Duke* was closest." He motioned for the cadet to slide his chair over and drew a seat to the table. "What d'ya say Sal? I'd sure hate to waste all this ale, maybe we have time for quick one." He poured himself a mug and winked at his companion. Camber and Hansil cheered as their friend sat down; the two cadets burst into song, followed by a laughing fit.

Sal spotted Dane and Bon throwing dice at the opposite end of the tavern, and grabbing a mug off the table he strode over to where his friends were enjoying a winning streak.

"The lad's a cheater!" A farmhand threw his coins down in disgust.

Dane greeted Sal as he scooped up the coins.

"What's that all about?"

He shrugged. "Poor sport."

As if on cue the gambler came back and slammed his fist on the table. "I want my money back - *Ranger.*" His three friends stood behind him. The tavern had suddenly gone quiet, all ears strained to hear Dane's response.

"Sorry, no refunds." He was at least half a head taller, but the man outweighed him by a good hundred pounds. "You lost fair and square. I'm no cheater and I don't appreciate being called one."

Bon and Sal were now standing, ready for whatever was going to happen next. They didn't have long to wait. The gambler swung his fist.

The archer ducked. "Miss me?" He popped up with a grin. A stupid look passed over the gambler's face and Dane hammered his jaw.

Camber and the others bounded across the room. Chairs went flying and tables were overturned as the cadets came to Dane's aid. The serving girl screamed when one of the thugs flew into the dish cabinet; and the balding barkeep, a mountain of a man with the foresight of a soothsayer, scooped the frightened slip of a girl under his massive arm and pulled her to safety, but not before she slammed her serving tray hard on the head of the hapless brute who now lay dazed across the upended dish cabinet. The sound of breaking dishes was completely drowned out by the cheers of drunken patrons, whooping and hollering at the cadets.

Camber dodged sideways, grabbing his opponent by the arm and twisting it in the opposite direction. The man let out a cry; his body contorted around his arm, causing further pain.

"Get off!" a muffled voice came from beneath Jules, who sat on the floor, heedless to the cries coming from his cushion. He tossed a chair leg to Bon, who used it to fend off the largest of the four.

"A little help here." Dane had pinned the gambler's arms behind his back.

"At your service," and Caleb smashed a full bottle of wine across his head.

"Thanks!"

"Anytime." He ducked to avoid a serving dish sailing across the room. It smashed against the wall near the entrance. As luck would have it, the door flew open at that exact moment the dish became acquainted with the wallpaper, and a very angry Captain of the Rangers and his bewildered Lieutenant stepped into the brawl.

At the sight of the figure standing in the doorway all combat ceased immediately. Tavern patrons and cadets froze in place. Dega's face hardened as he surveyed the scene. Dane was about to say something but the Captain's obvious anger made him think twice, and he shut his mouth with an audible snap.

"You, you, you, and you, OUT!" The excitement of the brawl quickly gave way to shame under the weight of the Captain's glare. Dega said something to Gareth, who left the room to stand outside with Caleb, Bon, Sal, and Hansil.

"Are you the Innkeeper?" Dega's gaze landed on the man behind the counter with a dirty dishrag on his shoulder. The serving girl peered nervously out from behind the barkeep, who slowly nodded his head.

"On behalf of Hartland's Rangers I apologize for my cadets." He glowered at the remaining three. "I hope we can make amends for the damage caused to your fine establishment." He pointed at Dane. "Give this gentleman all the money you have in your pockets."

Dane sighed, and drew out a sizable leather pouch filled with money left over from the day's shopping and the coin he had won playing dice. He handed it to the Innkeep.

"All of it." Dega prodded the archer.

He opened his breast pocket and dumped a few more coins onto the proprietor's serving counter. Another sigh; he really hated to see that money go.

"Now wait for me outside." Dega's lip curled back and he snapped at the three now exiting the door. "And DO NOT move!"

The stars were just starting to show amid the deepening blue blanket of twilight. The air was cool; a refreshing breeze stirred gently through the treetops, tousling the hair on their heads and clearing away the last wispy traces of inebriation. Camber stood at attention between Dane and Jules; he exchanged a look with Hansil, who he could barely make out on the far side of the buckboard. His eyes darted sideways; Dane to his right, and Jules on his left. Jules had predicted this. Why didn't he listen? Now look at the mess they were in. His uncle would be sorely disappointed if he were tossed out for something like this.

Dega came out after what seemed an eternity; he marched over to Gareth, said something, and the lieutenant saluted, then Gareth ordered Hansil and other three cadets onto the buckboard, tying Swishtail, Panther, and the packhorse to the back of the wagon, before mounting his own horse; he gave it a nudge and it started down the road at a trot with the wagon following close behind.

"I'm escorting you three on foot. A hard march might teach you all a lesson." Dega paced back and forth, turning sharply on his boot heel. "Furthermore, all your privileges will be stripped away, and although you will also graduate you will not be allowed to participate in the ceremonies." At this announcement all three cadets looked at each other; they were expecting a far worse punishment. "Be thankful I'm not tossing you out! Though I can't think of a single reason why I shouldn't." Dega stopped pacing. If eyes could smolder then his would surely start a bonfire. Catching the stunned looks of disbelief, he added, "No, I can't expel you from the Company. We've invested too much time with your training, and your heroics during the fire have already reached the ears of my superiors." It was true. He could not toss them out, not now. Not after sending out his latest report, which among other things, contained a glowing account of the action taken by his squad during the stable fire, commemorating the merits of each individual. "But," he continued. "I'm sure I don't have to remind you that you are still under *my* command."

Camber stared at the ground, he knew *exactly* what Dega meant, and entertained the notion that it might be better if he was tossed out of the cavalry.

Dega ordered his cadets to march single file, and they struck out along the road with the Captain bringing up the rear, passing quickly out of Hartland's principal district and down the road that led back to the garrison. The moon was floating high above their heads, lighting the way, but Dega could care less; he gripped his sword hilt, clenching and unclenching his fingers around its grooved pommel. He was furious! If Ravenhill caught wind of this it would be his head.

After they crossed the Whitewash he decided it would be quicker to cut across country, and when they reached the fork that split toward the outer farmlands or past Wildwood he steered them off the main path and onto a seldom-used trail. When they questioned his reason for doing this he had simply told them it would shave at least two hours off their travel time and since he had no intention of being on the road all night they had better double their pace.

Dane was following Camber, he could hear Jules laboring behind, his breath coming in short huffs. As they marched through the woods he thought he saw a shadowy movement off to the side. It was so quick that he told himself it must have been his imagination. *Or was it?* There it was again. This time just ahead of their intended route. He stopped suddenly and Jules bumped into him. He turned, half expecting Dega to snarl, but the Ranger's Captain had drawn his sword.

"What is it?" Jules whispered. His eyes darted between Dane and Dega, searching for some small reassurance that everything was fine, but both faces remained impassive. Dane looked at Dega, who nodded. The archer reached around for his bow and nocked an arrow. Camber had carefully retraced his steps so that he now stood between the two. He drew his blade.

Jules was the only one without a weapon; he hadn't bothered to take his sword. At the time he felt it would only be a hindrance, and why burden himself with more weight than necessary? Now he could only stand there and hope whatever it was would turn tail and leave.

A bolt of gray shot out of the bush. Its barrel-shaped body lunged, knocking Camber to ground. Moonlight bounced off long wicked teeth. Camber screamed, grabbing the Bounder by its leathery flaps. Spittle flew from its mouth, warm wet drops landing on his face.

"CAMBER!" Dega threw himself at the beast, knocking it off balance. It spun sideways, one forepaw still pinning its prey. Lips curled back, stretching its maw; teeth and fury; the bowels of hell shining red from within. The Bounder let out a long hateful note, raking its claws across the tops of his boots; another swipe took the sword clean out of his hands.

Dane dove onto its back. "GO!" he screamed at Camber. It let out an angry roar, turning its eyeless face at the archer. He threw his arms underneath its neck. "GO!" he screamed again. "I can't hold it." He bent its head backward, exposing throat.

Dega yanked his boot-knife free and plunged it deep. The Bounder's shriek hung on the air like a blast from another dimension. Teeth and claws tearing a frenzy. Blood spurted freely, covering them all in sticky wetness. The monster's throat gurgled, and Dega stabbed it again and again. Camber's fingers found his sword, and gripping it tightly he twisted away from the beast.

A warhorse crashed into the clearing hot on the Bounder's heels. Jules heard the noise the same time the creature lunged at Camber. He turned his head and saw the Easterling. With no time to find a weapon, he charged across the glade to meet the warrior head on. The Easterling whirled his steed and sent it speeding at the cadet. Drawing his sword, he made ready to run the boy through, but Jules dodged the blade, and grabbed the horse by its bridle, wrenching its head sideways, and bringing horse and rider crashing to ground. He pounced on the Easterling, grappling for the sword.

Iron-shod hooves churned up soil as the charger regained its footing, and it was only by a miracle that Jules managed to stay atop the rider, using his weight as leverage. But the Easterling was a fully-grown man and a veteran of many campaigns, and he soon gained the advantage over his inexperienced opponent when his horse gave one last lunge, kicking itself free. He now sat astride Jules. Centuries of hatred for the boy and all his kind stared through dark bitter lenses into the large brown eyes of the cadet. Cruel was that mouth, twisting into a smile as he drew a long sinister knife from beneath the folds of his cloak.

A rock slammed into his skull; his grip loosened, and Jules grabbed the knife, twisting the blade back to the warrior's throat. Hot red blood ran down his hand, splashing his face. With a grunt, he heaved the body off to one side, and picking up the sword he sprinted toward the action at the other end of the clearing.

The ground shook with force, sending Jules headfirst into the dirt. The earth ripped open, swallowing Camber, Dane, Dega, and the Bounder. With a cry of horror, he stumbled across the clearing, and reaching the spot where his friends had been only moments ago, he fell to his knees and stuck his face against the rock, yelling their names. The sound of muffled voices floated back from below. Tears of frustration welled up in his eyes; he clawed at the ground with bloodied fingers. He had to get them out! He called their names again and again, then pressed his ear back to the rock, but could no longer hear them.

A wave of panic spread from his gut, gripped by sudden nausea. *What to do? What to do?* Eyes darted about the clearing, back and forth, stopping on the Easterling's charger.

The need for action made him want to run, but common sense told him to go slow, and so he did, talking to the horse quietly and walking as slow as he dared. With a snort it flattened its black ears, but he caught its bridle, pulling the head low. Taking a deep breath, he swung into the saddle. The stallion reared, dancing wildly in a circle. It knew this was not its rider and tried to dislodge this new irritant, but Jules stayed in the saddle, for once his weight was an advantage.

"Okay boy. Let's see what you're made of." He shortened the reins and drove his heels home. Horse and rider sped back to the barracks, thundering down the last few miles. Jules was nearly breathless when he and the charger raced through the gates.

Gareth blinked in surprise when the cadet reined up on an Easterling warhorse. "Where's the Captain?" Jules repeated the events as quickly as he could, urging the officer to send out a search party, but Gareth was already shouting orders even as he was still relating the story.

* * * * * * * *

Camber rolled away from the Bounder as soon as he felt the earth shift beneath his body. He now sat on the ground (or below ground as was the case). He hadn't noticed that Dane and Dega took the tumble with him, or that the Bounder had met its death at the hands of three dwarves who were now hacking it to pieces. No, he hadn't noticed any of those things because he was staring at the strangely garbed man and the red-bearded dwarf standing over him.

"Welcome," the man said at last. A mop of unruly chestnut hair curled over his ears, and a goatee partially hid his sun-bronzed face, and though he appeared to be in his prime, the wisdom of the ages sparkled in his bright hazel eyes. He had a friendly reassuring manner, and Camber's initial anxiety subsided.

The archer stood, dusting himself off. "Snakes Alive! Where'd you come from?"

Dega put his hand on Dane's shoulder and stepped in front. "Where are we, and how did we arrive here?" Intuition told him to be wary, this man was very powerful, else why would he be mingling with dwarves.

"Aaah, yes. That was their doing." He gestured to his companions, now standing off to one side. "This is their warren and you have just fallen through one of their doorways."

Camber picked up his sword, and walked slowly over to his cousin's side. The stranger's eyes followed, seeming to scrutinize his every move. "You are Camber Bloodstone," he said; it sounded more like a statement than a question. Camber nodded.

Dane pointed a finger. "You still haven't told us who you are!"

"Do not be hasty young fellow. I mean you no harm. But if it helps, I shall introduce myself," and flashing a smile, he opened his palms outward. "I have many names but to most I'm Stornoway Hawker or just plain Hawker if you prefer. I am a warden of Astaria. Some call us wizards, or sorcerers, but we are really just the *Caretakers* for this world. I do what I can to preserve the delicate balance of *Life*." Hawker's eyes scanned the trio as he spoke. "This is my apprentice

Lockjaw, a dwarf from the Ironfist Mountains." The red-bearded dwarf stepped forward and bowed low to the group.

Camber had never seen a dwarf before, and his uncle's vague descriptions did them little justice. They were short, but incredibly muscular, maybe even more than Sergeant Weyland, if you were to shrink the stable sergeant down to dwarven height. All four dwarves were clad in armored breastplates and leather, and their broad-bladed axes were now tucked back into their belts. Lockjaw was the only one who, in addition to his axe, carried a long wooden staff.

"But I didn't think dwarves could do magic," said Dane.

"They can't," answered Hawker, and he frowned at his apprentice, like a teacher might when saddled with a pupil whose time would be better spent at manual labor than mathematical calculations. "But Lockjaw's heart is set on becoming a great wizard, and in exchange for his service I give him lessons."

Hawker's gaze swept over the skeptical faces of the three young men. "I see you still doubt me. Very well, we can do this your way." A bolt of blue shot from his finger and the Bounder vanished in a puff of colorful smoke.

"Snakes Alive!" Dane swore as he stared at the spot where the Bounder had been only moments ago. Camber stepped back, eyes wide, but Dega was well traveled and had seen his share of extraordinary sights before and was not as easily impressed by the sorcerer's magic. His body appeared relaxed but his hand rested lightly on the pommel of his sword. He spoke at last to the wizard. "I hope you plan on telling us why we've been brought here. I do not think it was by chance that we stumbled upon so secret a door."

Hawker blew a curl of smoke off his fingertip then rubbed his goatee. "Yes, of course. But the front porch of a dwarf-warren is no place for such a story. Come with me and we'll find a comfortable place to converse. You shall soon learn all you need to know."

* * * * * * * *

Gareth rode at the head of the search party with Jules. At last they reached the glade and the lieutenant dismounted. He took a minute to examine the Easterling, relieving the corpse of anything useful, then had Jules describe the events in detail while they retraced his steps to where Dega and the cadets battled the Bounder. Tears streamed down his blood-streaked face as he recounted all he had witnessed. Gareth listened carefully, his face could have been chiseled from stone for all the expression it displayed, even as Jules pointed to where the earth had opened up swallowing officer, cadets, and bounder.

The Lieutenant bent low, inspecting the ground. He pulled off a glove, running his finger carefully along the surface, tracing an invisible pattern; he paused for a moment as if calling something to memory, then put a reassuring hand on the young cadet's shoulder. "You said you heard voices. Is this true?"

"Yes!" Jules brightened. "I heard them. I'm sure of it! It sounded like they were underneath the rock." He put his ear to the very spot where he had heard Dane swear, half hoping to still hear voices. Gareth also put his ear to the ground, and then tapped on it with his knuckles. Jules started to say something but the officer cut him off with a "Shhh!" He bent his ear back to the rock and tapped again.

He stood, smiling, but the cadet said nothing, and so he explained. "The ground is hollow, that's why you heard voices. This must be a dwarf-warren." The lad seemed not to comprehend. "It means they're alive," the Lieutenant said.

Jules started to grin, but then his face darkened. "How do we get them out?"

"Not to worry, the Captain will see to that." He felt a wave of relief as he turned to walk back to his mount. He knew Dega would bring them safely back to the barracks. The Captain had survived far worse than this. He ordered the search party back to the garrison, tied his mount to a tree, and asked Jules to stay and help rid the area of any evidence that a battle had taken place.

* * * * * * * *

Hawker led them down the passage to a cleverly crafted atrium carved from polished marble, so exquisitely smooth that it might have been satin. Sapphires shaped the ceiling; each facet sparkling like an azure flame, illuminating the atrium in soft shades of blue. The circumference was easily as big as the barracks, if not larger; four corridors intersected from opposite sides leading to the four corners of Astaria: North, South, East, and West.

The floor appeared to be made of a singular piece of malachite - no visible cracks or seams, mirroring the company's reflection in depths of polished green as they passed over. A jungle of carefully cultivated plants sprang up in the center; green vegetation laced with a rainbow of flowers, and birds with bright plumage, all merging in a riot of color under that spectacular gemstone sky.

Hawker spread his arms wide. "Welcome to Stone-Haven. King Stonefinger's Warren and the greatest dwarven city of our time."

"There's more than one?" Dane spun in a circle, trying to see everywhere at once.

"Yes, of course. Men aren't the only people who build cities. There are at least six warrens still thriving in Astaria and all of them nearly as grand as this one."

Dwarven eyes followed as they strode along the garden path, making Camber quite uncomfortable with the attention their party had suddenly commanded; he tried not to look directly at the dwarves, hoping they would stop staring and go back to whatever they had been doing. Dane on the other hand, seemed to enjoy the looks of curiosity, and he gave his spectators quite a performance, cheerfully nodding his head and winking at any dwarf who had the misfortune of making eye contact. Dega brought up the rear, too busy memorizing the route they were taking to bother with the warren's inhabitants.

Two figures cast in bronze framed the South porch archway; on the left stood a formidable dwarf-warrior wearing heavy-plated armor and gripping a battle-axe in both hands; on his head, a gold helm encrusted with glittery gemstones. To the dwarf-warrior's right, a majestic lady, she as perfect and beautiful as the warrior was terrible and fierce. In one hand she held high a silver scepter capped with a round red jewel; in the other, a bouquet of freshly cut lilies, and on her regal head sat a crown made from clearest crystal.

"Who are they?" Dane placed his hand on the base of the warrior's pedestal.

"King Ironfist and his Queen, the beautiful Shale, Mother of all Dwarves," said a dwarf; he removed Dane's hand from the statue, then took a cloth, wiping away the sweaty print. "We place their likenesses at this entrance to guard against the evils of the Southlands."

Each entrance, including the North corridor they had so recently come from, had bronze figures on either side. "What about those?" Dane indicated the others.

"Aah," the dwarf who seemed to enjoy his role as historian spoke in his thick accent, rolling his rrr's and emphasizing his sss's. "The sentinels guarding *the North* are Goldpick and Whiterock, harbingers of Fortune and Prosperity; Three-Fingers and Longbeard frame *the West* and bring us Luck and Friendship, and the ones at the *East-*

gate, we consider the most important, for they are Slate-Eyes the Watcher, and Foe-Hammer, Guardian of Warfare." He huffed his chest with pride at doing his part to instruct these foreigners on an important piece of dwarf-lore, and he turned to further educate his young pupils; all this was wasted of course, since neither appeared to be listening.

"It's weird," Dane whispered. "Have you noticed that all the dwarves we've seen so far have been male? No female folk at all."

"That's because dwarxen are regarded with special reverence, for they are very few in number," said Hawker; he had heard Dane clearly even though he was more than twenty paces ahead. "You will not likely see one either, as they are more heavily guarded than any treasure the dwarves possess."

They crossed another atrium, this one not nearly as grand as the great dome but still beautiful with its sculpted gardens and ornaments, then exited through yet another arched doorway and down a long corridor.

"Sit. Make yourselves comfortable," said Hawker, and he ushered them into a round room with large pillows covering half the floor. "We have much to discuss, but for your benefit I've asked that food and water be brought."

Dane and Camber sat, but Dega remained standing. He caught the wizard looking in his direction more than once as he leaned casually against a carved pillar. Hawker took his seat. "The Captain is right about one thing," he said. "Your entry into the realm of the dwarves was no accident. I've been searching for you, Camber Bloodstone, though I did not expect to pull you and your friends through the doorstep of King Stonefinger's Warren."

Both boys opened their mouths to say something but the wizard brought up his hand. "Wait. Hear me out. There will be plenty of time for questions later." He turned his head. "You might as well sit Captain, this concerns you too." Dega shrugged, and took a seat.

"Camber, this may sound unbelievable, but you must trust all that I say." He waited for the cadet to show he understood the matter at hand was of utmost importance before laying the full impact of why he was so intent on finding him.

"You have a great and terrible power. For Good or Evil – *You*, Camber Bloodstone, have the ability to unmake this world."

IV

An Amazing Revelation

"How?... Wa... why?"

The wizard's words fell on his ears like a death-sentence, and somewhere in the back of his mind he imagined the click of a key turning the tumblers and locking a door.

"It's okay," Hawker said. "I did not mean to frighten you so. But you must understand, this is a very dangerous power. It comes from inside, and when something like that is born out of thought there are no limits to what the imagination will conjure."

"So what does that mean?"

"It means Dane, that I can pretty much obliterate anything in my path." It was too much to think about; dream no longer, his secret had been revealed.

"Well that explains how half the stables vanished," and Dega glared at him.

Hawker laid a reassuring hand on his shoulder. "This power of yours is nothing to be ashamed of."

"But why me? Why must I have it? " He looked at Hawker but all he got was a shrug.

"Destinies are not revealed until we begin them, and often it's too late to stop that which has been started."

The Captain tapped his foot, wondering just how much advice this Hawker would dole out that might be useful instead of the worthless drivel he was currently spouting.

"You view this power as a cruel punishment, one that's been placed on your shoulders for no apparent reason other than being born. But it is a gift, Camber. A gift."

Dega snorted, annoyance clearly showing on his face, but Hawker appeared not to notice. "Do not allow doubt to darken your heart. Stay true to your heart and you shall triumph over whatever evils are placed in your path," he was talking to Camber but his eyes were on Dega. "Make your decisions carefully and weigh all before you condemn your gift, your destiny."

Camber stared at his feet. "I don't understand. How can I control something like that?"

"You can't, not just yet. It comes under duress, and knows no boundaries, but like a wild beast it can be tamed. The Easterling King knows this; he will find you and make you his tool or he will break you."

Dega frowned. "But why should we listen to you? Camber has this power, so you say. All the more reason for him to stay under my protection."

"Have you *not* been listening? There are those who desire this power. Or did you not think it unusual for a Bounder to be this far north?"

"But what now? I can't just pick up and leave."

"Why not?"

"What? Leave?"

Dane nodded. "If you're not here then you can't be found."

"Yes," Hawker agreed. "You should leave. But I'm thinking that it doesn't matter where you go, you are a dangerous pawn in the wrong hands."

Dega started toward the door. "This is all very interesting, but I cannot see how hiding Camber will be of help. The Rangers will keep him safe, and once I get back to my outfit I can rally support and we can send forth an army to quell the Easterling King."

"I am truly sorry Captain, but I cannot let you go. You've already heard too much."

"Try to stop me." He turned on his boot heel and down the passage back to the atrium.

It was Lockjaw who spoke first. "Might I give it a try, Sir?"

Hawker nodded his approval, and Lockjaw pointed his staff at Dega. *"Dorno orn, Dorno nay can, Dorno Sine!"*

Nothing happened, and they watched Dega's retreating form grow smaller and smaller. *"DORNO SINE!"* repeated the dwarf. And Dega turned the corner.

"Lockjaw," Hawker spoke softly, and his pupil paused his

incantation. "Why don't you just go and retrieve our guest. We can work on that spell later." The dwarf nodded, and called the other three to come with him.

Lockjaw and his companions hurried after Dega; then Dane turned to the wizard. "If he can't do magic, why do you keep him as an apprentice?"

"Because dwarves are known for their tenacity, plus he's as strong as ten men."

"So he's your packhorse."

"No, not exactly. He carries my things from time to time, but in exchange for his service I teach him magic."

"But you said that dwarves can't do magic," Camber pointed out.

Hawker rubbed his goatee as he thought carefully. "All living things have the ability to do magic. It's the magic of *Life* that we take our power from. Whether someone, or some creature, has the ability to tap into that precious resource is an entirely different matter. Some, like Camber, are born with this natural talent, and theirs is the strongest. Others, such as the Easterling King, learn their skill over time. Elves are different, they weave their magic into talismans."

Camber fingered his locket until he felt Hawker's eyes on him, and he quickly dropped it back under his shirt.

"Then there are some who may never discover their hidden power. They live their lives to the best of their abilities, day in and day out, eventually growing old and leaving this world without any knowledge that they too have a special gift."

"Like I said," Dane grinned. "You're using the dwarf as a packhorse."

"Do you not believe me Thomas?"

"My name's not Thomas, it's Dane."

"My apologies. You remind me of another lad who went by the name of Thomas. He used to doubt me too."

Lockjaw and the other dwarves returned with Dega. He snarled at the wizard. "I'm guessing we can't go free until we do whatever it is required."

"Now that depends entirely on you, Dega Darkhawk." Hawker met his scowl with a look of his own. Dega raised his eyebrow; he didn't remember telling the wizard his name.

"I'm sorry Sir," Lockjaw dropped his head. "I have failed." He stood behind Dega, staring at the ground.

"In what way?" Hawker asked.

"The spell. It did not work for me."

"What was it you were trying to do?"

"I was trying to bring him back," he pointed to the irate officer.

"And is he back?" asked Hawker, cocking an eyebrow.

"Yes. But I had to go and retrieve him."

Hawker smiled warmly. "But you see, it worked." Surprise registered across the faces of the company but was reflected most keenly in the dwarf's squinty black eyes. "It did?"

"Yes. Well in a roundabout way," he stood and patted his pupil's head. "Not all spells are instant. Some work indirectly. And though you had to manually retrieve our guest," he gestured toward the indignant Dega, "you did so after you had cast the spell. The result of your efforts brought the Captain back. I would say the spell was a success." The dwarf beamed with pride, Dane rolled his eyes, Camber smirked, and Dega scowled.

"I certainly hope the safeguarding of Camber doesn't rely on your definition of magic." Dega's hand went for his sword, squeezing it tight.

"Perhaps you might enlighten us with your own philosophy on the arcane," replied Hawker.

"Can you really help me?" Camber turned, facing Hawker, wanting some reassurance.

"Yes and No. I can offer you my guidance. But the balance of *Life* is a precarious thing, and I will not upset that balance by taking a direct role."

"Then what can I do? I'm just one person."

"One person can do a lot given the right mindset. Fortunately, there are those who have a means to help and resources available to aid our cause. We shall depart at once for Illianther, last of the three great Kingdoms."

Dega was not pleased with this proposal. "And what can the Elves offer Camber that the Rangers cannot," he snorted.

"Well for one thing, wisdom. But it just so happens Illianther was the last known location of the Winterstone."

"What the hell's a Winterstone?" Dega relaxed his grip, resting his hand lightly on the haft.

"A talisman. But its whereabouts remain a mystery," answered Hawker.

"This just keeps getting better and better."

Hawker stroked his goatee. "We can consult the library at Illianther and perhaps gain a clue to where it might be found."

Dega grabbed the wizard by his cloak, twisting it around his fingers and drawing Hawker close. "I don't play games. And I don't play with people's lives. There better be a damn good reason for needing this talisman."

Hawker pulled away. "Camber's magic can be countered by someone who has the knowledge and skill to do so. The Winterstone enhances an existing ability and brings the user great power, one that rivals anything above or below Astaria. The King knows this, and he too is seeking the Stone." He pointed his finger. "Do you really think any of you will be safe once his armies cross the Barrier? Camber's very presence endangers your garrison, and all of Hartland. It may be in your best interest take this journey Dega Darkhawk."

The wizard had used his full name a second time, and Dega wondered just how he knew who he was.

"Besides," continued Hawker. "We will have need of your sword. If you truly are who I think you are then you will make the honorable choice regardless of whatever loyalties you hold dear with the Rangers."

"Very well," he said at last. "But in exchange for my loyalty I ask that my opinion be regarded equally in all matters." He was not happy about the trek to Elvenhome, and had no desire to seek advice from its patronizing people. But Camber could not stay here and the Rangers would be in good hands under Gareth's command. His Lieutenant would likely send scouts to look for them, *in fact he probably already has*. "We can cross at Whistlegate. But we can't go like this; we need supplies."

"Actually we need to make a stop along the way. Our journey will take us farther south, into the Borderlands of Caldorn."

He turned to the three dwarves who had accompanied Lockjaw and spoke to them in their language; they left immediately, eager to obey.

"We shall leave as soon as possible, for I fear time may be of the essence. Though I knew that the Easterlings were abroad I was surprised to learn that they had brought Bounders. This can only mean one thing," he tugged at his goatee. "Their King must know what he seeks is close at hand. He would never have sent his Bounders if this were not the case."

Hawker eyed Camber's torn clothing. "Roll up your sleeve. I have some salve that should take care of those scratches," he pulled loose a pouch from his belt and applied a sticky ointment to Camber's arm.

It was cool and carried a minty fragrance and Camber felt a refreshing tingle as the balm seeped into his skin. "What exactly is a Bounder?" Up till now he was only familiar with his uncle's fairytale depiction.

Hawker tucked away his pouch and sat down on the cushions. The others followed his example making themselves comfortable.

But it was Dega who spoke, having crossed paths with one prior to their recent battle. His first assignment as a serviceman was to map the region surrounding Tar Galleaon. After making a final study of the canyon he had surprised a lone Bounder hunting along the ravine. The scars on his neck were a visible reminder of that day. "Bounders are not a natural creature like a wolf or a bear, though they are in some way related."

"That figures," Dane added, "they look like the mating between a bear and a wolf."

Hawker nodded. "You are not far off from the truth young man. They are exactly that but with the added property of magic."

Dane exchanged a look with Camber. "But how is that possible?" he asked.

Hawker stroked his goatee. "Oh it's possible. As I said earlier, there are many forms of magic, inherent in all living things, be it tree or animal. The Easterling King has honed his craft over many centuries, and it was he who made the Bounders."

"But I thought he was a mortal man," said Camber.

"He is. But he is a mortal man with incredible power, and it's this very power that has allowed him to live a life many times greater than any mortal. But that is another story for another time, for now be satisfied in knowing that it was he who created the Bounders, shaped from the blood and bone of the snow bear and the cunning tenacity of the eastern timber wolf."

"They are bound by magic and without it they would cease to exist," added Dega.

The dwarves returned and Lockjaw sorted through packs, distributing the weight before handing each of them their own bundle. He hoisted both his and Hawker's packs onto his shoulders, said something in dwarvish, and Hawker nodded his head.

"King Stonefinger wishes to have an audience with us before we depart. Our war with the East is his battle as well, and therefore our venture is also his concern." He turned to one of the dwarves. "Go tell your King we accept his invitation." The dwarf bowed low and disappeared down the corridor.

"This warren is larger than most and it will take at least two days to reach the South porch. After we leave the safety of the dwarf-warren our progress will depend upon what we encounter above ground. With a little luck, we just might have the upper hand, for I suspect that since the Easterling King has sent his scouts this far north then it is unlikely he will expect you to be traveling south."

The wizard led them back to the grand atrium, and they crossed the plaza to the Western gate, but instead of traveling down the corridor they climbed a series of ramps cleverly concealed behind the bronze figure of friendship. Interlocking patterns embossed with silver flickered brightly as their feet passed over them. At the top they were led down a long hallway to an elaborately carved door framed by marble pillars.

A pair of warriors stood guard at the entrance. They might have been chiseled from granite, for they were completely motionless, but when the group approached they crossed their halberds preventing further access. Lockjaw and his companions dropped to one knee and bent their heads, but it was Hawker who spoke, addressing the guards in their own tongue; they uncrossed their weapons at once, allowing wizard and company to pass.

The King's chambers were made of white and blue marble. The same intricate pattern carved into the ramps was repeated on the polished floor of the room. Flowering plants scented the air with a pleasing fragrance while colorful songbirds jumped from branch to branch. The far wall was made from the same blue crystal as the dome and Camber's eyes were immediately drawn toward it. He marveled at the ingenuity of the dwarves as he looked out across the atrium.

"Greetings, Stornoway Hawker," a booming voice announced the arrival of King Stonefinger, and the dwarves immediately bent head and knee.

"Arise," he said. Stonefinger was almost a whole head taller than his kinsmen, coming right up to Hawker's shoulders. A mantle of winter fox pelts adorned his gleaming armor, and around his stout waist he wore a wide belt with a single sapphire in the center; he wore no crown on top of his balding head, nor was one necessary, for his very presence commanded attention leaving no doubt in anyone's mind that he was King.

"Your Majesty," Hawker took the King's hand, touching his ring to his forehead. "These are the men from aboveground," he made a sweeping gesture to Dega, Dane, and Camber. "It is they who I was seeking, and I'm grateful for your Majesty's help in this matter." The King wrinkled his white brows. "Hawker, I have known you for a very long time, there is no need to be so formal. You should know by now the dwarves will always aid you freely in your affairs." Stonefinger eyed the trio with a pair of cunning eyes that belied his ancient appearance. "I welcome you all to Stone-Haven. Though I regret it's not under more pleasant circumstances. Hawker and I have had many a discussion regarding certain tidings from the East and I am sure he has already informed you of the sorcerer's plans to renew his terrible war. His captains and bounders already invade the north, and it is only a matter of time before he grows bold enough to march his armies onto Stone-Haven's doorstep. For the safety of the lands and my people I have reinstated the dwarven armies, and messengers from my kingdom have already returned confirming allegiance with the warrens at Coldstone, Rockri, and Ironfist." The King sighed, and his voice softened. "I fear this war will be greater than the one that laid waste the plains of N'Amorr."

Dega's brow furrowed. "Pardon me for interrupting, your Lordship."

Stonefinger smiled at the cavalier. "Please speak freely; your words may hold wisdom for these old ears."

"I do not doubt this war will require the combined strength of all, not just the dwarves, and since you have the support of your brethren, I suggest sending an envoy to the Rangers as soon as possible. You can seek out my second in command at the former Ranger stronghold outside of Hartland."

Stonefinger stroked his long white beard. "Yes, I had thought of that myself but was not entirely sure who to contact. If you would provide the details I will send someone to your officer by the morrow." He called for his scribe and asked for Dega and Hawker to join him in private. They followed Stonefinger through an ornate door leaving the cadets with Lockjaw.

"This isn't exactly what I had in mind when I signed up," said Dane.

"I guess adventures never really happen the way you want them to." Camber stood near the window, shading his eyes to better view the chaotic scenes unfolding below; then turned to Lockjaw. "What do you people do for fun?"

"Fun?"

"Entertainment."

The dwarf shrugged. "What is entertainment?"

"You know, song, dance, games, that sort of thing."

Lockjaw's face brightened. "Oh! You mean Karpung."

"Karpung?" Dane rolled the word across his tongue.

"Karpung," repeated another dwarf, and all four nodded.

"What's Karpung?" asked Camber.

"It's a game, one that goes back to the earliest of days, long before the Easterling King's rise to power. We still play using the exact same rules as our ancestors did."

"How's it played?" Dane fingered his dice.

Lockjaw put his finger on the wall to illustrate the game. "You have two teams of fourteen dwarves. Here, and here," he made a crisscross in two places. "One team must carry a spherical-shaped stone past two upright markers." He drew an invisible line across the crystal. "The other team must stop them from crossing the markers. If they are successful then they are awarded a point. However, if the team carrying the stone crosses the markers then they are awarded a point and the other team has a point deduction. The first team to reach twenty points wins and the losing team must Karpung."

The other dwarves laughed. "The best part," one said.

A shadow passed over Lockjaw's face as he spoke. "The underground lakes look inviting, for they are very clear and very blue, but their waters are frigid and their depths unfathomable. The losing team has the honor of diving into the lake. That is Karpung."

"That doesn't sound so bad," Dane replied. "You dive into freezing cold water. So what?"

Lockjaw was quick to answer. "If the water was your only worry then losing at Karpung would not be such a huge disappointment and everyone would play. No, it is not the lake, however intimidating, but the fear of the unknown. *That* is the real force behind Karpung." Camber looked at Dane and the archer shrugged.

"Ancient and mysterious are the things that dwell in these lakes, far older and far stranger than any creature in this world. Even Stornoway Hawker cannot account for all life-forms, especially those that lie hidden beneath dark waters. It is what makes Karpung a game of chance." He opened his tunic, revealing a puckered scar that ran the length of his torso.

The door that led to Stonefinger's study opened and officer, wizard, and dwarf lord returned to where the cadets were admiring the view.

"King Stonefinger has graciously decided to form an alliance with the *Northern League*." Hawker tugged his goatee. "Messengers will be sent as soon as possible and Captain Darkhawk has drafted a letter to his Lieutenant with instructions to notify the other garrisons."

"Gareth is a good man and will put the cavalry in motion." Dega picked up his pack from where he had left it.

"You must be on your way as soon as possible." Stonefinger was speaking to the entire group. "So I will not detain you any longer. But know this. If you find that you are in need of assistance, whether it be that you have merely lost your way or your supplies are dwindling, or something much worse, make your way to a dwarf-warren if you can, and there you need only mention my name and you will have all the aid you require."

He pulled out a leather scroll. "This map shows the whereabouts of every warren in Astaria, though some are long abandoned." He rolled it up and gave it to Dega who tucked it inside his uniform.

"Remember," said the King. "The Dwarves have known for some time that another *Great War* is forthcoming and we have long been preparing for the worse. It's with steadfast hearts that we seek to unite our forces with your own, but I fear that even the greatest of armies can only accomplish so much. All hope must ride on the shoulders of fate. Go with my blessing, and above all, believe in yourselves."

Hawker shook his hand, thanking Stonefinger for his kindness, then led the company back down the ramps.

"The beauty of this place will stay with me forever," said Camber, his fingers reached out lightly brushing flower petals as he crossed the gardens of the atrium.

Dane agreed. "I would like to come back when we actually have time to stay for a few days," he turned to Lockjaw, "and maybe catch a game of Karpung."

The dwarf smiled. "Maybe you would like to play."

They entered the South-gate for the second time but instead of taking the side passage they kept to the main corridor. It was hard to tell exactly how long they had been walking since there was little variation in the passage to mark their distance, but Camber's legs were beginning to ache and he still had not fully recovered from his run-in with the Bounder. Just as he felt he could no longer summon the strength for one more step the company halted.

"We shall rest here for a few hours," said Hawker. "It's already been a full day since your arrival, and the Captain tells me it's been much longer since your encounter with the Easterling." There was a suggestive hint to his voice that he was aware of certain events that had taken place prior to their mishap on the road. Dega stood off to one side with arms folded and a disapproving frown on his face. It was clear that wizard and officer had come to a mutual agreement with respect to the supervision of their young charges.

The dwarves brought food out of the packs and they sat in a circle with Camber and Dane while Hawker and Dega conferred quietly across the other side of the passage.

"What do you suppose those two are talking about?" Dane asked.

"Don't know, don't care. I just want to shut my eyes. It's been forever since we had any sleep." Camber yawned, curling up against his pack.

"I can't sleep. I'm too wound up. I wonder if Jules made it back to the barracks, and if the Rangers are looking for us, and I can't stop thinking about all that's happened. Snakes and Spirits! Bounders, Easterlings, Dwarf Kings! And now we're off to Illianther." Dane's commentary was wasted, Camber was already sound asleep. He turned to one of the dwarves. "Do you play dice?" he asked.

After a brief rest the company resumed its trek to the South porch. Camber and Dane trailed behind with Lockjaw and the dwarves while Hawker and Dega were several paces ahead, discussing the newly formed *Dwarven-Ranger* alliance.

"See. I can touch both sides of the passage." Dane stretched his arms until the tips of his fingers barely brushed either wall.

"It is getting narrow," said Camber, they now walked shoulder to shoulder.

"It's the Whitewash," said Lockjaw, pleased to impart a little architectural insight to curious young minds. "It channels alongside this very passage and the engineers had to compensate; the result being that the passage is in fact narrow. And did you detect the slight rise in gradation? For we are now making our way uphill." He went on to further educate about the different styles of engineering found in the various warrens, and how to find the near-invisible markings in the stonework that allowed them to tell one warren's set of engineers from another.

Hawker, who had been talking with Dega, heard the beginning of Lockjaw's lecture on advanced dwarven masonry and abruptly put a stop to the monotonous rambling. "If I'm not mistaken, elven architects have achieved a new level in building technology," said the wizard, "they have done some amazing things with water that has to be seen before it can be believed." Lockjaw muttered something about elven architects and took a few steps back to converse with his brethren. Dane and Camber promptly sped up their pace to fall in behind wizard and officer.

"What exactly is our plan?" asked Dane.

"Plan?" Hawker repeated.

"Yes. Plan! And stop answering everything with another question."

"Well you needn't be so brash, but if you must know we are going to Illianther."

"Yes, yes, I know that, Elvenhome. What I mean is, what are we going to do once we get there? How can a library find this Whateverstone."

"Winterstone."

The archer rolled his eyes. "What sort of things can you find at this library?" Hartland had a library, but he never bothered with it. Nothing but books.

"We may find something or we may find nothing, but that's a chance we'll have to take. Besides, Camber needs to learn how to control his gift, and since Hartland is short on tutors, then Illianther is the most logical place to take him."

Camber pushed between the two. "How did you know where to find us in the first place?"

"What do you mean?"

"Who sent you?"

"Yes, wizard," Dega turned in mid-stride. "*Who* sent you."

"Nobody sent me. I sent myself. But I see you still don't understand. Perhaps if I explain why the fate of this world concerns me so, you might stop trying to doubt everything I say," these last words were intended for Dega. "Anyway it will pass the time while we journey to the South porch." He cleared his throat. "As I mentioned before, I am a Caretaker. We number six altogether, and while some of us are content to sit back and allow the world to remain as is, others engage in more active roles, directly playing a part in the shaping of Astaria. Such is my lot. I feel a kinship with nature, and with mankind, and I greatly desire to see the goodness and beauty in all things."

"Are you some kind of a God?" Camber stepped back in awe.

"Not a God," corrected Hawker. "A Caretaker."

"So you're not a God." Dane said.

"Take the potatoes out of your ears, boy! If I have to repeat every word it'll take a hundred years just to tell this blasted story."

"I'll be a hundred before we get to Illianther at this pace."

Whether Hawker heard this or not he gave no indication. "It was Atrilla, *Mistress of the Sky*, who was first to arrive, and *She* watched from above as we came into being one by one. Next came Pel Ak A Bar, whose very essence can be found in every drop of water, from the smallest of puddles to the vast blue sea. *He* enjoys a life of solitude and rarely do we see him. Shikkarri watches over the Eternal Flame and Defél lives in the crust of Astaria. Finally there is Norii who was one of the last to arrive, and it is *She* who governs the Dead."

"But what do you do?" asked Camber.

"I? I Care for Life." Hawker smiled, and he suddenly radiated a soft blue light.

"So why can't you just get rid of the Easterling King on your own?" Dane asked.

Camber was thinking the same thing. But the wizard was probably one of those high-minded types who made everyone else do the dirty work so that they might all learn some kind of valuable lesson. He rolled his eyes, no wonder Lockjaw has to carry everything.

Hawker stopped dead in his tracks. "I AM LIFE!" He repeated. "I make Life. I do not unmake it. To extinguish the gift of *Life* would go against everything that is my very essence and would be an affront to my own existence." The blue light disappeared and his face paled, giving his woodsy appearance a softer, humbler guise.

"But you have no problem using others to extinguish life," said Dega, he wasn't exactly buying into this Caretaker business, for one thing he had never heard of these Caretakers – Never.

"Yes, but that's different," answered Hawker. "I am not against Death. It's a natural phase and goes hand in hand with Life."

"But what of War?" asked Camber.

"Yeah," Dane agreed. "War counts as unnatural and un-necessary."

"Not unnecessary. Sometimes war is needed to expel the evils of the world."

"So that's where we come in," answered Dega. He knew it. They were all being used.

"Yes that's where you come in – No. Ah, it's not like that… " and he stopped suddenly, "We've walked far enough for one day; this seems to be good spot to rest."

Lockjaw laid out a blanket for Hawker who promptly sat down and waited for everyone else to settle comfortably before renewing his story. He spoke of Atrilla, Defél, Shikkarri, and Pel Ak A Bar, who came together as one and made the world. Atrilla created the sky and Shikkarri created the molten bedrock that Defél used to shape the world's crust, and Pel Ak A Bar added the oceans, lakes, rivers, and streams.

"And the world became this fascinating object that captivated the hearts and minds of its creators. Occasionally, Pel Ak A Bar would raise the oceans and Defél and Shikkara would change the landscape, excavating a canyon or calling forth a mountain, but the world that you call Astaria stayed somewhat unaltered for many tens and thousands of years. That was all about to change." Hawker paused to take a drink from his flask. "From whence I came I cannot tell you, for I know not myself. But here I was, and they drew me into their circle." His gaze wandered over the faces of his attentive audience until they came to rest on Camber. So young, so naïve; what a terrible thread Fate had placed in his hands. Even he did not know the pattern Camber was expected to weave.

"And… " Dane interrupted, eyes wide with disbelief, not caring if it was true or not, only that this was sure to impress the socks off his uncle, and even his friends back in Hartland, especially after he improved it with *his* version.

"Huh? Oh yes, where was I? Ah! Trees, flowers, insects, all came to life before our very eyes. The others marveled at these creations; it was all new to them, and to me. These growing things brought us great joy and we would sit and contemplate the smallest and the most simplistic of life-forms. A single blade of grass would keep us happily occupied for years; its green color spoke volumes in its vibrancy, and the complexity of each individual fiber yearned to be studied. A butterfly would bring even more fascination; its ability to procreate was a cause for celebration.

But Norii, who appeared on this world about the same time as I grew tired of my creations, and like a jealous sibling she waved her hand bringing an end to my living things. The others encouraged me to try harder, and so I did. These were more complex, taking on highly sophisticated traits, and so we started naming them: horses, birds, fish, deer, and the list goes on. The more advanced the animal the harder it was for Norii to undo their life-threads."

"Are you saying that you created *Mankind?*" asked Dane, this was sounding more incredible by the second.

"Mankind was an accident." Lockjaw answered.

"Wha... accident?"

The dwarf nodded.

Hawker held up his hand. "If it's okay with you Lockjaw I would very much like to finish my story by morning."

"I became frustrated with this *Life and Death* struggle and so I presented Norii with an idea. We would try something new. Make something that would come from the both of us. Norii agreed. For she was eager to explore new ways of using her abilities. We came together as one, and out of our joining came the race of Elves." Hawker smiled, recalling something from his past.

"The Elves carried the best of our traits. They had beauty, talent, and immortality. But we overlooked one factor; rational beings are not like dumb beasts, they need nurturing, understanding, and above all, education. They crave knowledge and have a natural desire to create and increase their own importance in the world, *and* eventually they outgrow their tutors. We all had a hand in their lessons, but they soon isolated themselves, wanting to be left to their own devices, and developing society to *their* liking. Thus we let them be, promising not to meddle in their affairs. We were saddened by this. All of us had enjoyed the time we had spent with our children, for that is what we had come to consider them, and every one of us longed for those days when our guidance had been needed."

Hawker took another drink from his flask. "Norii was infuriated. How dare they turn away from their mentors! She vowed to teach them a lesson. Though they were immortal they were not immune to death. Whether by accident or violence, Norii's hands wore the stain of her calling. I confronted her, gaining support from the others, for they loved the Elves as much as I. But she fled our circle. To where we knew not. And I was deeply worried, for she had taken all the knowledge I had taught her, and it wasn't long after that she started using it for her own dark design."

"And so I watched over the Elves from afar, like a caring father who wants to make sure his children are healthy and well looked after. I wanted desperately to be a part of their lives but at the same time I dared not break my promise."

Camber was touched by Hawker's sadness, and he suddenly felt ashamed for doubting the Caretaker's intentions. "Why didn't you just go to them and tell them how you felt?"

"I was too proud. I wanted them to come to me instead. But then Shikkarri and Defél asked me to breathe life into their children. Their Children! I had no idea they had created life of their own. And so it was that the Dwarves awoke from their stone-cold slumber."

A gasp was heard from the Stone-Haven dwarves. Their ancestors had not recorded the history of their people from the beginning like the elves and it wasn't until King Ironfist decreed it mandatory to keep an archive of the Dwarven Nation that anything other than stories by word of mouth had substituted for a documented (if somewhat exaggerated) history.

"But where do we fit in?" Dane was getting impatient. He wanted to know why Lockjaw claimed Mankind to be an accident.

"Yes, where do *you* fit in?" said Hawker, but he seemed to be thinking aloud to himself. "If a certain person would allow me to actually finish my tale rather than my having to restrain myself from turning said person into a toad, then we might all finally learn the history of Man's arrival in Astaria," and he raised his eyebrows at Dane.

"Ahhh, Mankind," sighed the sorcerer. "A simpler race of people but remarkably adaptable to any situation, and with a great thirst for knowledge. You never cease to amaze me with your diversity, your persistence, and your heart." His eyes glowed softly in the dim lighting of the warren, and his smile radiated warmth, reminding Camber of his uncle's own benevolent grin.

"After Norii's departure we enjoyed a long period of tranquility. The elven race was at its peak and had grown to numerous proportions, but even so, they were experiencing conflict among themselves and were now divided into three clans and would remain as such for all time. But the elves were no longer a concern for us. It was the newly awakened dwarves who occupied our hearts. We all took part in their education but they seemed to enjoy the guidance of Defél and Shikkarri the best, and they built their great halls under rock and mountain so that they might forever be close to the two Caretakers who they revered the most. It was the dwarves who taught the elves how to shape metal, and to this day the best weapons, armor, and ornaments all come from the forges of the dwarves."

Lockjaw and his brethren nodded, and Hawker held up his hand – the last thing he wanted was to instigate another dwarven lecture on old world craftsmanship. "But like the elves, the dwarves became restless, wanting to be left alone, and they strayed from the hands that would readily guide them. Once again we had been shut away from our own children. It was especially hard on me, for I care too much for all living things. I could not stay with the others, I needed to be on my own, and so I stole away to a secluded region and transformed it into my own private haven, and there I dwelt - *Alone*.

I missed much of the world as it evolved. And I cared not. Too consumed was I with trying to recreate the elegance and beauty we admired so much in the elves. But this time I would bind those traits with the loyalty and perseverance of the dwarves. I poured all my energy and knowledge into what I thought would be my greatest achievement. But nothing went right, and I couldn't seem to replicate Astaria's first-born, and after a few minor mishaps I had all but given up." He paused, and his eyes came to rest on Dega, seeking something in the Captain's steady gaze, but Dega only glared back.

"*Until one day* - I remember like it was yesterday, so clear it is in my mind. I was walking along a steep embankment wishing to call forth the children I desperately wanted, and at that moment I caught my own reflection in a pool of water, and it was then that I slipped. I fell and hit my head on a rock. When I opened my eyes I was staring at my own reflection, but it was no longer gazing back from beneath its watery setting. I was speechless! My deepest desire had been set free. I now had children of my own."

"Is that it?" Dega scowled.

"Well, yes and no," answered the wizard. "That is the short version. The Elves befriended the race of Men and accepted them into their fold like brothers, and called them Valastari, which means youngest of the world. Centuries swept by - a blur of civilization. But to me it seemed as if it had been only a few years, and the Valastari dwindled despite their longevity.

Once more we were faced with the prospect of populating Astaria. My ability to channel had increased significantly but time had diminished the potency of my powers. It was the same with the others. We had no choice but to try and come together as one (save Norii), and in this last attempt we brought to life the human race you are now familiar with. But this second wave was much weaker in mind and body; they never came as close to perfection as my Valastari."

Hawker's eyes misted, and his voice hinged on regret. "Ahh, the Valastari. They had the graceful majesty of the Elves and the strength and honor of the Dwarves. Plus something else, a kind of raw emotion, that when aroused, was the real driving force behind their greatest achievements. We loved them best of all. We could not help it. Their passion drew us like the stars draw the night."

Hawker stroked his goatee. "The world has changed; what was once paradise is now harsh and bitter, and all innocence is nigh beyond recall. But even so, there are still a few in this world whose lineage can be traced without blemish to my original Valastari." He finished his story and stood to stretch his legs. "Now I suggest we all get some sleep for we still have another day's march before we reach the South porch."

Dega agreed; they would need all the rest they could get if they were going to travel through hostile territory.

The next morning Camber felt fully recovered from his battle with the Bounder but his arm itched terribly from the salve. He grabbed his bundle and tossed it over his shoulders, scratching furiously at his now fully healed wound.

"Are you going to eat that?" Dane fell in beside him, eyeing the strip of salted pork. Camber gave it to the archer. "Are you turning into Jules now?"

"Maybe, but I have a long way to go," he patted his waistline.

Camber laughed. "I wish there was some way of knowing if he made it back to the barracks. I'm worried that something may have happened."

Dega hitched his pack and turned his head. "There's no sense in fretting over events that may or may not have happened. Most likely young Jules was either found by one of Gareth's search parties or he made it back on foot. He's not entirely incompetent, and I would like to think he picked up at least some orienteering skills during basic training." He forced a reassuring smile across his dour face. "And, I've sent a letter to Gareth. He will tell your friends that you are alive and well." That letter was worded *very* carefully, using a special code only he and Gareth shared; in the letter he told his Lieutenant everything, including where they were headed and why.

After hours of endless tunnel, Hawker stopped the company. "There is still half a day's march before we reach the South porch. We can either camp here and continue on tomorrow, or travel in darkness since it will be nightfall by the time we come to the exit."

Dega argued in favor of marching onward. "We can use the night to our advantage."

While wizard and officer debated over the best way to travel, Camber shut his eyes. He woke to find that he was alone. "Dane? Dane?" No answer. He picked up his pack. No sign of Dega, Hawker, or any of the dwarves. The lighting was dim and his sense of direction had deserted him, he was unsure which way the others had gone. *Why didn't they wake him? Did they forget he was there? Surely Dane would notice.*

"Da-ane! Dane! Anyone?" Panic at suddenly wondering if he could even find his way back to the Atrium. "Anyone?"

Shadows lengthened in the diminishing light, merging into a single black void. "This must be the right direction," his voice echoed along the empty corridor, the walls narrowing until they were only an arm's reach apart, closing in like a cage. Cold was the air. And foul. The stench of decay filling his nostrils. Evil filtered along this passage, touching his skin, breathing terror down the back of his neck. He woke with a sudden start.

Dane drew his hand away. "Are you okay?"

Camber blinked, staring at his surroundings.

"What is it?" he whispered.

"*The Dream.*"

Dane nodded, he knew which dream. "It'll be okay. I'm sure someone at Illianther will be able to help you." He took his cousin's pack. "I'll carry this for awhile."

Hawker watched Camber from across the tunnel; a shadow had passed momentarily, enveloping the cadet in its blackness; it gave him cause for concern, and he handed his pack to Lockjaw, resuming the trek in silence.

V

The Messenger

Gareth Comstock was in the Captain's office when an orderly appeared in the doorway.

"Sir. There's a dwarf wanting to speak with you. Says he's an ambassador. Says he has a message from Captain Darkhawk."

Gareth jumped out of the Captain's chair, and bolted past the orderly. The dwarf was standing just inside the receiving hall as he came charging around the corner.

"Welcome friend," said the officer. "I'm pleased to hear that you have a message for me." And though he was very much relieved that Dega was alive, his face remained unaffected by this news.

"My name is Strong-Arm," said the black-bearded dwarf, and truly his name suited him well as he flexed an impressive limb toward Gareth's open hand, pumping it mightily with a few quick shakes. "This is for you," and he handed a letter to the officer.

"Thank you," and breaking the seal he unrolled the letter. Though it seemed he merely glanced at the parchment before scrolling it back up; he had actually seen all he really needed to know for the time being. *One*: it was the Captain's handwriting. *And Two*: it was in code. He would read it later. The lieutenant led his unusual visitor back to the Captain's study and away from the curious eyes of the cadets.

"What news from the dwarven realm?" asked Gareth, he closed the door and motioned for the dwarf to take a seat.

"King Stonefinger wishes to form an alliance. The Easterlings are once again knocking on our threshold and it is time to cast aside our indifferences and unite our forces to fight this common foe."

Gareth nodded, but kept his arms folded as he leaned back in his chair.

"Your Captain has suggested that His Majesty put forth his request into your very capable hands," Strong-Arm continued. "I come as both friend and ambassador. Will you accept our alliance?"

"You've traveled a long way and it's getting late, if you would but dine with me and stay as our guest I'll provide you with an answer in the morning." He wanted to read the letter before he made a decision.

The dwarf bowed, accepting this proposal. He knew politics only too well; it was why Stonefinger had picked him to go instead of anyone else.

"Come with me then," Gareth said as he stood, "and we shall have a hearty meal and share some interesting conversation."

Gareth Comstock retired to his bedchamber at midnight. He pulled off his boots, loosened his coat, unrolled the Captain's letter, then reached for a fresh piece of parchment, a quill, and some ink.

Strong-Arm departed at dawn with a promise from Gareth that he would do all he could to ensure the alliance.

Jules could barely contain his joy as he bounded into the room he shared with Hansil.

"Jules, what's with you? You look like you're about to burst."

"Maybe they let him out of kitchen-duty," Bon said; he was reclining on Camber's cot reading a letter from home.

"More like they let him *in* to kitchen-duty," replied Sal.

"Well don't just stand there with a stupid grin on your face," Bon sat up. "Tell us what the Lieutenant said." The others nodded. All five cadets were on a break when an orderly had come to the room asking for Jules. They knew it had to be connected with his recent adventure and they all hoped for some news of Camber and Dane.

Gareth had made Jules promise not to tell anyone about the incident, he would address the recruits himself with a slightly different account, but Jules told Hansil and the rest of his friends; the seven cadets had sworn their loyalty a long time ago and did not keep secrets from each other.

"They're alive!" he said with glee. "And what's more, they're traveling west to Elvenhome!"

"What!!!" All four said at once.

"What do you mean they're traveling to Elvenhome?" asked Caleb.

"That's really all the LT would say. But he implied it was of great importance that they go and said the Captain was leading the adventure accompanied by a wizard and a dwarf."

"Incredible!" Sal was now standing, and his eyes were wide with disbelief. "They disobey orders, start a barroom brawl, nearly get themselves killed, and the Captain rewards them by taking them on an adventure while we're stuck here with nothing to do but stare at four walls. Of all the bloody luck."

"Well there's more," said Jules. "It seems that wasn't the only reason why the dwarf was here." He smiled to himself, having caught a quick glance at the letter addressed to Colonel Ravenhill on Gareth's desk.

"I think we might be going to war."

* * * * * * * * *

Rich red velvet, all the way from Dakshevi, trailed across the marble floor; its white trim now a filthy grey, gathering dust with each sweep from end to end, but the sorcerer paid it no heed. Somehow he had lost one of the invisible threads that had connected him to his Bounders; one moment it was there and the next it was gone.

He stopped directly on the mosaic centerpiece – gold and ivory tiles depicting the white staff and stars; his symbol of power. It could only mean one thing: someone has killed a Bounder. But who? Not the boy, not yet; he doubted the youth had learned to channel his power so quickly. He would have felt it. Just like before, when a blast of energy had suddenly erupted; a bolt of light in his mind's eye, making him instantly aware of this powerful presence.

So who was it? Dwarves? Elves? Maybe the Caretaker. *Perhaps it was He.* No, it couldn't be him. He knew Hawker would not kill, no matter how terrible the creature. Stupid fool had his chance to kill him once, but for his ridiculous morals, he had got away unscathed. He sat down at his table and pushed some of the clutter to one side, resting his head between his hands. *Who was it? Who was it? Who?* He opened his eyes. *Him!* The only mortal to have braved his borders. That man had killed a Bounder. He sat up, slamming his fist and rattling the table. "If it's him, he will know pain in *every* part of his body."

The door to his study flew open, and one of his captains entered. The two massive dogs feigning sleep on the floor stood; hackles raised and throats growling, they sniffed the cloak of the warrior; satisfied the scent was known, they returned to their place by the fire.

"I have news Sire," he said, pausing just long enough to determine his sovereign's mood. "*And,* I have also returned with a prisoner."

"What has happened to my Bounder?!"

"We've lost one man and one Bounder. I do not know how. I was not nearby when it happened, and I am told that when the others arrived at the location someone had already buried the body. There was no trace of the Bounder." He stepped back toward the safety of the entrance.

"FOOL!" The King struck an armored fist across his captain's face. "I have taken every precaution to oversee the safety of my Bounders. How could you be so careless with them? All of you are supposed to travel in pairs. MEN are expendable - Bounders are NOT!"

The captain dared not flinch, even as he felt the force of the blow shatter his jaw. Any show of weakness would mean death - *his.*

"Take me to this prisoner."

* * * * * * * *

A creaking like an old cartwheel in need of greasing, followed by a loud snap and a thundering crash, revealed the South porch exit. Millions of stars blanketed the nighttime sky welcoming the company back to the world above ground.

"It feels strange to be suddenly top-side after being down below for such a long time." Dane stared out at the wide open space.

Camber agreed. "Yes, I was starting to like the warren."

One of the dwarves who had opened the entrance slapped Dane on the shoulders. "You see, there's no better place to be than inside a dwarf-warren. That's why you long-legs never see us abroad. We have everything we need right here under the mountain."

"Everything except a sense of humor," muttered Hawker, knowing that his sarcasm was wasted as it would invariably travel right over the dwarf's head. "If I'm not mistaken. We can continue south toward the Ironfist Mountains. There is another dwarf-warren which we can pass through to reach the Borderlands of Caldorn."

"Now you get to see my home," beamed Lockjaw. "It's been many years since I've been back and I'm looking forward to seeing the Ironfist Mountains again." He said something in dwarvish to his brethren and they all answered back in their native tongue.

Hawker stood with hands on hips frowning at them. He finally interrupted their animated conversation. "If you don't mind Lockjaw, and if it's not too much trouble, then maybe we should be off, instead of wasting the wee hours of the night discussing the always fascinating subject of dwarven architecture." He pointed to his pack and the dwarf slung it over his back and followed the wizard out into the wilderness.

Dega brought up the rear, scanning the shadows for anything out of the ordinary - a dark patch of black against the soft gray treeline; the tell-tale flicker reflected from a pair of eyes. He strained his ears listening carefully to the night sounds, walking with one hand resting lightly on the pommel of his sword.

The company stopped just before dawn. Dane and Camber flung their packs to the ground, dropping overtop like dead-weight. Both cadets were sound asleep within minutes. Hawker and Dega were still debating about the best route to Illianther. Dega wanted to cross at Whistlegate; he was silently counting on Gareth's men waiting at the Pass, but the wizard pointed out that since they were too far south it would mean backtracking, making them much more vulnerable to enemies. Lockjaw suggested they cross through an abandoned dwarf mine located near the southern-most tip of the Borderlands.

"There's one small drawback," the dwarf said.

"And what would that be?"

"We'll have to cross the Red-Bone."

"I've crossed the desert before." Dega turned his face away to watch the sunrise. "Shouldn't be a problem if we carry enough water and some salt."

Hawker tugged at his goatee. "We can replenish our supplies at Ironfist."

Dega stayed awake while the others slept. It was twilight when Camber and Dane had risen from their much-needed sleep and he was preparing something to eat. Dane sat down beside him and he gave the cadet half the meat he was roasting on a spit.

"How far are we from this warren?" he asked.

Dega shrugged. "The dwarf says maybe a fortnight. Could be longer, depends on how much ground we can cover in an evening."

Dane frowned. It wasn't the answer he was hoping to hear. "I don't suppose there's any chance of stopping at a farmstead along the way and getting a real meal?" The officer stood, eager to be on the move.

"Welcome to the wilderness."

It rained for the next several days making for a rather unpleasant trek; supplies were dwindling, but Dega managed to trap few rabbits, and while the dwarves erected a crude shelter, the others gathered around the cook-fire. Hawker stirred a pot of boiling water, adding anything and everything into a bubbling brown concoction.

"Snakes and Spirits! That stuff stinks! What did you put in there?" Dane held his nose.

"I was fortunate enough to come across some silverthorn. It's very hard to find but has remarkable rejuvenating qualities."

Dane sniffed the pot once more. "It smells like an old sock."

"You don't have to eat it, which is fine by me, more for the rest of us. While we continue our journey feeling refreshed, you on the other hand, will have to stay behind from lack of nourishment."

The stew was finished and Hawker doled out a portion to everybody. Dane tried to eat, but every time his mouth was close enough to the bowl the stench would overpower his senses and he would gag. "Gaaa! It's as bad as it smells!"

Dega cleaned his bowl, then took out his hunting knife; he ran his finger down the edge. "Why don't you tell us what you know of the Easterling King?" The fire cast a hard shadow across his face; he knew Hawker was holding back and he wanted answers.

Hawker put down his bowl. "What is it that you want to know?"

"How did this mortal, if that is what you say he is, obtain such great power." It was a fair question. One that deserved a good answer, especially since they had been doing everything asked without argument and without hardly any reason given by this wizard.

"He is a mortal man. One of my original Valastari."

"But how can that be?" Camber sat up straight. "You said yourself that the Valastari were the first generation of Mankind. How can anyone but the Elves live that long?"

"I told you. He has learned to wield a powerful magic. Even though he did not come by it naturally, it's still very powerful, and he has only increased it over the years. It's this magic coupled with the longevity of the Valastari that gives him nigh-immortality."

"How did he obtain this power?" Dane had managed to consume the foul-tasting stew and pushed his bowl aside; when Lockjaw tried to refill it he quickly waved him off.

"I taught him."

"You?! But why?"

Hawker waved his hand. "It's not what you're thinking." Then tugging at his goatee, he added. "He wanted to use magic to make the world a better place. So I took him under my wing. And I can tell you that there is no better feeling than imparting a little knowledge to an eager pupil and watching that knowledge germinate until the student has mastered all he has learned." He sighed deeply. "How was I to know he would use all that I taught for his own terrible means."

Lockjaw stretched his hand to Hawker. "I will never use your lessons for anything other than the welfare of Astaria, Master."

"Ah, I know your heart is true dwarf. I have learned how to judge the integrity of people instead of taking what they say for granted. Sentash did not always have a wicked heart. No indeed, at one time he was a very righteous and caring individual. He used his power to strengthen the Valastari's relationship with the world. But something in him changed. Over the years he sought to make himself immortal like the Elves, who he secretly envied. He collected countless talismans and consulted various tomes on magic, spending nearly all his waking hours and sacrificing much of himself to unlock the secret of immortality."

"Immortality? Why?" Camber fingered his locket; he traced the rune, working his forefinger across the symbol.

"His need to prolong his lifespan consumed his every thought to where it very nearly killed him. The magic he yearned to do good with had finally corrupted him. He was no longer the same self-sacrificing man that was once my favorite student."

"But why didn't you stop him? Seems to me that you probably had more than one opportunity," said Dega; his head was bent as he sharpened the edge of his hunting knife against a stone.

"I did," replied Hawker. "But he had been preparing for our eventual confrontation and enlisted the aid of the K'Ahtars and all who opposed us. We chased him East and left him to face those barren lands on his own, but that proved to be a mistake."

"So now it's up to us to right *your* wrong," said Dega. Nothing like being a pawn in somebody else's game. Now made even more apparent after the wizard's confession that he was the one responsible for teaching the Easterling magic and setting him loose upon the world.

"You are all free to go once we reach Illianther," said the wizard. "Except Camber, he needs to learn how to control his ability. But I had hoped that you, of all people Captain, would at least help us fend off the evil in the East."

"And how do you propose I do this wizard? I'm too far away from my own Company to be of any use." He stopped honing his blade.

"Maybe your place isn't at the head of an army. Perhaps you were meant for greater things, Dega Darkhawk."

Dega grunted at the wizard and went back to sharpening his knife.

Camber slid his hand carefully along the surface of the wall. He turned the corner and suddenly stopped. A weird feeling came over his senses as he came to the next bend. He tried to turn but an invisible force prevented him from doing so. When he felt the cold rush of air on his fingertips, his heart lurched, sending a warning to his brain. The noise of blood pumped madly between his ears; beads of sweat trickled down his forehead, glistening on bare arms and chest, every muscle strained to keep from falling into black nothingness.

"Do not be alarmed," said Hawker, his hand softly woke the cadet from his nightmare. Camber sat up and looked around; the others were still sleeping, including Dega. Only the wizard was awake. "Do you know?" he asked quietly.

Hawker nodded. "I have known for some time," he said. "It's because of your dreams that I was able to pinpoint your whereabouts."

Camber sunk his head to his chest. "Does he know?"

The wizard shrugged. "Who can say? But I know for a fact that he felt you when you used your magic for the first time. We all felt it." His face darkened. "Camber, you must refrain from using your gift, for it calls his attention like a beacon." Camber nodded, and Hawker gave him a warm fatherly smile. "Good lad. Now let's see if we can do something about those nightmares." He laid a hand across his forehead and muttered a spell. Camber felt his head tingle. "That should help. But I'm afraid I could not completely rid them from your mind, for they are not your average dreams. Someone has bound these dreams with magic, and this magic is very potent and very old. About all I could do was hide them from your subconscious so you won't be bothered by them when you are sleeping."

At the sound of voices Dega and the dwarves awoke from their sleep. Dane still snored loudly. Dega scowled and gave the cadet a boot. "Ahh, what," the archer mumbled, and he rolled over onto his side. Another boot, this time a little less gentle, and Dane sat up rubbing his eyes. "You people don't believe in getting a proper night's sleep do you?"

The Captain ignored his complaints and fanned a fire to heat the leftover stew. Dane had decided berries would be preferable to what he now described as the vilest concoction ever to grace society. Camber rolled his eyes at Dane's ridiculous aversion to the stew, and he and Dega took apart the shelter, then carefully covered up any traces of the camp. As luck would have it the skies opened up catching them all under a downpour of rain.

* * * * * * * * *

Jules led the big black charger out of the stable. Every day began with a battle of wills, and this day was no different; he leapt swiftly into the saddle before the stallion had a chance to unseat him. The black protested when he shortened the reins, but once clear of the gates he cracked the ends and put spurs to flank, giving the animal its head and sending it thundering down the road to Wildwood.

Caleb was in the guard tower when Jules rode out – a gray and black blur becoming smaller and smaller until it disappeared from sight altogether. Hard to believe that this was the same cadet who had at one time been all but afraid of the animals. He went back to surveying the grounds. Even to an untrained eye it was obvious that military preparations had been stepped up at the garrison; the cavalry paraded in formation, riding around and around in circles, and cadets practiced mock duels on grassy fields, brightly colored flags wavering in the morning breeze. They looked pretty enough from high in the watchtower, but would any of that careful rehearsing be of use during a real battle? Somehow he doubted it. All the rehearsing in the world could not prepare them for the horrors of war. Death was not pretty.

Gareth was making plans to host a summit between the delegates from the Northern League and the Dwarven Nation. Almost five hundred years of hardly any contact between the two races and now they were about to gather under one roof with the single purpose of eradicating a common foe. And if the Captain really is headed to Illianther as his message implied then there was hope that the Elves might be persuaded to join the Alliance. The letter contained only bits of information with very little detail and Gareth had to piece some of the puzzle together from the events that had taken place with the Easterling and the small scraps he had gleaned from the dwarf. The rest he filled in with logic and reasoning. Upon reading the letter he had sent three of his best men to watch for the Captain at the Pass.

And young Jules left just this morning with a message for Ravenhill. Gareth Comstock leaned back in the chair with his coffee, taking a long sip; the only thing left to do was wait for all his messengers to come back.

* * * * * * * * *

The Ironfist Mountains loomed just ahead, snow visible on the peaks; a stark and naked whiteness contrasting sharply against a cold blue sky.

Lockjaw could hardly contain his excitement as he reached for the secret finger holds between two slabs of rock. Once the doorway was revealed the dwarf eagerly disappeared into the passage. Hawker sat on a boulder and the Stone-Haven dwarves stood at the entrance.

"Are we going in or not?" Dane's lack of patience finally got the better of his manners.

"In a minute," said the wizard, stopping the cadet from descending down the steps. "We must wait until Lockjaw returns. It's customary for a dwarf who's been away from his home for as long as Lockjaw has to be the first to enter. He'll be back with an escort and then we may all go inside."

Camber sat down on his pack; he hoped the dwarf came back with more than just an escort, he was starving. Dane slumped to the ground beside him. "As long as I get a clean bath and a bed I'll be happy," he picked up a handful of stones and started throwing them at the trees.

They didn't have long to wait. Lockjaw popped his head through the entrance; a wide grin looking absurdly comical on his bearded face. He motioned for the group to follow and introduced the two dwarves who had appeared with him. They greeted their Stone-Haven brethren and bowed low to the rest of the company. The dwarves then led them to a guest room filled with all the amenities required to refresh the party, including (to the delight of Dane) a heated bathing pool set deep in the marble floor.

"Rest here for the time being," said one of Lockjaw's companions, "and we will come for you in the morning. Prince Grimbeard will want to welcome you all to Ironfist himself." Lockjaw thanked the escort and they exited out of the room and back to the royal chambers.

"It seems Lockjaw has some kind of pull here," said Dane, he was already out of his clothes and enjoying the benefits of the bathing pool.

But before the dwarf had a chance to respond, the sound of running feet echoed down the hall, their quickened patter growing louder as they clipped toward the guest room.

"Lockjaw! Lockjaw! Lockjaw! It's really you!" A tiny figure bundled head to toe in velvet green darted across the room, latching onto the red-bearded dwarf.

"SHARD!" Lockjaw whooped. "Shard! What are you doing here?!"

"They said you were here. I had to come see for myself," said the figure, and she threw back her hood revealing a pretty face and a pair of glittery green eyes. "Oh Lockjaw – oh how I've missed you." It was evident from Lockjaw's reaction that she was not supposed to be seen as such in public; he quickly pulled the hood back over her soft flaxen tresses. She threw the hood off at once and stepped back a few paces from the dwarf. "Why have you been gone so long?" she demanded. It would have been comical watching the diminutive dwarx wave her tiny hand in the face of the powerfully built Lockjaw, but something in the dwarf's expression said that Shard's temper was not to be treated lightly.

"I cannot help it." Lockjaw tried to cover her head once more but she ducked away from his hand. "My position as apprentice-wizard-in-training takes me from one end of Astaria to the other. You know that." He took her by the hand, intertwining her delicate fingers with his. "You cannot stay here. If your father finds out you've left the safety of your gardens he'll be furious."

"I don't care," she argued. "Besides, I asked Sparkle to cover for me. I had to see you. Father can rage all he wants."

The room was quiet and every pair of eyes stared incredulously at Lockjaw, who at this moment was on the receiving end of a severe tongue-lashing from the pint-sized dwarx.

"You must go back now else your father will never grant us his approval." Lockjaw cupped her heart-shaped face with his hand.

"Oh my poor Lockjaw. If Father denies us our happiness I will run away. But for your sake I will not risk his wrath." She reached inside her cloak and pulled out a brilliant green stone set inside a crystal orb; it dangled from a silver chain, and she slipped it into his hand. "Take this," she said, closing his fingers around the amulet. "If I can't be with you in body at least I can be with you in spirit." She stood on her tiptoes and kissed the blushing dwarf, then threw her cloak over her head and darted toward the doorway, where she stopped to take one last look at Lockjaw before disappearing down the corridor.

"Snakes and Spirits!" Dane swore; he stepped out of the bath and pulled his clothes on. "Wow! I don't suppose you want to tell us who that was?"

"Dane!" Camber smacked the back of his head. "Have some courtesy. It's not polite to pry into other people's affairs."

"Shard is the moon, out of reach for a mere dwarf as I," sighed Lockjaw, he stared at the orb. "I must become worthy of such radiance before I can ask for her hand."

Hawker hunkered into the pillows, muttering a spell to muffle his hearing while the others gathered around Lockjaw, all except Dega, who seemed disinterested, and he positioned himself on the other side of the room across from the doorway.

The next morning they were taken to Grimbeard's apartment. The company passed through an atrium similar to Stone-Haven's, but the dome of Ironfist was made from emerald instead of sapphire. The layout was nearly the same with four archways located opposite each other, and like Stone-Haven, the same bronze statues framed each entrance. Straight lines of dwarven architecture complimented the beauty of the gardens. The atrium's splendor had a rejuvenating effect on the company, washing away all remnants of their trek.

The Prince was much younger than Lockjaw and the other dwarves, and he hadn't quite grown a full beard; his wavy red hair was gathered loosely at the nape of his neck, tied with a black silk ribbon. He greeted the party one by one, shaking hands and showing genuine enthusiasm, but when he came to Lockjaw he grabbed the dwarf with both arms and hugged him to his breast. "Brother!" said the Prince.

Dane jerked Camber's sleeve. "There seems to be more to Lockjaw than meets the eye."

"Ahh, Stornoway Hawker," Prince Grimbeard pumped the wizard's hand. "Still keeping my older brother out of mischief? When are you planning to return him? You forget that he has a warren to run." The dwarf waved his bejeweled hands.

"I have not forgotten my Prince," Hawker bowed. "He is free to leave at any time."

"And you should know by now dear brother that I have no desire to run a kingdom. You are the ruler not I."

"I guess I'll never understand your attraction to this wizardry business," Grimbeard sighed. "I've been told that your quest is urgent and I wish not to detain you, but you have all traveled a great distance and must still be weary from your journey. I ask that you stay a few days as my guests and join me in a celebration of welcoming for my brother; he's been gone far too long and there is much I wish to discuss with him."

"We are honored by your generosity, your Highness," said Hawker.

"Excellent. I'll be happy to restock your provisions before you leave." He put his arm around his brother's shoulders. "Come with me, and we shall feast together. My ears will be delighted to hear any stories that you happen to conjure at the table."

Grimbeard's table was already laden with food when the company sat down, and four dwarves dressed in silver and black waited on the guests, filling goblets with wine and taking away empty trays. Camber and Dane helped themselves to seconds, thirds, and fourths, which inspired more than one dwarf to comment on their hearty appetites.

"You haven't asked me about Shard," said Grimbeard.

Lockjaw stared at his plate, pushing his food with his fork. "I suppose you're happy now that I'm gone," and he brought his head up, meeting the eyes of his brother.

"Lockjaw," replied the Prince. "You know Stoutfist has already promised her hand to me. You could have had her a long time ago but you chose to follow this foolish dream of yours."

"It's not foolish!" he snapped, wanting his brother to know how he truly felt about what it meant to bend properties, for that is how Hawker described the working of magic, *bending properties*. More than anything Lockjaw wanted to take all Hawker had to offer and use it to heal the badness in the world and replace it with love. Yes, magic could do this – magic from the heart. He opened his mouth, but it was Hawker seated at the opposite end of the table who spoke.

"Though to some a wizard's quest may seem unfathomable and perhaps daunting, but we who wear the badge of Astaria's protectors do not feel this way. Lockjaw has been tried and tested many times over these last span of years and I am grateful every single day for his selfless loyalty."

"I meant no offense to you or your profession," said Grimbeard. "But I only wish my brother would realize how silly this idea of his wanting to become a wizard is, and by chasing this dream he is losing not only his right to rule but the dwarx he loves as well."

"Ahh, you do not know what your brother is capable of if he

puts his whole heart behind that which he perceives is his destiny." Hawker stood, smoothing his robes. "Come here Lockjaw." The dwarf obediently moved to his side. "Stretch forth your hand." Every pair of eyes turned to watch the wizard instruct his pupil. "Now concentrate on pushing this stone away from your hand." He produced a small round rock, about the size of a child's fist, and held it carefully above the dwarf's outstretched hand, then dropped it into Lockjaw's palm. At first nothing happened. And after a few minutes, nothing happened. Then still, nothing happened. Finally, after what seemed an eternity the rock rose a few inches away from the dwarf's hand.

There was polite applause from everyone at the table. Only Dega refrained from applauding, he had been watching Hawker, not Lockjaw, and noticed that prior to the rock rising, the wizard had wiggled his finger.

"I'm sorry I doubted your abilities," said the Prince, and Lockjaw broke his concentration causing the rock to fall back into his hand.

"Well," said Grimbeard. "Now that we have supped, and have had our entertainment," he nodded to Lockjaw. "We should discuss the real reason for your venturing this far south. I've received Stonefinger's request to mobilize our forces, it seems the sorcerer is gathering an army great enough to destroy us all. Do you see why I desire your presence brother?" He stood and made a sweeping gesture. "We have not gone to war since the time of Three-Fingers, and there is hardly a dwarf alive that remembers those times. How am I supposed to run this warren *and* lead an army?" He sighed softly, and suddenly appeared very tired.

"If I could stay I would in a heartbeat, for there is more than just the welfare of our people to keep me here." He thought of Shard. "But I am committed to this quest and will not abandon Stornoway Hawker while he needs me the most." Lockjaw put his arm around his younger sibling's shoulders. "Come, while I'm here, let's take advantage of our time together and ask Hawker and the Ranger's Captain to join us where we can discuss your concerns in private."

"Hey!" Dane sprang from his chair. "What about us? Don't we count for something around here?"

Hawker made a sweeping gesture. "If you can explain to me how your worldly experience will benefit the marshaling of dwarven armies, then by all means join us."

Dane glared at the retreating back of the wizard. "I guess it's just us again." But Camber had other plans, and for once was glad to be excluded. "Why don't we go down to the atrium."

Brilliant green sparkled across the Atrium, lighting the dome with verdant fire and welcoming the cadets into its spectacular setting. One of the dwarves took it upon himself to educate his guests on all things dwarven. "It's customary for us to wear our gemstone in battle so that the fallen can be recognized and burial rights respected according to the clan; the emerald is unique to the dwarves of Ironfist."

Dane stared up at the dome's starry glow. "It must have taken thousands of years and a hundred times that many emeralds to create all this."

"Yes," replied the dwarf, "and it's still not complete. We are constantly working on it."

"There is always room for another emerald," offered another.

"Aren't you afraid someone might ravage your warren for all this remarkable wealth?" Camber asked. Precious stones, silver, and gold were used in almost every piece of dwarven craftsmanship.

"No," said the dwarf. "Every one of us would give his life to protect that which belongs to us. Besides, this warren hides many secrets, and even if an outsider were able to find his way in he would not get far before he'd be begging for the nearest dwarf to guide him safely out again."

The dwarves had led them across the atrium to the Eastern corridor where they passed under the bronze statues of Vigilance and Warfare.

"Secrets?" Dane's dark eyes sparkled with sudden interest. "What kind of secrets?" A dwarf slapped the archer across his back. "Do you think you could find your way back to the atrium from here?" They stood at an intersection with three identical passages, and neither could agree which direction would lead to the dome.

"You see," said the dwarf. "But it's not just about having a good sense of direction, there are other things in the dark that one has to watch out for." All the dwarves chuckled, and an uneasy feeling crept along Camber's spine. He did not like this end of the warren and he suddenly wanted the atrium's bright glare. "I can certainly appreciate having a dwarf as a guide," he said, turning to leave, but to his great annoyance Dane had wandered on ahead and apparently found something of interest.

"What's down here?" he asked, ducking back into the corridor.

"Ahh, that leads to the forge," said a dwarf. "Would you like to see the Everlasting Flame?" Dane nodded, leaving Camber no choice but to follow.

An archway opened into a room with a very high ventilated ceiling. The air was stifling. So hot, that it immediately brought back unpleasant memories of the stable fire. Camber stopped at the entrance, staring wide-eyed at the greatest of all dwarven achievements: the legendary forge of King Ironfist.

Brilliant orange, brighter than the sun itself, roared to life from a circular pit in the center. Dwarves moved back and forth between the great pit and several smaller fires, working with rhythmic precision to the sound of heaving bellows and the chinking of metal; a mechanical melody punctuated by hissing water.

"This is where we craft our weapons. The ornaments that adorn the Atrium are made in the adjoining room, though gemstones are cut elsewhere then brought here to be placed in their settings." The dwarf directed Camber's gaze to the central fire pit. "Behold, *the Everlasting Flame*. Shikkarri's gift. And the reason why we Dwarves of Ironfist are able to shape any type of metal; there is nothing below or above Astaria that can withstand its heat." He paused for effect. *"And,"* he raised his finger. "It has never gone out."

The Stone-Haven dwarves wandered from station to station, engaging their brethren. Dane's insatiable curiosity took over, and in true Dane-like fashion he began poking and prodding at things. "What's this do?" He rested his fingers lightly on a lever protruding from the wall.

"Don't touch that!" The dwarf closest to Dane launched himself at the archer. Too late. Whether he meant to or not the lever came down.

At first nothing happened. Then suddenly a blasting roar as the Everlasting Flame rose up to the ceiling in a twenty-foot wall of fire! This action caused one of the dwarves monitoring the pit to jump back in surprise. He bumped into another even as the wall of fire had reduced itself to a sputter. The dwarf who was nudged had been hammering away at a chunk of metal. Across the room his hammer flew. As luck would have it, the hammer managed to strike the marble statue of Shikkarri with enough velocity to rock it sideways on its base. Its momentum increased with each tilt back and forth while all eyes watched helplessly from every corner of the room. Shikkarri's marble likeness wobbled four times before it finally toppled over onto a wheel-lock, turning it a complete revolution. This particular outlet was not used very often, for its main purpose was to tame the Everlasting Flame into a manageable level. But with no dwarven hands to restrain the outpouring of water a great stream poured forth. Under normal circumstances such an amount of water could not possibly put out Shikkarri's gift, but the once great fire had been reduced to a mere spark. The Everlasting Flame spluttered twice then disappeared in a single plume of smoke. A gasp was heard from every dwarf in the room, and Dane slipped his hand off the lever then quietly went to stand beside his cousin.

On the other side of the warren the *Dwarven-Ranger* alliance had just concluded. Grimbeard seemed pleased with the news his brother had shared, and decided to send the dwarves who had accompanied the group back to Stonefinger along with a few of his envoys. With a little luck, and a lot of preparation, the bulk of his army could be organized and ready for battle before winter. As he escorted the company back into the dining hall a messenger came running up to greet them.

"Sire," the dwarf bent himself low and his breath fell in short huffs. "You must come quickly! The foreigners have committed a great offense!"

"What?!" Hawker glanced about the room. Camber and Dane were missing. The dwarf took a deep breath. "They have been taken into custody. You must come quickly!" he repeated.

Hawker pulled the dwarf to his feet with a surprising amount of strength. "Take us to them. Now!" The dwarf bowed one more time, then sprinted out the door.

Camber sat with his arms wrapped around his knees. The floor of the detaining room was cold, and its only light source, a single torch, illuminated the only way out – a heavily guarded door on the other side of the room. "Do you have to touch everything?"

"It's not my fault," Dane answered. "If they don't want people pulling on levers then they should hang a sign or something."

"What do you suppose they plan to do with us? From what I gather, something like this has never happened before and they didn't seem too happy about it."

Dane shrugged, he was leaning against the wall. "Don't know. But I don't see what the big deal is. Why don't they just restart it with any of the other fires burning in the forge? Isn't it all from the same source?"

A beam of light filtered through a crack as the door opened. Two figures stepped into the doorway. Neither wizard nor Captain seemed too pleased about the situation. "Get up." Dega snapped. Hawker pushed his way in front of the officer. "You two have caused a lot of trouble. I cannot even begin to tell you how much. It's fortunate that I was able to repair the damage you've caused, and you should be grateful that Lockjaw and Grimbeard have both intervened on your behalf, else you would have found yourselves hanging upside down over a bottomless pit."

Camber looked at his feet, but Dane glared back. "We've done nothing wrong." In his mind he still faulted the dwarves for not properly marking the lever.

"Nothing wrong?!" Hawker fumed. "You destroyed half the forge! Damaged equipment beyond repair, busted a marble statue, and quenched a ten thousand year old fire! Not to mention you've just added another notch of distrust in the already shaky alliance of men and dwarves." He pointed his finger at the archer. "You're lucky I don't leave you here," and under his breath he muttered, "they probably wouldn't take him anyway."

Dega glared at the two youths. "Out!" he barked, and marched them off to one side. He stood before Grimbeard, squeezing the pommel of his sword. "I hope this will not in any way undo the bonds our two races have begun to rebuild."

Dane rolled his eyes. "The way he talks you'd think he was the same age as Chance instead of just five years older than us." Camber jabbed an elbow at the archer, Dane had caused enough trouble for one day.

Hawker was able to salvage a few embers from the bottom of the pit, coaxing a small flame, which became a larger flame, and then a fully restored Everlasting Flame. Because the fire had been restarted from *those* embers, it was still technically Shikkarri's gift, and after countless apologies the young men were forgiven for their crime, though Camber was still confused as to how he was to blame when he had been standing at the doorway the entire time.

After one more day of rest they were ready to start the next leg of their journey. The cadets were relieved; since the incident they had been confined to their original quarters and had begun to feel less like visitors and more like prisoners. Somehow Lockjaw had managed to mend the rift between himself and his brother. The only issue that still seemed to make the brothers uncomfortable was the mere mention of the dwarx who had paid a secret visit to Lockjaw on the first day of their arrival.

"Good-bye Prince Grimbeard and thank you for your hospitality." Hawker shook the young dwarf's hand then guided the company out of the South porch. Lockjaw waited until he and Grimbeard were the only ones left standing at the entrance. "Good-bye brother," he said. "Take good care of her."

Grimbeard pressed him close. "In the end it will be her decision. I believe her heart will choose you, though I have always hoped it might be me. I respect the fact that you had staked your claim long before I, and I will abide by your wishes as long as you are alive." He took hold of Lockjaw's hand, clasping it with his own. "But know this - if she needs an ear to bend, or a smile to chase away her tears, I will be here while you are far away."

Lockjaw sighed. "I know, and I forgive you. For I would do the same if our roles were reversed," and with a heavy heart he climbed out of the passage and into the world above.

VI

Janastari

Jules had just returned from Wildwood with a message for the Lieutenant. After handing the sealed parchment to an orderly, he led his mount to the stables and removed the horse's tack. Twice on the road the beast tried its best to unseat him.

"I see he's still giving you trouble." Sergeant Weyland handed Jules a brush from the young man's grooming kit.

"You don't know the half of it." He kept a wary eye on the horse as he spoke. "I've tried everything to win him over, but it's impossible. I don't know what else to do."

"Sometimes you have to earn your mount's respect before he will trust you," said Weyland, and he caught the charger by its harness and drew its head in close; he stroked the warhorse gently on the nose. "This animal is intelligent, and he knows you're not his true master and this is not his home. You'll have to prove that you are every bit as worthy as his former owner. It may be you might never get that chance, but if you succeed, I daresay that this horse will be your loyal companion for life."

The grooming done, Jules walked carefully around the stallion, keeping a safe distance from those iron-shod hooves. Weyland threw hay into the stall, and the sandy-haired cadet made sure his mount had fresh water, then he and the Sergeant walked back to the barracks.

"Hey," Hansil placed his quill on the table. "How was Wildwood?"

"You wouldn't believe it if I told you," said Jules. "If anyone had any doubts that we might not be going to war then one visit to Wildwood would clear their heads up fast." He sat on his cot, pulled his boots off, and tossed them to the corner. "I'm pretty sure the Lieutenant is planning some kind of a meeting. I overheard the Colonel tell one of his men to make arrangements for his departure. Though that's about all I know."

"Well you're right. The LT is planning a conference. Bon and I helped with the preparation."

The door opened, and Caleb entered with Bon and Sal. He plunked himself onto Camber's bed and the other two pulled up chairs. "Any news of our boys?" he asked.

"None so far," answered Jules. "I was just giving Hansil the rundown on Wildwood. They've been busy."

"How so?"

"Forging weapons for starters, bringing supplies in by the cartload. You should see it. Bloody hell! Plus Cambert's sending messengers back and forth almost daily. I even heard Thayneland stepped up patrol along the Barrier."

Bon whistled. "That's pretty serious stuff. Did Hansil tell you about the dwarf?" The cadet shook his head. "Well, he's supposed to be coming back."

Hansil nodded. "Ya. It's true. I was about to knock on the LT's office when I overheard him tell Bonner to make sure he was notified as soon as the dwarven ambassadors arrive. I waited to see if anything more was going to be said but the Sergeant shot out the door so fast he nearly knocked me flat."

"Hmmm... " Sal mused. "Sounds like a war council. Jules, since you're the only one who rides to Wildwood you keep monitoring their outfit, particularly anything to do with Ravenhill." He stood and gave orders to the others. "Caleb can keep tabs on anyone who enters and leaves the garrison when he's in the watchtowers. Can you do that?" He waited for the young man to nod. "Fine. Keep a quill handy so you can make a list. Bon, Hansil," the two cadets sat up, "you stay close to the LT, but be careful he doesn't suspect you're watching him, he's no fool."

"What are you going to do?" asked Jules.

"I'll infiltrate all the high-ranking officer's quarters for any information that may help us find the whereabouts of Camber and Dane."

Gareth sipped his coffee as he studied a map of the Eastlands. A sharp knock, and Bonner's face peered into the room. "Sir, everything has been prepared as you requested."

"And is there any news from the Pass?" Dega should have reached Whistlegate days ago.

"Sir, there has been no news concerning the party. But if you like we could send more scouts."

He shook his head. "No. We'll just have to trust the Captain on this one. We're going to need every available man right here at the barracks. Ravenhill's keeping this garrison as a back-up in case these boys are needed."

Bonner frowned. "They're still green. It'd be slaughter sending them to battle." Gareth sighed, running his hand through his closely cropped hair. "Let's hope it doesn't come to that."

* * * * * * * *

Sentash followed his captain down the spiraling staircase. A smile played across his face as he remembered the last time he paid the dungeons a visit. The agony of the man had been reflected tenfold across his face, *and* he had enjoyed every minute of it, stripping away the young man's remaining years and adding them to his own ancient span. Yes, the Valastari made excellent life-givers, but they were few and hard to find.

"This way, Sire." The captain lit a lamp and led him past a number of empty cells to the darkest corner of the dungeon. The air was dank, smelling of rust, iron, and rotting flesh, and somewhere within the walls a desperate cry blossomed into an agonizing scream. When they reached the last cell the captain gestured to the prisoner; the sorcerer took the lamp, moving in for a closer look. Fierce blue eyes met the eyes of the Easterling King, and right then and there he knew that *this* Valastari would provide ample entertainment while he devoured the years from his soul.

* * * * * * * *

The dwarves from Stone-Haven had stayed behind; they would be heading back to Stonefinger with messages from Grimbeard. Hawker and Dega led the company across field and stream to the outer region of the Borderlands. They stopped to converse, and after a few minutes a decision was made to set up camp.

"It's only afternoon," complained Dane. "Why are we stopping now?"

"Because we are now crossing through lands that although are not considered hostile, their inhabitants are a cautious folk and do not take kindly to strangers sneaking across their borders," Dega answered. "Or, if you prefer, we could march right up to their chief citadel and spend the next few days wrapped in chains explaining to their King who we are and why we're traveling through his lands," he raised an eyebrow to emphasize his point.

"I think that's his attempt at a joke but I'm not altogether certain," said the archer, and Camber laughed, maybe some of Dane was finally rubbing off on Dega after all.

They made a shelter inside a cluster of birch rooted between two grassy knolls. From a distance it appeared as though the trees were standing on a flat open meadow creating an illusion that the scenery was unvarying, screening their campsite from all sides. It was Dega who picked this location; skilled he was at moving unnoticed through foreign territory, and no stranger to the Borderlands; he seized the moment to instruct his cadets in the art of camouflage, and it pleased him to see that they enjoyed their lesson in this craft.

"If you look for specific flaws in the landscape you can almost guarantee yourself a safe haven." He pointed to a mound of rocks. "Too obvious, though you could certainly use it to your advantage if you were attacked. But look, just past the rocks," his hand indicated a ravine. "See the overhang? It might take some tricky climbing to get down it, but not a bad spot in a pinch." He walked them around the campsite's perimeter, scrutinizing it from an outsider's vantage point.

When they returned, Hawker had already prepared the meal. Dane was grateful that it contained no silverthorn; he ate what he was given, then had the nerve to ask for seconds.

The day gave way to dusk as the stars made their evening appearance. The night air was chilly and Camber searched his pack for an extra cloak to wrap around himself. Dega would not allow a fire, forcing them to make do with whatever clothing the dwarves had given them.

Camber and Dane would sit the first watch, then Dega. He was determined to take advantage of an early start and he woke the company in the wee hours of the morning. "We just went to bed," grumbled Dane. "I'll be glad when we reach Illianther, maybe somebody will let us sleep in."

"You're the one who wanted adventure," said Camber.

"Yes, but by adventure I meant living on the edge, flirting with danger, not running across country like a fugitive."

"Well if we stay here much longer then you may just get your wish," said Dega; he picked up his pack. "If the men of Caldorn find us they might just lop off our heads and ask questions later. Hang about if you like, but I prefer to stay alive myself."

"What about you, Lockjaw? What do you say?"

Lockjaw tucked his axe away; his heart was torn between following Hawker and leaving Shard. He stared miserably at the ground. "I have traveled many a lonely road and have always found the greatest reward to be the journey home."

The sky gradually lightened from pitch-black to midnight blue. One by one the stars disappeared giving way to a slate-gray sky and any hope of seeing the sun was quickly dashed as large raindrops began to fall. It rained steadily for the next few days; clothes were soaked to the inner garments, and did little to keep out the chill.

The company crossed an open field, which may have been solid at one time, but because of the rain was now a sloppy mudpit. Camber plodded in the tracks of the wizard, pulling his feet from the sucking sludge, only to place them back down again with a squelch. Mud oozed back into the indentation left by his boots, quickly covering his footprints. Warmth emanated from his forehead as the fever, which began yesterday, elevated his body's temperature well above comfort level. Dane was no better off, grumbling every time a sneezing fit racked his body. A constant stream of swearwords issued forth from his mouth reaching Camber's ears, but he barely had strength to acknowledge Dane's misery. Hawker pointed to a dark patch on the horizon. "We shall make for that forest up ahead."

The trees were very old, towering sentinels whose mighty tops graced the sky. Moonlight filtered through the branches, splashing an aura of majesty across the rough trunks of these ancient conifers. The canopy offered shelter from the elements; the rain had let up, and Dane was already feeling better now that he was dry, but his stomach rumbled, reminding him (and everyone else) that it had been nearly a full day since their last meal.

"Maybe we could hunt something," he said, breaking the silence. "I'm sure these woods are full of small game."

"No, we can't," replied Hawker; he stood still, as if waiting for something to happen.

"Why not?" Dane's voice rose, betraying his annoyance.

"Because," said Hawker. "We are the ones being hunted." As if to punctuate his words an arrow whizzed from the treetops and buried itself between the wizard's feet.

Dega went for his sword, but the sorcerer stopped him, and he dropped his hand.

"Show yourself Dark Elf," commanded Hawker, "for I know it's you. And you know me well enough that I come to your woods in peace."

"Step forward Stornoway Hawker," said a voice from somewhere above their heads, "and tell me why you bring a dwarf and three mortals into my realm." The wizard moved away from the company but both Lockjaw and Dega moved with him. He waved them back and boldly stepped to where the arrow had been launched.

"Come out of the trees so that we may talk Starlock," he said.

The treetops rustled and a figure dropped to the ground. The elf was dressed head to toe in black, with an impressive array of weapons glinting from leather braces. A single braid fell to her waist, blacker than midnight, but for the startling white lock which covered one eye, glittering like ice in the pale moonlight.

"Explain yourself Hawker," she said, keeping her bow taut.

"I had know idea we were in your woods." He brought up his hands to show he meant no harm. "We were merely passing through, trying to find shelter from the rain and..."

"Liar."

Dega stepped in front and made an attempt to grab the bow. The elf was fast, but not fast enough, and the Ranger's Captain was able to wrap his hand around the arrow. "If you try to kill the wizard then you'll have to kill us all. And there are five of us to your one."

She tugged at the arrow pulling Dega close. They were of equal height, and she met his scowl with one of her own. An ugly scar hid beneath the white lock of hair, running the length of her eyebrow to the top of her cheek, marring an otherwise flawless face.

"Do you think I cannot count, Ranger?" she snarled. "Do you really believe I would be standing here if I was not confident that I could take you all down," and snatching the arrow she sprang back two paces, dropping her bow and drawing the sword from its scabbard.

Dega's face hardened, daring her to come and cut his throat. And for a moment Camber wondered if she would meet the Captain's challenge.

Dane's hand reached for his bow and he pulled it carefully around front. Something shiny whizzed past his fingers slicing the bowstring. "Consider that a warning," said the elf. Dane dropped his bow, and Camber put his arm across his cousin's chest holding him fast.

"Enough," said Hawker. They were going to need the elf. "Starlock, I promise we meant no harm. We're merely passing through on our way to Illianther and it was my hope that you might join us. The others did not know about this, so if you must be angry with someone then be angry with me."

"Ha! Seems to me the last time you came stomping through here I ended up on a quest for your so-called *Fountain Eternal*." She placed her sword under his chin. "Come to think of it, I never did thank you for disappearing and leaving me to escape the Jungti hive on my own."

"Wait!" Hawker brushed the sword away. "I can explain."

"Well what of it - *Meddler of Affairs*. What do you want *this* time?" Starlock sheathed her sword and now stood with hands on hips.

"A word with you - o great and powerful elf." he said, taking care not to say anything that might cause an unwanted reaction, like his head suddenly being removed from its exalted position atop his neck. "I wish to seek passage through your lands with my companions."

"You said you were going to Elvenhome. Why?" she demanded.

"That business is my own."

"Go on. I'm listening." Her eyes darted around the company until they came to rest on the Ranger's Captain. He looked familiar. Had he been in her woods before? She quickly dismissed the idea, obviously he was as unfamiliar with his surroundings as the rest.

"It's a tale long in the telling," Hawker said, "and is best not spoken where the eyes and ears of the Easterling King might be lurking." He waited to see how she would react to the name, but she didn't even blink. "Sentash has regained his power and grows hungry in his quest for dominance."

"What do I care about the sorcerer? He will not cross my borders, and so is of no consequence."

"Aah, you are mistaken," said Hawker. "His armies number in the tens and thousands, and he will surely take your territory when all else is conquered."

"I will deal with the East when the time comes," her tone indicated that the conversation was coming to a close.

"Then you must already have the Winterstone. How else could you possibly defeat an enemy whose magic rivals the combined might of every elven talisman ever made, save one," and he counted softly to himself, one, two, three...

"The Winterstone?! Do you know its whereabouts? Or are you playing games?" Starlock pointed her finger. "Speak now wizard, and I might let you live."

"Only that it has yet to be found, and Sentash is seeking it."

"He cannot use it anyway," said Starlock. "It can only be used by an elf, for it was made by elven hands." Her eyes darted back to Dega standing beside the wizard.

"So be it. But what if he finds one that can wield it for him? Someone who carries the blood in his veins. Think of the power he could harness for his own."

"What are you saying?" Dane moved between them. "Is this why the Easterling King is after Camber?" Camber's mother was elvish, and his concern for his cousin became apparent as he placed his hands on the wizard and spun him around so they were face to face. Hawker shook himself free. "Yes, I'm afraid that is *one* of the reasons."

Now it was Camber's turn to show frustration. He was generally not hotheaded like Dane but he had his fill of Hawker's guessing games. "I'm not moving until I get some answers. You owe me some sort of explanation; after all, it's me the Easterling King wants."

Starlock chuckled. "It looks like you have a lot of explaining to do. Perhaps I should take you back to my place and if we are not all satisfied with your answers then I will gladly help them be rid of you."

Hawker tugged at his goatee. "Fine. But you must agree to accompany us to Illianther."

"You have my word," and she plucked the barbed star out of the tree behind Dane.

The forest was now so dense that it was impossible to navigate, and several times they were forced to stop and wait for the elf to return. At last they arrived at a clearing, an enormous chestnut stood at the center; its circumference was easily as big a house, with a skillfully constructed platform around its mid-trunk.

"Wait here," said Starlock, and she sprang lightly up onto the nearest branch. After a few minutes a rope ladder was tossed over the side. Dega was the first to ascend, followed by Dane, then Camber, and Hawker.

They were waiting for Lockjaw to climb when his voice floated up from somewhere below. "Might I try a levitation spell, Sir?" he asked.

"Go ahead," said Hawker.

And the dwarf began his spell. *"Munto... "*

"Minto," corrected Hawker.

"Minto." Lockjaw repeated. *"Minto farro. Minto farro. Minto Farro!"* About ten minutes later he repeated the spell. Starlock knelt beside Hawker waiting for the dwarf to rise up to the platform; she turned her head. "You still haven't told him he's not capable of magic have you?"

"He will learn. The magic I teach him is very different than your talismans. It takes many years to master even the simplest spell."

"And in the meantime he makes a great packhorse," offered Dane.

Hawker glared at the cadet, then promptly yelled back to his apprentice. "We can work on that spell later. Why don't you just climb the ladder for now."

After a few minutes Lockjaw's head came in to view and Dega pulled him to the platform. Starlock drew the ladder back and led them up a series of stairs shaped from living branches. When they reached the top, the branches widened and became a solid foundation; at the center they twisted into a hut. Lanterns hung from several limbs, bathing the house in golden warmth.

A shadow swooped down from above, landing on Starlock's outstretched arm. The falcon squawked angrily at the company. "This is Belia, and she has ever been my closest companion." She stroked the bird's head, and it shook itself, fluffing its feathers. They followed her into the hut and she placed the falcon on its perch. "I have something that will cure those colds and restore your health." She ducked into an adjoining room, "and then Hawker will tell us *everything*."

The cabin seemed larger than what it had appeared from the outside. The furnishing was sparse but comfortable, and one wall had nothing but shelves crammed with leather-bound books.

Dane was immediately drawn to a shiny cylinder in the corner. He turned it around and around, inspecting the surface, intent on finding a way to pry it open. Dega poked through an impressive collection of weapons stacked against the wall, and Hawker selected a book from the library; satisfied with his selection, he sat on a cushion and began thumbing through the pages.

Starlock came back with a tray of fruits and cheeses and a silver decanter. She put the tray on the table and immediately went over to Dane, now holding the cylinder up to his eye as he tried to peer into the small holes at one end of the tube.

"You might want to put that down," said Starlock.

"Why?" He tossed the cylinder into the air, catching it with his hands. "What's it do?"

"Do? It doesn't *do* anything. But the snake inside doesn't like to be tossed about, and if the lid pops off I'm sure you'll like it even less."

Dane promptly placed it on the stand, then plunked himself down beside the wizard. "Why would anyone keep a snake as a pet?" he asked.

"Because it comes in handy for making the poison I apply to my weapons," she answered, eyeing the Captain. He too, stopped what he was doing and came to sit beside Camber.

Starlock sat cross-legged at the table and it arranged itself to suit her comfort level. Small leaves wrapped around the legs, adorning it like green lace.

"Tell me about the Winterstone," she said, filling a glass and tilting it toward Hawker.

"Wise were the Elven Kings of old, and they poured their knowledge into..."

But she held up her hand. "I know its history! You said Sentash was looking for it. Then it must be true! The Stone was not destroyed."

"The Winterstone has resurfaced, but its whereabouts remain unknown. And since your patience is nearly as short as another in this company, whose name I need not mention, but has the attention span of a gnat, then I will cut straight to your question." While Hawker spoke he frowned at Dane, but the archer was captivated by the walls of the dwelling. As he put his hand near, the branches tightened until there were no visible gaps, becoming quite solid, but when he moved his hand away the branches expanded to their former position. He did this several times until he became aware that the room had suddenly grown silent.

Hawker shook his head. "Done?" he asked.

Dane nodded.

"Good." he said, clearing his throat. "Sentash has not yet learned of its whereabouts. When he does, nothing will be safe. Not even your own *Black Wood*."

"Ahhh, but as I already pointed out, he cannot wield its power."

Starlock stole a quick glance at Dega, who turned his head so she wouldn't think that he had been watching her.

"He will find a way."

"I suppose that's why his Bounders have been after Camber," interrupted Dane, and he went back to studying the wall.

"Bounders?!" Starlock's eyes widened. "You didn't tell me his Bounders are loose."

"He hunts the boy," he pointed to Camber. "But we've eluded him thus far."

"So you thought to hide out in my forest."

"I'm trying to get the lad to Illianther. I hoped you might be persuaded to join us."

"We do not need her help," Dega said. "We've made it this far on our own, and the reason for that is because our party is small. I'm quite capable of taking Camber to Illianther myself."

"Fine job you did leading them here. I was alerted to your presence long before I hailed the wizard. It's fortunate that I was in a mood for questions otherwise you'd all be dead right now." She stood and so did Dega.

"I somehow think not," his fingers curled around his sword.

"If you're their only protection then I worry for the boy's safety."

"I am aware of your abilities, o great and powerful Elf," he scoffed. "And good you are with a bow, and fast you are with your sword, but I am no green cadet."

She flicked her hand and a dagger appeared. "We could settle this now if you like."

"Lockjaw," said Hawker, and the dwarf looked up. Hawker held out his hand, and Lockjaw moved between elf and officer with arms extended.

"Now if we could all go back to being civilized we can make a decision to what is in Camber's best interest."

"Don't I get a say?" Camber stood beside Dane, staring incredulously at the trio who were now plotting *his* future without even asking for *his* input.

"No!" All three answered.

"Now Captain," Hawker addressed the officer. "If you would allow Starlock to join our company you will see that her skill will prove quite useful. And Starlock," he pointed his finger at the elf. "All I have told you is true. The Winterstone must be found. If Sentash finds it there's no telling what may happen."

"And who would you choose, wizard? Who do you deem *worthy* of the Stone?" Grim was her smile. "I don't think it would be me. Not that I would take it. Better if nobody claims it. Some things should stay lost."

"Snakes Alive!" Dane swore. "Did you just say that you can use this whateverstone?"

"Yes, of course," replied Starlock. "Anyone with elvish blood can wield it, even you."

"What?" Dane blinked. "I'm no elf."

"Actually Dane, you are. Remember Grandfather's side?" Dane nodded.

"Well," said Camber.

Dane's face changed, a sudden understanding – Thayne the Bold, hero of the Second uprising and his and Camber's great ancestor had taken Clearheart, the Nantastari, as his wife.

"It's not uncommon for Valastari and Elves to mix together," said Hawker. "In fact, all three of you have elvish blood, but Camber has the gift."

"Pardon me?" This time it was Dega who spoke. "The Darkhawks certainly do not have *any* elvish taint in their blood." The mere thought was abominable. "Besides, you said it was only the Valastari who mixed with Elves." His face grew dark.

"That's right," beamed Hawker. "Now we're getting somewhere. All of you are direct descendents of my original Valastari, and on both sides of your families. Do you realize how rare that is?" He rubbed his goatee. "And I might just mention, that you, Master Darkhawk, have the strongest connection since your lineage runs unbroken from father to son from King Brand."

"What in bloody hell! You can't be serious. My father never mentioned this. How could...." and Dega Darkhawk, Ranger Captain and Hartland's favorite son, came completely unraveled. He paused long enough to bring his emotions into check - then in a clear voice: "My father was a traitor. He sold military secrets to the enemy."

"No," said Hawker. "That's what you've been told. It was the other way around. Your father Drake Darkhawk was infiltrating the Easterling camp posing as a traitor so that he could gain valuable information for the Northern League. Only two other people knew about this other than myself – Glade and Chance Bloodstone." Hawker waited for some kind of reaction, but Dega just stood there, clenching and unclenching the pommel of his sword. "That story was made up to protect your father, and it gave him an excuse to leave Hartland for good. He was in danger the whole time he dwelt there and did not want his family harmed, especially his only child and heir to the throne."

Dega's hand shot up grabbing Hawker by the throat. His teeth clenched and he snarled at his face. "You Lie! You use words to manipulate people. None of this is true." He slammed the wizard hard against the wall. "NOT TRUE!" And he stormed out of the hut, slamming the door.

"I see you're as popular as ever," said Starlock, her gaze followed the cavalier as he stomped outside. She rolled her eyes; this had all the makings of another Stornoway Hawker escapade. Damn if she shouldn't just put an arrow through his forehead.

Both cadets regarded Hawker with a look of disgust as they followed Dega out the door. He was sitting on the platform dangling his legs over the edge.

"When my father was arrested and removed from our house I told him I was ashamed and never wanted to see him again," he sighed. "And he said to me that one day I would know the truth. From that moment on I hated him. I hated the fact that he was in league with the enemy. I hated your father and uncle for taking him away. And I hated you too, Camber." His face was dangerously hard; his eyes glittered like two chips of ice. "For years my mother and I had to endure the whispers, the finger-pointing, the guilt. I never thought I'd be able to rise above my father's infamous deed. Not until I joined the Rangers. I wanted to clear my family's name and make people proud of the Darkhawks again." He took a deep breath, and slowly blew it out. "I didn't care if I lived or died, as long as I did it with honor." It was all true. He strived to become a living legend, something all men would admire and measure up to. But most importantly, he wanted to distance himself from his father's past.

"Uncle Chance always said your family sacrificed more than anyone would ever know, but I never understood what he meant until now."

Dane nodded. "For what it's worth, I'm sorry," he added.

Dega shrugged. "It's all in the past, and nothing can change it now. I guess I owe you both an apology. I know I was hard on you, but I was only trying to make you earn your place, like I had to. I didn't want you rising through the ranks because of who your father and uncle were." He turned to Camber. "The night of the fire. Why did you save me?" From that moment on his opinion of the two cadets had changed.

"Why wouldn't I? You were lying face down. I had to do something."

Dane smirked. "Would you rather he had left you there?"

"If he had he could be assured of more than his share of late-night watches." Then Dega's voice became serious again. "So what now? It's your call Camber. Do we go back to Hartland or do we carry on to Illianther?"

"Since we came this far already then I don't see any harm in going to Illianther. Dane and I were hoping we'd find Chance there. And maybe the Elves will join the alliance."

"At the very least they might be able to help Camber."

Dega frowned. "Illianther?"

"Illianther." The cadets nodded.

The door of the hut opened and Hawker stepped across the tree to join them. "I have good news," he said. "Starlock has agreed to join our party."

Camber and Dane got to their feet, followed by Dega who had resumed his air of authority. "Fine," he said as he passed the wizard. "And we've decided to take the elf as a guide. But we need to replenish our supplies, especially water if we're going to cross the desert."

"Good." Hawker rubbed his hands together. "Let's all get back inside before someone falls out of the tree," his eyes moved to Lockjaw, who had just stumbled over a rather large knot.

Starlock was already stuffing bags when they returned from outside. She pulled the leather strap to tighten an already near-to-bursting pack. "I'll travel as far as Elvenhome even though I have not left my own forest in some time. I must leave you here for the night while I strengthen my borders. You may eat whatever you find in my kitchen or read the books on my shelf, I don't care which. But please do not step outside again until I return. It will not be safe," she whistled for Belia, and the bird flapped over to her shoulder.

Dane immediately went for the kitchen, followed by Camber and Lockjaw. Dega pulled a book from the shelf, blew the dust of the cover and carefully flipped its yellowed pages to a chapter on the Valastari.

Starlock returned the next morning, and Camber and Dane awoke to find all their belongings tied neatly to a pair of horses and the elf waiting with the animals on the ground.

"Where's Lockjaw?" asked Dane, jumping the last few feet from the rope ladder.

"He's combing the area for plants and healing roots that may be useful on our journey," answered Starlock. The cadet reached up to touch one of the horses, but it shied and gave a delicate snort. "Please be careful," cautioned the elf. "These are not domestic stock. They are wild horses from a nearby herd and are not used to being so close to people. It took a great deal of convincing on my part just to get them to carry our belongings."

Neither horse wore any tack except for two leather straps circling their underbellies holding the packs in place. Starlock watched the cadet with some amusement. "They have agreed to carry our packs as far as the Rivermarch. They will not, however, suffer the indignity of carrying a rider unless it is myself, and they do not wish to have either bridle or saddle placed upon them."

"I don't blame them. I wouldn't want to wear one either." Dane grinned, and Starlock gave him one of her rare smiles.

Lockjaw returned from his mission, showing his find to Hawker, who selected two, then tossed the rest over his shoulder.

Dega stretched his legs and stifled a yawn. It was time to be off, for they had wasted nearly the best part of the day and soon it would be midmorning. He had not slept well, and it was not because of the snores emanating from both wizard and dwarf, something else had kept him awake; a strange melody, not unlike someone singing, and unfortunately for the others it had soured his mood for the day. "If you don't mind wizard," he said, "we are not accomplishing much by standing here," and made a motion to depart.

Starlock took the lead, and the horses followed like tame pets. Above in the sky, Belia circled over the heads of the company. Hawker walked at the front, and Lockjaw fell in beside Camber and Dane, quite happy at being relieved of both his and the wizard's packs.

The journey was almost pleasant but for the constant bickering between Dega and Starlock, it seemed neither could agree on what the other proposed, and by day nine it was almost a welcoming respite when the company came to a halt under a canopy of dense jungle. The vegetation was a mixed variety of exotic plant-life rivaling the gardens of the dwarf-warrens, but unlike the cultivated flora inside the atrium these plants did not have gardeners, and they grew impossibly close, so that at times one could not even slide a hand through the greenery.

Starlock solved the problem by drawing a sword with a curved edge and cleaving a path.

Black flies buzzed in and around unprotected heads, their incessant humming adding to the drone of a sluggish atmosphere. Further in, sunlight failed to penetrate such dense cover, and as the day waned it was clear they could no longer continue, they were forced to set up camp under the pitch-black of night. Camber and Dane erected a shelter while Lockjaw chopped wood for the fire. Starlock unloaded the baggage, freeing the horses from their burden, they now combed the area in search of edible plants and grass.

The company was rudely awakened next morning to a sudden shower. It lasted all of fifteen minutes but had thoroughly soaked their belongings, not to mention the food. And as Camber soon discovered, the very second the shower stopped the bugs were out in full force. He slapped a mosquito off his neck. "I don't suppose you have any idea where we are?"

Hawker turned around, for some reason the bugs had left him alone and he was not bothered by their buzzing nor their bites. "No," he said, "and for the umpteenth time stop asking that question!" Apparently, bugs or no bugs, the wizard was still irritable.

They reached the edge of the rainforest as day gave way to night. An immeasurable expanse of sky dotted with stars was a breath of fresh air after the oppressive weight of the jungle, but Dega could care less, too busy brooding over matters concerning his family, particularly his father. Memories from the past suddenly resurfaced. Hadn't Glade Bloodstone come to his family's home in the wee hours of the morning just weeks before his father was arrested? And before that, was it just a coincidence that he and his father ran into both Glade and Chance while hunting in the Wildwood? His father sent him off to check the traps and he gladly obeyed, proud to show his father's friends that he was capable of checking and setting traps by himself. He squeezed the pommel of his sword as he walked. Yes, he now knew the real reason why his father had sent him away. So he could talk in private with his friends. And now everything he had believed about his family, about his father, was a lie.

The next few days went by in a blur, and at last they reached the fertile meadows of the Rivermarch. A gentle wind stirred the waist-high grass, bending gold and green stalks in half. The scenery shifted and the same dark green conifers found in the Northlands loomed on the horizon. They were now at the edge of the plains.

The sun had reached its zenith when they stopped at the muddy banks of a river twice the width of the Whitewash. Pockets of churning froth collected around jagged teeth of upright rock as the mighty *Icewind* sent forth its hungry tongue. The only apparent crossing was a small ferry conveniently moored to a dock on the other side of the shore.

"Just wonderful," muttered Dane; he threw his pack to the ground. Camber joined him on the grass happy to sit while the others figured out a way to get across. He turned his head, watching Starlock argue with Dega; it seemed they disagreed on everything, including the safest way to travel across country. "And you thought Dega was hard to get along with," he said.

Dane grimaced, remembering that first night in the Black Wood. Starlock was a force to be reckoned with and he wondered just how much of Hawker's bravado had been feigned when she had trained her bow on him. "My money's on Dega," he said at last.

"Explain."

"Dega's got a temper, any fool can see that. But he also has smarts," he tapped his head. "He thinks all the time. Always sizing up the situation, using his head instead of his sword." Camber tried to argue but Dane held up his hand. "Remember that fight in the tavern?"

"'Course, who could forget that."

"Well - did you notice that when Dega entered everyone stopped what they were doing? Nobody dared flinch."

"So?"

"So Dega's fame precedes him, and he used it to his advantage. He didn't have to do anything, and he knew this."

The afternoon sun was warm, not too hot, but just the right temperature for basking in the tall sweet-smelling grass; unfortunately their relaxation was about to come to an end as Lockjaw waded into the fast-moving water. It was obvious the dwarf was going to swim for the rickety raft that served as a ferry.

Hawker came over and sat down beside them, and Dane looked up at the wizard from his sprawled position, propping himself on his elbows. "What's Lockjaw trying to do? Drown?" Hawker shaded his eyes so that he could watch the dwarf muscle his way to the dock. "Dwarves are strong swimmers," he said. "They have to be if they want to survive under the mountains. Every male dwarf will at one time or another encounter an underground pool or river, whether it's because he lost in a game of Karpung or happened to fall into one while excavating a passage. So naturally they are taught to swim right from birth, and Lockjaw happens to be an exceptionally strong swimmer."

"As well as an exceptionally strong packhorse," said Dane. Camber laughed, and to his surprise so did Hawker.

Lockjaw had reached the ferry and was now untying the line that held it fast. He pulled the rope loose and quickly reached for the pole to steer the raft. At first it seemed the current would sweep dwarf and raft downstream, but after a few minutes of Lockjaw poling and twisting, the ferry slowly turned to where the rest of the company now stood ready to receive the craft.

Dega tossed a rope, and Lockjaw snatched it up, tying it securely to the bow. Starlock tied the other end around one of the horses, coaxing it into pulling the raft ashore. The others waited along the river bank, tugging on the rope and bringing the ferry to rest in the mud.

Starlock let the horses go, whispering a few words, then joined them on the raft.

"What was that about?" asked Camber.

"They wanted to know where I was going with such strange companions, and if the one with the perpetual frown on his face practiced at being unsociable," she answered Camber but her eyes were on Dega. The officer looked up from guiding the raft and scowled.

They gained the opposite shore and Belia landed on Starlock's shoulder squawking in her ear. She frowned, then bounded up the nearest tree.

"What is it?" called Hawker.

Starlock's voice floated back from the treetops. "Riders. Five of them. Their present course will lead them past this area."

This side of the river was more or less open with few trees, and nowhere to hide. Dega drew his sword and the others followed suit. Hawker tugged his goatee. "Wait," he said, then snapping his fingers. "If we all stand a few feet apart I can cast a spell which will make us appear as trees from a distance. However," he added, "you cannot move else the spell will fail. And if the riders happen to come too close then they will see through it."

"That's your plan? We can't move and they'll see us if they get too close? What kind of stupid plan is that? Why don't we just wave a flag!"

Hawker pointed his finger at Dane. "If you can think of an alternative

I'd love to hear it." He waited for the archer to speak. "Fine. I guess we go with mine."

"Might I give it a try Sir?"

A sudden wave of panic seized the beating hearts of all.

"Not this time Lockjaw."

The sound of air expelled from four sets of lungs as the wizard put his magic to use.

VII

Deserts and Dragons

The scouting party rode past without so much as a glance; all except one rider, who slowed his horse to a trot and veered toward the treeline. He stared at the clump of trees. Tired and saddle-weary after his second straight week riding the Rivermarch he failed to see why they had to be out here at all; obviously, if there was no sign of the Northlanders the first week then they probably weren't even this far south. But orders were orders, and who was he to argue with the higher ups. If Heyhrwulf wanted to kiss ass to the sorcerer in the East then that was his problem. Shifting his weight in the saddle, he could think of a hundred things he'd rather be doing, and none of them involved riding patrol. He was about to turn his charger back to where the others waited when the horse gave a snort, he stopped short and held his mount in check. What was that in the trees? A man's face? He blinked and the vision disappeared.

"Yo! Grundzen. What's keeping you?" One of the riders turned his mount. Grundzen waved him off, but he galloped up to where the soldier had stopped. "C'mon, we've leagues yet before we can report back," he reined his horse in beside Grundzen's.

"I thought I saw a face." Grundzen pointed to the trees. His companion looked in the direction where the man was pointing. "Bah! There's nothing there. We've already been through that area; you've been drinking too much skifft." The Southlander frowned and turned his horse to join the others.

"Aachoo!"
"Gesundheit!"
"I didn't sneeze."
Both riders wheeled their mounts around.

"Snakes Alive!"

"Cripes Dane, did ya have to go and sneeze." Camber drew his sword. Dega had already engaged the first attacker, and Lockjaw stood in front of Hawker with his axe in both hands. Grundzen whistled for his companions even as he rushed his horse at Camber. Before he could bring his arm down Starlock swung out from the tree and kicked him in the face, knocking him clear out of the saddle. The elf landed in a crouched position, as she rose something shiny flew from her hands. Blood spurted from his jugular, and Grundzen took three steps before he toppled over dead.

Dega barely had time to turn and meet his adversary. He drew his blade, bringing it up just as the Southlander's sword came crashing down. Sharp steel bit into his upper arm, but Dega knew from experience the wound was not deep and switched his sword to the other hand. The Ranger's Captain was one of those rare individuals who could use both hands equally well, and he took advantage at the distraction his sudden switch had caused, thrusting his blade through the opening and giving it a twist. Gore splashed his uniform and face; he stuck his boot on the dead man's body pulling his sword free.

Dane loosed a volley of arrows; all three hit their mark, and the man was down before the other riders had passed. A blur of brown fell from the sky striking a Southlander as he vaulted from his horse, but the falcon flew out of reach, spiraling high above the treetops.

Belia struck again, and the soldier swung blindly, hoping to connect by sheer luck; his sword met resistance from Starlock, and when he left himself open she kicked him hard in the groin, then lopped off his head.

"Listen!" she hissed. The sound of pounding thunder came faintly to their ears.

"Cavalry," confirmed Dega.

"We cannot fight them all." Blood streaked her face and hair, turning that snow-white lock into a scarlet candy stripe. "There's a bridge not far from here."

"I know that bridge," said Dega. "It crosses a ravine; we can cut it down once we get to the other side." He grabbed at the reins of the nearest horse. "Mount up!" The others rounded up the remaining horses, with Lockjaw doubling up on the back of Hawker's steed.

Now they could see a faint line of horses moving swiftly on the horizon; a dust cloud marking the distance, growing larger by the second as it rose high in the noonday sky. Dega dug his spurs in deep.

The bridge was close; they should just have enough time to gain the other side and then destroy it.

The horses were running flat out, but Dane's steed was barely keeping up. For the love of... why did *he* have to have the slow one? Something whizzed past his ear. He turned his head for a look, and wished he hadn't. The dark band of riders grew at an alarming rate, and the ones in front were drawing bowstrings. He flattened himself against the horse's neck, spurring it on with renewed vigor at the sight of the bridge.

Flecks of foam flew from his mount; lather covered its neck. Camber didn't think the poor beast would last much longer, but the bridge was coming up fast even as the riders behind narrowed the gap. The faster ones were fanning out on the sides hoping to cut the party off before they crossed the ravine. His horse had stretched its lead and it looked like he would clear the bridge just in time. With less than twenty yards to go, the charger stumbled, catching its foot in a pothole. Camber flew over its head, landing hard on the ground.

The shock of the fall was quickly replaced with the sudden realization that he was going to have to run for it. The bridge was still more than fifty feet away and the others were already across. Camber took off at a sprint; the ground trembling beneath as cavalry charged behind; the pant of horses, the jangle of steel, sweat, leather, and fear lending speed to his feet.

Dane pulled his mount to a halt. Where was Camber? Turning in the saddle he spotted his cousin running pell-mell for the bridge. Dega was already at the overpass, and Starlock was cutting the ropes that held it in place. Two riders gained on Camber as he struck across the bridge. Dane vaulted off his horse and drew his bow. One! Two! His arrows found their mark just as Starlock cut through the last rope holding the bridge.

Dega reached out to Camber. "JUMP!"

* * * * * * * *

"Jump!"

"I still can't see anything."

"Try again," Bon said, and Caleb readied himself for another attempt.

This time his head cleared the window and he briefly caught a glimpse before he landed.

"See anything?"

But before Caleb could answer Gareth walked over to the window and drew the shade across, preventing further attempts at peeking through the glass.

"Well I guess that ends that," Bon frowned.

"Maybe Hansil has something new to report," Caleb offered, and together they marched over to the supply hut where the cadet was on duty.

"Hey!" Hansil greeted his friends. "Didn't Sal ask you two to keep an eye on the summit?"

Bon flicked his white-blonde hair from his eye. "The LT has seen to that plan. We can't get a look from the outside, and he's posted guards down the hall so that no one without proper admittance can get within ten feet of the boardroom."

"What about you?" Caleb asked. "Any luck?"

"Nope. I haven't seen hide or hair of anyone. And there hasn't been one commission for supplies. I was told to check the list and I've done that twice already."

"Ahh, so here's where the slackers hide when there's work to be done." Sal entered the supply hut. "You'll never guess where I've been," and with a grin he held up some keys attached to a silver ring.

"Those are the Lieutenant's," said Caleb.

"Yep, and he doesn't know they're missing. In fact, I just came back from his quarters."

"You what?!"

Sal held up his hand. "Not to worry, he doesn't suspect a thing. At least not yet. I have to get these back before he misses them." As if worried that the Lieutenant might show up at any moment and demand his keys back, he quickly closed the door. "Now listen. This is what I found out. The dwarven armies are expected to meet up with Cambert, Janus, and Wildwood. While the armies are in the final stages of organizing their attack, Thayneland will send her warships up the coast to engage the enemy and thereby act as decoy. All the while the real invasion will be in the Southlands. The combined forces of the Northern League, the Borderlands, and the Dwarves will cross *the Hook* and take the East by surprise."

Bon whistled softly, "That just might work. But what about us? Are we going with them?"

"No," Sal continued, "we have to act as messengers and relay dispatches to all the other garrisons. And," he added, "we're backup. If the lines break, then we'll be the last line of defense between East and North."

"What about Camber and Dane?" Hansil was eager to learn any scrap of news concerning his friends.

"As far as I know they're alive and well. And I'm sorry I didn't learn much more, except that Rangers were sent to Whistlegate with orders to watch for them, but there hasn't been any sightings yet." He hopped off a sack of grain and winked at the trio. "But don't lose hope. I bet the Cap's taking good care of them. Anyway, I gotta get these keys back. Caleb, come with me and be my decoy." Sal stopped and turned as he and Caleb started out the door. "Jules will be back tonight and maybe he'll have more news."

Gareth was pleased at how well the talks were going. It wasn't easy being the mediator between three nations. He was glad King Silvan agreed to the alliance. The Southlanders were as much of a problem for the Men of Caldorn as the East was for everyone else, and by invading the Southlands first they would be doing Silvan a service. Too bad the emissary from the Borderlands had no news concerning the Captain. He scratched his head, still torn between sending more Rangers to the Pass and just waiting it out until the armies were under way.

As he turned the corner two cadets came flying down the hall; he tried to side-step and avoid an unwanted collision but they all ended up on the floor anyway. "Oops! Sorry Sir. Allow me to help you," one of the cadets pulled him up by his arm. Before he could say something they had disappeared down the next corridor. Gareth shrugged and dusted off his jacket. *Still innocent. They do not yet realize how this war will change them.* And he pulled his keys out of his pocket.

* * * * * * * *

"JUMP!"

Camber obeyed, pushing off with his legs and thrusting his body forward. The bridge went slack beneath his feet and his body pitched forward, just as the bridge itself, disappeared entirely, taking with it the two horsemen. A strong hand clamped his outstretched arm and he opened his eyes to see Dega holding onto him, dragging his body forward while his feet sought to find purchase on the loose rocks of the cliff. Dane was by his side in a flash. He reached over Dega to grab Camber's coat and together they hauled the cadet to safety.

"That was close." Several arrows whizzed past Dane's head landing in the dirt. "Too close."

"C'mon. We can't stay here." Dega was already astride his horse. Camber climbed onto the back of Dane's mount and they followed the others across the open grasslands.

The company rode for several hours, sometimes at a canter, sometimes at a trot, across fields of waist-high wild grass and over treeless hilltops until at last they reached a stream trickling down from the foothills of the southernmost peaks of the Dragonspine. Here they stopped to rest their mounts and refill their water skins. "We'll have to keep riding through the night," Dega was saying as Camber bent down to the water. "That ravine won't stop them for long now that they know we are here, and we don't want to get caught in the open."

"We should make for the warren that Lockjaw spoke of. It can't be far," said Hawker.

The dwarf agreed. "If memory serves me correctly, then we should reach Silverlake sometime tomorrow."

Dega spread Stonefinger's map on the ground; blood trickled down his arm, staining his uniform and dripping onto the parchment.

"Take off your shirt," said Starlock; she reached into her pouch for some salve.

Dega frowned, he had intended to take care of that later, but at last relented and removed his coat and shirt.

Camber and Dane were surprised at the hard physique of the Ranger's Captain. The last time they had seen Dega shirtless he was still in his teens, and though he had always been athletic, they had not seen him for many years and had not realized until now the difference the gap between their ages made. Biceps the size of grapefruits threatened to burst from under taught tanned skin; a solid chest complimented tight abdominals, each one a finely chiseled diamond, even the nasty scars along his neck enhanced his manliness.

Dega held his arm out for the elf to tend; she discarded her gloves, touching him lightly as she inspected the wound. After cleansing it with water she worked the salve slowly into the cut, and while Starlock poked and prodded, he held his breath, taking great care not to flinch, for some reason he felt it would be a display of weakness on his part. She bandaged the arm with a strip of cloth. Dega waited for her to finish, then slowly - *oh so slowly* - let his breath out.

Camber was fortunate to escape with only a few minor scrapes and bruises, but Starlock wanted to look at them anyway, and so he allowed her to administer her healing salve to his abrasions. She examined his knee with genuine concern, softly applying the ointment. Hard to believe this was the same individual who, only moments ago, lopped the head off her adversary without even batting an eyelash.

Starlock took her leave and went to join the others who were studying Dega's map.

"Here." Lockjaw pointed. "This is the location. But it has long been abandoned. I cannot say whether I will be able to open the entrance after all this time."

Silverlake had been home to a colony of dwarves renowned among their kind as the most skilled of miners. Unfortunately, they had only been a few, and of that few only a handful were dwarxen, and after a series of attacks by dragons, jungti, and even Southlanders, the dwarves of Silverlake had finally come to an end.

Hawker was looking over his shoulder. "Hmmm… " he tugged his goatee. "That is not far from where we are now. We could be there by sunup tomorrow if we ride through the night." Dega rolled up the map and tucked it back inside his coat. "Then we should leave now. But I worry that the cadets will not be able to ride all night without falling out of their saddles, not to mention that the horses are all but spent and will need more rest before they are fully recovered. They will not be of much use if we have to run from Southlanders again. I suggest we walk the horses until nightfall, then post a watch and resume our journey just before daybreak."

This was sound advice and for once Starlock agreed. "Belia can scout the area and warn us if we need to pull leather." She called for the falcon, and Belia sped down from the trees to alight on her arm. Starlock said something in elvish and the bird was away again, circling high into the bright blue sky.

The company stopped at nightfall and since Dega was feeling restless he took the first watch. Starlock had disappeared up the nearest tree, and Lockjaw and the cadets were asleep within minutes. Dega flexed his bicep, the arm was stiff, but at least the cut was not deep. A frown creased his brow as he reflected on the day's events; always good with a sword, he was not used to being put on his guard, and it bothered him that he had been slow on that duel.

"How's your arm?" Hawker asked.

"It's fine. A little stiff, but it'll heal."

Hawker rubbed his goatee. "I thought you and I might talk."

Dega raised an eyebrow. "All right," he muttered.

"I thought you might want to know something of your family's history." Hawker made himself comfortable by the fire.

Dega nodded, and the Caretaker told him about his family's beginnings, starting with King Brand and ending with his own father, Drake Darkhawk. Not one to wear his emotion, Dega tried to keep a straight face, but his eyes widened when Hawker revealed that his many-times great grandfather had been the best of friends with the Easterling King.

"In the end he betrayed your family and murdered Blacker Darkhawk with his bare hands. He fled west and took refuge in the south, then was driven to the Eastern shores where he built his fortress. From that day on, your family has always been at the forefront of the fight against Sentash, even at their own expense. A wise man once told me – *the greater need outweighed his own reputation*." Hawker paused, and placed his hand on Dega's shoulder. "That man was your father."

Starlock stretched herself along the length of the tree branch, curious to see how the Ranger's Captain was going to take this news. Would he explode, or was he going to be all calm on the outside and mad like a nest of hornets underneath. Either way she didn't care, it would be just as amusing to watch the outcome, whether she had to wait for it or not. She inched a little closer to hear what the young hothead was going to say.

"Is that it?" Dega snorted. Somehow it seemed more like a lesson in morals than an actual account of his family's history.

"For the time being, yes," answered Hawker. "But more shall be revealed once we reach Illianther. And there you shall know everything."

The branches shook overhead, and Starlock slipped to the ground. "I'll stand watch if the Captain would like some sleep," she said, feeling more than a little cheated by his reaction, she had really been hoping for some fireworks. Dega grunted a thanks and went to find a suitable spot to lay his bedroll.

The company got off to an early start, and Dega rode at the back of the group keeping a watchful eye, but there seemed to be no sign of the Southlanders. Even Belia, from her lofty position, failed to catch a glimpse of the army. Well that was okay by him; but if they were not actively pursuing the party then they must be planning something else, maybe an ambush, maybe something worse. He just hoped this dwarf mine wouldn't be crawling with Southlanders when they arrived.

Bright was the sun amid a cloud-scudded sky. It was going to be an exceptionally hot day; fortunately, part of it could be wasted inside the cool underground lair of the dwarf-warren. Lockjaw jumped down from behind Hawker and immediately began looking for the hidden spring that would trigger the opening. Belia landed on Starlock's shoulder as she dismounted, and the elf brought something out from a pouch and fed it to the bird. The others hopped off their horses to stretch their legs while waiting for the dwarf to open the entrance.

A *BOOM* blasted across the heavens. And a ball of light dropped from the sky. Sunfire radiated from the orb; the air grew heavy; it shimmered, and a figure crystallized before six pairs of astonished eyes.

The woman was tall, and elegantly attired in layers of fine silk cast in shades of midnight, but as she glided toward the wizard her robes shifted to a rich royal purple, sky blue, and many shades in-between. Upon her shoulders she wore a mantle of white clouds; blue-black hair floated around her head, held aloft by a gentle breeze.

"Jessa. I have found you at last," she breathed; her velvety voice could be heard by all, though it was not loud.

"Atrilla!" Hawker dropped the pack he was holding. "Why do you seek me?"

The woman lifted her snow-white arm and touched him gently on his face. Creamy alabaster contrasted sharply with sunbrowned bronze.

"Jessa. Oh Jessa," she whispered; the leaves in the trees rustled as the breeze became stronger. "Norii has taken Defél."

"WHAT?!" Hawker grabbed her by the arms. "When? How?"

Starlock narrowed her eyes. This was not good. Two powerful beings, fear on their faces, and an aura of doubt that a blind man could see.

As if reading her mind, Dega edged up beside her. "What is it?" he whispered. But she did not need to answer, for her look said everything. *And hadn't the wizard mention this Norii once before?* "Caretaker of Death," he said, and Starlock nodded.

"You must come with me at once Jessa. There's no time to waste. The others are waiting for your counsel and I have spent nearly all my resources looking for you." There was a hint of urgency in her voice, and as it rose, so did the wind rise up around them. The leaves blew off branches and small dust devils whirled around at their feet. Hawker turned to face the company. "I must go. You cannot imagine how important it is for me to leave right now. But know this - I will join you at Illianther." Atrilla raised her white arms and commanded the wind to bear them away.

"Wait for me at Illianther." Hawker's voice trailed out from the funnel of air that now enveloped them both, lifting them high into the noon-day sky.

* * * * * * * * *

"You will die. That much is certain. But do not worry, for you do me a huge service with your death, and know that you will not have died in vain."

The man who had been stripped naked and suspended by his heels from the ceiling stared at the Easterling King. Their heads were almost even; Sentash laughed as he saw that ridiculous defiant glare that so many of the Valastari wore while facing death's embrace. "Before you die," he added, and he placed a finger on his captive's forehead. "I will rake your mind for every scrap of thought that it contains. And afterward, if you can still manage to talk, you will beg me to release you from this world."

The Val clamped his jaw shut; he would not give this madman the satisfaction of even the smallest of whimpers.

* * * * * * * * *

"Now what?" Dane asked, as he walked over to the Captain.

"We go to Illianther," said Dega. "I promised to take Camber there and that's just where he's going." The archer nodded, they couldn't very well turn back now, and there were still the Southlanders to contend with if they did. He ran his hand through his thick black locks and smiled wanly at the officer. "Can we take a vote?"

Dega was not in the mood for humor and it showed. He started barking orders: "Round up the horses. Get them inside. Move it!"

The horses were reluctant to enter the tunnel, and for good reason, it was pitch-black, and as Starlock and Lockjaw lit some torches they saw the passage was in complete ruins. Part of the tunnel had collapsed; tree roots poked through cracks in the walls. Lockjaw shook his head; even though he had suspected that the warren was probably in need of repair he had no idea things were this bad. They led their frightened mounts through rubble and around twisting tree roots, but had not gone far when the dwarf suddenly stopped, causing everyone, including horses, to bump into each other. "Something's not right," said Lockjaw; he froze in place.

"What's that smell?" Dane sniffed the air; stale, earthy, but carrying a peculiar odor, not unlike the sharp tang that emanates from reptilian skin.

"Hssst!!!" Starlock recoiled in horror. "Tambril!" She drew her sword.

"Wait," Dega put a restraining hand on her shoulder. "One of us should go on ahead and see just how many there are. We still have to pass this way if we can. We cannot go back through the Southlands." Starlock sheathed her sword.

"I'll go." Lockjaw said. "We're in my element now, and there's no better guide than a dwarf when it comes to slipping about unnoticed beneath a mountain." Dega nodded his approval, and the dwarf disappeared down the corridor. The others waited in silence for Lockjaw's return. After a few minutes, he came back through the passage startling the horses. Camber and Dane reached for the reins to keep them from bolting back up the tunnel.

"We are in the East corridor. The guardians at the entrance are in ruins, but I recognized the face of Slate-Eyes. This is a small warren, little better than a cavern, but its corridors are short and straight." His face darkened. "You are correct elf," he growled. "It is indeed a nest of tambril."

Dega frowned. "How many?"

"The whole central atrium is filled with them."

Camber and Dane stared at each other. They knew from their own limited experience that in order to cross they would have to pass through the grand atrium.

"How many torches do we have?" Dega was already hatching a plan. Starlock glanced about the corridor. "None on these walls, but if the dwarf knows where we might find some then I will accompany him." She passed Belia from her shoulder and onto a gnarled root.

Lockjaw nodded; he had passed two intersecting passages further down the corridor; one was completely blocked but the other was open. Together elf and dwarf went in search for more torches. "How will torches help us cross?" asked Dane.

"Tambril do not like anything bright. They hide from daylight in places where it's almost always dark and they hunt only at night. If we carry enough torches they may just leave us alone," answered Dega.

"But aren't they a type of dragon?" Camber asked.

"In a fashion. But they are more closely related to bats than dragons." Dega's brows furrowed as he tried to recall all he knew about tambril. "They hunt in much the same way a bat might – by sound." Both cadets listened with interest. It was amazing the amount of information that Dega carried around in his head; he seemed to know a little bit about everything. "The tambril have limited vision at best and are extremely sensitive to light; they have no sense of smell, but their hearing is keen. When they attack their prey they let out a high-pitch squeal, when the sound bounces back they calculate their striking range. Ultimately, they can pinpoint their targets to within a hairbreadth." His body stiffened and his hand went to the pommel of his sword. But the faint noise he had heard was just the dwarf and the elf returning with three more torches.

"It's all we could find," said Lockjaw, and he handed them to the Ranger. Dega counted the torches; with the two they already had that made five. He took Starlock aside and they talked quietly, it was clear from her frown that she did not like what the Captain was proposing, but at last she agreed and they came back to the group.

"Lead on dwarf," said Dega. Lockjaw nodded, and Dane and Camber led the horses, following him down the passage. As they neared the end of the corridor the horses became agitated, and it was a struggle to convince them to move forward to where they instinctively knew danger was lurking. Starlock moved from horse to horse, placing a hand on each forehead and talking softly until they quieted and the cadets were able to lead them without further incident.

"We are not more than fifty feet from the entrance," said Lockjaw.

Dega nodded. He gave orders to light the torches, and he and Starlock undid the packs and distributed them amongst the company. Then to Camber's surprise they tore strips of cloth from their cloaks and blindfolded the horses. "What's that for?" he asked. Dega gave him that look that said to dispense with the questions and do as he was told. He quickly obeyed, and shouldered one of the packs around to his back as he received two burning brands, one for each hand. Dane also had two torches, and the dwarf held the fifth along with most of the baggage piled upon his shoulders. Dega and Starlock took the horses by their reins; they had discarded the rest of the tack onto the floor.

"We walk as far as we are able," Dega explained his plan. "When I give the signal, you three run for the Western gate. Keep running and *do not* look back." The orders were simple enough, and Camber and Dane nodded to show they understood. They followed Lockjaw out of the corridor with Starlock and Dega leading the horses.

Neither cadet was ready for the sight that lay before them as they stepped into the remains of the once beautiful atrium. The foliage was long gone, withered away into dry brown husks. Deep fissures split the walls, and busted marble lay strewn in every direction. Camber's eyes wandered to the top of the dome; its gemstones long since removed, and as his eyes adjusted to the torchlight he realized to his horror that the walls and ceiling were crawling with hundreds of dark shapes.

Dega's hand pushed him forward, and he stepped from the safety of the passage and into the terror of the tambril nest. At first nothing happened. Lockjaw led the group across the center to the Western corridor. And for a brief moment Camber thought they just might get across unscathed. He held his breath; the stench was overwhelming; he could taste bile rising in his throat as he forced himself to breathe the foul stink of tambril waste; it covered every square inch of the cavern in white sticky goo.

A shattering shriek violated the quiet, stopping them all in their tracks. "NOW!" Dega yelled, and Camber and Dane sprang forward brandishing their torches.

At Dega's command, he and Starlock stabbed the horses in their hindquarters; the frightened animals bolted blindly out into the center of the atrium. The ruse worked, buying them time to gain the passage. Elf and officer sprinted toward the corridor. Lockjaw was already at the far end, working on the door that would open the porch. Camber and Dane were waiting half way up the tunnel when Dega and Starlock came charging through the rubble.

"MOVE!" Dega yelled running toward them, and they raced up the corridor to where the dwarf was fumbling for the finger holds. It was no easy task; large rocks blocked the exit. Lockjaw lifted boulders, tossing them aside, searching for the trigger.

Starlock and Dega drew swords and turned to face the way they had come. "Throw those torches on the ground," commanded Dega, and he pointed to an area just in front of where he was standing. Camber and Dane obediently placed the torches out in front, but no sooner had they done so when two tambril entered the passage. A third crawled up from behind and clung to the ceiling. Dane fitted an arrow to his bow and Camber drew his sword.

The first one lashed out at Starlock; she swung her sword, slicing through its short scaly arm. Dega whirled, catching the second underneath its neck; he gave it a twist and his blade came free covered in gore. The passage filled as more and more tambril tried to squeeze into the narrow opening, now squawking excitedly at the prospect of finding such a meal.

Dane drew his bow and sent an arrow into a yellow eye; the fallen reptile screeched horribly, writhing in pain, and to his disgust its nest-mates scrambled to devour its flesh.

Sunlight spilled into the tunnel; hundreds of angry squawks rose up in protest at the bright glare. Camber and Dane were already out of the passage with Lockjaw, but Dega and Starlock were still caught between tambril. Belia screeched, narrowly evading snapping teeth; the beast opened its jaws wide and Dane sent an arrow from the safety of the doorway. It thrashed about, blocking the passage, and several of its kindred tore it to pieces trying to reach the party.

"Look Out!" Starlock charged at Dega, diving toward the exit and taking the Ranger's Captain with her just as a very large tambril detached itself from the ceiling, striking the spot where only moments before he had been standing. Elf and officer tumbled out the exit, rolling to a halt in front of the others. Dega landed on top with a bewildered expression on his face. For a brief moment he gazed into the depths of her startling blue eyes - and Captain Dega Darkhawk discovered something strange – something *he* had never felt before.

"Get off me." She scowled, and her boot came up flipping the cavalier backward. The elf jumped up and dusted herself off. "I do not think they will follow us now," she said, "but we must leave at once. It takes two days to cross this desert and night will be here soon enough. We may yet see the tambril again if they are hungry enough."

Lockjaw placed his hand under a slab of rock, closing the porch. As an added measure he rolled a couple of boulders across the front. "I fear that this will not hold them for long should they decide to come after us."

The sun was more than halfway across the sky and burning brighter than ever, signaling that there was maybe less than half a day before nightfall. Dega wanted to put as much distance between themselves and the tambril as they could and he did not allow the company to stop.

The Red-Bone was aptly named. Crimson sand covered the barren landscape as far as the eye could see; giant swells of sand lit by coppery fire and an endless expanse of blue sky only added to the illusion of this immeasurable empty space that lay forgotten by the rest of the world. Green prickly-spined plants grew in a variety of shapes and sizes, but no sign of animal life, except a few snakes and one or two small lizards.

The heat was almost unbearable, and Dane took his coat and shirt off and stuffed them into his pack. Dega warned him that he was better off leaving them on, but he ignored the officer anyway. The waterskins had been filled before entering the mines of Silverlake and so they were not bothered by lack of the precious resource. Dega also had the foresight to bring along some salt which he had obtained from Grimbeard, and made sure everyone had a small dose. The company trudged in silence, staring at the back of the person in front and thinking only about moving each leg forward in the sweltering heat. Finally Dega stopped the line, and when Camber turned to look back at the dwarf-warren he was surprised that he could no longer see the ridge where it lay hidden.

"No time to sit. We have holes to dig." Dega prodded Dane with his boot. The archer stood and grumbled to no one in particular. His lips were chapped, and his upper torso completely red from sunburn, and Dega gave him an 'I told you so' look.

"Dig?" was all he could manage.

"Yes, dig." Dega repeated, and he pointed to where the others had already started.

The archer hauled himself to where Camber and Lockjaw were excavating with their hands and fell to his knees to help. It seemed like a pointless task; sand would invariably spill back into the cavity almost immediately upon leaving it, but as the hole grew in size it was easier to keep the sand from sifting back into place, and when they were done the end result was a pit about a foot and a half deep and seven feet in length. But Dane was not allowed to rest yet, immediately they began working on another hole just like the first one, and as he looked over to where Starlock and Dega were digging he noticed that their hole was similar in size and shape to the one that he had just dug.

"What's going on?" he asked when Dega came over to inspect their holes. The officer handed him a long needle from one of the desert plants. "Unless you want to be a tasty tambril treat then I suggest you get in and lie still. I'll throw sand over you and with a little luck the tambril will think we're all just part of the landscape." Dane frowned; he hadn't liked that 'little luck' part. He lay down in the hole. "What's this for?" he held up the hollow needle. Dega gave him one of those *special* smiles. "You like air, don't you?" and the Captain threw sand over his face.

Sand filled every square inch of his clothing, and also the spaces in-between. But it wasn't just the sand that caused Camber to bite his lip. There were sandfleas, lots and lots of sandfleas. And other crawling things. It was lucky he couldn't see them, for he would probably go crazy trying to rid them off his body. He kept his eyes closed, breathing quietly through the quill. The hole wasn't deep, and if he wanted he could break free at any time. But Dega had warned them all to lie still and he was starting to appreciate the officer's invaluable experience.

Starlock and Dega had just finished burying Lockjaw, and tired as they both were they dragged themselves over to the next hole. "Get in," she said.

Dega's eyes widened, and he did a quick tally. They were short a hole! Now how could that have happened? "No, you get in," he told her.

"Look," she argued. "I can take care of myself, and there's not enough time to dig another, the sun will be down within minutes." She pointed at the sky, and as she did, it seemed the fiery globe dipped even lower. It now sat midway on the horizon.

"Exactly!" Dega snapped; he was tired of arguing, and pulling Starlock close he threw her into the hole, then landed on top, flinging sand. It wasn't much cover but it would have to do. Starlock pushed back, her rage rising up beneath him. Good, let her be angry. Whatever it takes to get them all to Illianther; he wasn't leaving anyone behind.

Starlock snorted, loud enough for Dega to understand that he had just committed the ultimate insult. Heart and hands made for war. Of all the elves, the Janastari were meant to be feared. She snorted again for good measure.

Lockjaw was not bothered by sand, or bugs, for they had a hard time biting through his thick dwarvish hide. It was Hawker that worried him. In all their years together the Caretaker had never left him, always, always, he stayed by Hawker's side, even sacrificing his love for Shard to be the wizard's apprentice. They shared many secrets, and Hawker did not keep things from him. Not like he did with the others, those he manipulated for the good of Astaria. As he lay in the sand pondering Hawker's fate the sound of screeching reached his ears. *Tambril.* Lucky the Ranger had foreseen this. Lockjaw silently mouthed a protection spell for all and waited patiently in his hole.

Dane heard the tambril shrieking and stopped his shifting; he held his breath, hoping to gods that they would fly past without incident. Here they were already stuck in the ground, waiting to be plucked from their sandy beds like vegetables in a garden. The tambril would have a field day. What was Dega thinking anyway?

Dega wasn't thinking anything remotely related to tambril. His thoughts were elsewhere as he pressed himself against the elf. He kept his eyes closed, but his other senses were alive, though he tried his best to ignore them. She shifted slightly in the cramped space, and his nose suddenly found its way next to her smooth, soft neck. She smelled of summer, and deeply did he inhale; sun sweet meadows and ripe blue skies. Silky strands of hair tickled the side of his face, and he was suddenly aware that he might crush this fragile creature with his own cumbersome weight.

Starlock turned her head. She couldn't wait to get out from underneath the Ranger. The stubble on his face scratched, and his breath fell heavy in her ear. With barely half an inch to move it was suffocation at its worse. She had no choice but to lie beneath his body and breathe his musky sweat.

The sun was shining brightly when Camber broke free of his sand-filled hideaway. Having heard the tambril last night he was relieved that everyone, including Belia, had survived. A dark bruise covered Dega's left eye, and he was just about to ask what happened when Dane came over and handed him a flask of water. "Don't say anything." Camber nodded, taking a sip.

Dega checked their surroundings, choosing the direction that would lead them to Illianther. For once Starlock didn't argue, in fact she didn't say much to anybody; the elf trailed the group keeping to herself. Belia circled high above the company, the little falcon had been instrumental in keeping the tambril away from where they had been buried. All through the night she had kept the creatures chasing after her trail, and Starlock knew this. When the bird landed on her shoulder the next morning she stroked Belia's feathers, thanking the falcon for her part in their survival.

"Will they come back?" asked Camber. Dega had finally stopped the company, allowing them a brief rest. "Probably," he said. He was not in the mood for answering questions. Dane caught his cousin's eye, and Camber shrugged.

"I just hope we don't have to put ourselves back in the sand. I'm already carrying half the Red-Bone in my shorts," said Dane; he shook his leg, spilling sand out from his breeches.

The day grew instantly hot. If possible, even hotter than the previous one, and it wasn't long before the company fell under the immense lethargy that accompanied such intense heat. They dragged their feet toward a mound of rocks that had sprung up in the middle of nowhere. Dega seemed genuinely relieved, and estimating at least three hours before nightfall and much to be done, he put them all to work hunting high and low for any scrap of wood or burnable material within the vicinity of the rock-island. Lockjaw chopped down all the small scrub trees that grew in and around the boulders, and Starlock dug up all the vegetation she could find while Camber and Dane retrieved tumbleweeds. Dega searched through packs, tossing anything expendable onto a growing pile of clothing and other flammable objects. He squinted up at the sun's position. It was almost level with the horizon.

"When they come, keep your back to the rocks and the fire in front of you," he said, pulling his sword from its sheath. Dane lowered his quiver so that his arrows were within easy reach.

"Give me those," said Starlock, and she held up a pouch. "Poison."

Dane nodded, and the elf quickly applied a small amount to each of his arrows. "Do not touch the tips," she warned. "You may think I just barely coated them but there's enough poison on each of those arrowheads to kill half a dozen men."

"Or bring down one full-size Jules," he winked at Camber, and placed the barbs back into his quiver.

It was decided that Lockjaw and Camber would light the fire and keep it fueled while the others would slay any tambril that managed to brave the flames. Belia sat on Starlock's shoulder; she would repeat her performance from the previous night and attempt to draw the main body away from the company.

The sky became a rosy pink as the sun slid beneath the horizon; a picture that only nature could color, but its beauty was lost to a rising trepidation as the stars blinked into existence one by one. Starlock stood at the top of the rock pile, watching for tambril.

A sudden cry triggered the company into action: Lockjaw and Camber lit the fire, fanning the flames until they became a roaring blaze; Dane raised his bow and nocked an arrow; Dega held himself ready - sword raised, knees bent, and Belia lifted into the air, flapping madly toward the east, where a dark patch spread like spilt ink, obliterating the stars above.

Tambril filled the desert sky. Camber's heart beat loudly between his ears; he clutched his sword, praying that the bright light and scorching heat of fire would keep the monsters away.

The first wave flew low over the heads of the company. Wind from tambril wings whistled loudly, rattling even Starlock's confidence. She held her sword aloft, ready for battle; bright orange mirrored in the depths of metal, coloring the blade in supernatural fire. The second flight came in for the attack, and though most shied away from the fire, many more came in from the party's unprotected sides. Starlock gutted the first beast clean across the underbelly, drawing her blade at the next gliding in from above.

Dane loosed his arrows one after another; the poison working almost immediately. He tried to collect his barbs, but tambril had beat him to it, savagely tearing into the dead until only gooey gore-covered bones remained.

"Look out!" Dane ran to where Camber fanned the flames, nailing another as it landed behind his cousin.

"Thanks." Camber drew his sword, backing up until he stood beside the archer. Dane nodded. "Stay close."

Axe crunched into bone as Lockjaw made quick work of the beast that had dropped down in front. He barely cleared his weapon when another swooped in; it was joined by two more; soon he had his hands full clearing the area of tambril.

Dega was covered head to toe in dripping blood, some of it his. He held the position on the far side, away from the fire. One after another the monsters came at him; he raised his sword over and over, using everything to drive his arms and shoulders past the limits of mere mortal men. He could not stop. Dared not stop. Lives depended upon his sword. Two tambril dove at once; he sidestepped one, then brought his blade through the second one's snout. Something silver whizzed through the air and the first beast fell over dead with a dagger in its gelatinous eye. He saw Starlock retreating back to where Camber and Dane were cornered.

The cadets had no place to go; tambril on all three sides and the fire behind them. Camber fell to his knees, swinging his sword. A claw caught his cheek, drawing blood.

"Camber!" Dane reached into his quiver but found nothing. He was out of arrows! Scooping a handful of rocks, he blasted them at the beast, hitting it square between the eyes.

The monster squealed, it turned its head, and Camber thrust his sword into belly. Another swooped in to take its place. To his horror he heard Dane cry out, then turned just in time to see the archer lifted into the air by his coat. "DANE!" He screamed. "DAAAANE!!!" He ran after the beast, now fending off its nest-mates while keeping a tight grip on its prize.

There was no doubt or fear this time; he simply allowed the magic to be. It consumed his body, filling his mind with that delicious white light he secretly craved. The beat of his heart pulsed between his ears; a steady thud thud, plunging Camber into a nonexistent plane. A host of scenes played out from every direction, all within his mind's eye. Starlock ran toward him, mouth wide open, but her words were lost to the hum drowning out all external sound. Lockjaw looked up from where he was hacking away at tambril. His face a mixture of surprise and wonder. Dega had turned to watch, his sword still raised above his head like a statue forever stuck in the same position. And Dane. *His flesh and blood.* Dane's hand stretched out toward him. On his face an expression that Camber had never seen before - *terror.*

When the power reached its bursting point, Camber directed it at the beast holding Dane. White light ripped through darkness wrapping itself around the reptile. In the space of a heartbeat the tambril was no more. Dane fell, landing with a sickening thump in the sand. He raised a barrier over the archer, and targeted several tambril, picking them off one at a time. Then three or four all at once. When that became too tedious, he started annihilating whole groups of them until they turned tail to flee. But he was not done with them. Not yet! They had attacked his friends and tried to take Dane. He would rid the world of tambril.

Something hit his head; he slumped to the ground, eyes glazed, losing their fire. Starlock had struck him with the pommel of her sword and she now held his sagging body in her arms.

Dega and Lockjaw carried Dane back to the rock pile. Slowly the archer opened his eyes. When he tried to sit, his arm sent a shock of pain.

"Careful," Dega said, and he pushed Dane back to the ground. "Your arm is broken." He was ripping his own shirt into shreds as he spoke. "Hold him still." And Lockjaw did as he was told, pinning the cadet with his strong arms. A flash of searing hot pain brought tears to his eyes; his chest swelled with air, and he wanted to scream. In seconds it was over and he was allowed to sit up. Dega gave him water and he looked at the splint on his arm. "Is Camber okay?"

"He'll be fine. He just needs rest," Starlock answered, and she came over to look at his arm. "I cannot do anything further for you here, but when we get to Elvenhome the healers can tend to your injury." Dega stood shirtless overtop of him. Tambril blood streaked his face and torso, and his jet-black hair was matted with gore. His jaw was set, hard and grim. "We are not far from Illianther, maybe half a day's march to the desert's edge. Rest now. We leave in a few hours." Starlock looked up at the young officer from where she crouched beside the cadet, but he turned on his boot heel without so much as a glance in her direction.

Dega washed some of the grime off his face with his waterskin and took a long swallow; he put his head down to catnap, but no sooner had he done so, when the toe of a boot kicked his foot. He opened one eye. Starlock sat down and picked up a twig, she started drawing with it in the sand. "I'm sorry," she said, meaning his bruise from earlier. Dega grunted; he had no time for games. "Don't worry about it. I'm not."

If one could read into the very complex mind of Dega Darkhawk, then one would be surprised to find that he *had* worried about it. But because he was a gentleman he decided it was best left not mentioning, and taking all things in stride until better suited to his needs, he had left the problem buried among other trivial items stored upstairs in the organized compartments of his mind. His lack of understanding for the elf's apology, however, was another matter. The Janastari are not known to hand out apologies on a regular basis, and Starlock was a little taken aback by the Captain's indifference to her words. With a snort, she kicked his boot again, only this time harder than before, then stormed off down the other side of the rock pile.

Camber opened a bleary eye; he was strapped into a makeshift stretcher. Gone was the desert; tall trees blocked the sun, shading his face as he tried to make out his surroundings.

"Have a nice nap?" Dane's face came slowly into focus. "What happened to your arm?" he asked, pointing at the splint. Dane smirked. "You dropped me."

Camber sat up. "I did what?!" He shook his head trying to recall the tambril attack.

"Well not directly. But when you let the tambril have it with your, er... *whatever*. I hit the ground. That's when my arm broke, luckily that's all that happened." His face paled at the thought of being carried off by tambril. "Cripes Camber, next time you try to help someone at least have the courtesy to give them a nice soft landing." Dane laughed, and Camber smiled weakly.

After a brief rest, Camber was allowed to walk, and he rubbed the lump on top of his head. Dane whispered. "Compliments of Starlock. You were getting carried away with your power trip."

Starlock raised her hand, halting the company, she stood in place, listening to the sounds of the forest. Belia dropped out of the sky, landing on her shoulder and squawking once at the elf.

"HOI!" Starlock hollered suddenly, and to everyone's surprise it was answered.

"Hoi, a'cha isvani Janastari."

And another voice in the common tongue added, "What brings the *Dark Elf* so far from home? It must be something truly important to bring her out of the gloomy reaches of the Black Wood and into the bright beauty of Illianther."

"I see you Lightfoot, for you have never been much good at hiding. Enough of your banter, it is not you I wish to see, but your King and Queen."

"Ah, as pleasant a disposition as ever, Starlock. You shall see Winterleaf and Dovetail, but first you must hand over all your weapons. You know the rules."

"Fine," she snapped, she had no patience for the insolent elf. "Come and take them."

"Don't be ridiculous Starlock. We have you and your friends surrounded. Though I never would have bet in a million years that you'd be taking up with a dwarf."

It was true. They were surrounded, and as Camber looked up at the trees he could see several elven faces, the glint of steel, and Lightfoot, who now made his appearance as he stepped out onto a great branch directly above their heads.

"Hoi. Lightfoot stop teasing our guests, and you Starlock, sheathe your sword and play nicely, else we won't have you back," a different voice, deeper than Lightfoot's, caused Starlock's face to pale.

"Warblade?"

"Greetings Starlock," said the voice.

"But how?... you're alive... I thought you ... "

"Dead?" Warblade finished her sentence, jumping down from the tree to land neatly on the ground in front of the bewildered elf. He was tall, and fair of face, and he glided with the grace of a cat. A full mane of silver hair shone like the snow on the highest peaks of the Dragonspine, and upon his brow he wore a circlet of silver. Though his face appeared youthful, his green eyes said differently as his gaze swept across the company, stopping lastly on Dega.

"Nay. I am not dead," and he walked right up to Starlock, standing only a hairbreadth from her face. "Maybe next time you toss someone off a cliff you should check to make sure the deed is done before you leave."

"Well perhaps I'll get another chance to heed your advice," she snarled, and her hand went for her sword. His hand landed on top of hers. "Enough," he said. "You are in Illianther now not your Black Wood, and we were sent to intercept you. We mean you no harm." He turned to face the entire company. "You are all welcome to Elvenhome. Winterleaf has been expecting you and requests that you be brought to him immediately." And his eyes moved back to Starlock. *"Unharmed."*

"You may all keep your weapons," Warblade continued. "But know this. Anyone whose intentions are harmful will have his, *or her*," he eyed Starlock, "weapons removed and sent into solitary confinement. Now if you please, we have but a small journey before we reach Illianther."

VIII

A Question of Honor

Eight other elves appeared on the ground with Lightfoot and Warblade; one was sent back to let the King and Queen know their guests had arrived. Camber and Dane immediately struck up a conversation with one of the elves who bore an identical resemblance to another in the group.

The elf grinned, noticing the look on Dane's face. "I'm Crescent," he said, "and *he* is my twin, Frost-Eye."

"You really are twins."

"That's right. But if you ask most everyone they will tell you that I'm the better-looking one," and he winked at the archer.

Frost-Eye overheard his brother and was quick to reply. "He is handsome to be sure, but sorely lacking intelligence."

"I can't tell either of you apart," said Camber.

"If you stay here long enough you will learn which is which, one is more annoying than the other." At this remark all the elves laughed, and so did the cadets.

Dega walked behind Starlock and Warblade, his gaze never wavering from the two, and the only time he spoke was when Lightfoot had asked for his name; he told the elf, but his tone indicated he was not one for talking and Lightfoot wisely let him be. Dega did not like Warblade. He sensed a falseness, and though he could not put his finger on it, something told him that he would be wise to guard against this elf. He clenched the pommel of his sword until his tanned knuckles were white, all the while pondering over the connection between Starlock and this silver-haired warrior.

Warblade carried himself with the sureness of a jungle cat and the arrogance of a lord, expecting others to step out of his path. Warblade served only Warblade, and everyone else mattered only when he needed something he couldn't otherwise obtain on his own.

"Nothing has been heard from you in nearly five hundred years and here you show up unexpectedly among the strangest company to set foot in Illianther since the time of the second uprising. Now tell me Starlock, how did someone like yourself, who never sets foot outside her wood, unless it's to pick off men from the Borderlands, come to be mixed up in all this?" He meant the Caretaker's business with the boy.

Warblade was no fool; he had lived a very long time and was twice Starlock's age, and he knew many things. Things most Janastari would not find all that interesting, unless it involved bloodshed. But he was different. Over the centuries he had gleaned every scrap of knowledge from the other two clans; reading all the books he could lay his hands on, and secretly honing his newly acquired lore; he was particularly interested in the *Threads of Destiny,* for they bound Brightwing's only child to the Fate of the World. He, himself, had uncovered that slender thread at Elvenhome shortly after his return from a long absence. He winced at the memory. *A long and painful absence.* Waiting for shattered bones to mend. It was strangely ironic that he had found aid and comfort from the last person who he had least expected to befriend.

"I am not mixed up in anything," she snapped; her frustration at seeing Warblade alive was overwhelming. *He should be dead!* A flashback of that day came rushing back, leaving a sour taste in her mouth. After she discovered the secret he'd been hiding, she fled. How could he be trusted after keeping such a thing from her? Her! In true Janastari fashion they wound up battling each other in a duel to the death. His! After she threw him over the cliff she rode until she came to the borders of the Black Wood. The trees comforted Starlock, and the creatures that dwelt there became her only companions; silent witnesses to the outpouring of grief that fell heavy from her heart. Over the years she swept all bitter remnants of Warblade to the blackest corners of her mind, buried like a wanted thing forgotten.

Lightfoot fell in beside Camber and Dane. "How is it that you managed to cross the desert?" he asked. The others gathered close, for they all wanted to hear about the crossing, and Dane did not disappoint, entertaining the elves with *his* version of the events that had brought them to Illianther. For some reason, they had laughed loudest when he told them about the mishap in the forges of Ironfist. By the time he finished his tale they had reached the entrance to Elvenhome.

Twin waterfalls running swiftly overtop sheer rock three hundred feet high, marked the entrance into the oldest and last of the three Elven kingdoms. Illianther belonged to the Nantastari, the record-keepers, but the Candastari dwelt there too, and many Janastari also claimed it as their adopted home.

The path into Elvenhome was cleverly concealed, and only those who dwelt there knew where to cross, stepping carefully over slippery rocks. Rushing water fell like thunder; a steady resonance echoing off the walls of a secret chamber hidden within. Mist sprayed gleefully up on all sides, distorting the air, creating mini rainbows that danced in the sun then vanished under cold shadow.

Rich voices rising in harmony welcomed the company into Illianther. A procession of elves lined either side of the garden walkway, and at the end of the path under the shade of a majestic tree stood the King and Queen.

The face of nature, in all her beauty, now humbled in the presence of the royal couple. The King was tall and fair, and in his face and eyes were compassion and understanding. Of all the Elves, the Nantastari King was the only one who actually looked old, though not old as a mortal who has grown weary after too many years; more like that of a sage who knows all things, all secrets, and has all the answers to every question ever asked, like Hawker, he appeared youthful and ancient at the same time.

"I am Winterleaf." He took his lady's snow-white arm, "and this is Dovetail."

The Queen curtsied low. "Welcome to Illianther." Flowing red hair glinted rich crimson hues that shimmered in the afternoon sun and tumbled in wavy cascades past her beribboned waist. She spoke again in soft tones, this time addressing only Starlock in her native tongue.

"It has been a long time since you last visited Elvenhome. Have you now found some happiness little cousin?" Deep green eyes looked upon the other elf with sadness.

Starlock had to look away from the probing eyes of the Elven Queen. *"Nay Lady. I came to Illianther only as a favor for the Elder."*

Dovetail nodded, then said quietly, almost in a whisper, *"Stay *as long as you like. You may be surprised to find the key to your happiness is right where you least expect it."** She smiled gently, then gestured toward the entire group. "It is an honor to meet you all, and especially you Camber Bloodstone, for someone waits for you even as we speak."

Dane stepped up beside his cousin. "Well if Chance is here why doesn't he show himself?"

"And you must be Dane Strongbow," Dovetail laughed, sweet and musical, like the tingling of a thousand tiny bells.

"His reputation for cheek is already well known around here," added Winterleaf, and he too laughed, wrinkling his wise eyes with merriment.

Dane's ego would not go unchecked by this remark, and he of course, had to have the last word on all things Dane. "At least I'm famous for something."

"Where is Hawker?" Lockjaw had hoped to find the wizard at Illianther, but his friend and mentor was nowhere to be seen and he dropped his head. "He promised to be here."

Winterleaf glided across the garden path to stand beside him. "Do not fret," he said. "I have known Stornoway Hawker for many years, even as a young elfling. He is both resourceful and sincere. If he has gone, then it's only because he perceives the matter at hand more urgent. He will return, you'll see." He laid a hand across the dwarf's shoulders. "In the meantime, if you would like to continue your studies I would be honored to guide you, though I doubt my scant knowledge will be quite as rewarding as Hawker's."

Lockjaw smiled. "I accept your generous offer. Thank you."

Winterleaf nodded. "It is my wish to visit with each and every one of you during your stay, however long or short it may be. As is our custom we will honor the return of the ruling house of the Janastari with a celebration. And mayhap we will see new bonds of friendship formed and old acquaintances reunited."

Dovetail took Camber aside and whispered into his ear. "Go now with Lightfoot. He will take you to the one I spoke of." He turned to wait for Dane, but the Elven Queen gently squeezed his shoulder. "Do not fret; you will meet up with each other later." With a sigh, he picked up his pack and followed Lightfoot across the greensward.

After introductions, the King and Queen had their guests escorted to rooms in the palace. New clothes were laid out while old ones were taken to be repaired. Dane's arm was made whole by the healers, but when they had tried to heal Dega's wound he brushed them aside, wanting to keep the scar for personal reasons; a small reminder that he had left himself open – a mistake never to be repeated.

"Look Lockjaw," Dane flexed his bicep. "Good as new."

"Perhaps you should have asked for some muscle." Lockjaw flexed his own arm, and a big round rock rose up thrice the size of Dane's bicep.

"Well it can't be his eating," said Dega; he walked out of the bathing area, his face now smooth and devoid of hair. "He eats enough for an army." He ran a comb through his wavy black locks, pausing for a moment to reflect whether it needed cutting; he liked it just below ear level, then grabbing his coat he strode out the door.

"Where's he going?" Dane asked.

Lockjaw was now thumbing through one of several books given to him by Winterleaf. "Don't know," he said.

Lightfoot led Camber to a room on the second floor, and left him at the door. He raised his hand to knock, but the door opened of its own accord. An elf maid, flaxen tresses and fair of face, sat beside a window gazing out at the gardens below. She turned as Camber stepped into the room; her bright green eyes staring directly into his. A skip, and a beat, his heart stopped when he saw those eyes.

"Mother... MOTHER!"

"Camber!"

He ran to her and she caught him in her arms hugging him fiercely. In those eyes he saw love, and suddenly he understood that she had always loved him. "Father... " he said. She shh'd him. "I know." Eighteen years of missing her and thirteen without his father had taken its toll, and he did the only thing he could possibly do. He wept. And she wept for him.

Finally, she let him go, and they sat on the bench side by side. She asked him about his childhood in Hartland, and about Dane, and she knew things that Chance had told her. He in turn asked her the question that had always been foremost on his mind.

"I left because I was afraid for you, Camber," a tear rolled down her cheek. "Shortly after you were born I had a dream. A terrible and frightening dream. And no amount of reassuring from your father could chase away the dread I felt." She took the amulet from under his shirt and held it in her slender fingers. "Do you know why you wear this?" He shook his head. "I placed it around your neck to protect you from the Evil that was trying to find you. But even as I did so I knew in my heart that it would not be enough. It would never be enough. I had to leave, lest I draw the Evil to you unknowingly." Her eyes brimmed with tears and Camber thought his heart would break. "Your father wanted me to stay. He begged me to stay. I could not... I had to go. Without me near you would be safe."

"But why? Why me?" *Yes, why him.* Why did *his* mother have to leave. Why did *his* father have to die.

"Because Camber," she said, tucking his hair behind his ear as she spoke. "It runs in our family." She held his face in her hands, savoring every detail, locking it safely away in her heart. "It skips every second generation," she said softly. "I did not receive the gift, though now I wish I had instead of you. Your grandfather had it and so did his grandfather, but I did not think you would be cursed since your father was mortal." She turned her face away. "No. I did not think you would be the one. But the magic proved me wrong."

"But father's heart was broken," Camber said, his face near to tears again. "He left. He went after you to bring you back."

"I know," said Brightwing. "Chance told me. Your father was the love of my life. I miss him with all my heart." She sighed, and her eyes gazed longingly out the window searching for something lost and knowing it will never be found. She drew Camber to her breast once more and hugged him tightly. "But now you are here, and I see much of the man that was your father, and my heart is glad."

Dane was reading over Lockjaw's shoulder when Camber walked in accompanied by an elf who bore a striking family resemblance; with a broad smile he strode over to greet them both. "Dane," he said, embracing his aunt.

"And this is Lockjaw. The dwarf I was telling you about," Camber added. Dega was not in the room. "Where's the Cap'?"

"He's gone outside for some fresh air. Just up and left with barely a good-bye." The archer glared at the door, then reached across Lockjaw's shoulder to snap the book shut. "Thank the gods you came when you did! I'm tired of looking at four walls and a dwarf. Let's get some fresh air," and his mood brightened at the thought of finding someone who might like to throw dice.

Dega wandered the gardens, relieved that Dane had not followed. He needed some time alone; away from the two cadets, away from

Lockjaw, and everyone else. He whistled as he strolled, not because he was happy, which he was, (though he did not know why) but because it seemed the only way to release the tension, now running dangerously high since leaving Hartland. And so, as Dega Darkhawk strode through the richly cultivated grounds of Illianther, the Elvenhome, he whistled a favorite song.

The sound of whistling came faintly to Starlock's ears, assaulting them with an inane tune that she tried to ignore as she punched at a sand-filled sack hanging from the tree, working her body physically and spiritually through the rigorous training of *Dar-Ginne*. This time she spun, landing a high kick hard against the sack.

Dega stopped whistling, he paused, listening to the wind, the twitter and chirp of birds, *and something else* – heavy breathing, falling in short labored huffs, coming from just a few feet away. He was about to turn and leave, but curiosity got her way with a poke and a prod, and he tracked the noise to a clearing. As he peered through the bushes, a shock of surprise played momentarily across his brow – Starlock pummeled a sandbag, oblivious to all else. Sweat glistened over her taut, trim frame; hard and athletic, not soft and willowy like Dovetail or the other elvish maids. *And aggressive.* He leaned in for a better view and a twig snapped underfoot.

Starlock whipped her head around. "Who's there?!" To her surprise, the Ranger's Captain stepped awkwardly out of the bush. He looked different... did he rid his face of the bristles? Too bad, she rather liked them. "Were you spying on me?" she asked, hands on hips.

"No." Dega answered, feeling more than just a little foolish. The sun beat down upon his brow, and his face flushed several shades of red.

"So you always sit around in bushes? Is this some kind of a hobby?"

"No. Of course not," he snorted. "I thought I heard something – heavy breathing." *Blast. That was stupid.* "A panting noise, uh loud breathing." *Even stupider. He should just shut up now.* "Um, what's with the sandbag?"

"It's for combat practice," and she went into a lengthy explanation of how Dar-Ginne, as it was called, was the first form of fighting among the Janastari, long before the forging of steel.

"But how is it possible to use this skill against someone with a weapon?" he said, avoiding her previous interrogation.

"Easy." Spotting a branch in the grass, she tossed it to Dega. "Here. You come at me as though you mean to attack."

Dega shrugged. Okay, now he was going to have to humor her. He took the tree branch and swung it at the elf. In two strikes she had the branch out of his hands and he lay on his back.

"Let's try that again." He took his coat off as he got to his feet and rolled up his sleeves. Starlock came at him a second time, but Dega was more than ready; he dodged her first blow then countered with a strike across her thigh. As his hand came away, her boot came up, and he went to grab it; the boot was a decoy, and her left leg swung around, connecting with his chest, and knocking him flat. But Dega was resourceful, and snatching her ankle, he pulled it hard. She lost her balance and landed on top.

He was expecting her to get angry, but instead she stroked his brow. "Does it hurt?" she asked. *What? His eye?* "No," then changed his mind. "Yes. Err, sometimes."

"Really?"

The pounding of his heart beat loudly in his ears, seconds became minutes, and minutes ticked into eternity, but still she lay on top of him. Should he shove her off? Roll over? Their lips were almost touching, and Dega's shirt collar was uncomfortably hot.

"Hoi!" said a voice, and Lightfoot stepped into the clearing. "I found them. They're over here." Two bodies shot out of the grass as Lightfoot made his presence known. "We've been looking all over for you. Winterleaf wants you both in his chambers." Eyes roved from elf to Ranger, now standing a good space apart. "Is that yours?" He pointed at a lump of grey, and Dega stooped to snatch his coat, wearing a telltale flush he couldn't disguise.

Starlock kept her eyes trained on the back of Lightfoot's head. But her thoughts were not as easy to control as her eyes, and she wondered what the Ranger might be thinking as they followed the elf back to Winterleaf's quarters.

Camber and Dane strode through the palace with Brightwing, and they were soon joined by the twins, who were delighted to have finally found someone, *two someones*, younger than themselves.

"What's this for?" Dane lifted an orb from its pedestal and held it aloft.

"It's a scrying eye," said Crescent. "There are several scattered throughout Illianther," and reaching up, he touched the crystal. "Look now. Do you see anything?"

Dane peered at the orb. At first nothing happened, then it became a fuzzy colorful swirl that brightened as a picture of someone slowly came into focus. *Dega!* "Snakes and Spirits!" The picture expanded to reveal Dega lying on the ground with Starlock.

"Let's see that," said Camber, and he reached for the crystal.

"Umm, it's not working," he shook the globe, erasing the image. "Here. Take it," he gave it to Frost-Eye, who shrugged, and placed it back on the pedestal.

"Would you like to see King's Hall?" Crescent offered.

"As long as there's no Degas."

The twins led them down a long hall lined with tapestries, richly embroidered, and depicting the history of the three clans in brilliant colors. One featured a man riding at the head of an army with several scenes woven around the central figure, including the same man kneeling before a raven-haired beauty in pale green.

"Thayne the Bold," said Brightwing, gliding up to put her hand across Camber's shoulders. "I made this tapestry myself," she added. "See. This is you and your father." She pointed to a man holding a baby. Camber recognized his father's face, his eyes moved around the tapestry, taking in every detail. Another scene showed his father and mother dressed in white robes standing before Winterleaf and Dovetail. "Who's that man with father?" He pointed to another figure, a mortal, not an elf, to his father's right; the man had dark hair and a familiar face.

"That's your father's best friend. Drake Darkhawk."

"What?!" Both cadets leaned in for a better look. "It looks like Dega," said Dane.

"Why didn't father ever mention this?"

"He was protecting you from peril, much like I had by leaving Hartland. He believed the less you knew the least amount of danger you would draw to yourself."

A chill ran down his spine, and he took hold of his mother's soft hand. One of the twins suddenly became aware of his unease and suggested they continue to King's Hall.

The walls were transparent, but not because they were made of crystal or glass. These walls were made entirely from falling water. The twins laughed as they watched Dane extend a cautious hand.

"It will not bite you," said Crescent, and he walked through the wall.

He now stood on the other side completely dry. "You try." Frost-Eye gave the archer a push. Dane held his breath and walked through the wall, followed by Camber and Brightwing.

"That's amazing!" He went back and forth several times. "How does it work?"

"Magic," said Crescent. "This hall is the pride and joy of Illianther and is used as a place for socializing by most everyone who lives here."

King's Hall was nearly double the size of Stone-Haven's atrium, and its gardens were every bit as breathtaking. Musicians seated on a platform played a melody that lingered on the air like a light summer breeze. The twins led them up the stairs and they stood beneath a domed ceiling painted with murals depicting a medley of exotic pictures that shifted slowly, transforming into a kaleidoscope of enchanting scenes. From this vantage point they could see that white pillars circling the hall and not the walls of water were responsible for bearing the weight of that spectacular ceiling.

Thrones fit for royalty sat at opposite ends of the Hall, adorned with gold stitching on red velvet cushions and emblazoned with an elaborate insignia on each gilded back.

"Who sits there?" Camber recognized the Darkhawk crest on one of the chairs.

"Aah," said Crescent. "These are the seats of the three ruling houses. And the fourth one," he pointed to the chair that Camber had indicated, "is for the house of the Valastari. It was added afterward to honor King Brand."

Dane marveled at his surroundings, he let out a low whistle. Never in his life had he been around so many lavish things. His mother didn't even like it when he sat on the "good" furniture in the great room. She always kept the stuff covered up with long floral sheets and would yell if either him or his father stepped foot into the room. "What's down there?" he pointed at several tables laden with fruits, sweetmeats, and cheese.

"Those are refreshments, and all are welcome to enjoy," said Frost-Eye, and he led the cadets down to the lower level. Dane took a seat, and winking at Camber, brought forth his dice.

"What's this all about?" Starlock's tone was harsh, angered that Lightfoot had been sent to fetch her as though she were a mere elfling.

"See. I told you she'd be all thorns and bristles. We should have left her in the woods."

"That's enough Lightfoot. Sit down Starlock. And you too, Captain." Winterleaf gestured to the empty chairs. Elf and Ranger sat, but not beside each other, and Dega found his face had cooled considerably as he realized this had all the makings of an important council.

"I have called you here to discuss the next step that must be decided in the likelihood that Stornoway Hawker might not return." Winterleaf's cool gray eyes settled on the faces at the table. "It's entirely possible that he will be unable to reach Illianther and we do not have the luxury of waiting for him to guide us into the next phase."

"But he will return. He gave his word. I know Hawker better than anyone here and I will attest to his sincerity."

"No one doubts his integrity dwarf," replied Winterleaf. "I am just stating a possible reality. One that we need to be prepared for."

"And if the wizard doesn't come back. What then?" The Candastari King sat beside Warblade, and his unsettling gaze fell upon Lockjaw.

"He will return. Have faith!"

"Enough!" Winterleaf commanded. "We are only discussing our options if Hawker is delayed. I for one believe we need to strike fast. Sentash will not be expecting a confrontation at this time and mayhap he will not be ready."

Dega leaned back in his chair. "Then you plan to marshal an army?"

"Yes, this has been talked about for sometime between Willowsnap and myself."

"Then allow me to suggest an alliance with the Rangers. The dwarves have already sent an envoy, and with the union of all three races Sentash will not be able to withstand an attack."

"A wise and noble idea, Captain."

"Bah!" Warblade scoffed. "Can we really afford to trust the mortals with such an undertaking? They are as unstable as the cities they dwell in."

Dega's hand went for his sword but found nothing. He had left his weapons in his room; there was no reason to be wearing them while in Illianther. "Can you afford not to." It wasn't a question; it was a statement. He shot out of his chair and leaned over the table. "I have ridden with men who would not hesitate to put their lives on the line for King and country; gladly would they exchange their valiant hearts to rescue even a pathetic soul like yourself if it meant they would be ridding the world of the Easterling King."

Warblade stood. The elven warrior met the cavalier eye to eye, and knew then and there that this man would be his greatest adversary.

Winterleaf cleared his throat. "Sit down. Both of you. This is no place for a rivalry."

"May I make a suggestion," Starlock glared at Warblade as he took his seat.

Winterleaf waved his hand for her to do so.

"Since the dwarves have sent an ambassador, then it's only fair we send one too. That way, if there is an alliance forming we will not be left out. *And*," she eyed the Captain, "if the Janastari take up arms then the Alliance will be assured they fight alongside the only army that can defeat the sorcerer. But our only hope to truly rid the world of Sentash is with the Winterstone. You know this as well as I, Winterleaf."

"Very good," the Elven King nodded. "This is sound advice. The Winterstone was to be my next point of discussion, but where it lies no one can say for sure. Rumor has its whereabouts in the East. Whether true or not I cannot say. If this is indeed where it is then we have little chance to recover the Stone, and therefore must not count its awesome power for our own."

"Why not?" Lightfoot stood. "Sentash does not have it. At least not yet. Why can't we send someone to get it?"

"But even if the stories are true, we can't just march into Tar Galleaon." Willowsnap left the table to stand beside a map on the wall. "Sentash will spot an army before they even reach his citadel." His finger indicated the region all around the eastern capital.

"Perhaps therein lies our hope. It may be we can use this to our advantage."

"Yes," Dega answered suddenly. "An army can act as decoy, engaging the enemy and keeping his forces distracted. Then there is a chance, albeit a slim one, that someone might be able to slip through undetected."

"But that's absolute madness! We don't even know its exact whereabouts. And who would take such a dangerous quest?" Willowsnap could not disguise his fear, the Candastari were not warriors, and his eyes darted back and forth from Winterleaf to the Ranger's Captain.

"Yes, mortal," Warblade sneered. "Who would take such a quest? You?"

Before Dega could answer, the Candastari King turned to Lockjaw. "Does your Master know where it is?"

"It lies in the East, but that is all I've heard him say."

"But what is the harm in waiting for Hawker? Perhaps the sorcerer does not yet know the boy has come to Illianther." Lightfoot countered.

"He knows," said Dega. "We were chased by Southlanders before we gained the safety of the dwarf-warren at Silverlake."

"And his Bounders are on the loose. It was so when Hawker and I came across them in the North."

"Bounders!" Winterleaf had lost some of his composure. "Starlock. Why didn't you mention this?"

"You never gave me a chance. Besides, I didn't see them. It was the Ranger who encountered the one in the North."

"Are you sure it was a Bounder?" Warblade did nothing to hide his disdain. "Perhaps you were mistaken, it may have been a bear."

"It was a Bounder." Dega felt his anger rising, clenching and unclenching his fist, lest there be one less silver-haired elf in Illianther. "I have killed one before."

Starlock raised an eyebrow, and Lightfoot was equally impressed and he said so.

Dega did not want to talk about either Bounder attack and quickly switched the subject to whether or not they should wait for the wizard. "Maybe we should hold for a few days to see if Hawker will show."

Lockjaw and Starlock also favored this, and Winterleaf agreed. "We shall wait for the new moon, and if Stornoway Hawker does not materialize by then we will hold another council and decide our next course of action."

The meeting now came to a close, and Winterleaf asked Dega if he would stay and counsel him on whom to contact at the Ranger garrisons. He grunted a yes, and sat down again, but his eyes followed Starlock as she exited the study.

Starlock strode down the hall and back to her room; she planned to go as soon as she was free to leave, back to her home and far from the troubles that plagued Illianther and the rest of Astaria, and more importantly, away from the likes of Warblade and the Ranger. As she walked the corridors she reflected on the day's events; one in particular, chewed at the loose threads of her thoughts, fraying her most vulnerable strands. The scar above her eye deepened as her brows furrowed. *What if Lightfoot hadn't crossed the clearing when he did?*

Dane and Lockjaw were throwing dice when Dega came in. The three of them were sharing a guest suite and Camber was staying with his mother. The Ranger's Captain walked right past without a glance.

"Care to..." Dane started.

"No!" followed by a slamming door.

Dane shrugged at Lockjaw. "Guess that'd be a no, then." When he looked at the dice something was not quite right; he was sure that had been a seven. "Hey! Are you cheating?"

Camber and Dane spent the next several days touring the grounds of the palace. Brightwing went with them, as did the twins, and they were introduced to many of the folk who dwelt there.

The palace was the heart and soul of Illianther, but it was more than that, an architectural wonder; timeless and untainted. Marble pillars shaped interior and exterior, lining the portico leading to the grand entrance, capped by an arch and adorned with life-like sculptures.

In the courtyard stood two fifty-foot pillars, carved with the history of Astaria winding upward in a spiraling scroll. To read the columns one would have to start at the bottom and walk around and around until finishing at the top. Though it seemed like a daunting task, the twins assured Camber and Dane it could be done.

"I have read it several times," said Frost-Eye. His brother rolled his eyes, "Please don't ask him to recite, else we'll be here all day." Brightwing pointed out some of Camber and Dane's history, and they eagerly circled the columns looking for more.

"It's rumored that if you read the inscriptions backward you will discover a hidden message," said Frost-Eye. "But no elf I know has been able to do this. The artisans who built the columns infused them with magic to confuse anyone who tries to unravel the mystery."

Dane walked backward around the first column. All he succeeded in doing was making himself dizzy. Camber had some help from Brightwing, and together they circled the column, but after the first few trips around the pillar he felt an odd sensation and completely forgot what he was doing.

"See?" said Frost-Eye. "It happens to anyone who tries."

Dane snorted, "A challenge is it? Well one day I'll come back and solve it. I give you my word."

"You'd best learn how to read elvish first," laughed Crescent.

"A minor inconvenience."

Brightwing placed her hand on his shoulder. "I can help you with that. But for now be content to enjoy the beauty around you and don't try so hard to interpret everything you see, tonight's celebration will be entertaining enough and you shall find much to satisfy your thirst for amusement."

When Dane arrived back at his suite he found clothing fit for an elven prince laid neatly across his bed. The shirt was soft, made from an unfamiliar fabric, smooth and slippery, white in color, but with a hundred different hues that shimmered from within; the buttons were made of pearl, and were repeated on the dark green waistcoat, and when he tried it on it was a perfect fit. There was even a fine gold belt and a pair of sleek black boots to accompany his new breeches, and taking one last look at his 'handsome' reflection in the mirror, he strode out of his bedroom in style.

Dega and Lockjaw were already dressed and waiting. The dwarf wore a green velvet tunic with black breeches. Gone was the chainmail and broad leather belt, in their place he wore a mantle of dark gray fastened at the front with an emerald brooch. A matching silver belt with small emeralds embedded into each link completed his resplendent attire. His beard was neatly braided in two long forks, and around his neck he wore Shard's amulet.

Red embroidery decorated the sleeves and hem of Dega's deep black waistcoat. The Darkhawk crest was sewn on either side of the high collar, and he looked every bit as imperious as Winterleaf, and maybe even a little more so, as he glared at the cadet with those piercing blue eyes. "Let's get going," he gruffed, and Dane smirked, noticing that *the Captain* had removed the spurs from his old boots and had fastened them to his new ones.

Elves were filing into King's Hall, filling the tables in the gardens below. Lockjaw took his place atop the same platform where the musicians had performed only a few days ago. "I feel foolish," he said, waving a hand at the faces staring up at him.

"Do not be," said Lightfoot, pulling up a chair. "It's been nearly five-hundred years since Whitebeard's visit and there hasn't been a dwarf since. They're all just curious; it'll pass."

Dane and Dega took their seats alongside Camber and Brightwing and were soon joined by the twins. Winterleaf and Dovetail sat at the head of the table, warmly greeting their guests.

"It is a pleasure to meet you all again," she said, a tiara of gemstones twinkled brightly, jealously dimmed by her fiery-red hair, now piled elaborately on top of her head. Winterleaf also wore his crown. He searched the table end to end but did not see Starlock. As if on cue, the elf appeared through the water-wall.

No longer the seasoned warrior, but a vision of regal beauty, commanding attention from all as she stepped lightly across the floor. The Janastari's reluctant heir wore a velvet gown of midnight-blue, no jewels, except for a circlet of silver around her waist and the diadem of the Janastari nestled into her long black mane, now unbraided and falling in heavy cascades down her back. She glided up to her seat, and Dega stood to hold her chair while she took her place.

Winterleaf smiled. He was pleased Starlock had decided to show, *and* in formal dress; he knew she despised such displays, most Janastari did. "Welcome to Illianther." Winterleaf raised his goblet and Starlock did the same.

"May the Sun always smile brightest on your throne." She clinked his cup with her own.

"Never in my dreams did I imagine *the Houses* would be reunited, and though I worry for what the future might bring my heart is glad to be a part of this day." Dovetail smiled, and Willowsnap lifted his cup. "I remember the first Valastari, and when they left for the Northlands I wished for the day they would return. As I sit here and see the faces of our beloved friends I am warmly reassured that these men are all equal to their forefathers. It is an honor to finally meet you, Camber Bloodstone, son of Brightwing and Glade. And you too, Dane Strongbow, for I see something of Thayne the Bold in your face and manner. And as for you, Dega, son of Drake, I have met your father, and can tell you that he is truly among the admirable. I hope we might yet have a chance to talk in private, and I will tell you stories of your father's deeds that you won't hear anywhere else."

"Thank you, Sire. I look forward to conversing with you before I leave." Dega clinked his cup, but did not taste the wine.

The talk at the table was jovial and no mention of the Easterling King or any such trouble was allowed. Dinner was served; a golden broth with sweetbread for dipping, followed by sea bass stuffed with shellfish; the skin basted with a paste that gave it a savory flavor. A selection of pastries and fruits came last, signaling the end of the banquet

Winterleaf made a speech, welcoming the returning Houses of Janastari and Valastari, and acknowledging Camber, the son of Brightwing and Glade, as well as Dane, a grandson of Thayne the Bold, and finally introducing Lockjaw, heir to the throne of Ironfist. This was followed by applause, and several folk came by to pay respect to the honored guests. The orchestra launched into a lively ballad while folk mingled among the upper and lower levels of the hall. Camber and Dane followed the twins from table to table, and Brightwing now sat beside Dovetail; the two bent their heads in quiet conversation.

Starlock excused herself, then glided down to the lower level and out the far wall. Dega turned his head, watching her go. Willowsnap was still talking and he turned his head politely back to the Elven King.

Warblade was seated at a table on the lower floor when Starlock passed, excusing himself, he followed her outside.

"Starlock. Wait"

"Warblade?" She turned in midstride. *"Well what do you want."*

"You know what I want."

"Stay." Her hand came up.

"I need you." he stepped toward her.

"I do not feel the same as you."

"You loved me once."

"That was long ago, before I learned the truth. Before I knew you left my father to die."

"I did what I had to. He knew I could not help. He sent me away."

"Do not come any closer, or I'll... "

"Or you'll what, Starlock. Kill me? You tried that once before, remember?"

She made to take another step, but rough bark scratched her skin, pressing from behind, she could go no further.

"You and I were meant to be together," his voice breathed hotly in her ear. *"There is no better match in all of Astaria, and I will not take no for an answer."* His arm moved quickly, trapping her against the tree.

Starlock took a deep breath, fighting to control her pounding heart. Anger swelled beneath her breast - and something else... *fear?*

"Do not play games with me Starlock. For even you do not know what I am capable of now," and he placed his lips on hers. Remembering a time and place from the past, she pressed against his mouth; but her mind quickly recovered, her body went stiff and she pushed back, shoving him away.
"I am not your prize Warblade. Stay away from me."
Warblade's eyes followed her as she stalked angrily away from the clearing. *No. You are wrong about that Starlock.*

Dega left the table, and went to find Starlock. There was much he wanted to discuss, and he stepped through the water-wall hoping to catch up before she made her way back to her apartment. The moon overhead silvered the garden path bathing each individual blossom, each leaf, in soft radiance, but Dega paid no heed to the garden's nighttime beauty; too immersed in what he would say when he caught up with Starlock.
Twice he almost turned around. What was he doing? *Stupid Fool!* He stopped. *Voices.* He listened. Elves speaking in their native tongue. One was Starlock, and he poked his head through the tangle of foliage, then quickly pulled it out. His knuckles went white, clenching and unclenching. And when he got to his room he nearly yanked the door off its hinges.

Dane left Camber with the twins and walked back to his suite. What an evening! The music, the food, the entertainment! Yep, this was the life, given a choice it'd be no contest, he'd take it in a second. Dega was in his room and Lockjaw sat at the table. The archer yawned, said goodnight, and made his way to bed.
Lockjaw held Shard's necklace in his hands, caressing it as he pondered over his troubles. Too much was happening way too fast. He needed reassurance from his mentor. *Where was Hawker? Why hadn't he tried to send a message? Why... why was the emerald in his hands tingling?* The charm vibrated between his fingers, and his eyes opened wide as a beautiful face appeared. Shard! He smiled, gazing at her deep green eyes. She knew him better than he knew himself. Another smile, then a frown. This war with the sorcerer had to be won. It must be won. Else everything, all hopes, dreams, all he held dear, and especially his precious Shard would be lost. "I promise to see this business to its end, with or without Hawker, and when I

come home it'll be for good." The necklace vibrated once more, then Shard's lovely countenance disappeared.

The next week went by quickly. Too quick for Camber and Dane, and not quick enough for Dega. The evening air was crisp, and Dega knew winter was probably not far off. He wandered through the gardens alone. The cadets had gone with Lockjaw to watch a concert in the Hall. As he came to the spot where a pristine pond acted as a natural boundary between untamed treeline and Illianther's cultivated landscape, he picked out a silhouette sitting on a rock. Moonlight limned the figure in soft silver; he recognized Starlock's form and walked silently up to where she sat with her back to him.

"Greetings Captain," she said.

"How did you know it was me?" he asked, taking a seat beside the elf.

"Your spurs."

He smiled softly, he had forgotten the disadvantages to wearing spurs. "Where have you been?" It was a fair question. Nobody had seen Starlock since the night of the banquet.

"I? I have been busy contemplating a number of things." She held the diadem of the Janastari in her hands, rolling it over and over between her fingers and staring out at the dark waters of the pond.

"Winterleaf is calling a council for tomorrow."

"Yes I know. I was hoping Hawker would be here before then, but I am sure whatever the decision it will be the right choice."

"You speak as if you're not going?" Then noticing for the first time she was dressed in her leathers and fully armed, he added, "Are you leaving?"

Starlock stopped fingering the diadem and turned to look directly into his eyes. "Yes."

"You can't." The unflappable Ranger's Captain was shocked. "What about the Winterstone? I thought you wanted to retrieve it. Help us defeat the Easterling King."

"I never said that," she whistled for Belia and the falcon appeared out of nowhere, alighting on her shoulder.

"You promised Hawker."

"I promised to take you to Illianther. I have done just that."

His heart was in his mouth. She had every right to leave. She had fulfilled her half of the bargain. But still, what about the rest of it? How could she turn a blind eye against the entire welfare of the world? Everything depended upon finding that talisman and ending the sorcerer's reign - this time for good. "What about your people?" he asked. "You wear the crown of the Janastari. You are their leader – what of them?"

"This?" Starlock held the diadem aloft, it flickered brightly as the moon's silvery light bounced off its polished surface. "A mere trinket. My people live here now, under Winterleaf's protection. This has no meaning, except maybe as a symbol of the past." She flung the crown out into the pond; it hit the water with a smack and a sploosh, then slowly disappeared, sinking into its watery grave. Small undulating rings marked the spot where the diadem had vanished, gradually growing larger until the water's surface became smooth as glass once more. "I owe them nothing," she said, walking away.

"But you do," he called after her. "You owe them everything. You owe yourself. You who live in your Black Wood, shutting out the world around you. This is your hour to redeem yourself and make peace with the world." His words were wasted as he watched her slip into the shadows. A sigh fell heavy from his lips, and he took one last look at where she had vanished into the night.

IX

The Quest Begins

The next morning saw the return of the company's traveling clothes, and Dane marveled at his Ranger's uniform, cleaned and repaired it looked almost new. His bow had a new gut, and his quiver restocked with arrows; and to his surprise, among his articles - a new dagger. Blades from dwarven-steel are rare, and are almost never given to outsiders; but this particular blade had a history and its former owner would be proud if he knew that it now lay in the hands of his many-times great grandson. The level of craftsmanship surpassed even that of the dwarves, for the Candastari took great pride in the quality of edging, and nothing was overlooked, right down to the perfect detailing on the haft. Lockjaw also had his staff and battle-axe returned; he carefully ran his fingertip across the edge admiring the skill of the elven bladesmith.

Dega had switched his spurs back to his old boots, and even though Camber and Dane found their new footwear to be far more comfortable than their regulation cavalry boots, the Captain was a service man to the core and he opted to keep his required military gear.

The whole business of last evening occupied his thoughts, even to the point of Dane reminding him that they would be late for council if they didn't leave now. And when the cadet prodded his Captain with an outstretched arm, (he wasn't stupid enough to stand within snapping distance) the officer merely nodded his head. But Dane could not have known that his Captain's legendary fire had been temporarily vanquished by the vapors of disillusionment. Dega had begun to believe Starlock was something other than what she pretended to be, and that the elf who had traveled with them to Illianther was one who upheld the mark of honor with both hands high. *He was wrong.*

The shade of an ancient oak marked the very spot where Winterleaf and Dovetail had greeted their guests only a few weeks earlier; a marble-topped table had been transported from King's Hall for the occasion and was filling up fast with those whose wisdom would help decide the next course of action against the Easterling King.

Dega did a quick survey of who was seated where and pulled up a vacant seat directly under the shady side of the great oak; its gnarled and knotted branches spanned across the gathering like a giant's misshapen hand, casting dappled shadows of doubt across the fair faces of the council. Dane and Lockjaw plunked themselves down on two more empty chairs. Only one seat remained unoccupied.

Winterleaf cleared his throat, noticing the empty chair. "Where's Starlock?"

"She's not coming," said Dega; he glared across the table at Warblade. The silver-haired elf barely acknowledged his stare, and instead, seemed bent on tracing a path on a map that lay unfurled across the table. Dega could not read elvish, but he could tell even upside-down that it was a map of the Southlands, featuring the natural land-bridge known as *the Hook*.

"What? Why is she not coming?" Winterleaf looked more crossed than surprised.

"She left."

"She's back," said a voice, and Starlock swung out of the branches, landing neatly beside the empty chair. *Blast the Ranger's Captain for making her feel guilty.* Belia floated down from the treetops and landed on her shoulder.

Starlock pulled up the remaining seat beside Dega, and she cocked an eyebrow; a reply to his unspoken question. The Captain nodded; he understood completely and would not pursue the matter further.

"Good." Winterleaf nodded. "There is much to discuss so we best get started." The King of the Nantastari gave a brief history of the Elves, and of the coming of Dwarves and Men to Astaria. Winterleaf was only the second King to rule over the Nantastari. His father, Silverwise the Just, had reigned over all who had come to Illianther, from the time of *the Great Gathering* until *the Separation*.

"It was thought that we could benefit from each other's wisdom, and out of the hearts and minds of a united people Illianther was raised. *Illianther*. Its name means First City. And it was always meant to be the first and best home of all Elves. *First*, as it was built - and *Last*, as it now stands." Winterleaf paused so all might understand the significance of his words. Illianther was the cradle of civilization. If Illianther were to fall then all else would surely fall with it.

"The restlessness of the Jans would not manifest until later. Man had not yet made his appearance, and we were still learning much from our tutors. How we revered the Caretakers! They who were above us in all things. We wanted to please them, emulate them, but at the same time we wanted to be free of them; the Jans rebelled, and it wasn't long after, that Shadowshot took his people and left the confines of Illianther, going west over the Dragonspine, and there he built Bruinther. The Candastari followed, and soon we were a people apart. Though the Candastari lived relatively close, the Janastari did not. And we saw little of Shadowshot and his people." Winterleaf cleared his throat, and one of the elves waiting upon the council poured water into his cup.

"The Candastari quickly befriended the dwarves." Winterleaf spoke directly to Lockjaw, more than any other elf he knew the value of dwarven friendship, it was a rare gift to be 'owned' by the mountain folk, for that is how they regard friendship – a priceless possession. "The dwarves taught them the secret of forge and flame."

Lockjaw nodded. He knew the story of Iron-Hyde and the elves. The famous dwarven-smithy was instrumental in solidifying the bonds between the two races, and it remained steadfast until after the second uprising.

"With dwarven-steel we were able to renew our bonds with Shadowshot's people, and thus it was that our old familiar ties were strengthened."

"But the alliance between the Jans and the other two clans has never been strong," said Willowsnap, his voice held a hint of disdain for the warrior clan.

"Yes, but differences aside, we are all Elves just the same, and it was the Jans that came to the aid of your people when they needed them the most," said Winterleaf.

"The Black Barbs." Warblade pointed a finger at the Cando's King. "It was they who came to Khollinther's rescue, slaughtering her attackers, every last Bittite, every last K'Ahtar. You owe them your gratitude, if not your allegiance. Remember that, the next time you toss your head with contempt."

"Does it really matter?" Starlock tried unsuccessfully to hide her anger as she rose from her seat. "The laws of the three clans are a thing of the past. Look around you." She waved her hand at the faces gathered at the table. "Nantas, Candos, and Jans all sit at the same table. We live, eat, and sleep under the same sky. How many Candastari or Janastari cities have been built in recent years? None."

"Just because you prefer to be a recluse doesn't mean the rest of us have to be," Warblade scoffed. But Starlock did have a valid point. He eyed the faces around him, they might have all been cut from the same cloth, so nondescript. All followers of Winterleaf. He wondered if Snowblind and the Barbs now took orders directly from the Nanta's King.

"You all have lost your identity!" she snapped. "As I see the faces of my people, I see the composed tranquility of the Nantastari not the fire of the Janastari. I see the dignified refinement reflected in the actions of the Candastari, not the lighthearted gaiety that defines its people." She pointed her finger at Willowsnap. "When was the last time you even had a thought all your own?" Her face twisted with disgust. *"And you,"* she snarled at Warblade. "You who were second to only my father as the greatest of warriors. Where is your honor?!"

"Calm yourself Starlock." It was Dovetail who spoke. She stood, and her lavender silks rustled softly as she did so, gathering about her splendid form like the petals of an exotic flower. "No Elf that lives in Illianther has become less for doing so. All are free to come and go, and we do not quell the passions that make Candastari and Janastari unique." Her tone was motherly, but her voice hinted at unimaginable strength. Strength amplified over thousands of years; only Dovetail was as old as Winterleaf. "We do not begrudge your solitude, and we do not force you to live among us. Nor do we force anyone else to remain here, or be other than what they choose. You, yourself lived here as an elfling with your father."

Starlock's blood went cold, and she turned away from Dovetail's bright green eyes. Her father had come to Illianther after her mother's sudden death. Night-Raker had lost a little something of his fiery spirit afterward; a mirror of the once battle-ready elf on the outside, but nothing of the blazing warrior inside; he was but an empty shell, devoid of passion. He left Illianther only once and never came back. Her eyes narrowed into angry slits as they sought their intended target: *Warblade*. To this day he still called it an unfortunate accident.

"You only see things in black and white Starlock. You always have," said Warblade. He folded his arms across his chest, tired of the speed at which the council was proceeding. "I thought this was to be about our next plan of action, not a history lesson." Only he dared to speak at Winterleaf in such a mocking tone.

"We are getting to that Warblade. But in order for important decisions to be made freely, and without prejudice, all must know what it is we are fighting for."

"I for one am glad you are relating our history. There are a few at this table who have not heard it though some of us have lived it."

"Thank you Brightwing. I will dispense with the Separation and start from the Betrayal."

Dega sat up. *The Betrayal.* That is what Hawker had called the death of Blacker Darkhawk.

Across the table Warblade smiled, as if the retelling of how Blacker was murdered at the hands of his closest friend held some secret tidbit that only he was privileged to know.

Blacker had been tutored by Sentash; as the boy grew to a man, and the man became a King, the bond between teacher and student transformed into that of adviser and ruler. Blacker permitted Sentash to counsel him on political matters, and in return, the Valastari King enjoyed great prosperity. But Sentash had other plans, and while he allowed Blacker to think he was running the kingdom by his own decree, it was really Sentash holding the reins. The star pupil of Stornoway Hawker now controlled the royal vaults as well as the Valastari army. All that remained was to be rid of the King.

Dega's hand clenched and unclenched the pommel of his sword, but a gentle touch on his fingers from Starlock caused him to stop. She tilted her head toward Winterleaf, and dropping his hand, he gave his attention back to the Nantastari King.

"This evil act of cowardice was the thread that unraveled the Valastari. The tale in its entirety is a complex one, long in the telling, and our time grows short. I wished only to touch on certain events for why you are gathered here today. There's no point in discussing all the atrocities committed by Sentash, for that would take days. But all of you are familiar with his tyranny, and all have been affected by it in some form or another."

"How come he wasn't stopped?" All heads turned to look at Dane, who shrugged at his own question. "Someone should've stepped in."

"Aah, it was what we had originally planned when we drove him out. But then he went underground until he was strong enough, while securing the armies of the Eastern and Southern empires for his very own." Lightfoot was now speaking, and his face darkened as he recalled the *War of Sorrows*. "I was too young at the time to take my place on the field. Instead, I stayed at Illianther and made friends with the young charge that Thayne Bloodstone bade us guard. He who was next in line to the throne."

"Darius Darkhawk," said another elf.

"Darius, Blacker's only child." Winterleaf added.

Yes, and my great ancestor, thought Dega.

"Thayne Bloodstone brought him to Illianther fearing the boy would be next. Then we mobilized the largest army ever assembled. Nantastari and Candastari took up arms for the very first time under the guidance of Night-Raker's Barbs. And when King Ironfist caught wind of what we were doing, he too, quickly joined our ranks, convincing his neighboring warrens to rally to our cause." Winterleaf paused to point at the map. "Here." His long finger indicated the Dragonspine. "This is where the armies came together, on the other side of the Pass. We marched down to the Southlands along the banks of the Gambolin, which men call the Whitewash. More dwarves swelled our ranks as we crossed the Ironfist Mountains and into Caldorn, where the Valastari enlisted the aid of their distant cousins in the South, men of the Borderlands who already fought to keep the Easterling King from overrunning their territory. The men of Girt took up arms joining our growing numbers as we turned east; by the time we reached the Hook we were already sixty thousand strong. We met his armies on the fields of N'Amorr."

"It was all we could do to keep the mortals from running when the sorcerer brought forth his dragon," sneered Warblade.

Dane caught the scowl on Dega's face and he decided to say something before his Captain strangled the arrogant elf. "I was taught as a child that Thayne the Bold led the charge, and he, himself, slew the dragon."

"You are correct young one. If it were not for the stout hearts of the Valastari we might not be here today," Winterleaf frowned at the silver-haired elf. "After we drove the two Kingdoms apart we chased the sorcerer back to the safety of his citadel. But we were not prepared for his final showdown, for he enlisted the aid of another - *a Caretaker!*"

"What?" Camber sat up straight. "One of the Caretakers?"

"Yes. We had little hope of routing both Sentash and Norii. One of them alone would be a challenge, but together they were nigh-unstoppable."

Lockjaw sat unhappily at the table fingering the amulet around his neck. "He was going to tell you." He kept his head bowed so as to avoid eye contact with the angry Captain.

"When? Before or after the Rangers stormed Tar Galleaon!" Dega exploded. "I have the welfare of my men to think about! If Norii is aiding the sorcerer then we have lost." He cursed Hawker for not mentioning this before.

Winterleaf touched his fingertips together so that they formed an arch. His smooth brow furrowed for but a moment, then he spoke his careful reply. "If we can locate and retrieve the Winterstone then mayhap there is hope for us yet."

"And now we come full circle back to the Winterstone. And its whereabouts lay somewhere deep inside the Easterling King's realm, yes, yes, we've heard all this before. It's obvious our only hope is to recover it. What I want to know is how long have you been planning this Winterleaf? You and Hawker." Starlock's tone indicated that she knew all along why she had been sent to Illianther, and it wasn't just to guide the boy to Elvenhome; he just happened to stumble along at a convenient time to move them all down the garden path. "And who do you intend to send?" But even as she said this she knew she would have to go. Yes, they had even selected the company; she could see it in his face. And Winterleaf confirmed her thoughts by a nod so slight, so subtle, it appeared as though he was merely drawing a breath of air.

"What are you proposing Winterleaf?" Willowsnap asked. Starlock raised an eyebrow, was it possible that even Willowsnap had not been informed of the plan? Interesting that Winterleaf would keep such a thing from the Candastari King.

Camber leaned forward in his chair. He too wanted to know whom Winterleaf would send. What was it that Hawker had said? That he, Camber Bloodstone, could destroy the world. Had the wizard already foreseen such an event? Or would this talisman be his undoing? He looked at Dane who grinned back at him, clearly enjoying their adventure, but up till now they had managed to get through unscathed. How could he live with himself if he knowingly marched his cousin and best friend to his doom. He now wished Dane had stayed at Stone-Haven; perhaps it was not too late to send him back.

"What needs to be done is less talking and more action."

"Our decision must not be rash, Warblade." Winterleaf frowned at the elf. "And so I shall ask Starlock to locate the Stone and place it in the hands of the one person who has the gift to control such power and the mortal balance to resist its seduction." Winterleaf stood. He was tall even for an elf, and he radiated an inner strength, unbending and unyielding, and when he spoke all ears listened. But as he looked at Camber, and drew the young lad's large green eyes to his elfin-fair face, he suddenly appeared shrunken, dried up, very old, and very ordinary. All ethereal light had fallen from his noble countenance; the starlight behind his eyes lost its gleam, as he asked, rather pleaded, his request. "Camber, will you accept this duty? That which was ordained to you long before your birth. *Your Destiny.* It might lead to your destruction, or possibly the end of the world. And it pains me greatly to put this burden before you, but I ask you to choose freely."

A single leaf falling from above drifted lazily from its lofty perch; it hovered momentarily, then landed with a thunderclap.

"I will." Camber stood. His voice sounded like it had come from somewhere far away and not from his own lips, and out of the corner of his eye he could see his mother, a single tear staining her soft complexion.

Several elves at the table gasped, then all at once everyone started talking. Winterleaf raised his voice and held up his hand. "Then all that remains is to decide who will accompany Camber on a quest that mayhap some will not finish." His heart lightened, knowing the first and most integral part of Astaria's destiny had just been made true. All else would surely fall into place. *It had to.*

"I will go." Dega said. He did not like the idea of letting his cadet wander aimlessly through the wilderness, even if that cadet had the power to obliterate everything in his path.

"Oh no way - I'm not staying behind." Dane stood, and folded his arms in a display of stubbornness that his father claimed came from his mother's side.

Lockjaw held Shard's amulet, caressing it with his fingers. "I will go. For I believe Stornoway Hawker will soon return. He would be greatly disappointed if I did not watch over the boy as I promised." The amulet vibrated gently in his palm.

"I'll go too. It's been too long since I've set foot outside of Illianther, and I'm curious to see the world, particularly the dwarf-warrens. I wonder if all dwarves are lacking a sense of humor, or is it just the ones they keep sending here." Lightfoot nudged his bearded companion.

Winterleaf rubbed his chin thoughtfully. "Yes. All of you may go. And Lightfoot too, if only to act as messenger should the need arise. And perhaps Starlock will consider the twins. None can compare to their tracking abilities, and they are a valuable asset for this skill alone." The twins were delighted with Winterleaf's decision and it showed on their faces.

"One more should go. Another warrior to guard the backs of the others. Where one Janastari leads the quest, then a second Janastari should accompany the party and use sword and shield to protect he who will wield the Stone."

Starlock glowered she knew who Winterleaf meant, and he looked at her with all the arrogance and conceit of which could only emanate from such as he. True, she loved him once. But that was centuries ago, and he had been a different elf then. Now she saw through his brittle façade; a shallow reflection mirrored from a handsomely striking countenance, and the real Warblade made her heart feel like cold dwarven stone.

"Warblade. Do you accept this task which is appointed to you?"

"I will go. But only if Starlock asks for my aid."

"Starlock?"

For a moment she considered saying no, but the look on Winterleaf's face showed that he had already guessed what she was thinking and was ready to overrule her decision. "Fine. Warblade, we ask you to join our quest." Warblade said nothing; instead he nodded his head in a show of acceptance.

The talks now turned to marshaling the Black Barbs under the command of Snowblind, Starlock's kinsman, and when the council finally broke it was dark, but groups of elves still sat around discussing the day's events. And though no one would ever admit such a thing, all who attended harbored a grave fear for the safety of the world, and any outsider looking down from above would see the strongest evidence reflected on the face of Winterleaf as he walked beside Dovetail, shoulders slumped and brows knitted with a sense of doom, knowing that he, Winterleaf, son of Silverwise the Just, had just pinned the fate of the world on the slim shoulders of a boy.

Camber left with his mother, and they wandered along the gardens back to the palace. A heady bouquet of floral scents wafted lightly on the evening air, and Brightwing stopped to pick a flower. "You do not have to do this," she said. "There are other ways. Other things we could try. We have warred with the East before."

"I know," said Camber.

"I do not want to lose you," she kissed the petals, and tucked the flower into his coat.

Somewhere above, an owl made its presence known, hooting louder than the chorus of crickets in short solitary protest. Camber sighed, rubbing the velvet blossoms in his pocket. "I want to do this. If I have to be the one, then so be it. Father would have done the same."

"You are brave, but you are young, and your father would not want you to risk your life this way."

"If I don't do this, we might never get another chance. The Winterstone might end up in the wrong hands, and I would have to live with the knowledge that I could have been the one to prevent this War, but instead, did nothing." He stared at his feet. "What then? How can I turn a blind eye, when you, Dane, and everyone I care for might never walk this world again." Brightwing said nothing. She wrapped her arms around her only child and held him close.

Dega lay awake in bed. He could hear Dane and the dwarf snoring deeply. Arms folded behind his head, he stared out the window at the stars peeking through dark treetops. An endless stream of troubles swirled inside his head, and try as he might, he could not shut them out. *Camber was the Key.* He had known this since the night of the Bounder attack, but had left it buried beneath a growing pile of other problems. *A never-ending supply of problems.* Gareth must be warned. They must not march on the Easterling King. Not until he could figure out a way to restrain this Norii. *Caretakers and Sorcerers!* How could they possibly win against such odds? Fighting he understood. Magic he did not.

In the morning Dega Darkhawk looked like he hadn't slept. He hadn't. The Ranger's Captain sat astride his mount with a dour expression on his face while the good-byes were being said. The Elves had made sure the party was well equipped and carried enough supplies to keep them on the road through winter.

Starlock led the company out of Illianther and stopped just outside the waterfalls. It was decided to cross at Whistlegate, if only to avoid Southlanders. From there they could travel along the Whitewash and stay close to the foothills until they cut across country to the Razorhones, and finally the Hook, that barren land-bridge that connected the East to the rest of Astaria, and which was nearly impossible to cross without being seen.

Camber turned in his saddle. Tears brimmed his eyes. Eighteen years of not having a mother, and now he had to pick up and leave. So many questions and not enough time. *Not enough time.* What if something happened and he couldn't return? He clung to his mother's image, still fresh in his memory as she hugged him for the last time; her parting words repeated over and over inside his head. *Trust your heart, for there you will find your answers when there are none to be found.* He clutched the locket. Would he ever see his mother again?

Dane reached over and shook the sleeve of his coat. "You okay?"

"I'm fine. Just wish I could have spent more time here."

"Hey, look on the bright side, maybe we'll run into Chance. Didn't Winterleaf say he had left just a few months ago? My guess is that he probably went back to Hartland, found you gone, and is now out looking for you."

"He's gonna have a hard time finding me then, we've been all over this wilderness."

"You should've left a note."

"And say what? Dear Chance, gone on a field trip with Dane, Dega, a host of elves, and a dwarf, be back before dinner."

"You left out the Bounder."

Camber rolled his eyes and nudged his horse. Lockjaw looked up as the cadet rode in beside him; a frown creased his bearded face. Dwarves rarely ride, and Lockjaw was no exception; to make matters worse Lightfoot found the dwarf's discomfort amusing.

"I would give a mountain of gold to be off this beast and walking where it's safe," he huffed.

"Depends where you walk," joked the elf, "you might find yourself stepping into something you wouldn't like," he pointed to horse droppings along the trail.

Camber laughed. Lightfoot's easygoing nature was a far cry from Warblade; the warrior kept mostly to himself but never missed an opportunity to take a jab at Dega. In fact, he was mildly surprised that the Captain had not lost his temper thus far. All things being equal, he figured it was just a matter of time. Dega was proud, and refused to bend to no one; he took his task seriously, and expected everyone else to as well.

The company made its way down to a valley, here the trees grew tall and tightly spaced; tanglebrush grew between the gaps, making it difficult to maneuver past, and the speed at which they had traveled earlier had slowed considerably while horse and rider stepped carefully through the dark green canopy. By late afternoon they had reached the edge of the forest; the trees had thinned and the soft dirt floor gave way to a hard-packed path that wound its way alongside a noisy stream. And while the others refilled waterskins and saw to the horses the twins went on ahead to look for the best possible trail.

Crescent galloped back to the company. He spoke to Starlock in the lilting tongue of the elves and she sent him on ahead to help his brother prepare a campsite.

"I see no point in stopping so early in the day," said Warblade, nudging his horse up alongside Starlock. "We could easily ride until nightfall."

"Hmm, funny I don't recall asking for your opinion, and since this company is under *my* guidance I've decided to rest now and spare the horses. We do not know what we might find when we cross the Pass and I would just as soon have fresh horses if we need to take flight."

"She's right," Dega said, riding up from behind. "You were not with us when we crossed the Southlands, and do not comprehend the need for caution. By now the Easterling King has had word of our whereabouts. It would be folly to pass on such a location only for a few more hours of traveling time when we might not be able to find as good a spot farther along." Warblade snorted at the Ranger's comment and spurred his horse up the trail.

The twins were already clearing an area for horses and packs when Camber and Dane joined them. Together they readied the campsite while Lightfoot built a cook-fire. Camber sat beside the fire, Starlock and Warblade were still out hunting to supplement the company's provisions. He shivered and wrapped himself in his cloak. The seasons were changing, and a chill touched the nighttime air, a faint reminder that snow would soon be making the trek through the Pass treacherous.

Dega looked up as the outline of Starlock materialized in front of him. She held two rabbits out to the Ranger. He took one of the proffered hares, brushing his hand across the back of hers, and for a brief second their eyes met; he quickly averted his gaze, pulled out his hunting knife and started skinning meat from bone. "Where's Warblade?"

"He's not back yet." Starlock snapped a branch from above and whittled it to a point.

"He's been gone a long time," observed Lightfoot. "You left well after he did. And if I'm not mistaken, I have never known Warblade to be that bad of a hunter."

"He's not," said Starlock; she spitted the carcass and laid it across the fire.

"I'm right here." Warblade's voice floated through the trees as he stepped into the clearing. "No need to fuss." He threw three more hares onto the grass and chose a spot across from Dega. "I suppose you'll be wanting to head straight for the 'hones, but I might remind you that there is jungti to watch for. *No wait.* You probably already thought of that. Afterall, you *are* a veteran of the wilds."

Dega ignored the elf. He had far more important things on his mind, and would worry about jungti when the time came. They were still hundreds of leagues away from anywhere near the 'hones, and between here and there they were vulnerable as long as they were crossing through open territory. "We need to set a watch. Dane. You and Camber take the first shift. The twins can take the second. Lockjaw and I will take the last. Tomorrow we rotate with Starlock, Lightfoot, and Warblade." That being said, he stood to stretch his legs, and chose a spot to lay his bedroll. Dane shrugged at his cousin, and pulled out his dice. "Wanna play?"

When Camber finally lay down he was mildly surprised at how accustomed he was to sleeping out of doors, and as he looked up at the stars he wondered if his father would have been proud knowing that his son was following in his footsteps. He chuckled softly, well almost in his footsteps, he and Dane had been thrown into the mix without a choice. He yawned and rolled onto his side.

Dega woke them all just before dawn; pink clouds quickly gave way to a dull gray overcast that threatened the company with rain. Much of the scenery looked the same and the following days swept by as a blur, blending together under a rather bland looking sky.

They rode along in silence under the shadow of the mighty Dragonspine; its snow-capped peaks like the points of a monarch's crown against a purple-gray backdrop. It was easy to understand why the Candastari had built their city so close to these mountains. Starlock took them past the ancient walls, and they paused a moment to pay respect to glorious Khollinther.

Thus it was that Camber found himself standing amid the ruins of the fabled city. He sat on a chunk of broken rubble; the remains of a marble monument. Part of the face lay half sunk in the ground with moss growing between cracks in the stone. Flecks of paint, the tint of color still visible, gave a vague impression of what the statue might have looked like when it was whole.

Dane flopped down beside him, and the two sat in silence, pondering the awesome weight of Khollinther's destruction. "Why?" Dane said at last. Camber knew what he meant. He shrugged; it was something he did not understand either. All this waste. The wars with the East. Why would anyone want to destroy such a thing?

"It is difficult to explain, but perhaps I can offer an attempt," said Lightfoot, and he joined the cadets, sitting cross-legged on the largest piece of the statue; it made a convenient chair, and the elf made himself comfortable using the detail of the folds to set his pack.

"You see, even though we Elves have clearly become three separate people, we are still of one mind and spirit. Whether it's because we had been the first to arrive in Astaria or we are immortal, or both, I cannot say. But know this: all Elves are aware of each other at all times. We may not always know what the other is thinking, but we are in tune with each other's presence; the bond between us is always there. Dwarves are different, but they too share a bond through the riches of the earth. And then there is Man. The Valastari, the first-born sons, lived in close proximity to the Elves of Illianther and had the fortune of being favored by the Caretakers, especially Stornoway Hawker, who spent hundreds of years among them. But the second wave did not have the wisdom of the immortals to guide them. Nor did they share a special connection between their race, and they grew as a people apart, governed only by their leaders, little more than barbarians. They fought among themselves, and too, had to fend against the Janastari who dwelt in Bruinther and hunted them, and mayhap this contributed to their hatred. Who can say? But I will tell you this – always their hatred of all things Elven was foremost in their hearts, and they soon discovered how vulnerable Khollinther was; her doors wide open for all to enter. And to these men especially, it was as if we were flaunting our wealth and superiority over them.

In the end the city was laid to waste, despoiled of its riches, and the Candastari were left with only memories. But those memories do not die, and the Candos embrace them, and celebrate their joy in ways that do not involve elaborate festivals; we keep the happiness alive in our hearts, and that is something that can never be taken from us."

"But it's still a waste," said Dane. "Why can't the world live in peace?"

"Aaah. Because without strife there can be no change. Without evil there can be no good. It's a fine balance between the two, and the world cannot survive without either one. From bad things spring forth heroic deeds, and it is in times like these that the hearts of the brave are truly put to test. And do you suppose that even if we win the battle against the Easterling King and finally rid the world of Sentash, that some new evil will not rise up to take his place? This I can assure you. For without the horrors of tyranny we cannot truly appreciate our freedom. Hmmm... and I can see by the scowl on Starlock's face it is time for us to leave." Lightfoot jumped to his feet, picked up his pack, and went to collect his mount, leaving the cadets to ponder his words.

Another day's ride brought them to a rough path that hailed the start of the trek through Whistlegate Pass. The ground became increasingly difficult for the horses to climb, and the main trail was no longer a proper road but a narrow footpath strewn with loose rock.

A wintry chill forced the company to layer themselves with extra clothes. But even wrapped in a blanket over his fur-lined cloak failed to keep Camber warm, and he could no longer feel his toes. When he did move them, sharp pins of pain jolted up from the tips to the very roots of his hair, reminding him that they were still attached to his feet, and yes, they were still quite frozen. Dane grumbled – something about not feeling his... *wait,* why were they stopping? It couldn't be time for a rest just yet. But as he reined in his mount he could see one of the twins waving the white and green flags the elves used as a form of communicating over great distances.

"What's happening?" Dane asked, and he trotted up beside his cousin, somehow he managed his mount with both arms tucked tightly into his chest and the reins wrapped around the saddle's horn.

Lightfoot shaded his eyes from the glare of the sun bouncing off the snowy peaks of the mountains. "If I'm reading the flags right then there is something blocking the path and must be moved before we can carry on."

Starlock came charging back to where the others were waiting. "Crescent has discovered some bodies at this end of the Pass. They appear to be Rangers."

Camber and Dane exchanged a fearful look. "Do you think it's Chance?" Dane asked. Camber shook his head. Chance was not in uniform, and Starlock said the bodies were Rangers. "No," he answered, but silently prayed they were nobody he or Dane knew.

Dega had reached the bodies first. The Ranger's Captain was already off his horse, inspecting the frozen corpses when the cadets reined up.

The bodies had been badly mutilated; only one of the three was recognizable. "Portsmith," said Dega, and he turned the remains over in the snow.

Crescent and Frost-Eye were down on their knees brushing away debris. "It appears as though a large animal, maybe a snow-bear, attacked these men."

Dega stood and went to where Frost-Eye had cleared away most of the cover, revealing a clear impression of a large animal paw-print. He bent down to study the size of the predator's print, and recognized it immediately for what it was. "This is no snow-bear," he looked up at the rest of the company now gathered around him. "It's a Bounder."

X

At Whistlegate Pass

"Impossible!" snorted Warblade. "There is not enough evidence to prove this was done by a Bounder." The silver-haired Jan bent down to trace his finger along the imprint. "This could be almost any large animal."

"I think I know what I'm talking about, I have seen these tracks before." Both stood, and Dega's hand rested lightly on the pommel of his sword. "In the Eastlands."

Lightfoot stepped between elf and Ranger. "If it is a Bounder then perhaps we should get off this path."

"These tracks are weeks old. I do not think we are presently in danger," Starlock said. "However. Just to be sure." She called Belia to her arm, muttered some elvish, and released the bird. The falcon spiraled up into the sky then disappeared from view. Within minutes she was back. Starlock looked up at the bird circling overhead. "There are no Bounders or anything else that poses a threat in the immediate area."

Dega buried the bodies with help from the others. His face never showed anything more than a controlled frown on the outside, but inside he was troubled over the death of these men. He knew Daryl Portsmith, smart fellow with a bright future and a young family. What a waste. He wondered if Gareth would send any more men to the Pass. *Doubtful. He probably has his hands full.* The Captain hoped his latest letter would find his Lieutenant in time.

By the time they finished clearing the Pass the sun was already setting, and they quickly made camp just as darkness replaced the last rays of light. The evening sky was clear, promising yet another good day for travel, and billions of stars twinkled across the blazing blue-black of night. But the beauty of the cosmos was wasted, and so was the cheerful warmth of the campfire, for each person in the company, including the good-natured Lightfoot, seemed uncomfortably silent as the sobriety of the day's events weighed heavily on each brow. Thus it was, that supper was consumed in silence; and those on watch huddled within their blankets, not wanting to converse, or otherwise.

The next day was clear but much colder than the day before, and though the sky was sunny, dark storm clouds moved in just before dusk. "I don't like the looks of those clouds. We might get hit with snow if they stick around," observed Lightfoot.

Camber couldn't agree more. They certainly had the look of bad weather. "Rather snow than rain," he said.

"Ha. Be careful what you wish for. If we get snow now we could find ourselves trapped up here until spring." Lightfoot grinned at the cadet. "I'd rather splash along through water than trudge through snow drifts any day."

"I don't think it's gonna snow," Dane shaded his eyes as he peered up at the sky. But no sooner had he spoke then the first fluffy flakes began to fall.

"Well that settles it. I guess we better hope the end of the Pass is not much farther, though I'm afraid we are still a few hours ride from the halfway mark." Lightfoot tapped his horse with his heels and cantered up to the front of the company.

The snow continued to fall, coming down faster with each passing hour and blanketing the ground in quiet whiteness. It was now dark and the company had no choice but to keep moving. Dega urged them onward. He knew the Pass well, and recalled that a shallow cave once used by smugglers and caravan thieves lay hidden just beyond the bend.

When they finally reached the old hideout the snow was already midway to calf and showed no sign of stopping. The cave was deep enough to allow the company, their belongings, and horses, to take shelter from the outside. A fire was built, though wood was lacking, but Lockjaw had brought along dwarven fire-blocks, made from coal and used mainly to keep the cook-fires burning. He'd been saving the blocks for such an emergency.

"Why didn't you bring these out before?" Dane took a block and tossed it in the air.

"We had plenty of wood and were not in danger of losing the flame." Lockjaw caught the block and placed it back in the pit.

"But I had to burn my clothes. MY CLOTHES!" fumed Dane.

"And if I had used the blocks then. What do you suppose we would be using for fuel now?" The dwarf eyed Dane's fur-lined cloak. Camber slapped his cousin on the shoulders. "Think of it as restitution for the commotion you caused in the forges."

Dega and Lightfoot found some blankets heaped in a corner, and a wooden crate, which remarkably, still contained a supply of grain.

Starlock, Crescent, and Frost-Eye were still outside covering up their trail. She followed the twins into the cave, threw back her hood, and shook the snow off her mantle. "It doesn't look like it's letting up anytime soon. We've done our best to hide the tracks, and the snow will cover what we could not; but if there is a Bounder nearby and it catches the scent of horses it may be drawn to our location."

"What do you suggest then?" Warblade sat cross-legged beside the fire. He was honing the edge of his blade across a stone, his chain-mail and cloak were cast aside; the glow from the fire lit the contours of his long sinewy arms: muscular, hard, and corded, they complimented his warrior's physique. He paused for a moment while he waited for Starlock's response.

"We must secure the front of this cavern." Her eyes darted around the cave until they came to rest on a slab of rock. The elf took two of the horses and fashioned a makeshift harness, and with Dega's help she coaxed them into moving the stone so it now blocked the entrance. "That should keep most things out, but we'll still have to post a watch."

The cave was warm and snug, and slightly cramped with wet horses and baggage, but by far the most comfortable spot they had chosen as a campsite since leaving Illianther. After dinner, Lightfoot brought out a flute from somewhere within the folds of his coat and played a lively tune. He was soon accompanied by the twins, and even Camber picked up part of the chorus; it was in elvish, but that didn't stop him from lending his soft tenor to the music anyway.

"Well done, Lightfoot." Warblade's face appeared softer; the elf inside the warrior had enjoyed the entertainment. "How about a story? We might as well pass the time with one of your tales."

"Fine by me, but I would not wish to bore the others with my stories, which can be rather long in the telling."

"That has never stopped you before," said Crescent.

"To be sure," Frost-Eye warned, "sometimes there is no end to his talking, though I doubt he even realizes it."

"Well if you don't want a story... "

But the others pleaded, and at last he relented. "Then I shall tell you the tale of Sharp-Glance and Feather. It is a love-story, though I warn you, the ending is not exactly a happy one." The intriguing tone of Lightfoot's voice caught the interest of all, including Starlock and Dega, and both stopped what they had been doing to come sit beside the fire and enjoy Lightfoot's tale.

"Many ages ago, long before *the Separation* and well before the time of ruling houses and such. There dwelt along the shores of the Western Sea a village of Elves who were a fishing people by nature. Each family maintained their own boats and nets though they shared their catch with the community. And all who dwelt in the village knew the sea intimately, but as some were reliant on fishing, others were hunters. Game was plentiful, and when winter storms kept the boats moored, all benefited from the bounty of the woods. Such was the way of life among these elves. All worked together, contributing to the village, and not one among them, be he sick or no, would go without a full belly or a warm blanket." Lightfoot paused; an expert storyteller, he chose his breaks carefully, allowing the tale time to settle into the imagination of his audience.

"In the heart of this village lived Feather. She with a crown of golden hair and lively blue eyes to match her sunny disposition, and though her nature was always kind and caring, it was her voice that endeared her to the hearts of those who dwelt by the sea. When Feather sang all would stop and listen, including the woodland animals, and too, the birds in the sky; for they, themselves, were no match in song.

It was because of this gift that she would accompany her father each morning, and while he made ready his nets she would sing to the waters attracting large schools of fish, enchanting them with her sweet velvety tones and drawing them out from their hiding places in the deep. After the fishing, Feather would take the rowboat by herself and drift dreamily along the shore thinking up new songs for her friends and family.

Today her thoughts were only of Sharp-Glance as she glided her small craft into a lagoon on the far side of the village. It was his Naming Day and she wanted to sing a song that would be worthy of he. *Sharp-Glance.* He who commanded her heart.

Sharp-Glance was no fish-trapper. A mighty hunter was he. Under his watchful protection the village remained safe from the wild beasts that roamed the woods. Strong, virile, and full of life's fire, but in the presence of his beloved Feather, the lion was but a gentle cub. And it should be said, right here and now, never has there been a better match in all the world."

Warblade smiled, and he stared at Starlock from across the fire.

"As Feather sat in the boat she sang. At first a jumble of muffled words, then slowly the song began to take shape, forming itself into pure joy. A song of adoration inspired by her love for Sharp-Glance. The sea calmed itself, and the afternoon sun shone directly over the boat illuminating the small craft rocking gently on the waves. Seabirds landed on the bow and fish flashed silver beneath the waters, and it did seem that all the world paused in its preordained pattern so that only Feather's enchanting voice might be heard.

As she sang her eyes swept outward along the depths of the blue-green sea; something dark bobbed out of the water, and they stopped their travel, staring wide-eyed at the elfin-fair face that had suddenly appeared beside the boat. Startled by the vision, she let out a fearful scream, and the strange sea-elf dipped beneath the dark waters. Bravely, she began to sing anew, and the face reappeared. It was an Elf!

How she managed to keep the music flowing, only the Elders knew. Slowly the elf came up to the boat, popping his head above the waves. Feather stopped singing, mesmerized by his saucer-shaped eyes, curiosity supplanting caution. The sea-elf's gaze followed her as she sat in the boat and she looked at him as he bobbed up and down on the crest of each wave. Delicate was that face with its large green eyes - glossy and unblinking, and his skin, a pale blue-green, blending perfectly with the sea. It was then she saw the tail; an iridescent jewel of spectacular proportions, twice the length of his upper torso, and with a fluke-span wider than the boat.

After several minutes of wide-eyed staring the sea-elf finally spoke; he introduced himself as Ak-A-Bric-Nan - *He Who Braves The Giant Sea Swells*, a Prince from Hap-Nic-Nan - *The City Below The Sea*. He asked Feather to sing, for he had never heard such sweet music in all his life. She gladly obeyed, fascinated by Ak-A-Bric-Nan, but the day was waning and she knew Sharp-Glance would come looking for her if she remained too long, so she took up her oars and bid the sea-elf farewell, but not before accepting his invitation to meet again the next day.

It was dark by the time she reached the great house where the community gathered, and she was met at the door by none other than Sharp-Glance. He was just about to go looking for her, and his handsome face, all planes and angles - made more so by its dour expression, showed signs of relief for her safety as she entered the hall, and taking her hand he led the object of his heart's desire to her cushion at the table.

"I have something for you," he told her, and produced a small bouquet of yellow flowers with tiny triangular petals that smelled of springtime. Sharp-Glance knew Feather liked to bathe herself in the scented blossoms of the sunspun, and though they were exceedingly rare, he had come across a batch while hunting deer. As her face lit up brighter than the yellow petals he now placed in her arms, he knew it had been worth the trouble to climb down the cliff and retrieve them, if only to see Feather's radiant smile for a mere moment.

Feather was delighted, but not surprised, for such was the way of Sharp-Glance, who doted on her every whim. Thus she inhaled deeply of the sunspun's scent, and as was her wont, recited the day's events to the strapping young warrior who listened to every detail, savoring each word as if they were a treasure for his ears, and his ears alone. But Feather found herself skipping over the extraordinary encounter with Ak-A-Bric-Nan. And Feather, who had never before kept anything from Sharp-Glance, tried to bury her shame from those piercing black eyes by hiding behind the song she had composed for his Naming Day. It was a powerful song, charged with her feelings for the young hunter, and it brought tears of joy to all, especially Sharp-Glance.

After the evening meal, and the last of the Elder stories, Sharp-Glance escorted Feather back to her family's hut. He kissed her gently on the forehead and said his good-nights. But the hunter was no fool either, and as he walked back to his own dwelling he reflected on how unresponsive Feather had been. It was not like the elf-maiden to be so secretive and guarded, and it gave him cause for concern.

When Feather accompanied her father to the sea the next day she could hardly contain her excitement, and this was not lost on her father who commented more than once on his daughter's apparent eagerness. But the elf-maiden only smiled at her father's needless worry and kissed him gently on the cheek before summoning the day's catch with song. If Feather seemed hurried through her musical duties it did nothing to take away from the usual effect her melodies had on the denizens of the deep, and none but her father seemed to notice his child's apprehension as she untied her rowboat and stepped lightly into its bow, maneuvering the small craft away from the pier and out to sea.

Her nervous excitement would not stay hidden as it rose up in song. A splash revealed the dark head of Ak-A-Bric-Nan, and he greeted Feather with a ready smile.

And so it happened each morning after she sang to the waters, Feather would go off in secret to meet the strangely wonderful elf, who called his people, *Kinakkin*, the sea-dwellers. But her disappearances and unusual behavior did not go completely unnoticed. And so, on this particular day when Feather had gone off to meet Ak-A-Bric-Nan she was followed. Sharp-Glance trailed her path by land, his coal-black eyes smoldering with jealousy while he watched his beloved from the shore.

Feather was oblivious to all as she conversed with Ak-A-Bric-Nan under the brilliant blue sky. Over the past few weeks she had learned many things about this sea-elf and his people, *and,* she had discovered something else. A feeling had been steadily growing in her heart, not unlike her feelings for Sharp-Glance."

Lightfoot's voice drifted softly through Camber's ears, working its story-telling magic. The cadet imagined himself standing on shore watching Sharp-Glance, Feather, and Ak-A-Bric-Nan, from afar. A private play unfolding before his very eyes.

"It was at that precise moment, when all the world seems perfect and anything is possible when willed by the heart of a young maiden that the unthinkable did happen. Ak-A-Bric-Nan reached up into the boat and took Feather by the hand, speaking softly in her ear as he guided her down into the depths of the sea. She knew how to swim, and very well, but they were traveling below the ocean's surface at a startling speed; she let out a cry, but stopped when she realized she was still breathing air. A frown crossed her fair face, not understanding this anomaly that bent the laws of nature, and her bewilderment caused Ak-A-Bric-Nan to laugh. He told her that he was a creature of the sea, and therefore had the power to control his environment. Fright soon gave way to fascination as she found she could converse and breathe under the sea, and she allowed Ak-A-Bric-Nan to guide her to his city.

Tall spiraling towers sprang from coral in hues of pink, white, and red; gemstones glittered from rooftops, arches, and porticos.

Brightly striped fish darted past as they glided up to Hap-Nic-Nan's entrance; its gates of pearl swung open, allowing Ak-A-Bric-Nan to lead his bewildered beauty across the threshold and through doors of polished abalone.

Sharp-Glance watched in horror as his beloved Feather slipped beneath the sea. Strong were his strokes, driven by anger, bringing the hunter through those great gates of pearl just as they were closing.

Ak-A-Bric-Nan took his maiden by the hands, confessing his love, and asking her to stay. She shook her head; golden hair, caught by the current, unfurled around her face like a halo. In her heart she wished not to leave her friends and family, all of whom were dear to her.

Tightly did this Sea-Prince weave his spell, trapping his prey deep within his net, and there he made Feather promise never to reveal the location of Hap-Nic-Nan or tell a soul about the Kinakkin. He kissed her forehead and whispered such sweet words, that she gave into his request, pledging her loyal obedience to never reveal a word.

Sharp-Glance crouched behind two giant oyster shells, rage rising in his veins. The words of this stranger burning his ears until he could no longer contain his anger; he pounced at this creature who dared to claim Feather for his own. But Ak-A-Bric-Nan was in his element; under the sea he was twice as fast as the grass-walker; he whipped his mighty tail, striking a blow, and knocking his rival across the ocean floor.

The Sea-Prince delivered another strike, then glided over to where Sharp-Glance lay, hovering over the fearless hunter with a spear he pulled loose from its place on the wall. A cry from Feather, as she made her choice, throwing herself overtop her true love.

Ak-A-Bric-Nan paused, then grew angry as only a Prince of the Sea could. He cursed Feather and all her kind, and reminded her of her promise. And to make sure she would forever keep her word he wove a powerful spell and set it loose upon the young lovers before casting them back onto the beach.

Feather awoke to find she was lying in the sand. Sharp-Glance cradled her head; the fearless hunter caressed her brow, but his gaze wandered off in the distance. She reached up, gently touching his face. *He flinched.* Sensing something wrong, she sat up; he jumped at her sudden movement; she asked if he was injured, or at least tried to, but when she opened her mouth no words came forth. She tried again. Still no words! Tearfully she waved her hand in front of his face, but he saw it not. She wept as a sudden understanding of what

Ak-A-Bric-Nan had done to make sure she kept her promise – she could not speak, therefore, she could not tell a soul about where she had been, and Sharp-Glance, whose piercing black eyes fueled his passion for life, could no longer see. Tears streamed down her face but even the smallest of sighs could not escape her delicate throat. The warrior held her fast, whispering his love over and over until she fell asleep in the comfort of his strong embrace.

When Feather awoke for the second time it was night, and Sharp-Glance lay asleep at her side, one arm curled protectively around her waist. In her heart she knew she could never be free of guilt, knowing those fearless eyes would never again see the brilliant colors of a sunset, nor the moon's silver sheen, or scan forest, hill, and plain. No longer would he be the hunter, the provider, the protector. Tall and proud, he would forever be dependent on the village, stripped of his virility. If only there was a way to make it right again. If only for Sharp-Glance.

But there was! It came like the fleeting beat of a butterfly's wing – one chance to make things right. Slipping carefully out of his arms, she kissed his lips for the last time and unfastened the necklace he had made for her the day he had first professed his love, and placing it in his hand, she closed his fingers around it. Then taking one last look at Sharp-Glance, her love, her life, she waded into the depths of the sea.

Sharp-Glance opened his eyes, the sun beat down upon his brow, confusion played across his thoughts, for he had no memory of the underwater palace, or of Ak-A-Bric-Nan. He looked at the shells in his hand. It was then that he spotted Feather's rowboat. It bobbed up and down on the water; one oar lay across the gunwale and the other floated to and fro as the tide gently pushed and pulled it to shore. *Where was Feather?* He scanned the beach but did not see her; in a panic, he dove into the sea, swimming the length of the lagoon, but she was nowhere to be found.

Thinking she may have gone back to the village he sprinted for home. The entire community was in the midst of forming a search party when Sharp-Glance appeared; and they were surprised to see him. They told him that he and Feather had been missing for two days. The warrior took charge, and with the aid of Feather's father, the two of them organized all who could be spared. And it must be said, that everyone in the village wanted to join the search for the missing maiden, for she was the jewel of their community and loved by all.

Days went by. Then weeks. Then weeks became months. And months turned into years. And it was agreed by most that Feather must have fallen overboard and now lay in her watery bower under the sea. But Sharp-Glance would not give up. He would never stop searching as long as his heart still beat within his breast. He left the village never to return. Over mountains and through the woods he went, calling her name until he could speak no more. As the years passed quickly his path led him back to the very beach where Feather had placed the necklace in his hands, and though he did not know it, he now stood on that exact spot where she had kissed him good-bye. Weary from the weight of his sorrow, Sharp-Glance lay down in the sand to die.

But Atrilla who watches all from the sky took pity on Sharp-Glance as he mourned the loss of his Feather. She came to him, and taking the grief-stricken warrior, she placed him among the stars. *The Hunter.* And there from his lofty perch does his watchful eyes search forever for his beloved Feather."

Lightfoot finished his story. The cave had grown quiet. The sting of Feather's sacrifice, and the heartache it caused, had left them all feeling the sorrow of Sharp-Glance. Lightfoot asked Dega if he could take the first watch and the Captain nodded. As the others fell asleep around the warmth of the fire the elf stared up at the crack between cave and rock, and there he did spy in the nighttime sky, the Hunter watching from above.

XI

Separate Ways

"Look. Tracks!" Dane was the first one out as soon as the rock blocking the entrance had been removed. Paw prints crisscrossed over the snow, back and forth along the path.

"Wolves," said Crescent, and he followed them to where they disappeared into a thicket. He came back after a short while and reported his findings to Starlock. "The wolves circled the cave; the tracks disappear farther up the Pass and leave the main trail; they appear to be heading south."

"South?" Starlock frowned.

"Yes. And they weren't hunting game; they stayed within close proximity of each other and had lingered longest near the entrance of the cave."

"Why didn't we hear them?" asked Dane.

"Maybe they didn't want us to." She was already forming her own ideas about who sent the wolves and why.

The snow had let up but the going was slow; more than once they came across snow drifts deeper than the hocks of the horses. They saw no further sign of the wolves, but as an added precaution Starlock had Belia survey the area from above. They did not linger long at midday, stopping only once to retrieve food from packs and allow the horses to rest.

The beauty of the wilderness in winter did not go unnoticed. Snow covered rocks, trees, and the bare branches of tanglebrush; the leaves long gone, now exposing the twisted prickly sticks that gave the bush its name. Small rivulets of water trickling down from the mountain's sheer cliffs transformed into ribbons of ice, forming jagged icicles;

sparkling like glass under the sun's prismatic beams. The wintry world was breathtaking in its brilliancy, and Lightfoot was especially moved, composing a song inspired by this white wonderland.

The day waned, and Starlock had the twins search for a suitable place to set up camp. They found shelter from off the Pass and guided the others to the site. Darkness came quick, clouds moved in blotting out stars, only the moon could be seen. A fire was built, and the evening meal consumed in silence.

A dismal cry sent neck hairs on end; it was picked up by a chorus of long cheerless wails. The horses panicked, pulling at their tethers, and Belia took to the trees.

"Wolves!" Starlock had her sword out.

"Backs to the fire," said Dega, and the cadets jumped to their feet.

Four silver-tipped wolves made their presence known, braving flame; several more moved around the outer edge, eyes glinting in the dark. The largest of the four bounded in for the attack. Then all at once the pack came at the company, leaping out of the dark. Dega cut the leader clean across its belly, clearing his blade just in time to receive the next.

Starlock stood in front of Lightfoot, who had only a bow and not enough space between himself and the wolves. Her boot came down on snapping jaws, followed by steel, clearing away lupine attackers and allowing Lightfoot to shoot.

"Camber!"

Camber turned at Dane's warning. A ball of grey sprang out of the shadows. The wolf spun sideways, launching into air. Something whizzed past his ear, and the beast dropped dead, felled by an arrow. Steel and flame kept the wolves at bay, bodies piling off to the side, until the last one turned tail, fleeing into the night.

Dega examined his arm, sleeve torn and bloody, he took off his shirt and splashed the wound with water, then bound it with cloth. "We can't stay here."

"A horse is down, and another is missing," said Lightfoot. He took the packs from the downed charger and threw them across his own mount. Camber, Dane, and the twins, collected the remaining animals, checking packs and saddles.

As Warblade mounted, a hand reached up, snatching the reins. Starlock stood beside his leg, and she looked up at him. "You didn't seem to be doing much fighting back there."

"I didn't need to. You seemed to be doing enough for everyone."
"If you try another stunt like that. I'll make sure you get left behind. *Permanently.*" She let go of his horse and he kicked its flanks sending it to the front of the line.

They rode for a few hours, then moved off the path just before dawn. The fire was kept small and a watch posted, and it seemed everyone slept lightly with weapons close at hand.

Starlock took to the trees but did not sleep. She sat huddled in her cloak peering out at the early morning sky. The elf remembered a time when the world was a very different place. Warblade had been different too. Slowly her thoughts melded into that not quite asleep but not wholly awake dream state, where memories come unbidden, whether welcome or not. Warblade, handsome and striking as her father's fearless *Second*.

When she came of age this dashing warrior had captured her heart. And with Night-Raker's approval, Warblade began courting Starlock. Tender he was, and they shared many a starry night hunting the plains and forests, wrapped in each other's arms watching the sun as it came over the horizon. They talked as lovers do discussing all manner of things; and sometimes they would just sit in silence, content to be near each other as if nothing else mattered.

And when the Black Barbs marched against Sentash, whom men now called the Easterling King, she worried for both her father and Warblade. But Warblade came back and her father did not. The years went by and she mourned her loss, finding comfort in his arms. And he, so caring and gentle as was his nature then, made her forget her tears.

But another Janastari had set his designs on the daughter of Night-Raker, and wanted Starlock for his own; Moontrekker, a proud and distant cousin of Night-Raker, and a mighty warrior in his own right. His lands stretched away west across the plains, not far from the white cliffs where the Black Barbs now camped. And with his brother Windstalker, the two of them could often be found patrolling their borders and hunting the great fanged cats of the plains for sport. So it was, on one particular morning that Starlock had chose to visit Warblade, whose own lands lay adjacent to Moontrekker's, she encountered the arrogant elf as he and his brother returned from the hunt.

"Hoi! Starlock," he called, as she rode past. "Come be our guest and grace our humble castle with your beauty. We will dote on your every wish, for no request is too grand or too much trouble for the daughter of Night-Raker."

Starlock reined in her horse, stopping a good distance from the brothers. Though she had no fear of the elf or his brother, she was not well armed; she had only a bow and a short dagger, and they were both well equipped and highly skilled with their weapons. Caution played upon her words, not wanting to sound as if refusing the offer, for Moontrekker was sincere and might easily be offended. "I am truly sorry Moontrekker, son of Striker, I cannot tarry on this day. Gladly, I would sit by your fire and enjoy your hospitality, but I have other matters more pressing that require my presence. Another time, perhaps?"

"And what matter is most urgent? Is it something that we the sons of Striker Doomslayer can be of aid? What troubles the jewel of the Janastari?"

"Nay. Do not fret for me. For it is something I must see to myself. But I thank you kindly for your concern. Good day to you Moontrekker, and to you as well Windstalker. Honorable is the House of Striker Doomslayer. May it stand forever," and she turned her horse away.

"We thank you for your blessing, and we grieve the loss of your father; he was surely the mightiest of all the Kings who came before him. But you should not so easily dismiss our worth Starlock, for we are Princes of the Blood and are sworn to protect our sovereign at any cost." Moontrekker had guessed where she was going, for he knew whose home lay in the direction she was riding, and he called her bluff once more. "I have decided to come with you. I do not wish to see you in any danger, though skilled you are with your bow, you have no weapons other than the dagger you wear and you may find yourself in need of a sword," and he adjusted his own sword so that she might catch his meaning.

She struck the flanks of her mount; the animal reared, taking off at break-neck speed. But Moontrekker and Windstalker would not be so easily rebuffed and made to look as fools. Away they sped, chasing after across the plains.

Starlock bent low, clutching tightly to mane, and it seemed for a moment that she had lengthened the gap between herself and the sons of Striker Doomslayer. But the brothers were expert riders and their horses of good breeding stock. In the span of a heartbeat they had all but caught up to her. Windstalker whistled an arrow past her head to show they meant business. Down a steep embankment she rode, her mount stumbling as he lunged headlong down the slope to the rocky waterbed that crossed below. Moontrekker and Windstalker followed, laughing in sport while they gave chase.

Across the riverbed she splashed, and up the bank on the other side. A rider astride a dappled charger rode up to meet her. Warblade! Wind whipped his silvery mane, framing his noble face; a scowl formed upon his fair features at the sight of what his eyes beheld. Anger came fast; he pulled his sword loose, and bade Starlock to stay behind as he came to greet the sons of Striker.

"You have been a thorn in this fair maiden's side far too long, Moontrekker. Go now and be spared your heads, else I'll cut you and your brother down where you stand. Go now and trouble Night-Raker's daughter no more."

But Moontrekker only laughed, and he said in a voice loud and clear and meant especially for Starlock's ears. For he guessed that she had no idea the wicked deed that Warblade's hand had done, else she would not be holding it so tenderly.

"And will you protect her the same way you did her father? You who abandoned Night-Raker in his hour of need and left him to die!"

"You do not know what you speak of. It did not happen that way."

"Did you think by ridding the King you could slip in and take his place by stealing the heart of his only child? Bah! You are no better than the Valastari." He laughed as he saw the look on Starlock's face, knowing his words had inflicted damage that could never be repaired.

"What is he saying Warblade? Is this true?" She started to back her horse away from the warrior elf, he who was her betrothed and her father's best friend. And then it suddenly seemed to Starlock that maybe all of Warblade's love and concern for her well-being was but a charade. Could it be that his true desire all this time was for the crown of the Janastari? Why else did he evade her questions whenever she brought up the subject of her father's death? "What have you done Warblade?"

Moontrekker laughed and he turned his horse back to his own lands, but not before calling over his shoulder. "Beware Starlock. Do not trust in the words of this murderer lest you find yourself in the same fate as your father."

Warblade's explanation came in a flurry of emotion, but her ears were numb to what he was saying. She turned from him and kicked her mount hard. Warblade followed, begging forgiveness, but Starlock rode until she had crossed into lands not often traveled by elves, and there she breathed a sigh of relief, believing she had out-ridden her pursuer.

On the peaks of the Razorhones he finally caught up, and vaulting from his saddle he ran to catch her in his arms.

"Leave me." She drew her dagger. "I have nothing more to say to you."

"Starlock, wait. Let me explain..."

"Explain what? Why didn't you tell me? All this time you led me to believe it was an accident, a casualty of war. You! I trusted you." She backed away, her father's death weighed heavy on her heart, a burden amplified by Warblade's secret deed.

"Forgive me."

"No forgiveness. Death-Match!"

"You are upset. I will not accept."

"You cannot refuse. By Janastari law you must accept, or be banished for life." She lunged, knife in hand, and though the blood of Kings flowed strongly through her veins, she was still young and fresh and not the seasoned warrior that Warblade was, and he grabbed her by the hand, giving it a twist; the blade jumped cutting across her eye, her fingers let go, dropping it hundreds of feet to the rocks below.

Warblade pulled her close. "Listen to me. I did what I had to. Night-Raker could not move. Both his legs were shattered; his spine snapped. He told me to finish it, go see to your safety."

"No! I don't believe you. You LIE!" She whirled in his grasp. "Let me GO!"

"It's True! I swear by all that is pure in this world." His hand came up, gently sweeping away the blood trickling down her face.

"Betrayer! Your word is tainted, just like your honor." Tears filled her eyes, mixing with blood, she pulled away, but Warblade held on. Anger came fast, and her leg came up, sending him over the cliff.

Her eyes snapped open as she realized she had been dreaming. Everyone was still sound asleep except Warblade. It was supposed to be his watch, but as she looked out of the branches of the tree she saw no sign of the Jan. She slipped to the ground and waited for his return. "Where have you been?" she snapped.

"Been? I haven't been anywhere."

"Oh no? Well you haven't been at your watch, that is certain."

"Bah! I heard a noise and went to check it," and he dismissed her questioning with a wave of his hand.

"Don't play games with me Warblade."

"Games? You're the one who plays games. You've been playing your own game since that day you left me for dead."

"As you left my father? AS YOU LEFT MY FATHER!"

Starlock's words might have stung if Warblade had been that same Warblade from long ago. But he was changed. And the new Warblade only laughed as he watched her stalk away. "Go. Go now and enjoy your freedom while you yet have it. A new day is dawning and you will find yourself under far different circumstances than which you now fare." *And,* he added, *the only decision that you will be making will be how to best fill your days to better serve me.*

Dane woke to the sound of elvish voices arguing in their own tongue. Soon the others would be up and they would all be on their way. He yawned and looked up at the morning sky and thought about everything he had experienced since leaving Hartland. Things he'd seen that most people only hear about in fairy tales. Dwarf-warrens! Elven cities! And even Bounders!

What tales he would tell when he finally returned home. He smiled as he thought of what his mother would say: *"Dane Strongbow! Stop making up stories and go to your room. Honestly, the things you say. You get more and more like your uncle each day."* He missed his mother, and his father, and Jules. He wished he knew for sure whether Jules had made it back to the barracks. *Probably, if he was hungry enough.* He chuckled softly. The first thing he'd do once he got back was buy his portly friend the biggest steak his eyes had ever seen. But if he was going to do that then he best start finding a way to win some coins; he sat up and patted the dice in his pocket, then frowned, he'd have to be extra careful, the Captain seemed to delight in taking away all his hard-earned winnings.

Starlock bade them mount up, and they traveled the Pass without further incident, coming to the end just as darkness fell. Camber sighed as he ate his rations cold. Frost-Eye and Crescent sat down beside him and the three of them passed the night in quiet conversation while they watched Dane try to cheat Lockjaw and Lightfoot out of their valuables.

"Do you have any family?" asked Camber.

"Yes," answered Frost-Eye. "Our parents live just outside of Illianther. Not far from the falls. We came to Illianther to study when we were of age."

"Of age? You mean you're still in school?" Cripes! He and Dane finished school over a year ago.

"An elf's education is a lengthy one, and it takes years to complete even the most minor requirements, but we visit our folks as often as we can spare it."

Crescent grinned at his brother. "I at least visit them. You have not been home since your Naming Day."

Frost-Eye lowered his head. "Ahhh, to deprive them of my good looks whilst they are forced to look upon the not-so-fortunate other son, 'tis a tragedy."

"What's a Naming Day? Is it like a birthday?"

"Not a birthday but something like that," said Crescent. "We Elves are immortal and count only certain birthdays. The Coming of Age is considered by far the most important milestone. It is generally celebrated at the one hundredth year after birth and is also the day we select our names."

"But I don't understand. If you have no names before that then what do your kinfolk call you when you are elflings?"

"We have names, but on this particular day we are given a choice to keep the name we've had all our lives or choose a new one. The name we choose on our Naming Day will forever define who we are."

"Crescent and I both changed our names to what they are now," said Frost-Eye.

"Each milestone after that is referred to as our Naming Day and we celebrate our individuality not our age."

Camber liked this concept rather than counting birthdays. "So how do you celebrate your Naming Day?"

"It depends," said Frost-Eye. "Each elf celebrates his or her day in a special way. I like to sit quietly and reflect on my place in the world."

"And I like to be around friends and family," Crescent chimed in.

"You have always been too flamboyant."

"And you are far too reserved."

"Both of you are tiresome," said Lightfoot as he rolled the dice. "C'mon doubles!"

The next day the company skirted the Dragonspine, soon they would have to turn east and then cross the Razorhones. As they neared the ridge that marked where Thayne the Bold had led his people, along with a host of Elves and the armies of the Dwarves into the Southlands, the Ranger's Captain changed course so that they now traveled adjacent to the Ironfist Mountains and the snow-capped peaks of the Dragonspine were behind.

The landscape transformed from sloping hills dotted with towering evergreens to rolling grasslands with few trees, save for white-barked beech and stunted alder. A bitter flavor lay heavy on these parts and even the horses felt its wretched taste as they plodded single file, heads bowed low and tails dragging.

At last they crested a hilltop crowned with broken boulders and rubble that may have been part of a wall; a single slab of granite stood upright like a finger pointing at the dismal sky. They stored their packs on either side of the stone, forming a barrier that did little to keep the chill from their bones.

"What is this place?" Dane asked, somehow he had acquired, not one, but two blankets, and he wrapped them around his body, exposing only his face.

"It was once a settlement; tall and proud were its people. But the jungti came down from the mountains and raided their village, and they were forced to fight or flee. In the end they were no match for the jungti who were many and the people too few." Lightfoot's words were short; he too felt the weight of gloom.

"Jungti," repeated Dane. It was a familiar name. Yes, even in Hartland the jungti were known. The name itself was used to frighten small children into behaving, though he suspected his own mother used it a bit too freely. There was only so many times one could threaten that the jungti would come and take you away before the warning lost its effect.

"Bah! Jungti." Warblade sat down between them. "One of the Elder's many mistakes."

"What do you mean?" Dane huddled further into his cocoon.

"When the Caretakers were running about messing with the world while it was still in its infancy they created all manner of creatures. Some intentional, some not. The jungti were a mistake. They have the look of men but the mindset of animals. Think of them as a type of Man that never evolved, like your Captain over there."

Dega caught the tale-end of the insult and was about to reply when Lockjaw grabbed him by the wrist. "Leave it alone. He's only goading you."

The dwarf turned to Warblade. "Hawker has at least admitted to his mistakes, and he takes full responsibility whatever the outcome. But *you* - you have much to atone for, and this is probably the only reason Winterleaf sent you on this journey."

Warblade started to say something, but Lockjaw held up his hand. "Ah. I see you readily defend yourself. I wonder how much I say is true?"

The silver-haired elf scowled at the dwarf. "And where is your master now? He has abandoned the boy, and you as well. You should count yourselves fortunate that I am here. You will need more than the skill of a Ranger's Captain to see you safely through these lands, and you forget that I have seen more battles than anyone here. I stood on the fields of N'Amorr, against the greatest host ever assembled under that black banner. We fought day and night, for how long I cannot tell you. There was no end to the sorcerer's armies and they came at us in great waves, and with each renewed attack we were sent closer into the arms of our demise. And there by the grace of all we stood for - the free people of Astaria would have fallen but for the swords of the Janastari. By my bloodied hands are each of you alive today." Warblade stood, towering over Lockjaw. "Something for you to think about Master Dwarf before you open your mouth again," he flipped his cloak over one shoulder so the haft of his sword was clearly visible, and turning on his boot heel he stalked away from the group.

That evening Dega set the watch so that this time he had the last shift, and more importantly, he was by himself. The Ranger's Captain needed to reflect on things, and for this he needed some privacy. He stared up at the early morning sky. The stars were visible with no clouds to dim their bright lights. The Great Bear chased The Serpent across the path of Lightfoot's Hunter. Fall was over and winter was here. *Winter.* Had they really been gone for four and half months? He stood, walked the perimeter of the campsite coming full circle, then leaned against a tree.

War. It was happening so fast. And because of what? *A boy?* Not just a boy, one who harbored a lethal power with enough force to destroy us all. *Camber Bloodstone.* Dega laughed quietly, remembering a time when he used to go out of his way to make trouble for Camber and Dane. Now here they were again. This time under a far different set of rules. He was their Captain. Sworn to protect them. Bring them out of danger or die trying. Do whatever it takes to put a stop to the Easterling King. *And this War.* Would it really decide once and for all who wins and who loses? Somehow he doubted it. Too much killing.

Always too much killing. Dega surveyed the sleeping forms huddled around the fire. His eyes came to rest on Camber and Dane. They shouldn't be here. Far too young to be mixed up in this business.

He sighed softly, recalling his first kill. It had not been glorious. It hadn't even been heroic. *It had been senseless.* A waste of a life. The boy not much older than himself at the time (and they not much older than Camber and Dane) belonged to a band of Southlanders who were ambushing traders and taking their goods.

Dega, fresh out of training and this his first mission, was the youngest and the least experienced, and the officer in charge made sure he stayed well behind the others when they launched their attack. But the boy had somehow broke through the line, and he drew his blade and came at Dega. The Captain had been sorely tested that day, taking more than his share of steel, and had very nearly lost his life, right then and there. It might have been the end of Dega Darkhawk, but for a freak accident that had suddenly turned the tide in his favor.

The young Southlander tripped on a tree root and pitched forward onto Dega's sword. He slumped unceremoniously to the ground, leaving Dega to wonder what had just happened. He drew his blade from the boy's soft stomach; its shiny surface now sticky red with blood.

The shock at seeing the gore-covered blade and the boy's body collapse to the ground was too much. He grabbed the youth by the shoulders and shook him vigorously. But the fire was gone, replaced by death's lifeless gaze, and he realized that this boy would not be waking up. He had taken a life, and it made him sick. Without any regard for his own safety, Dega dropped his sword to relieve the contents of his stomach on the grass. The commanding officer in charge had come up behind him, and placing a hand on his shoulder he had said. "Do not take it personal son. When all is said and done, War is just a business like anything else, and killing is just part of the package."

Dega frowned, the first of many burdens to come; he woke the others, everyone except Starlock. She had slipped off earlier and he wasn't about to go chasing after her.

"Have you decided on our intended route?" asked Lockjaw, appearing beside the Ranger.

Dega shook his head. "No." He started to walk away, then turned. "What are we fighting for? Your people. My people. The Elves." The dwarf looked up, and Dega spoke softly. "What is it that we hope to accomplish? What are we fighting for?" He had to know. Whose idea in the grand scheme of things had decided what side was the side of right.

Lockjaw was slow to ponder the Captain's question, such was the nature of dwarves, who believe anything worth considering should not be rushed. At last he simply said, "Love."

Dega nodded, and went to saddle his mount. Lockjaw watched him go. "Love," he repeated. Shard's locket vibrated gently in his hand.

The Razorhones were well named; sharp and jagged like lion's teeth; narrow trails with many twists and turns that if not for the nimble feet of the horses would likely see someone fall to his doom. There was no turning back, and no possible way to do so on the ledge they now traversed. As they shuffled around the next bend the path widened so two could ride abreast. One of the twins was away in the distance and he signaled Starlock with the flags. "A chasm separates the trail and there are signs of jungti near the crossing." The elf made a motion with her arms. The flags moved again. "The bridge will not support the horses."

"What are you saying?" Dane asked, he did not like where this was going.

"We'll be turning the horses loose once we reach the bridge."

"What?! So now we have to pack everything on foot? Isn't there another way around?"

Dega frowned, he too didn't like the idea of having to leave the horses, but he knew that if they were going to chance it through the jungti hive then they would not be able to bring their steeds. "How much farther?" he asked.

Starlock waved at the other elf. The flags answered. "About an hour's ride, not far."

"Then let's break here and divvy up the packs. We'll have to travel as light as possible, which means we will have to discard everything except food."

The company rode a little further then dismounted where the trail widened into a flat grassy glade. The horses were stripped of their packs and quickly went to work on the grass. Dega and Starlock searched through saddlebags, tossing much of what they had brought aside while Dane hovered nearby, pestering the Ranger's Captain while he rifled through the bags.

"You're not chucking that are you?" He picked up a hatchet that Dega had thrown off to the side.

"It's only good for splitting wood. We don't need it," and he snatched the axe out of Dane's hands, tossing it back to a growing pile of discarded items. Dane waited until Dega turned his head then quickly rescued the hatchet from its lofty position atop the unwanted items; he tucked it into his belt (under his cloak) and went back to peering over the Captain's shoulder.

Camber sat on the grass with Lightfoot and Lockjaw and they busied themselves with separating the foodstuffs into equal portions. The twins were waiting near the chasm, watching for jungti. Warblade had disappeared. The silver-haired elf finally came back just as they were about to leave. He said not a word to anyone as he pulled the saddle off his mount and leapt aboard the stallion's bare back. They rode the rest of the way in silence and were greeted by the twins at the edge of a glade.

"We had best let the horses go here," said Frost-Eye, surprising Camber by suddenly popping out of the landscape. The cadet looked around but did not see Crescent until the elf rose from where he had been waiting in the shadows. Starlock nodded and they dismounted, pulling the last of their tack from their mounts and stowing it in the brush.

Long stalks of grass concealed the company; Starlock lay between the twins peering out at the bridge. "What's the layout?" she asked.

"There's just the one crossing and it's guarded by jungti at both ends. Four at this end and two at the cave's entrance."

"Six. Shouldn't be too difficult, but I estimate only three hours till sunset, which means if we don't gain entry soon then we'll have to deal with the entire warrior class if we're discovered." Starlock turned away from the chasm. "Jungti sleep during the day so we may be able to use that to our advantage."

"Exactly what are you planning?" Dane wasn't sure he was going to like whatever she was proposing. It sounded like they were going to have to go into those caves and sneak past the jungti.

"We are going into those caves and sneak past the jungti," said Starlock, and she turned her gaze back to the bridge.

Dane blinked. "Okay I've seen enough. How about you Camber? Should we call it a day? Camber and I are leaving now. I do hope you people have a pleasant journey. Be sure to write." The archer started to back away on his knees and elbows.

Dega grabbed him by the cloak as he wriggled past. "Quit fooling around."

Camber peered over the rise at the four guards who sat backs to one another in front of the bridge. "How are we going to get by them?" he asked.

"It's not going to be easy." Starlock crawled up beside him.

A brown and black bird spiraled out of the sky landing a stone's throw away from the guards. It tried to flap its wings but appeared to be injured, and they sat up with interest. The falcon was small but would make a nice snack. Two of them carefully surrounded the bird and they quickly dove to catch it, but the falcon was fast, flapping just out of reach. The warriors chased after, bent on catching their prize. As they disappeared into the bush, two arrows whizzed from the treetops and into the gurgling throats of their companions. In an instant, garments were changed and the twins now stood at the end of the bridge wrapped in animal hides. To the jungti at the other end, it looked as though two had gone off to hunt and the other pair were merely stretching their limbs.

The bird was entangled amid a gathering of ivy creepers and had no chance for escape. The larger of the two warriors bared his sharp yellow fangs, drool formed across his tongue, dripping down his painted chin. This little bird would make such sport before he devoured it. Long brown hands reached out to trap the bird. White light filled his brain, then blackness reached in erasing all thought.

Starlock kicked the body aside and gently retrieved Belia from her entanglement. She cooed softly at the little bird and set it atop her shoulder. The other jungti lay not far from the first one. Dega wiped the gore from his blade on its garb. "Make yourself useful and undress these bodies," he snarled at Dane.

The body was surprisingly heavy, though it looked to be all sinew and bone, and he grunted while Lockjaw fumbled for the leather thongs holding the animal skins. "It looks like a wild ogre, all painted like this." Long lines of red paint, dotted with white, covered every inch of the jungti's tawny skin; colored beads and hemp held each mud-plastered braid in place, and around its neck it wore a necklace of teeth and bone.

Lockjaw handed the skins to Dega, who put them on over his uniform. Dane let the body drop, and Warblade stood impatiently to one side, dressed in the other guard's clothing.

Starlock tied something to Belia's leg and whispered elvish to the falcon before letting the bird go. "She cannot come where we now go, and though she would follow I would not risk her life. I am sending her back to Illianther with news of our location."

The twins kept watch as though nothing important was happening, and the guards at the other end of the bridge hailed their brethren as Dega and Warblade approached. Dega waved, and one guard greeted him with a throaty grunt. The Captain grunted back, but by the time the guard noticed that these were not his nest-mates, it was too late. Dega pulled his blade free, and wiped it on the animal skin, then flipping off the headdress; he motioned for the others to cross.

The air was stale and carried an incredible stink. Wet walls, barely visible in the dark, had not the straight precise lines of the dwarf-warrens, but rather a roughly hewed and irregular appearance. The twins went up the tunnel first, using hand signals to warn the others what lay ahead. Starlock went next, followed by Dega, Lockjaw, Lightfoot, Dane, and Camber. Warblade brought up the rear; he moved his sword so it now fastened across his back.

The company came to an abrupt halt. "One of the twins has signed to Starlock that we are coming up to a nesting area," Lightfoot whispered. "We will have to crawl to avoid being seen."

Dega nodded, he knew these caverns; dark twisting passages that wound their way deep into the heart of the jungti hive. The Captain hit the ground when he came to the next bend and the entire company wriggled forth on their bellies down a sloping culvert strewn with loose rock.

At last they were able to stand, but the path was narrow with a sheer drop on one side. "I hope we don't have to come back this way," whispered Dane, and Camber nodded.

"This trail leads down into the belly of the mountain and who knows where else," said Lightfoot; he took a torch from the wall. "But your Captain has assured us that we will gain the other side by following the stream," he pointed to running water trickling down the passage.

"That's only if we can stay undetected," Warblade's voice came up from behind. "It's only a matter of time until one of them finds the garments then discovers the guards."

They scrambled across slippery rocks and into another chamber, this one unoccupied. A perfect square. All debris had been removed from its smooth dirt floor; a stone block with a flat tabletop marked the chamber's center. Deep grooves in the floor, an inch and a half in diameter, ran the length of the room from table to corner where they converged upon a trough covered with wooden bars.

"A ceremonial altar," muttered Starlock, running a finger through sticky black grime covering the table and coloring the crude drain.

"What kind of ceremonies do they hold here?" asked Dane.

"Sacrifices," answered the elf. "Humans mostly, sometimes elves."

"The jungti are a bane to dwarves as well," said Lockjaw, and he spat on the altar.

The twins signed all was safe, and they began another long descent down a winding path. *The hive*; a honeycomb of intersecting tunnels and open caves. *One slip – one sound* – they would have no chance against the swarm of jungti huddled in the pockets below. The noise of rushing water grew louder, and the air, heavy and damp – no way around the waterfall and no going back.

"Blocked!" said Lockjaw; he studied the waterfall, then leaned out as far as he dared. "Ah, all is not lost," he added. "I can see a way around." He turned his bearded face to Starlock, wet from spray. "But we have to swing across, then down."

"Rope," she said, holding out her hand, and Dega dug into his pack and pulled out a thickly twined cable; he uncoiled it and passed it to the elf. "Master Dwarf," she said, addressing Lockjaw, "do you have anything that we can fasten to the other end?"

"Here." Dane pulled out the hatchet.

"Where'd you get that?" Dega frowned at his cadet.

"Ummm… waste not, want not?"

Starlock tied the rope to the hatchet. "Come here boy, we have need of your talent," and she motioned for Dane to come join her at the very tip of the ledge. "Can you see the gap between those boulders?" Dane nodded. "Do you think you can hit them? You have only one chance. If the rope drops then we risk alerting the jungti."

The mist around the falls lay heavy, distorting his line of sight and slicking his grip, but Dane let instinct be his guide; he carefully calculated the angle and speed required to hit this target, and swinging the rope three times, he released it with an outstretched arm. The hatchet landed with a 'tink' on the other side, and he slowly drew back until he felt it catch, then giving a tug he handed it to Starlock.

Camber let his breath out. "Will it hold?"

"I'll go," Warblade volunteered. "I can secure the line from the other side," he gave Starlock a smile, "and if I should happen to fall then Starlock will get her wish." He took the rope and clambered as far down the rockface as he was able, then pushing off, he disappeared into the wall of water. A few minutes later the rope reappeared and Lightfoot caught it up. One by one they swung out over the gap and through the waterfall, and each time Lightfoot reached out into the dark to retrieve the rope. Finally it came to be Lockjaw's turn, and the dwarf's face blanched as he took hold of the line. "Perhaps I can go the long way around and meet up with the group later," he said.

"Bye-bye," Lightfoot pushed him off the rock.

"I'm not readayyyyyy."

The rope swung back and the elf passed it to Dane. There was no need to coax the cadet; he took the rope and pushed away with the same enthusiasm reserved for the young and the bold.

"Your turn," Lightfoot said.

Camber climbed down to where the elf was perched. His knuckles whitened as he gripped the rope; he shut his eyes tight the moment he felt himself airborne. Water splashed his face as he passed through the falls; he opened his eyes when he felt a strong tug on the rope as Dega reeled him in. In moments Lightfoot had joined them.

"Now what?" Dane untied his hatchet. "The path doesn't cut through here. It looks like we've reached another dead end." The ledge was little more than a precipice; solid rock rose up around them, and far below, the river coursed angrily between its narrow bed.

"We go down," said Dega, and he secured the rope just below the rock shelf. "I'll go," he said, and lowered himself to where he tied the line. For some reason he felt it necessary to be first since Warblade had already tested the swing across the falls. Down the rope he went, dropping the last few feet into the water below.

Camber went last, twice he nearly fell, but for a miracle he managed to hang on. Big shiny droplets clung to his lashes, blurring his vision; friction burned his palms, and when he ran out of rope he let go, dropping into the current and losing his balance. Someone grabbed his shirt and he found his feet.

The roar of the river was truly deafening, words were wasted since the only objective seemed to be finding a place where the company could climb ashore. Starlock brought up her hand. She pointed to the embankment. A jungti warrior stood near the entrance of another tunnel, his painted torso was turned away from them, and he did not see Starlock take Dane's bow, nor did he see her rise up out of the water on Warblade's shoulders, but he did hear a loud whistle. He turned at the sound just as the arrow pierced his throat. The company splashed ashore, and Starlock put her finger to her lips; she sent Frost-Eye down the tunnel.

The elf reappeared, he held up four fingers then pointed to the warrior. Starlock, Warblade, and Dega drew swords. They followed Frost-Eye down the tunnel; the glint of steel marking their progress until they disappeared from sight.

The waiting was almost unbearable; the silence a heavy reminder that they were unwelcome guests in the heart of hostile territory.

A shout erupted - cut off in mid-pitch. Three sharp whistles followed on the heels of the dying note.

"GO!" Lightfoot jumped to his feet. Down the tunnel they sprinted to where Dega and the others were waiting. More than four, Camber counted the bodies as he ran after the Captain and around the base of an ancient fountain; the natural geyser sprang from the very core of the rock splashing mineral-enriched water on the faces of the dead.

They raced through the cavern, stumbling over uneven ground and squeezing through openings no bigger than cracks in the mountain. The alarm had been raised, and now the entire hive joined the chase.

"We stay close to the stream," Dega breathed; his chest heaved, gulping air into his lungs. He led them down the sloping path, but pulled up short when the path suddenly divided into two separate forks. "Dwarf!" Dega yelled. "Which Way?!"

Lockjaw put his bare hand on the rock. His fingers felt their way down into the very heart of the mountain, reaching into its memory back to a time when it was newly raised. It was very old and had many stories to tell, and he sifted through them all until he came across the one he was searching for. The mountain spoke of a great river that led to the open sea; mighty it was, cutting through rock like a knife. "This way," Lockjaw said, pulling his hand away. Behind them the sound of jungti grew louder; the discovery of their slain nest-mates only served to fuel their hatred for the intruders.

Dega sensed the exit was near. Something in the back of his mind niggled at the familiarity of this particular passage. Years ago he had passed this way and had come out on the other side, though his travels had taken him on a different route. But this path he knew! It led to a great opening in the...

"A Dead End." Lightfoot announced the obvious.

"It can't be!" Dega stared dumbly at the rock blocking their exit.

Lockjaw examined the barrier. "This was not done by the jungti, it was a natural occurrence in the bedrock."

"The water still flows out underneath. We can follow it," and Dega pushed Camber and Dane over the edge and into the river.

Shouting now filled the narrow opening. A spear came whistling through the tunnel, and the sound of many feet not far behind.

"GO!" Warblade yelled, drawing his sword.

"Warblade, you cannot take them all!" Starlock drew her own sword.

"Go. They need you. They do not need me, and I owe you much – though you no longer love me."

Starlock watched as he charged up the tunnel to meet jungti head-on, and in that moment she was reminded of the fearless Warblade of old. "You are wrong," she whispered, and dove into the fast-flowing stream. The current pulled her under and she swam along the floor until she came to the base of the mountain, and found an opening with just enough room to squeeze between and out into the strong current of the mighty *Nic'Ash*.

The river seemed to have a mind of its own, and it took great delight in tossing its captives downstream, dashing them against the rocks of its toothy grin and drowning them in the eddies of its open maw. Like a roaring beast it carried the company to the open sea. Camber latched onto Dane, and the two of them were sent spinning over and under the powerful surge. Foam splashed into eyes, momentarily blinding them; water forced its way down throats, beating the air out of lungs.

A volley of arrows greeted Starlock as she and Dega scrambled ashore. It took but a moment to realize what was happening.

"Ambush!" She drew her sword. "To Me! To Me!"

Dega and Lightfoot drew weapons. Jungti poured out from the hills, descending on the party as it gained the shore. Lockjaw swung his axe, fending off the few who got past the Captain and Starlock, and giving Frost-Eye a chance to climb out of the river.

"Where's Camber!" Dega yelled, turning just in time to avoid a spear. It whizzed past his head and buried itself in the soft muddy banks of the Nic'Ash.

Lockjaw turned, but did not see the cadets. Before he could answer, a horn rang out, blasting across the valley like a mighty gale. The jungti broke and ran, but they did not get far. Over the grassy plain rode an army, swift and proud. Moonlight bounced off shield and armor, illuminating the tips of a hundred lances, glinting steel on long wooden shafts impaling jungti as they sought to escape.

"What then have we here?" the leader commanded; he spoke the common tongue slowly, as if he had to think of the words first before putting them to speech.

"We are allies of the Men of Caldorn, and of your Kingdom as well, my Lord." Dega bowed as low as he would for any man. He knew by their leader's accent that these men were kin to King Silvan's people.

"How can you say so?" The chieftain said, and he pointed his lance directly under the chin of Starlock. "You travel with the strangest company. How can I say you are not then spies?"

Starlock looked up at the horseman, and she slapped away the lance and raised her sword. "NO!" Dega tried to stop her. But she already held it out, ready to strike down the warrior. In a blink of an eye, no less than fifty lances hemmed the Janastari from all sides.

"*Bind them!*" The Chieftain commanded in his own tongue, and in the common tongue he said to Dega. "You have the look of a soldier. I do not doubt your word. I have seen this uniform before. But know this," he paused to make sure he chose his next sentence carefully, so that there would be no misunderstanding, "you are now our prisoners, and we will take you to sit before our King. It will be upon his judgment whether you speak the truth or not, and he will decide your fate. But if escape you try, I will take this matter into my own hands."

Dega nodded; he handed his sword to the two soldiers who moved in to tie his hands. Following his lead, the others stood quietly while weapons were confiscated and their arms bound. For a moment he thought Starlock might try to resist, such was her nature. But she allowed herself to be tied to the back of a packhorse without so much as batting an eyelash. Dega could see her face clearly as he rode alongside, and knew she was already planning an escape.

XII

Foreign Affairs

Gareth closed the door to his room. He had to sit and think for a minute. A sharp tap at his door, and Bonner's head peered into the room.

"A messenger is here," he said, saluting the Lieutenant.

"Where?"

"He's waiting in the boardroom. It's urgent."

"Fine. Tell him I'll be there in minute."

Bonner nodded, and turned to go.

"Corporal," Gareth called, and Bonner stepped back into the room. "Is it another Elf?"

"No. It's one of Thorson's people."

Gareth nodded, Admiral Thorson commanded Thayneland's fleet. He splashed his face with water; the stress taking its toll in the form of discoloration around his hazel eyes; that and lack of sleep. He quickly changed his shirt, grabbed his overcoat, took one last look in the mirror and strode out the door and down the hall to where the naval commander's man was waiting.

"Hurry!" Sal ushered his friends up the stairs to the LT's private suite. That messenger couldn't have come at a better time. He tried the door handle.

"Locked!" whispered Jules, that was fine by him; he really wanted no part of this.

"No problem," Sal winked, and he produced a metal pin about an inch long. Jules rolled his eyes as he watched his friend jam the pin into the keyhole and start jigging with the lock. Success! The door creaked open.

"Watch the corridor, if you hear someone give a low whistle then try to stall them."

"I hope you know what you're doing," Hansil was about as thrilled with the plan as Jules.

"You two have no sense of adventure. I should've brought Bon and Caleb. Now go." He directed them to their places and slipped inside the Lieutenant's apartment.

The cadets stood at opposite ends of the hall; every time footsteps echoed down the corridor they exchanged a fearful look; the tension playing across each face like the painted hand of guilt would not subside until the footsteps had retreated to another room. Jules mopped his brow; sweat streamed down his forehead in big wet droplets.

Sal came out of the room and called his companions over, he checked the doorknob, then took Jule's handkerchief and wiped the handle. "There, that outta do it," he handed the cloth back to the portly cadet. "Let's go find the others."

Gareth gave the messenger his reply and returned to his quarters, *echh... it's wet...* his fingers slid off the doorknob and he wiped his hand on his coat, then trimming the lamp by his bed he wrote the entire conversation with Thorson's messenger in his diary. Gareth was a thorough man; he left nothing unchecked, part of the reason he and Dega got along so well; the brooding officer trusted him with the sort of information he would never reveal to anyone else, not even his superiors. Such is why he happened to know certain details about Camber Bloodstone that even his friends were unaware of. The power the boy could channel was jaw-dropping, and he shuddered at what might happen if the cadet were ever to fall into the wrong hands.

He flipped to his notes on the Captain's last message. *The Hook.* Seems risky. Here they were practically marching the boy into the hands of the sorcerer. Not Dega's decision, but some council; he knew the Captain would never place a green cadet in danger, and certainly not send such tempting bait. Might as well dangle the lad on a string. But Gareth found something else disturbing in the Captain's latest letter. Dega had also advised against sending troops into the Eastlands until he deemed it safe. He ran his finger across the page. Yes, here it was. *Change of plans – his ally is an Immortal – Death waits in the East.* Gareth frowned as he reread the words. It had to be someone, or something truly evil, else Dega would not have sent the warning. He read the next line – *Hold the South.*

Hold the South. That's just what their forces have been doing over the past few months. Already five thousand men had joined

Stonefinger's armies, and even now he knew the Elves would be with them soon. This was shaping up to be a bloody campaign that would make N'Amorr seem like an afternoon at the county fair.

Gareth closed his diary and placed it back in the drawer. He buckled on his sword, and went to find Bonner. Thorson's man had said the sorcerer's warships had already engaged Thayneland's fleet, and pockets of Eastern troops had been spotted on this side of the Barrier. War was underway.

"But how are they supposed to cross the Hook?" asked Bon. The five cadets had gathered in the room that belonged to Jules and Hansil for their "after-supper" talks.

Sal held up his hand as the other cadets started pondering the possibilities of such a move. He quickly called their attention to the fact that Camber and Dane were traveling with a band of elves, and a dwarf, and of course the Captain. His face flushed with pride at gleaning this tidbit from the LT's room. "It just might be foolhardy enough to work," Sal explained, hopping off the table. "Think of it. Who's going to notice them sneaking through the sandbox when there's a bigger problem, like a fleet of warships in your backyard." He paced the floor. "I wish I knew exactly what the LT is planning for us. It makes me wonder if we'll have a larger part to play in this war yet."

"You don't suppose we're going to have to join up with all them that's traveling down to the Borderlands do you?" asked Caleb.

"No," said Sal, and he stopped his pacing. "No, I don't think so. Remember, we're the last line of defense for the North. But it is possible that we may see action if an attack were to come from another direction. Let's hope Thayneland keeps her guard up. I don't really want to think about the possibility of the Eastern armies coming down from the North."

"They can't."

All heads turned, and Jules blushed violently at having to take center stage.

"Why not?" asked Bon.

"Because. It's all snow and ice up there. Even if they get past Thayneland's fleet their ships would still have to travel through miles and miles of frozen ice. Don't you people ever listen? We discussed this exact same topic months ago."

"But what if that's exactly what they want us to think? What then?"

said Bon, and he hopped to his feet. "And what about the Bounder that attacked you in the woods? How do you suppose it got here, it had to come from somewhere."

Sal shook his head. "There's no sense in stewing over something that hasn't happened yet. I'm sure this matter has already been tossed about at the War council and there's probably a plan in place that we don't know about yet. 'Sides, that's not our biggest worry. I found out the real reason for the Bounder attack."

* * * * * * * *

The image grew fuzzy then disappeared as the door to his private chambers flew open. Sentash glared, and the messenger stopped short of the entrance not sure whether it was wise to continue. "Sire, you have a visitor. It is *She*."

The sorcerer knew exactly who *She* was and he nodded to the guard to take him to where *She* waited, but not before strapping on his sword. No fool was he, and he trusted no one, especially *Her*.

They crossed the courtyard to a building adjacent to one of the castle turrets. Sentash stopped, removed his gauntlet, and placing his hand on the door he let his *mind's-eye* penetrate wood and metal and into the room where a solitary figure waited in the shadows; he could detect nothing else, and so he entered.

The shadows moved, and the figure stepped into the open; heavy robes rustling softly as she turned to face the sorcerer. "Sentashhh," a voice, husky and vapid, greeted him by a name no other dared to use. A tingle ran up his spine; a reminder that he was in the presence of a being who could extinguish his life-force with a snap of her fingers. His hand clutched the hilt of his sword and there he did find his bravado.

"Norii." He kept his eyes on her as she threw back her hood, revealing a face of smoke and shadow and not much else, save two holes that reminded him of eyes; they glowed a dull green and he felt sick to his stomach if he stared too long. He sucked in his breath, hiding his unease. "Why have you come?"

She glided up, touching his face with her cold dead fingers. "I've come to tell you that I've kept my part of the bargain." Her breath blew gently in his ear, a faint trace of evil, softly assaulting his senses. "I have captured *He* who dwells in the earth, and imprisoned him within his own element. You are free to act as we planned. The others will not hinder you, for they are preoccupied with their search. They will not find him. I have hidden Defél well, though it has cost me much."

"And Stornoway Hawker? What of him?" He drew back until he felt the safety of the door pressing from behind.

"Jessa is with them, so will be of no consequence. Do not fear. If he steps in then I will be waiting." She held aloft a black metallic globe in her shadowy hands. "*Look*. Look what I have brought you." She waved the orb in front of his face. "This will help you win the War. I will show you how to make them, and you shall arm your forces with these spheres, and they will inflict damage upon your enemies far greater than any thrust by sword."

* * * * * * * *

Three men dead and two mortally wounded. The Chieftain of the Fighting Blue-Feathers surveyed the carnage with an experienced eye.

"Why don't we execute her now and be done with it," his second-in-command voiced his demand for justice.

"No."

"Why not?!" Two of those dead men had been his friends, and for good measure he kicked the elf in the ribs.

"Enough." Gerharte stopped his second from inflicting more damage to the prisoner, who lay with hands and feet bound on the blood-stained grass where she had taken as many men as she could in her attempt to escape. "You know the law. Only King Halstaff can decree punishment for such a crime. All must be brought before him to be judged." He checked the ropes. "Keep two men with this one at all times." As he stood he grabbed the sleeve of his subordinate. "Do not take the law into your own hands Tharn, otherwise you be no better than the Easterling."

Dega winced as the soldier kicked Starlock. He did not understand their tongue, but the looks on their faces said as much. Starlock's fate was linked with theirs; one more attempt at freedom might win them all a death sentence. He hoped she had sense enough to realize this when she woke up. He studied his surroundings through a swollen and teary eye, compliments of Tharn, who blindsided him the moment he had leapt to his feet to aid Starlock. But there was nothing he could do, so he did the only thing possible, sit quietly and observe everything while reflecting on the events that had put them all in jeopardy.

Starlock made her bid for freedom sometime during the night. The Janastari gave no indication to what she had been planning since their capture three days ago, barely saying anything to anyone, even when Lightfoot and Frost-Eye spoke to her in the lilting tongue of the elves. If anything she seemed quite willing to do as she was told, something that Dega would never have guessed the elf capable of, especially when handled with such brute force by her captors. But that had suddenly changed as they saw their window of opportunity to find the others grow smaller and smaller while they were transported further away from the banks of the Nic'Ash River.

Starlock carried what Dega considered to be a ridiculous amount of weapons, and not all of them immediately visible. This was overlooked by the men of Girt, and she quickly cut her bonds at first opportunity, and while the encampment lay sleeping, she slipped behind the two guards keeping watch and silently slit their throats. Dega woke when Starlock cut his ropes, but a cry from one of the soldiers returning from his "business" in the woods had quickly roused the others and she was forced to flee or fight.

Dega pulled his hands free, and he jumped to his feet, but did not see Tharn until he felt the blow from his fist. His legs wobbled and he fell to his knees just as Starlock caught another soldier in the eye with one of her stars. It stuck out of his head like a tiny pinwheel; the poison killing him before he had time to blink. The elf sprang onto the back of the nearest horse and took off at a gallop. They brought her back at dawn, unconscious but *alive*, and he whispered a small prayer of thanks for her safe return.

Lightfoot and the others had also been wakened, and they were forced to lie belly down with hands tied behind their backs. They talked quietly, speculating on their fate once they reached Girt, and whether Camber and Dane had survived. Frost-Eye confirmed that his twin was alive but did not know the fate of the cadets. "Crescent and I share a special bond as we are more than just kin, we are twins, and I would know instantly if he were no longer among the living."

"If Crescent has survived then its possible Dane and Camber are alive," Dega said.

"What now?" asked Lightfoot. "Starlock has surely angered these men and I doubt their King is going to welcome us with open arms."

"That is something we cannot control, but we might be able to gain their trust if they can be made to see we fight the same cause

- *against* the Easterling King. From what I gather they think we are his spies, and we must prove we are no such thing. I have not traveled to Vintnorr and have no knowledge of the men of Girt except they are related to Silvan's people in the Borderlands."

"I know something of these people," Lockjaw said, he lowered his voice to a rumble. "Their King has no love for Stornoway Hawker."

"Why doesn't that surprise me," mumbled Lightfoot.

"Shhh," Dega warned. "Why not?"

"They had a falling out over a minor disagreement."

"How minor?"

"Ummm... the King accused Hawker of manipulating his resources in order to bring them under the crown of the Valastari."

"And?" Dega knew there had to be more.

"And... there was an incident."

"What kind of incident?"

"Vintnorr sort of caught fire, but it wasn't all Hawker's fault," insisted Lockjaw.

Dega scowled, it seemed Hawker was a thorn in everyone's side.

"Kind of a meddler isn't he," said Lightfoot. "Though I wish he were here, perhaps he might repeat his performance and extract us from our current situation."

"Dwarf. Is there anyway at all that you might be able to contact Hawker?"

Lockjaw shook his head. "Hawker will show when he's ready, and not a moment sooner. I do not know what is keeping him, but have faith - he will return." The soldiers guarding them broke up their quiet conversation; they untied the ropes that bound their hands and bade them mount up. A day's ride brought them to the outer farmlands of Girt. They would be in Vintnorr by sundown tomorrow.

No fanfare, no parades, no celebration for the men of the Fighting Blue-Feathers. The best warriors in all of Girt; tall and fierce, bright armor, gleaming helms, and the long blue plumes that gave them their name; many wore the scars of battle proudly, quick to put courage on the tip of a sword. The people of Girt regarded them with awe, but such men did not believe in pageantry and frowned upon any such display. Out of respect for their Blue-Feathers, Vintnorr did its best to ignore the soldiers and went about business as though it was just another day.

Gerharte, Chieftain of the Blue-Feathers, marched Dega and company up the steps of a heavily fortified fortress. Six men, dressed in uniform and fully armed, guarded the great bronze doors that led to the King's chambers. They saluted Gerharte as he climbed the steps, and he stopped to speak to them in his own tongue. The doors parted, allowing the company to enter, then closed with a thunderous crash.

Two more guards stood at the arched entrance leading into the royal sanctum and no less than twenty-four lined the carpeted path to the throne. A man who appeared well past his prime sat on a high-backed throne atop a dais. Instead of a crown he wore a circlet of laurels on his snowy head, and in one hand he held a scepter fashioned from ebony, made to look like two dragons, whose serpentine bodies twisted around each other until the tops of their heads met, jaws stretched open, nose-to-nose, capped with a blue jewel sparkling from the space between.

The King stood as the company was made to kneel before him, and Dega could tell by his size and his quick-sure movement that this man had been, and probably still was, a formidable warrior. He carried himself with the grace of a gazelle; his speed belied his age as he navigated the many steps down to the floor to stand in front of the Ranger's Captain.

"I'm told that you were found sneaking across the very edge of my realm." King Halstaff spoke the common tongue perfectly, without the strange accent that plagued the Chieftain and his warriors. "You do not have the look of a Southlander, nor do you look like one of the Easterling's spies. Your uniform tells me that you are a Ranger from the Northlands. Is this true? And if so, what are you doing traveling across these lands in such strange company."

"Sire," said Dega, also with an air of authority, ingrained into his nature over several hundred centuries through only the purest blue-blood though he was not aware of it, and his fierce gaze caught the bold gray eyes of the King as he spoke. "Your wisdom is infallible. We are not Southlanders or Easterlings, and we are allies of neither. We are here by the most unfortunate of circumstances and not because we wish to cause your kingdom trouble. I serve with the Rangers up north and have traveled far and wide, and always with only the welfare of Astaria foremost in mind." Dega paused briefly, and gestured to the others. "These people who stand before you are my companions. We were sent by a council to undertake a very dangerous quest, one that could undo the reign of the Easterling King. I ask that you allow us to leave as friends and not interfere with our task, one of utmost importance for all of Astaria, including your own kingdom of Girt."

Not used to being talked to in such a manner, and only then by someone whose lineage equaled his own, and guessing there was more to this man than meets the eye, the King was careful to disguise his own surprise with his captive's assertive demeanor. "I do not doubt your word. Your face and eyes tell me much," and though he had to stretch his neck to keep his gaze level with Dega's, he did not allow the cool control of his face to lapse into anything less than a superior scowl. "But this one," he pointed his scepter at Starlock. "This one has killed three of my people, and as is the law of this land must be judged for her crimes."

"I understand your concern, I too am saddened by what has happened, for we now realize that the Men of Girt meant to harm us not. But we did not know this at the time of our capture and the elf is a Janastari and sought only to escape so that she might continue the task appointed to us by the Elven Kings." Dega was careful not to mention anything that would include the rest of the company; the less anyone knew about Camber the better chance he had - *if he's still alive.* He meant to find out, but for now he had to abide by Halstaff's wishes until he was free to leave.

"I cannot allow this one to go free without trial, for it is the law of my land handed down by my fathers of old. To do so would invite chaos among my people who would see it as a means of taking matters into their own hands since my word has become so worthless that even outsiders dare to disregard it. You must respect my rule, as do all who abide in these lands. Therefore, I say to you stay here as my guests and move about unhindered through my city, but the one who has committed the crime will stand trial on the new moon, and as is the custom of Girt shall be imprisoned until that day." He watched Dega's face as he spoke, but the Ranger gave no sign that he was affected by Halstaff's words.

"So be it," Dega bowed to the King. "We will abide by your law and accept your invitation." The others bowed, including Starlock, much to the surprise of her companions. Halstaff then dismissed the group asking they join him at his table for the evening meal. Dega nodded, and watched as Starlock was led away.

XIII

Welcome to Shady Haven

Camber rolled over onto his back, something sharp jabbed between his shoulder blades and he sat up. He spotted Dane as the archer got to his feet shaking sand and rock from his soaking wet clothes. Crescent or Frost-Eye, he wasn't sure which, lay face down in the sand not far from where Dane had staggered to his feet. He rushed over to where his cousin now crouched beside the lifeless form and they rolled the elf over.

Crescent! A huge welt across his forehead appeared grossly out of place on his elfin-fair face. Bright red blood flowed from a shoulder wound, staining his torn tunic.

"We need to make a fire," Dane said, and he pointed at the sky. "It'll be dark soon and we need to dry our clothes and keep Crescent warm."

"What happened to the others?"

"Danged if I know. I'm still trying to get my head together after that wild ride down the rapids. We're lucky we came out with only a few bumps and bruises."

"Do you think the Cap will find us?" Camber eyed the banks of the river but saw no sign of the others.

"If I know Dega, he'll find us alright, even if it's just to punish us for disappearing on him," the archer grinned.

They dragged the elf up to where the trees afforded some shelter, then scanned the area for kindling. Camber's sword was still firmly in its scabbard and he used it to chop branches from a nearby ash. Dane had his bow, but had lost the quiver and all its arrows. Both cadets still had rations wrapped in packets, now soggy and even more tasteless than before, and Dane was relieved at finding his dice and he challenged Camber to a few games while they chewed on strips of salted pork.

They awoke next morning to the sun's warming rays beaming brightly on their faces. Dane stood and stretched his legs and was delighted to see that Crescent had opened his eyes. "Can you sit?" he asked. The elf moved to a sitting position; he brought his hand up to touch the crude bandage wrapped around his head. Dane passed the waterskin, and he drank a few drops.

"We lost the others," said Camber.

Crescent nodded as yesterday came storming back like the wild waters of the Nic'Ash. Dane produced the last packet of pork and offered it to the elf; he ate what he could and folded it back inside its wrappings.

"Camber and I are trying to decide whether we should stay here and wait for the others or find a way out of these woods?"

"I do not think it would be wise to wait here," Crescent's voice sounded weak, and he strained to make himself heard. He pointed to the ridge of mountains rising against a smudge of gray. "The 'hones are at our backs and the sun is straight ahead; we have landed on the Eastern shore, whether near the Hook or not I cannot say, but it's best to keep moving. I fear if we stay in one spot too long we might become easy prey for those who serve the Easterling King."

"But what about the others?"

Crescent put his hand on Camber's shoulder using it as a crutch. "I cannot tell the fate of the others but I know my brother is alive. Part of me thinks that he is too far to be catching up with us anytime soon." Camber and Dane allowed the elf to lean on them while the trio hobbled along the forest path. "How can you be so sure?" asked Dane. Crescent winced as a sudden bump jarred his body. "Because we share a bond. All elves are in tune with each other at all times, and Frost-Eye's presence is always next to my heart. But this time it's different."

"How different?" Camber asked.

"It's as if he's far away. Like a fine thread that slips through my fingers. I know he is on the other end but I cannot draw him near."

"Do you suppose he's with Dega?" Dane frowned; he did not like the idea that the others may be farther than just a swim up the river.

"I cannot say for sure, but if Frost-Eye is alive then likely your Captain has survived. And Starlock. It may be they are trying to find a way to cross the river."

After a few hours of walking, Crescent was tired and they lowered him to the grass. Dane went off in search of edible plants while Camber tended the elf's injuries. "It looks like the swelling has gone down." The welt had receded but still appeared nasty.

"Ai! If it were only a head wound I doubt that I would feel so drained, but I fear my shoulder has been clipped by a jungti arrow." He touched the wound, pushing the spot where dried blood crusted over skin.

Camber lifted the torn cloth. "It doesn't look too bad, in fact it's starting to scab over."

"Ah, you probably wouldn't know this," Crescent said; his voice growing weaker, "jungti tip their weapons with poison." He chuckled softly, "Not enough to kill, just enough to render their prey powerless."

"We have to find you help!"

"If you can find me a healer that would be a start."

A sudden noise startled them both and Camber drew his sword. The branches moved and Dane emerged from the bush.

"Berries!" He held up a pouch filled with the fruit. "And look," his other hand proudly displayed several plants with white star-shaped leaves. "Silverthorn."

"I thought you didn't like silverthorn," Camber remarked.

"Not for me – Cripes No! For Crescent."

The elf managed a smile. "I don't care much for it either, but at least it will help slow the poison."

"Poison?" Dane repeated. Camber nodded, and explained about the jungti arrow. They plunked themselves down on either side of Crescent and made a meal of the berries and leftover pork. They did not have any pots, or anything at all that could be used to hold boiling water for the silverthorn, but Crescent showed them how to prepare it without cooking by grinding it up into fine powdery bits and pouring just a dab of water overtop to make a foul-tasting paste.

"The path through the woods widens into a road of some sort. I think it might lead to a village or some homesteads," said Dane, since he had no arrows for his bow he was trying to make a crude sling from his torn cloak and a piece of leather. "Perhaps we'll find a healer if we head in that direction."

"Have you forgotten where we are?" Camber asked. "It's not like a day trip to Cambert."

"I already thought of that. And it occurred to me since nobody knows who we are, no one will suspect we are foreigners if we just act like we belong."

"Except one thing."

"What's that?"

"We have an Elf."

"So?"

"So do you suppose that there are many elves in the East?"

"No problem. We just keep Crescent's head covered."

"Alright. We'll find a village. But if we get caught I'm throwing you at them first since it's your idea."

They let Crescent sleep until it was time to leave, and under night's starry blanket they struck out along the forest road. As they walked they relayed their plan to Crescent. "Dane's right," he said. "There's little chance of anyone finding out who we are if we just blend in."

They had not gone more than a few miles when the path widened into a proper road, and Crescent was able to walk on his own for the first time since they had come ashore. Evidently the poison was still doing its work but had been slowed by the silverthorn.

Dawn filtered across the sky; the air was cool and cloudy, threatening with rain, and by Camber's estimation they had traveled nearly twelve leagues since leaving the forest. Dane had gone on ahead to find a safe place for the three of them to take cover, but as Camber and Crescent walked over the rise of a hill his cousin came in to view wildly waving his arms. At first he thought it meant scramble for cover, but soon realized Dane was demanding they step up their pace, apparently he had discovered something of interest.

A sign hung upside-down by one of three brackets attached to a tilted post. The writing, practically illegible from years of weathering, read: *Welcome to Shady Haven*. Or at least that's what it would have said if someone hadn't painted *Not* above the Welcome part.

"See, we're closer to a town than what we thought." Dane righted the sign so he could determine which way to Shady Haven.

"Funny name," Camber remarked. "I wonder what kind of place it is."

Crescent looked at the sign. "Probably a coastal town. There are many such towns along the Barrier, they thrive on trade with each other and have little in the way of wealth, and so the sorcerer does not bother with them."

"Good. Then we can blend in with the locals until we figure out what to do next." The prospect of a warm bed and a hot meal brightened his spirits, and Dane was pleased with himself for taking the role of leader. "Let's walk a few more miles before we find shelter, if that's alright with Crescent."

"I'm okay for now."

"I would never have guessed there would be villages like back home. I always thought the people here were either soldiers or slaves," said Camber.

"Towns like Shady Haven sprang up during the time of Khollinther. Trade has always been an important commodity and there was no bigger venue than the Candastari city."

"But what about the Easterling King or the K'Ahtars?" asked Dane.

"Sentash had not yet come to power, and not all these lands are governed by tyrants. It wasn't until the end of Khollinther's glory that the strongest emerged as warring factions."

The trio stopped at a fork in the road. Nothing to indicate the way, no helpful sign pointing to Shady Haven. As they pondered their chances at taking the left or the right, a traveler came in to view leading a donkey loaded with far too many packs. The poor animal dragged behind on its lead, head lowered and tail drooping, it stopped, sat down, and protested with a series of long-winded brays until the old man cracked a branch across its dusty hide. Camber's first reaction was to get off the road and take cover. But it was obvious this old-timer and his half-starved beast posed no threat, and as he approached the trio Dane signaled him to stop.

"Excuse me sir. Could you tell us which road leads to Shady Haven?"

"Why?" The man looked mildly surprised at the question.

"Because that's where we're headed," answered Dane.

"Why?"

"What do you mean *why*?"

"'cause any decent folk knows Shady Haven is the armpit of the world," and he spat a chunk of chaw that landed beside Dane's boot.

"Pardon?" If the man had simply said don't go there, or it's not your type of place, he would have been less taken aback.

"Now if you folk be decent, which you seems to be… you ain't spies are you?" They shook their heads. "No, I guess not. You ain't got that spy look. Well if you had any brains a'tal you'd git out of the East altogether. There's a war brewin' and most folk are leaving these shores. Me – I'm hoppin' aboard the next boat that'll have me, and I'm hot-footing it to Girt."

"We need help. Our friend needs a healer," said Camber. The stranger bent his bearded face close and peered at the elf. Crescent's hood partially covered his head but his face could not disguise his suffering. "Yee – he looks like a sick 'un. You might find help in Shady, but I doubt it. Mostly everyone in Shady's out fer themselves, and those that have no jobs are thieves, cutpurses, or worse. Even them that upholds the law are crooked – *some* more than the citizens."

"Well that's where we're headed."

"Head that way then," he pointed to the right. "South fork'll take ya there faster. Ask around for Doc Sudi, folk call him "Stitches" he's about the only honest Doc in town if'n he still be there. And 'luck to ya." He doffed his hat. "C'mon Mabel," he pulled the donkey's lead, leaving them standing along the roadside.

After several hours of walking they came to the first cottages bordering Shady Haven. Most of the houses were little more than rundown shacks; those that were at one time painted had long been left to weather on their own. Windows were boarded, and yards unkempt; weeds growing waist high in some places. A face or two peered out from half-opened doorways as the trio passed, shutting doors tight after deciding the strangers were of no particular interest.

Close to the town's center, tall brick buildings, three or four stories high, towered side-by-side as if to squeeze out the remaining single dwellings. Garbage, bottles, and vermin littered alleyways, spilling into the streets.

"Look out!" Dane grabbed Camber by the sleeve and veered him away from a man lying on the doorstep of what appeared to be a drinking establishment. The drunk rolled his eyes, then vomited all over the sidewalk, splashing Camber's boots.

"That's nice," he said, and turned quickly as two youths ran between Dane and Crescent, nearly bowling him over as well.

"Give it back," said a voice. And a girl, (at least he thought it was girl) grabbed one of the boys with an outstretched arm and held him out to Dane like a butcher holding out a choice chop. The boy struggled at the end of her reach, but she kept a grip on his collar. "Give the man back his coin pouch," she repeated. With a sigh, he handed Dane his pouch. "Sorry 'bout that," she said. "You really gotta watch these streetrats. New in town?"

Dane stared at his pouch then the boy... *how the blue blazes...*

"Ummm, yes," Camber answered. "We're just passing through. Our friend here is very sick and we need to find a healer."

The girl stuck her hand out. "Name's Elspeth Danelle Tonni Charante, but most people just call me Tonni."

"Camber. This is Crescent." He shook the girl's hand.

"And you are..." she looked at Dane.

Snakes and spirits... how did... "Uhh, oh Dane." He tucked his pouch back inside his pocket. The girl grinned. "Pleased to meet you."

Shady Haven, deemed less perilous by day, was dangerous none-the-less. Most of the evening's unsavory element had long disappeared, now replaced by shopkeepers, customers, and carthorses, all crowding the streets. Somewhere in the distance a whistle sounded above the drone of a coal factory; its tall pipes pumping black smoke into a dismal skyline. People pushed and shoved their way around Camber and Dane as they supported a shaky Crescent.

Tonni stuck her hand across his pallid cheek, and a look of concern softened her brow. "We should probably get your friend inside."

"We were told to find a Doc Sudi, I think he also goes by Stitches," said Camber.

"Yes, I know him, but his home is on the east-bank on the other side of the Plaza. Your friend looks like he needs help now." She ran her hand through her closely-cropped hair. "Okay. I probably shouldn't do this, but you can take him back to my place and he can rest while I fetch the Doc."

"How do we know you won't try to rob us?" Dane was still skeptical, securing his coin pouch tightly to his belt.

"Trust me." The glint of steel suddenly appeared in her hand, and she pointed it at the archer. "I could have done that a long time ago."

Camber smiled, but it was Crescent who spoke. "Looks like Dane has met his match."

Dane's face turned three shades of red, and he muttered something about girls who dressed like boys. "Nothing but trouble," making sure she heard that last part.

They followed the strangely garbed girl; she with the boyish haircut and upturned nose wearing breeches and boots instead of flowing skirts and an apron.

"Hola! Tonni – where you be going with three handsome men?" A women's voice called.

"If you're looking to unlock her secrets you'll be sadly disappointed, she'd just as soon give you a black eye for your troubles," another voice belonging to a blonde joined the redhead at a window on the top floor of a seedy looking establishment. The sign on the front read: *Haji's Nest* above a silhouette of two women holding a bottle of wine.

"Come up here. We'll fix you right," and the redhead leaned out the window showing a goodly amount of cleavage. Both girls laughed when they saw how their words had caused the boys to blush.

"You bangtails mind your own business or I'll tell Madame Haji that you're spending more time hanging out windows than on your backs!"

Both heads disappeared promptly. "What was that all about?" asked Camber.

"Oh don't mind them; they get a little excited when they see new folk in town." Tonni stopped at a fruit vendor and stuffed a couple of apples into her shirt, then picking up a third, she walked over to the proprietor who had been busy with a customer and handed him a copper.

"What's a bangtail?" asked Dane. For some reason she laughed at this question as she handed them each an apple. "Whad'ya mean? Bangtails are whores."

"What are whores?"

"You know, women who sell favors." The look on their faces clearly said it all. They had absolutely no idea. She tried again. "Sexual favors."

"What?! Why would someone do that?" Camber asked.

"For money of course," she answered. "Some girls are sold to brothels, others have no choice; their husbands have left them, or worse. Better to be working in a parlor turning tricks than on the street." Tonni gave Camber and Dane an incredulous look. "Don't tell me you don't have whores where you're from? There must be at least one girl you know that'll probably never marry."

"Bridget," they said at the same time.

"She won't settle for anyone unless it's Dega."

"And that's not likely to happen in this life-time," added Dane.

"How will she support herself?"

"It's not like that in Hartland. Bridget lives with her parents, and once they're gone she'll probably run the Sandyman farm with her brother. And even if she had no where to go then the community would pitch in and help out."

Dane nodded. "Everyone in Hartland helps everyone else. We take care of our own."

"Must be nice," muttered Tonni. "I'd like to live in Hartland." She crossed the road and they followed, and she held the door while they carried Crescent inside.

"This is a drinking parlor." Dane waved away a waft of smoke as he entered.

"Welcome to the *King's Arms*. My room's upstairs."

"You live in... in here?"

"Kinda slow isn't he," she said to Camber. Then pushing Dane past several tables filled with the biggest, brutish men he had ever seen, and packing more weapons than even Starlock, she led them to a long flight of rickety stairs; half the rail was missing and the newel on the topmost banister had been broken off.

"It's a favorite haunt of the local patrol. Get's a little rowdy now and then, but it's probably safer than most places given the fact there seems to be a never-ending supply of *off-duty* law-enforcers from the local guardhouse down the street."

They started up the steps until a gruff voice from behind stopped them. "Girl, where's my money?" Tonni motioned for them to keep going and turned around to face the barkeep standing at the foot of the stairs. He did not look all that friendly, especially with that eye-patch covering half his scowling face, and Camber thought it wise to keep moving. "I told you I was waiting for a job. I have one set for tonight, and you'll get your money tomorrow."

"You're three days late on your rent girl. It'd better be tomorrow or I'm throwing your things out the window and lockin' the door." His one eye traveled up the stairs until it came to rest on Dane, Camber, and Crescent. "There better be no trouble either."

"No trouble Patch. I swear."

"Tomorrow. Don't you forget."

"I won't." She turned to follow the boys who waited at the top of the stairs.

A door opened, and a burly man in uniform came down the hall escorted by a buxom blonde wearing a robe and reeking of too much perfume. He kissed her hard and slapped her buttocks. "Till next time," he said, squeezing once more for good measure, and down the stairs he sauntered, pushing Dane out of his way as he passed.

"Well, well, well, what do we have here?" purred the woman, and she sidled up to Dane, wrapping her arm around his.

"Hands off Liselle. These are my guests, they're not for you." Tonni flipped a key out of her pocket and stuck it in the door across from the stairs.

"Three? I've never seen you with any man and now you have three?" The blonde narrowed her eyes; black paint on her lashes so thick they hid their soft brown color. *That, and the garish green on the eyelids,* thought Camber as he watched his cousin extract himself from her naked arm.

"What in the Gods are you up to Tonni?" she crossed her arms.

"Here's a penton," Tonni flipped a shiny coin at the woman. "Keep your mouth shut and mind your own business." The blonde snatched the silver from the air and tucked it into her ample bosom. "You could at least let me have the dark one," she pouted, and took her coin downstairs.

Tonni ushered them into her room and shut the door. "Better put him on the bed," she said. Crescent's face had gone completely white.

"Where?" Dane surveyed the mess; was there a bed under those clothes?

Tonni lit a lamp and placed it on the nightstand; she threw the clothes off the bed and onto the floor. Camber removed Crescent's cloak and helped him to the bed.

"He's an Elf!" she cried. "You didn't tell me he's an elf!"

"Does it matter?" The archer sat in a chair.

"Well yes - and no," she said, staring at Crescent. "We don't get many elves in Shady. If the sorcerer finds out then we might as well kiss freedom good-bye; he'll lock us up, or worse."

"I'm sorry we put you in jeopardy but Crescent needs help," said Camber.

The girl paced back and forth along the creaky planks of the floor. She was not very tall, and her slight body had straight hips and no curves. "Yes, I will help. I said I would. I have to leave soon and take care of some business, but I'll bring Stitches back with me. In the meantime make sure you stay in my room. And for Shikra's sake keep his head covered!" She went into an adjoining room that served as a washing up area and shut the door.

Her voice trailed out from behind the door. "How did you come to be traveling with an elf anyway? And what are you doing in Shady Haven?"

"He's our friend and we ended up here by accident," answered

Camber, he looked over at Dane, not sure how much he should say, but the archer only shrugged.

"That's obvious," she said, coming out of the room. She had changed into black. Black breeches, black high-collared shirt, black boots, and a black cloak to complete the black ensemble. "I meant what are you doing in the Eastlands, most people are leaving these shores not the other way around." She strode over to the far side of the room and pulled a dresser away from the wall.

"Camber and I are Rangers from up North," Dane said, watching the girl pry loose a board from the floor. "We were sent here to do something very important but became separated from the rest of our company." She pulled something out and replaced the board. "You look awfully young to be Rangers, and younger still to be trusted with some kind of mission." She pushed the dresser back over the spot and placed the bundle on the bed.

"What about you?" Dane huffed. "Your not that old either. Yet here you are."

"Ha! I've been on my own for the past five years!" Tonni pointed her dagger at Dane. "Don't forget who rescued who," she snorted. Around her waist she wore a belt (black of course) with many leather thongs, and she began taking items from the bundle and tying them to her belt.

"You didn't rescue us," Dane said. "You probably set that whole thing up just to meet us." She turned to face him with hands on hips. "Why o why would I go out of my way to meet the likes of you!"

Dane stood, pointing a finger at her face. "That's what I would like to know."

She glared at the archer and he raised an eyebrow. All the while Camber watched with a smile, it wasn't often that Dane lost his cool and he couldn't help but laugh.

"What's so funny?" Both turned on him.

"Nothing," he rolled his eyes to the ceiling.

"I've got some stuff to take care of, but when I'm done I'll bring the Doc," and she walked over to the window, opened it, and climbed out onto the ledge.

"Ummm... isn't the door that way?" Dane pointed.

"Yes. That's the door."

"Then how are you going to get down from there."

"I'm not going down. I'm going up." She hoisted herself from the ledge and disappeared from sight. "Stay in the room and don't answer the door. And watch out for Liselle, I think she's sweet on you."

"Women!" Dane flopped into the chair, kicking at the clothes on the floor.

Crescent smiled weakly, "You should watch what you say to the fair sex, they seem to hear only what they want to and everything else is redundant. Ask your Captain if you don't believe me."

Dane was only half listening, his gaze wandered about the room, which was in good need of a cleaning, but nothing short of a fire would probably be of much help. Clutter lay on the floor, on the bed, hanging out of drawers. His eyes roved back to where Tonni had pulled the dresser away from the wall. The archer went in for a closer look and moved the dresser exposing the floor underneath.

"Dane!" Camber jumped to his feet. "Put that back!" Too late. The floorboard was removed and Dane had spotted something. He reached in....and...

"OWWW!" Dane pulled his hand out of the hole. A mousetrap clung to his fingers. "Get it off! Get it off!"

"Serves you right," said Camber; he de-sprung the trap, and placed it back in the hole.

"Bloody hell!" Dane waved his fingers in the air.

"Shouldn't have stuck your hand where it doesn't belong." Camber shook his head as he replaced the floorboard then pushed the dresser back over top.

"I only thought there might be something in there that would tell us more about Tonni."

"Why don't you just try asking her when she gets back?"

"Which makes me wonder what the blue-blazes is she up to that requires her to climb out the window instead of walking out the front door like a normal person."

Tonni scaled the building with ease, having gone this route dozens of times and no longer needing the rope except to cross rooftops when the distance was too far to jump. Rooftops! The most underlooked mode of travel in a city such as Shady Haven. Plus it offered all kinds of advantages, not just for avoiding people, but it afforded a view like none other. You could see for miles in any direction and observe people and places without being seen.

The nighttime breeze offered a myriad of scents that wafted her way, somehow made a little less offensive than the nauseating smells of daytime by the light cool touch of fresh air, and she breathed deeply, washing away the stink that was Shady-Haven. She gave the moon a wink, loving the night, loving the dark; and in a way, the darkness loved her, wrapping its pitch-black arms around its most ardent follower.

A little more than a month ago a ship arrived carrying precious cargo, gemstones to be exact; not the first-rate ones that you'd find in places like Tanebe, nope, these were headed for the only jewelry shop in Shady Haven – pretty baubles for the not so upper class. And Shady Haven, being the type of town it was, did not have long to wait for the rash of thefts and muggings that followed, causing the local pawnshops to triple their regular business.

Tonight Tonni was headed to a particular pawnshop in the Plaza. In that shop she would find a pretty trinket whose stones would fetch a fine price once she removed them; the gold she would give to Patch. *And that should shut his mouth about my rent for the next two months.*

Leaping across two rooftops, she stopped at the edge of the next and took the rope from her belt, swinging it in a wide arc and aiming for the stovepipe across the way. It caught, and she tugged. *Good.* The sudden rush of adrenaline felt wonderfully exhilarating as she launched herself into the air. Better to fly from above and risk getting caught than to be smothered beneath a man. Booted feet hit the side of the building with a soft thunk, and she scrambled the rest of the way up, freeing the rope and fastening it back to her belt.

Two more buildings, then down. The stars twinkled overhead, silent witnesses wrapped in velvet, reminding her she was not alone, and she laughed as she lowered herself down the rope to land neatly on the shelf of the window she had cased only a few hours prior to her run-in with those Rangers. And the tall one had the nerve to call her a child! She took her favorite cutting tool, and using its specially crafted diamond-edge she cut a nice round circle in the glass. Stupid boy, she should've let the little streetrat pick his pocket, that'd teach him a lesson. She chewed up a wad of gum and stuck it to the window, and tugging gently, eased the glass from the pane. *Success.* She reached inside, turning the window's handle. "Child am I? I'd like to see what he'd have to say to me now," and she climbed into the pawnshop.

Dane paced back and forth. The room was small and he had to turn after eight strides. "She's been gone a long time," he said, avoiding a wooden crate in the middle of the room. He paused, the sound of slippered footsteps, too light for a man's, tipped down the hall. He put his finger to his lips and Camber nodded. A soft knock tapped lightly on the door. "Yoo-hoo anyone in there? Boys? Boys?" Liselle's smoky voice filtered through the keyhole. "Nuts!" The slippered feet continued down the hall.

Dane mopped his brow with his coat sleeve. "Hope she doesn't find us, I can't imagine anything worse than being smothered by those oversized melons." He went back to his pacing and Camber sat on the bed examining his father's famous sword. The ruins were remarkably clear even after centuries of wear, and he ran his finger along the haft stopping at the sword's razor fine edge. He grinned at his reflection, noticing the stubble on his chin. The hairs on his face were very fine, not coarse like Dega's or Dane's, and he had to stare hard just to see anything at all. He wondered what it would look like if he decided to let it grow.

"I can't wait any longer!" Dane snorted, his tolerance for boredom was not very high at the best of times, but coupled with the increasing pressure at having to wait on someone else it was almost non-existent. "I'm going downstairs."

"What? You can't. She said not to leave. Besides you don't know the people down there, or this town."

"You worry too much. I just want some fresh air, I'll be right back." He opened the door before Camber could object any further, and down the stairs he went.

Crescent opened his eyes. Fever heated his body and he rolled weakly onto his side, Camber couldn't leave the elf in his present condition; he would just have to trust Dane to come back on his own.

The common room was busy, and none of the gamblers tossing dice, nor the off-duty guardsmen pawing painted women on their laps, or the less than honest mercenaries discussing business with unsavory clients in dark corners seemed to notice the archer.

"Hey! Hey you!" The baritone voice belonged to Patch, and he moved his monstrous form between two tables as Dane passed, but luck was with the cadet and a fight broke out in the corner; the barkeep suddenly had his meaty hands full as he tried to break it up. Dane slipped out the front door and into the quiet dark of night.

Left or right - both directions appeared to lead straight into dead-ends, so he crossed the street and headed back to where he and Camber had first run into Tonni. He laughed as he pictured her; the top of her head barely reaching mid-chest, and here she was ready to go toe to toe with him. What kind of girl runs around in men's clothes anyway?

He passed between two tall buildings emerging on the other side of a square lined with shops, boarded and closed for the evening. *This must be the Plaza.* He started to cross, and quickly turned at the sound of footsteps. Two thugs came up on either side, and Dane sprinted the rest of the way through the Plaza and down the next two streets.

But Dane did not know Shady Haven's labyrinth of twisting streets and the two men had this advantage; they quickly took another route cutting off his escape as he turned the corner.

"Hand over your money punk." Both men were armed, and they backed Dane into an alley; his shoulders pressing against the rough texture of bricks. "Now where ya gonna go?" A piece of steel flashed brightly at his face. The mugger laughed, showing a mouthful of rotten teeth. He moved closer, and as he did his face changed from grin to grimace, his eyes rolled up, his legs buckled, and he slumped to his knees. Dane struck with his knife, sticking it to his belly, but the man was already dead from the dagger buried between his shoulder blades. A shadow fell from above, landing on the mugger's friend, detaching itself just as the body fell forward.

"I thought the cavalry was supposed to rescue people *not* the other way around," Tonni retrieved her dagger from the first thug. Before Dane could answer, a voice hollered into the alley. "Hola! Who goes there?"

"Night-watch!" she said. "Quiet now. Let me do the talking."

"Hola! We're just heading home."

"Elspeth? Elspeth is that you?"

"Just wonderful," she muttered, rolling her eyes. Only a handful of people used her real name. "Yes Braun." Of her seven brothers, two were dead, one had moved to the Southlands, and four served in the guard. As luck would have it the youngest of the four, and the most patronizing, (him being a whole two years her senior) surveyed the scene with a critical eye; his gaze came to rest on Dane.

"Who's this?" His hand went for his sword.

"He's a friend," she said.

Braun nudged one of the bodies with the toe of his boot. "What happened?"

"These two were all set to rob me, and my friend here came to my rescue."

Dane thought she sounded overformal, and he wondered how much of it Braun believed.

Braun bent down to examine the face of the closest thug. "This 'un is a known felon," he stood up and drew himself to his full height but still came up a half head shorter than the cadet. "Said you were heading home?" he asked. Tonni nodded. "Then you wouldn't happen to know anything about a break-in at one of the pawnshops near the Plaza, would you?" Her costume raised his suspicions, and he was already forming his own thoughts on what actually happened.

"Couldn't tell you," she said with a shrug.

Braun looked as though he didn't believe her. "I better escort you home then."

"It's okay Braun, I can take care of myself. Now run along and get back to your duties like a good little patrolman."

"Actually we were going for the doctor," Dane butted in. "We have a sick friend who needs his help."

"Stitches?"

"Now look at what you've done," Tonni punched his arm. "Now he's gonna want to come with us."

"Yeah. Do you know him?" The archer ignored her.

"Well his house is on the east-bank, a good walk from here. But you shouldn't be walking through that neighborhood at night; it's not even safe by day," Braun answered, and he and Dane started walking in the direction of the doctor's house leaving Tonni standing by herself.

"Hey!" She glared at their backs.

"Your sister's kinda strange."

"I know. She's wanted to be a boy since she was five. I remember this one time, before our parents died, she crawled down a well...." Braun's voice rambled on in the distance.

"I'm not deaf you know!" Her wrath was wasted, since both young men were now several feet down the road discussing her less than redeeming qualities.

Shady Haven at night had all the charm of a festering sore, and Dane was grateful that Braun had decided to come with them; his uniform cleared a swath through painted ladies and drunken revelers, who upon noticing the double-banded stripes of the night-patrol, quickly stepped out of the way instead of finding some excuse to accost the trio.

If Shady Haven was the armpit of Astaria, then the east-bank was its pimple. An abysmal blight in the middle of a wretched stew; two miles of condemned rubble – unfit for humans, or otherwise.

And the Stink! Dane thought he was going to lose the contents of his stomach right then and there. The stench of human waste and the cadaverous stink from a nearby charnel house had no effect on Tonni or her brother. *Must be used to it.* He brought his sleeve up to his nose as they crossed yet another patchwork of streets identical to the last three intersections; the only difference being that the buildings on this street were fewer and farther apart.

"Well here you be," Braun muttered; he held open the rusted iron gate in front of the Doctor's house. Surprisingly, it was one of the few places that seemed well cared for, even the patch of grass looked recently manicured. Braun led the way across the flagstones and banged his huge fist on the door. Dane stamped his feet; the evening air was cool and the thrill from his recent adventure had already ebbed away, taking with it the rush of adrenaline that had kept him warm.

A peephole in the center of the grainy door opened and an eye looked over the trio, this followed by a fumbling of bolts and chains and the door opened to a narrow slit. "Yes?" a man's voice asked.

"Stitches! It's Tonni. Open up. A friend of ours is really sick. He needs help – Fast!" Tonni pushed herself inside, jamming her boot against the door and wedging it firmly in place.

"Tonni? Tonni and Braun Charante." The door opened allowing all three to spill into the hall. "What in the name of Shikra are you doing here so late... and who's this?" A middle-aged man of average height but with an impressive build, the underlying bulk of muscle still noticeable despite his advancing years, carefully eyed the trio with his penetrating gaze. This was not a man who could be fooled, and something told Dane that he had better tell the truth or they would receive no help from this stranger.

"Excuse me sir," Dane interrupted. "We have a friend, a traveling companion, who is in dire need. He's been poisoned by a jungti arrow and we are unable to move him. We ask that you come with us. I'll pay whatever you charge at this hour."

"A jungti arrow? What? Where are you from boy?" No sooner had the Doctor asked this, then another voice shouted from the next room. "Dane?" A head popped around the corner. "Dane!"

"CHANCE!" Dane jumped passed the Doctor and grabbed the figure now standing in the hallway.

"Dane... what the... how... " The former Ranger shook his nephew; astonishment gave way to concern. "Why aren't you in Hartland?"

"Camber and I... "

"Camber! Camber's here with you?!"

Dane nodded.

Chance held the cadet at arm's length, his face lost its initial warmth; in its place was a serious frown. "Where is Camber now?" he said, and Dane felt a shiver run down his spine. Never had his uncle been so grim-faced in all his life.

"He's in my apartment," Tonni shoved her way past Stitches and stood with hands on hips staring at the dark eyed stranger; she fingered the handle of her dagger as if trying to decide whether he was friend or foe. Braun's hand came up and landed on her shoulder, squeezing it with just enough force to cause her pain and reminding her that this man was no cutpurse. She took her hand off the hilt but kept a wary eye on the man who Dane had embraced.

"He is safe then?" Chance said, and Dane nodded. "Is he sick?"

"No," the archer answered. "Our friend is the one who's been poisoned. He's an elf." Both Sudi and Chance exchanged a look. "Listen son, maybe you better tell me the whole story." Chance put his arm around Dane, guiding him into the kitchen. "All of you had better come in."

Stitches agreed. "I'll get my bag and you can tell us everything." He turned to look over his shoulder as he started up the stairs. "Jungti arrow?" Tonni nodded. "It's a good thing he's an elf then. The poison will not have harmed him as much as it would a mortal." He bounded up the stairs to retrieve his kit.

"And we've been traveling on our own since." Dane finished his tale and waited for his uncle to say something, as if hoping his adventure might have made an impact on Chance's own wealth of heroic deeds. But Chance just sat there rubbing his jaw, and it seemed he knew more than he let on, particularly with what the wizard had told Camber on that first day of their meeting.

"Hawker eh?" Chance said. "I daresay there's more to come."

A shadow moved against the window, so quick that it might have been a flicker from a candle; but Chance knew better, and he kept talking while he moved about the room, acting as though he suspected nothing out of the ordinary. "It was Hawker who sent me here to find Drake," he said, and slowly walked to the backdoor, resting his hand lightly on the knob.

"Drake? Dega's father?" Dane asked; why in the blue-blazes was his uncle standing by the door. "Is he still alive?"

"Yes and yes." Chance said, and he opened the door and launched himself out into the night. All four jumped up from the table and followed him outside. There on the ground just under the kitchen window rolled the former Ranger struggling with a smaller figure; it bolted out from under Chance and made a run for the gate, but Braun was already on top of him, taking his feet out from under as he dove toward the ground.

"Braun! Look out!" Tonni yelled.

Braun saw the glint of steel and he twisted the man's arm toward his own throat. A gurgle and a grunt escaped the would-be stalker. "He won't be spying on anyone else tonight," and the burly patrolman pushed the body aside.

"No. But his faerie might!" Chance pointed at something no bigger than a man's hand - except it had wings – and flapping madly to get away – but the wings were bent and it could not gain enough height.

"Grab it!" yelled Chance. They chased the bug-sized critter around the yard until it flew through the open door and into the house.

"Get the door!" yelled Chance. They cornered the little winged monster as it rested atop the bookcase. Chance threw his coat over the faerie, and Dane reached in under the coat.

"No Dane!"

"Owww! It bit me!"

"I told you."

"What? That it bites?" He reached back in, and held the squirming creature with both hands. "Try that again and I'll rip your wings off."

"Nooooo… " the others shouted, but the warning came too late, and in the blink of an eye the room lit up with a gassy odor that smelled of moldy bread and rotten cabbage.

"Gahhhh… Ech! What's that smell?" He wanted to bury his nose in his sleeve but wasn't about to let the bug loose.

"Faeries have few defenses. They can usually outfly anything chasing them," his uncle sighed. "But the one thing they do have is an incredible stink that comes out when they're frightened." The others held their noses nodding, who could not know that?

"How do we make it stop?!" Dane asked, the smell became stronger with a hint of green apples.

"Get it to tell you its name," said Chance.

Dane opened his fingers so he could see the green and blue bug in his hand. It actually looked quite human, like a little man about four inches long with iridescent wings. A craggy face stared up at him. *Ugly little bugger,* he held it up to his eyes.

"What's your name?" he asked.

"Why the *@%&* should I tell you?"

He nearly dropped it!

"If you don't I'll pull your *@%&* wings off." If curses were coin then Dane would be a wealthy lad indeed, and the faerie was not expecting such language from someone as young as this mortal. It blinked twice, not knowing whether or not Dane was bluffing but in the end it decided not to take chances. The face still appeared craggy, but the creature's buggy eyes said everything. "No. Don't. I will tell you." Its gruff voice sounded remarkably strange coming from such a small creature. "It's Buttercup."

Dane opened his hands and the faerie perched upon his finger. He looked over at his uncle. "Now what?"

"Now relax. He won't go anywhere; you have his name. Once a faerie gives you his name he's loyal to the one who asks for it," answered Chance. "But be careful. Just because he's given his allegiance doesn't mean he won't try to trip you up. Remember, he'll always be looking for an opportunity to escape his bondage, even at your expense."

"That's nice." Dane shook his hand but it stayed in place, wrapping its long toes around his finger. "Now how do I get rid of it?"

"Rid? You can't. At least not yet. It knows too much, and we don't know what else it heard under the window," Chance replied. "Faeries are notorious for lying, cheating, and stealing, *and* they have big mouths to boot. No son. You're just gonna have to keep it."

"Hey! Ya big dolt. Why not keep me?" The faerie walked its way up the sleeve of his coat, much to Dane's disgust, and perched itself right next to his ear. "I've gotta thing for people. I'm a real people person. You and I will make a great team. Why I could teach you things you never imagined – like what women really want," and it whispered something in Dane's ear causing the archer to blush.

"I think we better collect Camber and get you two into hiding before we run into any more trouble," said Chance, and he picked his coat up off the floor.

"Yes," the Doctor grabbed his bag, "and your friend is in need of my care." He ushered them out the front door, locking it behind them.

They traveled back to the King's Arms by way of back streets and alleys, avoiding unwanted attention. But Buttercup had other ideas, and he did all he could to thwart their plans to remain undetected; he whistled loudly at the ladies of the evening and shouted obscenities at anyone passing by. Twice Braun and Chance had to draw swords to ward off an unwanted fight. And after the last commotion, Tonni undid the leather sack attached to her belt and shoved it over the faerie. She tied the end and handed it to Dane. "If you're gonna have a pet then you best learn how to look after it."

Most of the patrons had already left the King's Arms; a handful of regulars sat together, *diehards*, some with heads slumped – there was only so much a man could drink (even if it was watered down).

Patch spotted Tonni, and his good eye fell upon the faces of the newcomers; one he recognized as Tonni's brother, the other Doc Sudi. Before he could enforce the house rule about the number of people allowed upstairs she strode over and slammed something into his hand.

The whole necklace – Curse It! She was planning to remove the diamonds first, but seeing the look on the Innkeeper's face and predicting the trouble that would surely follow forced her decision to hand it over, jewels and all. Shikra's Fate! This had better be worth it. The Ranger owed her. *Big time*.

Patch stared at the sparkle of gems that tickled his palm, momentarily lost in their priceless twinkle and forgetting about Tonni and the troop that trailed her up the stairs.

"I thought you told your brother you didn't know anything about a burglary," Dane whispered.

"I didn't say that," she whispered back. "I said I couldn't tell him, and that's true, I couldn't. He's a patrolman. I'm his sister. It would put his job in jeopardy."

She opened the door and the others stepped in after. Camber jumped to his feet. "It's about time you got… " he stopped in mid-sentence as his eyes followed the faces coming through the door.

"Look who I found," Dane grinned.

"UNCLE CHANCE!" In three-and-a-half bounds he was across the room wrapping himself around his uncle.

"Camber! Son!" Chance hugged him back.

The bond between uncle and nephew rivaled that between parent and child, made stronger yet by a common thread: the loss of a brother and a father. Camber had grown up under his uncle's watchful eye, and owed all that he was to the man who had carefully guided him through his most vulnerable years.

Chance touched Camber lightly on the cheek and smiled that warm fatherly smile. It seemed he had left the boy only a day ago, but in reality it had been nearly a year, and in that year the boy had become a man; the weight of responsibility ingrained upon his brow. He knew what lay hidden deep inside. And now as he looked into those large green eyes he knew that Camber had finally discovered his unusual gift. "It's good to see you son," he said, and gently nudged his nephew out of the way so Stitches could get past to tend the elf.

"What's that?" Camber pointed to the leather sack Dane was holding. It was moving. And was that muffled swearing?

"Oh this!" His cousin grinned. "I almost forgot." He stuck his hand in the bag and pulled out the faerie. "Camber meet Buttercup – Buttercup – Camber."

But Buttercup wasn't listening, instead his yellow eyes went wide as saucers; he hissed at the elf lying on the bed and scrambled to the top of Dane's head, digging his claws in sharply.

Crescent rolled over and opened his eyes and the faerie gave a shriek. The room filled with a noxious odor. Tonni rushed to the window, throwing it wide open.

"Stop that!" Dane plucked the tiny critter from his hair.

"Aeieee! An Elf!" Buttercup flapped his wings.

"He's a friend. He won't hurt you. Now stop that stink or I'll stuff you back in the sack."

The odor drifted out the window, mixing with the smells of the city, much to the relief of everyone.

"Snakes and Spirits! What is that thing?!" Camber eyed the tiny critter.

"Snakes and Spirits!" Repeated Buttercup in a squeaky-clean voice. "Is this kid for real?" He looked over at Chance. "You running a daycare?"

Dane frowned. "It's a faerie," he sighed, "and apparently I'm stuck with it." He glared at Buttercup. "For now."

The Doctor brought out several glass vials from his bag and an empty jar, then began mixing liquids, carefully measuring out portions until he reached a desired result; white foam bubbled over, and he poured a small amount into a cup and handed it to Crescent. The elf drank it and sat up. The concoction had worked its magic and his speedy recovery surprised even Stitches. "Well that's a first, usually it takes a day or two before someone's back on their feet."

"Maybe it was the silverthorn," said Camber, and he gave Crescent his arm to lean on while he stood.

"Yep, silverthorn will do that. Lucky you found some; it's quite rare in these parts." Sudi poured the rest of the liquid out the window. "Doesn't keep well," he muttered, and shoved all his equipment back into his kit.

"Now the question is just what to do with you boys." Chance rubbed his brow, pulling something from memory. "Ah! Wait – there's an abandoned homestead not far from Shady. It's well hidden in a gully, I doubt anyone's been there in years. But we'll need horses. We have to move fast while time is on our side."

"I can be of some assistance there," said Braun. "We have spares at the stables, and I'm sure with some help I can find a way to bring them to the Doctor's house – *unnoticed.*"

"Please tell me you don't mean Jax and Garth," Tonni scowled at her brother.

"Would you rather I asked Tam?"

"No."

Tam was the oldest of them all and the most militant. There was no way in the world that he would allow them to get mixed up in something that he deemed "wizardry business" even if it meant they were siding with freedom.

"Listen," Braun said, he was excited about being able to do something to aid the cause against the Easterling King and the prospect of such an adventure appealed to his boyhood fantasy of gallant knights and heroic deeds. "If I go back to the guardhouse I can probably get four horses to Sudi's in less than an hour. The sun won't be up for another three hours, so you'll be clear of Shady Haven if you leave right now."

"The lad makes sense," nodded Chance.

"We shouldn't go downstairs all at once," warned Tonni. She knew Patch would be asking all kinds of questions the next day; questions she'd just as soon not answer. At least my rent's paid – *for the next six months.* Tonni sighed. She had big plans for those diamonds and now she was going to have to wait for another job to roll her way, and who knows when that would be. "At least split into groups," she added.

Chance and Sudi took Crescent with them, and Tonni followed with Dane and Camber. Braun went back to the guardhouse to find his older brothers. And a pair of heavily made-up eyes, loaded with black liner and bright green shadow, watched them leave one by one from behind a barely opened door.

Once past the Plaza, the trio caught up to Chance as he and the doctor half-carried, half-walked, Crescent between them. He was still shaky, but by the time they reached Sudi's house the effects of the poison had faded away.

"I didn't know Dega's father was alive, everyone in Hartland thinks he's dead," said Camber.

"That's what your father and I told people when he left. But in truth he went to Illianther and stayed there for many years before traveling to the East. It was Hawker's plan to have me bring him back; it was hoped that all the smaller Kingdoms and the Northern League would unite under the crown of the Valastari."

"Hawker," Camber repeated. "Have you seen him then?"

"No. I saw him last in Illianther and that was long before you two came there." Dane had filled him in on the entire adventure at Sudi's though he suspected that his nephew had left out parts and embellished others.

"We lost Dega and the others. I don't even know if they're still alive," sighed Camber. He glanced over at Dane who was preoccupied with Buttercup. The faerie had crawled down his shirt and he was trying to get it out before its talons wreaked havoc on his unprotected skin.

"If Dega is anything like his father then I'm sure he's still alive. I remember him as a boy and I know of his deeds as a Ranger. I don't doubt that he's probably looking for you now."

The sound of horses clopping down cobblestones caused Tonni to jump from her seat and peer out the window. "It's Braun," she said, and went to the door. The others picked up their belongings and followed, all except Sudi, he was not going and he said his good-byes to Chance. "If I hear from our friend," he meant Drake, "I'll send him to the hideout. In the meantime, I'll set some false leads to make it look as though your trail has gone back across the Hook. That should buy you some time."

"And I'll send word once we've decided our next course of action." Chance mounted his charger. "Keep your eyes and ears open for any sign of the others. They'll need your help if they gain these shores." Sudi nodded, and Chance kicked his horse, leaving his friend to continue his work aiding the Northern League while under the guise of Shady Haven's only honest physician.

Jax and Garth rode with the company until they reached the outskirts of town. They handed over extra bags, hastily packed with supplies, and bade them good luck.

"Aren't you going with them?" Tonni asked.

Braun shook his head. "Nah, I got the short straw."

"What's that supposed to mean?" she snapped.

"Someone has to babysit."

Dane laughed until she scowled at him and he shut his mouth with a snap. Braun rode up and slapped him on the shoulder. "Don't take it personal. She just can't stand being on the receiving end of a joke. But if it's the other way around, then look out! You'll hear about it for weeks on end." Then in a louder voice, intended for his sibling's ears, that remarkably, were growing redder by the minute. "Maybe you'd like to hear about the time she got her head stuck between the fence."

Morning broke across the sky, cold and grey; no longer could they see the coal stacks billowing smoke over the city with its jumble of brick buildings. By now they were clear across the southernmost tip of the Eastlands, and as far as Camber could tell, still heading south to whatever great ocean reared its turbulent waters on the other side of Astaria. "Where exactly are we?" he asked his uncle.

"We are currently on course to Brugund which is very near the Galtic Sea. But we'll be stopping long before we cross that territory."

"Brigund?" Camber let the word roll off his tongue.

"Brugund," corrected Chance. "The people that live there serve only the Easterling King and would be quick to capture any of us if they happen upon our company."

"Then why are we heading straight toward them?"

"Because the best place for a lamb to hide is in the lion's den."

"Then what?" asked Dane, he looked quite comical with Buttercup riding on his head, but as long as the faerie didn't scratch he pretty much let it go wherever it wanted.

"Then we decide whether to wait for Dega or go back to Illianther or do what you came to do."

"It would be a shame to have come this far without completing the task bestowed upon us," said Crescent. "The Easterling King's army has grown to such a size that the combined forces of the free world will not be able to quell it. It was so fifty years ago, and it has grown larger since. We need the Winterstone. I fear there will never again be such an opportunity."

"Wise words, Master Elf. But the decision has to be made by all of us." Chance shaded his eyes with his hand. "Look there. I see the two arched elms marking the path we must take."

Braun had chosen four of the most surefooted steeds in the guardhouse stable, and his own horse was equally agile; they followed single file behind Chance's gray down a steep embankment. The rocky trail wound its way to a gully where once a great river had overflowed its banks but now only dry dust and scrub trees filled its stony bed. Around midday they reached a path that meandered through a wooded area and finally to a sod-covered cottage.

Chance dismounted and removed his horse's bridle; the charger quickly went to work on the grass. The others did the same, and Braun and Dane brought the packs inside. It was dark and musty, and Chance lit a candle; he and Camber went through each room looking for anything useful. They returned to where the rest of the company now sat on chairs and packs. Camber found an old lantern and some rope, and Chance had stumbled across the former tenant's weaponry: the sword and the dagger were rusted and useless, and the bow needed a new gut; the quiver and arrows he gave to Dane.

After a light meal of bread and cheese the talk turned to whether or not to wait for Dega. "For the sake of an argument let us suppose that the others are alive," said Chance. "Sudi knows where we are; if we stay put then there's a better chance that Dega will find us."

"If we stay put then we're sitting targets for the sorcerer," reminded Crescent.

"Not if he doesn't know we are here."

"Well he won't hear about it from Jax or Garth." Tonni felt the need to defend her brothers. "But," she added, and turned to Braun. "What about you? Won't you be missed at the guardhouse?"

"It's been taken care of," he said. "Jax is going to tell the Captain I suffered a lethal blow from an altercation – thanks to the mess you two made in the alley those thugs are perfect testimony to my disappearance."

"What if Dega doesn't show?" asked Dane.

"Then we must decide to go on or go back to Illianther."

"But the Stone's within our reach," Camber pleaded.

"Do you know where it is?" asked his uncle. The cadet shook his head. "Then without that knowledge we have very limited choices.

How long do you think we can continue evading the Easterling King until we stumble across the Winterstone?"

"It's under his castle," said a voice from behind Dane's ear. The archer plucked the faerie from his shoulder and held it out in front. "What'd you say?"

"It's under the dolt's castle," repeated the faerie.

"How do you know?" asked Dane.

Buttercup flapped his wings but Dane had a strong grip. "How do you know?" he repeated.

"Because bub, I've seen the *@%&* thing."

"And if you've seen it, then why haven't you already told him?"

"Why should I make it easy for that lump-head? I've no part in his war. Besides it's hilarious watching you big folk pound the crap out of each other."

"Can you lead us to it?"

"Ask nicely." The faerie stood with his tiny arms folded over his chest waiting for the archer to plead for help.

"How 'bout I squash you instead?"

Buttercup's bravado suddenly deflated, and he looked up at Dane with his wide buggy-eyes, "You wouldn't," he squeaked.

"I would," said Dane. "But I'll make a deal with you. Show us where the Winterstone is and I'll release you." Chance had said the faerie would stop at nothing to escape its thralldom and he tossed in the jailor's key.

"Deal!" Buttercup resumed his air of self-confidence.

"Can we trust it?" Tonni didn't like the idea of hinging such a dangerous plot on the mischievous wings of a faerie.

"A faerie never backs down from his word," snorted Buttercup.

"I think so," Dane answered.

"We'll have to sit tight for a few days. And I want to remind all of you that this is no picnic in the park. There are ways to bypass the protected region near his fortress but the paths are dangerous, and there is still the risk of being discovered. If anyone wants out he *or she* should go back to Sudi's." Chance eyed all the faces in the room, each one filled with a grim desire to find the talisman.

That evening Chance sat in his chair watching the others sleep. He hardly slept anymore, the former Ranger catnapped when he could but hadn't had a decent night's sleep since leaving Hartland. Where was Drake? His sources had led him here to the Eastlands, but the man he and Glade swore their allegiance to many years ago was nowhere to be found. Too much was happening way too fast. It was as if a giant hand had taken the world in its terrible grip and spun it like a top, and all who held the cards of chance were suddenly colliding with destiny, whether the outcome would mean the demise of the Easterling King or the end of the world only the cards would tell. *And in whose hand would that last card fall?*

XIV

The Hand is Dealt

An army - five thousand strong - camped along the northernmost tip of the icecap. Many more were still coming across. The Easterling King had been transferring his forces for months using the least expected route - *the Narrows;* a turbulent passage between one hundred foot glacier walls and miles of treacherous sea.

While his ships engaged the Northern fleet off the coast of the Barrier, his cargo crafts, equipped with metal skirts, cut through miles of frozen ice to go where no ship dared go before. And thanks to the dark arts, he was able to soften the ice-flows, allowing his fleet safe passage.

Along the Hook an impressive fighting force equipped with his latest weapon, exploding palm-sized globes, which would turn the tide in his favor, marched tirelessly across the divide, gathering strength from his Southland allies.

Only one piece of the puzzle remained. Somewhere between the 'hones and the Hook the boy he very much wanted still roamed free. His captains reported the company had now split but they had lost track of the boy. He sent them out again. But not before gutting the hapless fool who dared deliver the news of their failure. There would be no more botched attempts.

* * * * * * * * *

Dega wandered the gardens of Vintnorr; his feet led him down a cobbled path to the steps of a crypt housing the bodies of Girt's ruling families. Moonlight illuminated the doors, bouncing softly off polished marble; a ghostly breath that silvered the edge of night.

He sat on the steps, staring up at the stars. More than ever Dega needed reassurance from his father. But he had no father. His father had left. The shame shadowed his footsteps, riding his shoulders like a two-ton chip. And always, behind his back, behind closed doors, he heard the whispers. Now he would give anything just to hear his father's voice.

He sucked his breath, the air was cool and it smarted a little. "I've failed," he said to the stars. It was true. Somehow he had lost all control of the company. Camber was gone. He might even be dead. And Starlock was locked in a dungeon. He and the others were given permission to leave with fresh horses and all the supplies they could carry but Starlock was to remain and stand trial. He was free to go – but stay he did. Dega would not be leaving anyone behind.

The sound of slippered feet tapping down the garden path roused him from his thoughts, and Dega Darkhawk let all emotion slip back into storage as the shape of a woman came into view. *Helena.* The comely flaxen-tressed maid was one of two concubines given to him by Halstaff. Of course he refused both women right away – he was not *that* sort of man.

Women were considered property, and under Girt law, Helena belonged to the King. She and her infant son came to live at the palace after the death of her husband, a Fighting Blue-Feather, who left to defend his homeland and never came back. Dega did not understand (nor did he want to) the barbaric laws that governed these people. Halstaff had been mildly amused over Dega's refusal to keep the women, but not surprised, for he had guessed the Captain's nature and had already deduced the outcome.

Helena found him sitting on the steps of the royal tomb; she lifted her voluminous skirts and sat down beside him. Even though he had dismissed the women, Helena had refused to leave. She slept on the divan at the foot of his bed and brought him his meals. But Dega felt uneasy with all this attention and he had taken to avoiding her whenever he could.

"Here you are," she said. "I could not find you so I gave your supper to the dwarf."

"I needed some air," he stood to take his leave.

"Don't go," she placed her hand on his cheek.

And Dega drew back. "I'm sorry. I cannot."

"Oh. Forgive me. I have made you uncomfortable." She lowered her gaze. "I did not mean to cause you alarm, you have made it clear you wish not to bed me, and I accept your decision. But know that I cannot stand idly by whilst you struggle with your conscience."

Dega turned his head away and looked up at the moon, anywhere but into those luminous eyes. If he wasn't careful they would draw his most guarded secrets from his soul.

"You love her don't you?" She reached up and turned his face to hers.

"Who?" But he knew whom she spoke of.

"The prisoner. The Elf maiden."

He walked away.

"I will help you."

"What?" He came back and grabbed her by the shoulders. "What did you say?"

"I will help you," she took his calloused hands in her own. "Tonight. I will help you free her, and all of you can leave together."

"Why would you do this?"

"I miss my Erik. My heart – my soul. Nothing can ever replace a love such as we had." She looked into his eyes, and a tear slid down her cheek. "My Erik is gone, but you and she have a chance to have what we could not. If I can save a love meant to be, mayhap it will ease my own heartache."

"You do not have to do this."

"I do so freely." She pushed him. "Go. Go now and do as I say. Send your friends to the east wall. They will find horses there. I will meet you at this spot in one bell's time, and bring only the dwarf."

Dega left her standing in the garden. He did not look back, but if he had he would have seen compassion in its purest form, standing with her hands clasped, and looking on with sorrow. Helena lifted her skirts and skittered back to the palace. There was much to do and only a short time to fulfill her promise to the Ranger. Secretly she desired to go with them, leave Vintnorr, but she could not leave her son, Erik's pride and joy; the last traces of the father slept soundly in the King's nursery.

Dega returned to the gardens with Lockjaw. Helena was already there. She handed them their weapons. "Where did you get these?" He strapped his sword back to his belt, and took the blanket which held Starlock's things.

"I have my ways," she said, not wanting to tell the young Captain how she had obtained the weapons, it would only demoralize her character in his eyes, and she wanted him to think only the purest thoughts of her and not tarnish it with how she offered herself to the orderly who's job it was to keep the weapons under lock and key. *Yes, that man had never had a King's concubine and would probably never have such an opportunity ever again, given his status, and for his brief moment of pleasure he gave her all the weapons with a promise that she would come back and bed him whenever he wanted.*

"Come with me. We must go quickly," she motioned for them to follow as she stepped lightly down the garden path and across the courtyard. They entered a building which served as a prison, though rarely used since Girt's populace were well aware of the consequences for breaking the King's law. Helena led them down a hallway, stopping only to light a torch. "The hour is late and only one guard will be down here," she pointed to a staircase that disappeared into darkness. Dega nodded, he knew exactly what she meant and there was no further need to discuss the plan. He drew his sword. "No," she whispered, gently touching his wrist. "Not that way. No killing. Let me go first and distract him." She led them down the stairs, and put a finger to her lips, then stepping out into the room she made her presence known.

The man on duty was not a Blue-Feather. He was on the same pegging as the weapons orderly and those that did the more mundane tasks around the palace. And he was bored. He turned his head at the sound of footsteps and the rustle of silk. One of the King's concubines stepped into the room. She beckoned him forth, unlacing the bodice of her gown. Could his fortune be so sweet? A grin split his face as he circled his prize, like a child admiring a new toy.

A hand came out of the dark, and the pommel of a sword crashed down upon his skull. Helena quickly re-laced her gown and grabbed the jailor's keys. Dega snatched them from her fingers and ran over to the cells. The elf lay crumpled in the corner. He could not see her face, and he wondered for a moment if she were dead. "Starlock!"

"Dega?" her voice warbled and she rolled over.

He fumbled through several keys and finding the right one he stuffed it into the lock. It turned with a snap. Dega rushed to her side and pulled her up from the filthy floor. "What have they done to you!" He stared at her bruised and battered face.

"Nothing I didn't already deserve," she muttered. "Get me out of here."

Lockjaw gave Starlock her weapons, and he and Dega held her up while she fastened them to her straps. Helena stood at the foot of the stairs, keeping a wary eye on the turnkey. "Hurry," she whispered.

"Wait," Lockjaw called. He grabbed the guard by his feet and dragged him into Starlock's cell, then shut the door, locking it and leaving the keys on the chair.

Helena doused the torch, then led them outside and around the back of the building staying within the shadows, and all the while she thought of how proud Erik would have been that she had bravely organized this daring rescue.

They reached the east wall without incident where Lightfoot and Frost-Eye waited with horses in tow. Starlock took one and Dega hoisted the dwarf onto the back of his steed.

"Take the road through the forest. There is a ravine to cross but no guardpost to past. Once clear of the ravine, ride hard and fast, and with a little luck they will not find out about your disappearance until morning."

"I thank you from the bottom of my heart," said Dega, "I will not forget your kindness, nor your bravery. I hope you find your peace."

"Go quickly," she said, looking away so he could not see her tears. She started back to the palace, then turned to watch Dega's retreating form as he led the others into the forest.

* * * * * * * *

"We're under attack!" A messenger sprinted down the South porch corridor. The sound of metal on metal clanged inside the dwarven city. A horn rang out, rousing Grimbeard's people out of slumber. The young Prince was ushered into his most private chambers where he would be safe. "This is an outrage!" he cried. "I need to be among my people. We are under attack!"

"You can't Sire!" Rockhand, his personal servant, stood in front of the door barring his way. "You are heir to the throne. You cannot take the chance."

"We need every available dwarf," he snapped, and tried to push past the valet who was twice his size. "My army is already a thousand leagues from here. There is no one to protect the dwarxen!"

"Sire the dwarxen are being brought to these chambers. There are enough dwarves in the mines and firepits to see to their safety and hold off the attack."

Shard was asleep when the alarm sounded, and Sparkle came rushing into her boudoir with fear in her blue eyes. "Mistress!"

"I heard the alarm," she said as she sat up. "What's happening?"

"Mistress we're under attack!"

"Attack?" She sounded the word out loud, thinking that perhaps she was still dreaming.

"Quickly!" Sparkle grabbed her robe and tried to wrap it around her. "We must go."

But Shard had already jumped to her feet and she bounded over to her closet pulling out the clothes she wore when she wanted to sneak out of her rooms.

"Mistress! What are you doing?!"

"What's it look like?" she asked, pulling leather boots overtop her father's old breeches.

"You cannot go down there!" Sparkle shrieked as she realized what Shard was about.

"We have no dwarves, save the workers. Who is going to stop them?" She reached under her mattress and pulled out a very long and deadly blade, it glinted menacingly in the dimly lit room. She bounded out the door with Sparkle running after.

The dwarxen had gathered in the central hall of their enclosure. Several dwarves carrying axes and wearing chainmail had already started to herd them to the Prince's apartments where they would be safe. When Shard burst into the room a wave of silence filled the air; dwarf and dwarx stood still, mouths open, staring at the petite figure who, by all accounts, should not be armed with a sword.

"You are mad!" Sparkle's eyes were truly wide with terror.

"Mad? Do you want to spend the rest of your life in chains?" Shard jumped onto a pedestal with Shale's likeness, wrapping her arm around the statue for support. She raised her sword high above her head. "Or will you join me and fight. Fight for your home! Fight for your people! Fight for freedom!" A cheer went up. "I will not be taken! Who is with me?!"

Something happened. Something that had not happened since the time of Ironfist. One by one the dwarxen took up arms, grabbing whatever they could use as weapons. Pots, bedpans, a ceremonial dagger, brooms, goblets, trays - anything and everything. They followed Shard out of the compound racing toward the Atrium with their armed escort in pursuit, not quite believing what they were seeing. "Fight!" she urged. "Fight for Freedom! Fight for Shale!"

At the mention of the revered Mother; the dwarxen sent up a loud cry as they swarmed down the staircase coming to the aid of their menfolk.

* * * * * * * *

Shard's amulet began to vibrate. Lockjaw fished it out from inside his tunic. It hummed with great ferocity in the palm of his hand, sending tingles throughout his entire body. *Something's wrong.* He sensed it. A shadow grew heavy on his heart, shrouding it in a cloud of worry; he mouthed a safeguard spell and kissed the amulet. It was the only thing he could do; he just hoped it would be enough.

"Hang on." Dega grunted; his horse launched itself in the air landing cleanly on the other side of a steep bank. Lockjaw felt himself sliding back across its haunches as the charger scrambled up the embankment. He squeezed the Captain as another jolt nearly dislodged him from behind the saddle.

A whole day had passed since their early morning escape and it was now too dark for even the horses to pick their way through the treacherous ravine. "We can't go much farther," said Starlock. Purple and yellow bruises covered much of her face, and Dega suspected the rest of her body had also taken a beating. He nodded. She was right. They could not risk the climb in the dark. "Let's keep a watch posted," he said.

Frost-Eye took the first shift, then Lightfoot, Lockjaw, and finally Dega. They had all agreed that Starlock get as much rest as she could. While they had slept in soft beds and eaten their fill, Starlock had not; she had slept on filthy straw and had been given only one meal a day.

But Starlock did not sleep. Her eyes followed the stars high in the sky, and she deemed them her adjudicators. "I have failed at this simple task handed to me. How can I ever follow in my father's footsteps? The line that remains unbroken from Shadowshot has lost its potency through me. Ah – the futility of it, I could not even manage to look after one boy." Her face grew angry and she wanted to yell back as they twinkled from their lofty position. "What would you have me do?! I never wanted this in the first place!" She snorted and stood, part of her wanting to run. Run home. Run back to the Black Wood.

"What is it?" asked Dega. He moved cautiously toward the elf; she like a wild animal that might bolt at the drop of a hat.

"It is nothing. I cannot sleep."

"Are you in pain?"

"No it's not that...." she sighed. "I have failed everyone. The boy is lost and so is any hope of destroying the sorcerer. He will surely find the lad and then use him against us. It's not even a war that I know how to fight. Swords and bows are of no use."

Dega knew what she meant. "You did not know. None of us thought it would end like this." He placed his hand gently on her shoulder with the same light touch he might use to reassure a skittish colt. "Frost-Eye is certain his brother is alive and for that reason alone we should believe hope still lies within our reach."

"I am sorry," she said, dropping her gaze. "I do not feel as confident as you. It's as if a stone has been around my neck since the day Hawker brought you all to my wood."

"You say that I am confident about this quest. But it's only because I must believe it will succeed. The true power in changing the course of destiny is believing you have the ability. If you had asked me five years ago what I think now I assure you it would be a completely different answer, but I have seen a thing or two, and I know that even a sorcerer has a weakness. All we need is to find it."

"You say everyone has a weakness. And you believe this?" Starlock looked at Dega as if seeing the Ranger for the first time. Ice-blue eyes wandered into foreign territory, seeking answers.

"Yes."

"Even you?"

"Especially me."

Neither seemed aware that their bodies had moved closer; she pressing up against him and he breathing softly in her ear. Their heads turned at the same time bringing their lips within a heartbeat.

"And what is your weakness?" she whispered.

His chest pounded; hot was the blood that boiled deep in his veins; he was just about to give her his answer.

"Good morning," said Lightfoot.

Elf and Ranger quickly moved apart. Dega glowered, and Lightfoot smiled, nodding his head in cheerful greeting, and giving no indication that he had just interrupted something of great importance. At the sound of voices Frost-Eye and Lockjaw joined them; horses were saddled and the company started the steep climb up the other side of the ravine. Lockjaw was now sitting behind Lightfoot so that Dega's horse could rest. "I feel like baggage," he complained.

"But you look like a sack of potatoes," said Lightfoot, and he kicked his horse into a jarring trot much to Lockjaw's dismay.

"Will they follow us?" Frost-Eye rode up beside the cavalier.

Dega shrugged. "They might. I'm sure by now the turnkey has been found, but it depends on whether they think we are worth the trouble or not." He hoped Helena had not been found guilty of aiding them. Bad enough he had already collected more than his fair share of weighed-down responsibilities, but adding innocent bystanders left a sour taste in his mouth.

They rode until dark, and by this time they were well and clear of the ravine and far away from Girt's sprawling grasslands. Frost-Eye found an ideal spot to take cover and they set a watch. This time Starlock took the first shift and Dega the last. The next few days went by quickly and they stopped only to hunt small game. By the end of the fifth it was evident the Fighting Blue-Feathers had not been set upon their trail and the party resumed at a slower pace.

Suddenly Starlock signaled to stop. "Can you hear it?" she asked. Both Frost-Eye and Lightfoot nodded, but Dega and Lockjaw heard nothing. She jumped off her horse and stuck her ear to the ground. "An army!" She looked up at Dega. "A large one."

Dega frowned. "What direction?"

"East."

"If we continue riding toward the Hook we will surely run into them," said Starlock.

"What of Camber?" asked Lockjaw. "I hope he hasn't been captured."

"No. I do not think they are close by," answered Frost-Eye, and he joined Dega and Starlock on the ground. "Crescent is much farther away than this army. His spirit seems to be moving in the opposite direction."

"It's possible they're not traveling together, or have been taken prisoner and are being sent to Tar Galleaon," said Dega; he rubbed his jaw as he tried to weigh the possibility of the trio evading capture versus the likelihood they had been found. "We must decide right now our next course of action." He gripped the pommel of his sword. "We can continue to follow a non-existent trail based on our assumptions or go back and warn Halstaff that an army is marching on Girt. For that's where I believe they are headed since it's the only empire in these parts that still opposes the Easterling King, and it would be an ideal location for a military base."

"I fear you are right," said Lightfoot. "But why not send me back, since my part in this company was to be messenger, then messenger I shall be."

"No," said Dega. Though he loathed the thought of returning, and especially for Starlock's sake, he knew it was the only answer. "We must all go together. Halstaff will be angry, and if only one of us returns he may be inclined to think it a trick. No, we will all have to return," he looked at Starlock expecting her to disagree.

"The Captain is right," she said, "and though I may have to endure confinement, what needs to be done must be done. If the Easterling King takes Girt than he will have a powerful hold in these lands and nothing will stop him from advancing on the surrounding territories and the rest of Astaria."

"Our hope lies in the fact that Halstaff will need every sword he can to defend his city, and mayhap he will allow Starlock to remain free for this alone." Dega eyed the group. "Now then, we must decide."

"Girt," said Starlock.

"Girt," repeated Lightfoot.

"Girt," Frost-Eye and Lockjaw agreed.

Dega nodded and mounted his horse. The others followed. Darkness had fallen but they rode through the night at a hard pace. Time was of the essence and it would take more than a few days for Halstaff to organize his forces.

* * * * * * * *

Camber rolled his eyes as he listened to Dane swearing up a streak. Apparently Buttercup had caught on quickly to his favorite pastime and was enjoying a winning streak with the dice.

"Not fair!" Dane snorted. "I think you're cheating."

"Hand over the coins kid," the faerie stuck his hand out and Dane gave him the two silver pieces he had placed as his bet. "You're just a bug, what are you going to do with money anyway?"

"Why take it away from you, that's what." He flew each piece to his stash on top of the cabin's support beam.

The door opened, and Chance came in from outside. He stomped the mud from his boots and threw his cloak onto the back of a chair.

"Well?" asked Camber, turning his head.

"No word on Dega or any of your friends," he said. Braun frowned. "Maybe I should head back to the guardhouse."

"You can't ya big idiot! You're supposed to be mortally wounded," Tonni snapped. "But you do have a point. If someone can get word to Jax or Garth maybe they can ask around. Perhaps I could sneak back to town and…"

"No." Chance raised his hand. "No. We can't risk it. We don't know who's watching."

"Well if I stay holed up here much longer I'll go insane." Three days of sheer boredom had chipped away anything remotely akin to patience, exposing her frustration with certain members of the company, chiefly Braun and Dane.

"Ha! Feel for us then. You're the one who snores like a …"

"That's enough Braun," said Chance.

"We've decided to wait three more days." Crescent removed his cloak, aside from the dark circles under his eyes, there was no trace of the poison that had nearly left him paralyzed.

"We don't know what may be keeping the others from reaching these lands, but we cannot stay here much longer for fear of discovery," added Chance.

"Then what?" Dane asked. He was ready to leave now; he hated waiting.

"Then we set out to retrieve the Stone."

Six pairs of eyes waited for the last candle to be extinguished. Tikri waved his men into position; at least the whore was good for something other than horizontal sport. The sorcerer would pay handsomely for such a find. But he'd wait until after he had things well under control before telling any of those Easterling bastards. If he didn't, they'd probably feed him to their bloody hounds and take the reward for themselves. Tikri was no fool. He'd make sure his stash was secure then demand to speak only with the sorcerer himself to solidify the deal.

The sound of breaking glass and a shout woke Camber from his sleep. Shadows erupted from the darkness. He kicked at one, and rolled across the floor, away from the woosh as a sword narrowly missed his head. Half jumping and stumbling to where he left his own sword, the cadet bumped his way past two more shapes and was shoved roughly behind his uncle. Chance had only his dagger but in such a confined space it was a better weapon than the swords carried by the intruders. He slashed and kicked, allowing Camber time to grab his own weapon.

Braun tackled one of the men to the floor. A dagger flew from Tonni's hand stopping another thug from splitting her brother's skull wide open; his throat made a gurgling sound and his hands dropped the axe.

Something hit the back of Dane's head, knocking him forward. A painful scream sounded from behind, and the man who had taken a swipe with his buckler reeled backward landing on Braun.

"Pick on someone your own size!" Buttercup detached his talons and flew back to stand protectively atop Dane's head.

"Thanks," the archer said; he was at a disadvantage since there was no way he could use his bow, so he took cover behind the table and used his slingshot.

"Just looking after my investment," said the faerie.

The last two intruders had been dispatched, and someone lit a candle. The bodies on the ground were not in uniform but Braun recognized one of them as a patrolman from his unit. "Tikri," he said in disgust.

"Do you think he told anyone else?" asked Chance.

"Hard to say. He wasn't well liked by anyone in our outfit and it was said he had connections with the sorcerer. I guess this proves it."

"Then we had better leave tonight just in case," said Chance. "Gather up weapons and anything else that may be of use. I think the decision has just been made for us."

* * * * * * * *

"To Arms! To Arms!" A rider galloped into the old Ranger barracks and dismounted, he had taken several arrows and fell face forward to the ground. Caleb grabbed the knotted rope and rang the tower bell. Gareth was already on the scene shouting orders. Officers and enlistees poured out the barracks, running to their stations. Several men were dispatched to neighboring homesteads with orders to round up as many people as possible and take them to the shelters.

"Quick! Get him inside." Gareth pointed to the wounded soldier; one of Ravenhill's men. "Wait," the rider said, he grabbed Gareth by his uniform as the officer hunched over him. "Easterlings....ca... come... tried to... stop... " his eyes rolled up and his head dropped.

"Take him to the infirmary," ordered Gareth. "Jules," he caught the cadet by the arm as he ran past. "Ride to Wildwood, see what the situation is. Bring back reinforcements if you can."

Jules saluted, then took off, sprinting across the yard and in through the double doors of the stable, nearly colliding with Sergeant Weyland who held tight to a pair of horses that spooked at his sudden entry.

"What's going on out there son?" asked the officer.

"A soldier from Wildwood met with Easterlings! I have to make a run to their outfit." Jules went for his tack. Which horse to take? Swishtail or the stallion? He still hadn't named it. Swishtail was reliable while the warhorse was not. But the stallion was faster. Weyland followed him still leading the two horses. "Take the other 'un," he said as Jules went for Swishtail's stall. "He's fresh and can make the trip faster." Jules nodded, opening the stallion's door.

The horse snapped its teeth, flattening its ears. At least he didn't try to kick this time. He threw the blanket across the charger's back and cinched up the saddle. Weyland handed him his bridle. "Take these," he gave Jules a knife and some rope. The cadet nodded, he had no weapons and there was no time to go get one. "Luck and speed son," said Weyland, and as was his nature, always thinking of the horses first, he added, "and mind that mouth, he's got a soft 'un, so don't saw on the reins."

The stallion snorted, taking off like a bolt and clearing the stable fence with room to spare. Horse and rider dashed out the front gates and down the road to Wildwood. Jules clung to the stallion's neck as they thundered along the muddy highway. Easterlings this far north! It couldn't be... it just couldn't be happening! He prayed for the safety of his family. "Please don't let anything happen to them." The stallion's ears flicked at the sound of his voice; the only sound except for rhythmic hoofbeats and the drumming of rain coming down in great sheets.

The charger came to a sudden stop, nearly unseating the cadet. Jules clicked and kicked but the horse refused to budge. *Now what?* He cracked the reins across its sweaty neck but the stallion only snorted and danced in a circle. Finally he dismounted, and holding the reins tightly, (he wasn't about to let it bolt back to the barracks leaving him stranded) he ventured forward on foot. The ground was soft, and as he walked a little farther he could just make out part of the road in the fading light; winter rains had washed it away, leaving a gap too wide for the stallion to jump. The Whitewash rushed heavily alongside;

its cold waters rising dangerously high at the banks and threatening to wipe away the entire path.

"Guess we can't go that way," he said, stroking the horse on its nose, and he mounted the charger and turned it around. Soft black ears pricked forward at the prospect of heading back to a nice warm stall, but flattened angrily when Jules clucked him into the woods. "Sorry fellah, but I've got orders to go to Wildwood and that's just where we're headed." He guided his mount through the trees and onto a seldom-used trail that would likely add three or four hours to his ride, depending on how treacherous the footing.

At the top of a hill they turned southeast. The route was rocky but fairly straight and the stallion was able to keep moving at a tireless trot. Jules rose expertly in his stirrups, landing softly on the downbeat; horse and rider glided across the hilltop like a ghostly apparition, and it was times like these that Jules really appreciated those long hours in the saddle. That, and the extra time he spent in the practice ring on his own. He had discovered something about himself that he would have never known existed if it weren't for the Captain – he loved riding. "Better not tell Dane," he smirked, then his face fell flat. "Hope I get the chance to make that choice."

A snort from the horse roused him out of his reverie. It flattened its ears and rolled its eyes, showing the whites. Another snort. It smelled something on the wind; a smell it had known before. A gray shadow bolted from the trees. The warhorse reared, letting out a fearful scream, then wheeling around on its hind legs, it took off at a dead run. Jules turned, and saw with horrified eyes the Bounder hot on their heels.

The stallion careened in a zigzagging path through bush and tree. Jules gave him his head. Small branches whipped smartly as they thundered across the hilltop. The Bounder howled from behind; its mournful cry only served to spur his frightened mount faster.

The ground was soft; a dull grinding of earth, and suddenly the trail crumbled. Horse – Rider – and Bounder – all went over the side! Jules flew from his saddle, landing hard against rock. His horse scrambled forward, its forelegs barely holding the rest of its body onto the small platform; the Bounder right next to it, also trying to gain a foothold. Wrapping his arms around the stallion's head, he kicked the Bounder in the face, sending it howling to the rocks below, then pulled the charger onto the ledge.

Not much room on this ledge and a good ten or fifteen foot climb up a muddy slope. Not impossible, but not an easy one either; he doubted the horse could manage it. *Rope!* Thankful for Weyland's foresight, he untied the stallion's tack, everything except the bridle, and taking the knife, he cut loose the saddle's cinch and one stirrup, then sent the rest over the edge.

"I don't know if this'll work but you have to help me out here. No biting, kicking, or fussing," he spoke calmly, using his most reassuring voice. Surprisingly, the stallion just stood there, allowing Jules to place the cinch around his belly. After securing the rope, he gave the horse one last pat and spoke gently in its ear. "Be quiet now. I'm trying to help you." The horse nickered nervously it knew there was only one way out and that was up.

Jules climbed the slope, careful not to go too quickly. It seemed like hours had passed before he finally gained the top. No time to rest. He took the rope and circled it around the nearest tree until it was taught, then used the stirrup to lock it into place.

"Now your turn," he tugged gently on the rope, and was answered by a snort, then the sound of hooves struggling up the incline. He pulled, straining heavily on the rope. The stallion's head and forelegs appeared at the edge of the embankment, and he gave one final heave, using everything he had; the warhorse scrambled to safety.

Exhausted, he sat down, not caring if the charger stayed or took its leave. But it stood there, as if contemplating, then walking over to where the cadet lay sprawled in the grass, it stuck its soft black muzzle against his chin and blew gently on his face. Laughing, he got to his feet, giving the black a scratch behind the ears. "So you wanna be friends now? Is that it?"

The stallion's ears pricked forward, and then Jules heard it too. *Drums!* It could only mean one thing. He vaulted onto its back and dug his heels into the flanks. But the horse needed no urging, in three mighty bounds it had reached full gallop, speeding down the hillock, and back to the road that led to the barracks.

XV

The Cards Fall

"You! At the gate. Open up!" Dega rode up to the watchtowers overlooking Vintnorr. A horn sounded, and a dozen Blue-Feathers rode out of the gates quickly surrounding them. One was Gerharte; he reined in beside the Ranger's Captain. "You are all under arrest."

"Wait!" Dega brought his hands up, opening his palms in a gesture of trust. "We've come to warn you of the Easterling King's army. It's crossed the Hook and is making its way to Girt."

"How do you know this?" asked Gerharte, his eyes narrowed, and his distrust was passed on to his charger; the big bay champed its bit and danced in a circle.

"We were headed in that direction to continue our quest but the sound of foot soldiers and cavalry reached our ears as we pondered which path to take."

"Listen," Lightfoot intervened, "you do not have to believe us but ask yourself why we would come back if we had successfully gained our freedom."

Gerharte nodded. "Come with me." This was true. Such a man as this Captain would not have returned unless the need was greater than his own commitment, and surely the elf would not have returned at all; pride ruling out any shred of compassion. He ordered the gates to open and led them across the courtyard to the second set of gates.

A jangle of armor and the clopping of hooves announced their entry back inside the fortified city. They dismounted at the great bronze doors marking the entrance to Girt's seat of power and handed their horses over to the Chieftain's men.

"If what you say is true then we must see the King at once." Gerharte's scouts had confirmed exactly what Dega had just reported. The Easterlings and their allies had always been under close scrutiny; their intentions made clear over the centuries. This was not news so much as an announcement that war was underway.

This time Gerharte signaled for Dega and the others to wait at the entrance to Halstaff's chambers and he went on ahead, nodding to the guards to permit his admittance. He needed no such approval or special announcement, for the Chieftain of the Fighting Blue-Feathers was allowed to come and go as he pleased, but for formality's sake he waited patiently as one of the heralds announced his arrival and stated his business.

Upon hearing that the foreigners were once again in his custody, Halstaff demanded they be brought before him. Gerharte ushered them forth, and removing his helm took a knee in front of his liege, the others followed suit, all except Starlock, who refused to bow to no one, no matter how important the personage, and did not her own royal presence negate his?

This act of defiance was not lost on Halstaff. "Ah, I see you have returned, and with news that merits your sudden friendship." His gaze wandered over the group, coming to rest lastly on Dega. "Stand then, and tell me why you think Sentash looks upon Girt with his vengeful eye."

"Sire," Dega began, he was not one to be intimidated, and still angry over the abuse Starlock had endured, and when he spoke it came as though he were berating an orderly and not confronting someone of equal rank. "We've encountered the vanguard of the sorcerer's host this side of the 'hones and they are surely headed to Vintnorr. With nothing to stand against them, save a few small villages, the occupation of Vintnorr will give him the toehold he needs to bring the North and then all of Astaria under his will. You must fortify your towers and prepare your armies; a battle is imminent."

If Halstaff was taken aback by Dega's words he did not show it. The King who had seen more than his share of campaigns stood up from his chair and strode down the steps to stand in front of the officer. "Know this," he said as he marched up to the only man who could get away with lecturing him in such an abrasive manner. "I believe his eye *is* fixed on Girt. But that does not give you the right to make decisions concerning my kingdom. Girt is mine. Under my rule. I will say when and where we will meet the sorcerer. Not you.

Not them," he gestured to the others. "This one is still my prisoner and must stand trial as is our custom," he thrust his staff at Starlock. "However, under the circumstances, I have far more important duties to secure my attention. I command you all to stay, and not venture forth as was your intent. My gates are closed to anyone leaving the city and I will give orders to kill anyone who tries."

"You do not understand," Dega countered. "You have only a matter of days before his armies reach you."

"I will not be spoken to in such a manner. I will send out scouts to confirm your reports, and until then you will all remain as prisoners. Take them away," he ordered Gerharte.

"Then you will lose valuable time in preparing for battle and he will have the advantage," said Dega.

"Sire," said Lightfoot. "If I might make a suggestion." He kept his head bowed and waited for the King to nod. "It seems you have all the fortification to make a stand right here. The natural surroundings make for a perfect location to withstand a siege."

"That is obvious to all, and is why my forefathers chose it," said Halstaff. If his words carried a hint of disdain it was only because he would not be made a token – be it Man's destiny or Elvish influence. The wizard had tried to secure his kingdom nearly thirty years ago and he was still sweeping up the mess Hawker had left behind.

"Then if your plans are to subdue the Easterling's armies you will need someone to marshal the confrontation once the battle begins."

"I have my Blue-Feathers," he snapped, his irritation with the foreigners beginning to show plain on his bearded face.

"Starlock is a Janastari - bred for war. And our good Captain is a Ranger, perhaps you might make use of their talents."

"Sire, now is not the time to be proud," Gerharte agreed, being a commander himself, and knowing the foreigners would not have risked their lives to return unless they deemed it necessary, he had every reason to believe in Dega's demand for immediate action. "If we waste time sending forth a scouting party then it's true we will not be prepared. I will send a handful of my Blue-Feathers while we fortify the city. If the Captain and the others can be of some assistance then it would be folly to send them to the dungeons."

Gerharte's sudden endorsement for the foreigners forced Halstaff to reconsider, at last he relented. "I will grant you this request if you take full responsibility for their actions," he said, and Gerharte nodded. "The men of the North and the men of the South have never been on the best of terms. Too much has muddied our trust in each other and not all of it the fault of mortals. If you pledge your allegiance to me then I will be grateful for whatever the outcome, good or bad. But know that I will not tolerate disrespect, especially by outsiders." This last comment was put forth to remind Dega who really held the reins of power and who he would answer to when all was said and done.

"You have my word. We will obey your strictest command, but on one condition."

"What is that?"

"Starlock remains free to aid your cause, and if our valor proves to be some assistance then you must allow us to leave without hindrance."

"Done."

Dega bowed politely, and Halstaff gave orders to prepare their original apartments.

* * * * * * * *

A blanket of cloud blocked any orienteering by stars, but this did not faze the former Ranger, no stranger to the Eastlands was he, having traveled far and wide while in the service of Hartland's cavalry. He stopped his horse, checked his position, then resumed at a walk down the dried riverbed with the others trailing behind.

The pace was agonizingly slow, too slow for Camber. He was growing weary swaying to the rocking motion of his mount as it picked its way through the channel of a long depleted tributary. The banks grew steeper, and he wondered if they might not be able to get out should the need arise; trapped between two towering layers of sediment.

At last the sun's golden face peeked over the horizon, not that it made a terrible difference, the haze that blanketed the Eastern sky thoroughly blocked any cheerful radiance the sun might provide.

An outcropping of rock resembling the skeletal remains of a beast served as a place to make camp, and while the others slept, Chance came to sit beside his nephew, handing Camber a strip of cured meat.

"How's your mother?"

"She's well," he took the jerky, but did not eat. "I'm glad I finally got to see her, but… "

"What's the matter son?"

"She told me about father, about why she left, and lots of things."

"Things? What kind of things?"

"You know, the magic and where it comes from."

"Oh - yes that." Chance smiled. "You must be careful Camber," he laid an arm across his shoulder. "Do not be tempted to make the wrong choice because you think you are doing the right thing."

"But what is the right thing?"

"Not to use it," said Chance. He gave his nephew a friendly pat on the head. "Get some rest. We have a good long ride ahead of us."

They broke camp at dark and Crescent guided them out of the riverbed and up a steep slope. The lone call of a bird dared break the quiet of night, and though the company rode in silence, not everyone could refrain from disrupting the peace, and every now and then Tonni found a reason to make some such remark regarding her run-in with Rangers, particularly Dane. Her brother would then come to his rescue finding some amusing tale about his sister's past to compensate for her jabs. "Then she ended up ass-over-teakettle in the pig pen with the slop-bucket over her head."

Dane howled, and Tonni glared red-faced at her brother, wishing he had stayed in Shady Haven. "If either of you had even half a brain you'd watch your tongue, or did you not notice that we are practically in the sorcerer's backyard, and I'm sure every pair of ears conceivable has heard you both from five miles out."

"Listen to the lady," chimed Buttercup. He sat on Dane's shoulder and was obviously enjoying the entertainment. "Any fellah knows there's nothing sweeter than when a beautiful lass has the final word," and he paused for a fraction of second then added, "yep nothing finer than a silent dame."

"Why don't you sh... " Tonni never finished her sentence, Chance held up his hand, halting the company.

A canyon opened up stretching its maw for miles with no apparent crossing in sight.

"We cannot go farther," said Crescent. "We should rest here, and I'll go on ahead and see if there's another path."

"There's no suitable spot to hide the horses," answered Chance; he was just about to suggest they backtrack to the edge of the forest when a sinister howl rose on the wind, reaching a pitch that sent shivers down Camber's spine. He knew that howl and so did Dane.

"A Bounder," whispered the archer.

"Wait." Chance barked. He held up his hand. Only the occasional stomp from an impatient hoof or the blowing of air through equine nostrils marked any evidence of the company's presence. The hollow wail was answered by another.

"Two," said Crescent.

"We're downwind so they probably haven't picked up our scent." Chance held up a finger, testing the breeze. "But if the wind shifts even a little, then they will have us." He thought for a moment. "Dismount and strip the horses of their tack. Throw everything into the canyon." They did as they were told and Chance set the horses running. "Quickly! Climb down the rockface!" He sent them down the canyon wall, and one by one they landed on a shelf that hid the entrance to a cave. Chance stood just outside the mouth of the cavern and listened intently to the sounds that fell upon the early morning silence. Sure enough, frightened whinnies gave way to bloodthirsty Bounders.

* * * * * * * *

"Brace yourself," said Dega. "Here they come." He stood with Gerharte on the outer wall surrounding Vintnorr, wrapping around the city like a protective hand. Only one side remained free from solid stone; the canyon was too treacherous for an army, but bowmen camped along the divide ready to thwart any attempt.

Hartland's favorite son and the Blue-Feather's Chieftain had found friendship through a common thread – *war*. The last eight days had uncovered a mutual respect shared by soldiers who have seen service.

Gerharte was impressed with Dega's numerous deeds and he said so, and Dega was intrigued by the ideology behind the Brotherhood of the Blue-Feathers. Born from a necessity to foster a trusted companion, the Brotherhood transcended the boundaries of simple military camaraderie; tied by bonds sworn on spilt blood, they belonged to each other. Men of the Brotherhood teamed in pairs; a left mate and a right mate; each *Blood-Spirit* fiercely linked to his companion's soul.

Gerharte's own Blood-Spirit (his left-side) had been Helena's Eric. By rights she should have gone to stay with his household, but her exceptional beauty caught the eye of the King, and Gerharte had to give in to his liege.

"Then did I grieve," he said to Dega. "And even now I find only emptiness in my heart. A piece of me has left this mortal world, and

I am now half a man. Lo, do I miss his comforting presence; but it is in battle when I miss him most, always I look to my leftside and expect to see Eric's ready grin and bright sword."

"Can you not partner with another?" asked Dega.

"No." said Gerharte. "Only in death will the two halves be reunited."

A constant stream of refugees from neighboring lands had swept through Vintnorr's gates: months, weeks, days, before the predicted onslaught. To the kingdom's capital they came like the precursors of doom heralding the impending storm.

Those who could fight were quickly stationed. Women, children, and the elderly were sent to the bunkers below the city. It was here that Helena had taken her infant son. The days following Dega's escape had placed her under close scrutiny, leading to questioning and confinement to break her will. But this could not be done, and she was set free only to be sent to cower in the dark with the rest of the women and children.

There were no intricate levels of class, not here, not in the dim lighting of the bunkers. Concubines and women of wealth sat on straw among scullery maids, cooks, and washerwomen. Babies cried incessantly, yowling from hunger. And each time the impact from a catapulted rock shook the very foundations of this fortified city, threatening to bury all in a cataclysm of debris, the women would shriek and huddle like frightened rabbits.

Helena sat atop an upended apple barrel. Her blue eyes filled with disgust at their all too predictable behavior. She hugged her son to her breast; he slept soundly, and even upon waking he kept quiet. He had what Eric had called *tam,* an ancient word for a warrior's heart.

Another boulder rocked the bunkers, and a striking redhead whom she recognized as Gretchen, the wife of Gerharte, Eric's Blood-Spirit, came to sit beside her.

"They do not fare well," she meant those gathered in the bunkers not the soldiers.

"They are scared, for they know not what is happening and they fear the worst."

"Yee. That is true. I myself would be *more* worried if all were quiet. At least I know that our walls are still standing, else they would not be trying so hard to bring them down." Gretchen lifted the baby's blanket. "He is the very image of his father."

"I know," sighed Helena. "I see more of my beloved Eric everyday. But my duties require that he stay in the nursery while I attend the King."

Gretchen put her hand on Helena's shoulder. "Would that I could change your fate and remove you from your prison. Gerharte and I... we hoped for you to come live with us, but... "

"Say no more," Helena smiled softly. "My fate is fixed... or cursed, but I will hear no more of your sadness on my account. Be happy my son is well cared for. In time, my looks will fade. I yearn for that day! Only then will I be released from my cage."

"Then my home shall be yours," offered Gretchen with a smile. "But what of your handsome Northerner? Surely he could persuade the King?"

"Nay. His heart belongs to another." She dropped her gaze and stared at the straw-covered floor.

"I am sorry," said Gretchen, and hugged her tight.

"NOW!" Arrows launched into the night, raining down upon the host that stormed below. It was answered by a volley targeting those on the walls. Starlock and Frost-Eye fired back; the elven archers aiming for the heads that commanded the siege towers moving ponderously up hill.

Soldiers with long wooden poles moved to intercept ladders thrown against the walls. Easterlings swarmed below, scrambling up the wall, but for every ladder pushed aside three more landed successfully against the bulwark.

On the far side, Lightfoot picked off any heads that made it across the first wall, but Lockjaw was forced to wait, axe in hand; no bowman was he, and he paced back and forth.

"Careful, Master Dwarf," said Lightfoot, stretching his bow, "if you stumble over the wall I might mistake you for an undersized Easterling."

"If I fall off this stonework it won't be because of my feet. Dwarves are one with rock, and here my feet are grounded like the roots of a willow deep in an underground spring. No, Sir Elf, it is not my feet that are cause for worry, but your head, which seems to grow larger each second of the hour; it is only by a miracle that you have not yet floated away."

Lightfoot laughed as he released another arrow.

Starlock found herself amid a host of Easterlings, each blow, a counterstrike. Eyes roved back and forth looking for an exit. *Above* – no place to go. *Below* – a fifty-foot drop. *Across* – a corner tower. She struck her foe; he dropped his sword doubling over to clutch his belly, and she kicked him in the face sending him over the wall. An arrow whizzed past as she made a giant leap. Fingers brushed against stone, and Starlock gripped the rock, heaving her body around its side. She clung for a moment, then let go, landing neatly on a ledge circling the tower's middle.

Black smoke billowed into the sky, blotting out stars. Siege towers hit by naphtha erupted like orange volcanoes, sending men jumping from their fiery tops. Ballistae rolled to the front replacing the towers and firing back at the defenders.

Cavalry charged out the gates turning the Easterlings back. But as more and more shore up the front they advanced again, beating the horsemen back to the walls.

Lightning rent the air, striking with precision at the towers, at the walls. "It has the feel of a wizard's touch," remarked Frost-Eye, another zigzag of blinding white struck the wall.

"Look there!" The man who had been fighting near his side pointed wildly at the front lines. Explosions buffeted the ancient walls, threatening to crumble them to dust. Frost-Eye stared through smoke-tearing eyes half in wonderment at this new trickery conjured by the Easterling King. Hand-sized globes were tossed at the wall, exploding on impact.

One flew up to where he stood. "DOWN!" He yelled at the soldier, but the man just stood there not comprehending the significance of this new weapon, and he reached out to touch it. With the speed of a diving hawk, Frost-Eye swept up the globe, tossing it back from whence it was hurled, then lunged at the soldier bringing him to ground. The globe exploded while still in the air, and elf and soldier felt a ripple of heat wash over them.

Chunks of rock flew outward, Dega ducked, narrowly avoiding a blow to the head. Easterlings spilled into the courtyard, widening the gap as more of the wall gave way.

"We cannot hold the front wall much longer!" Gerharte came running, sword in hand, striking at the mob, and allowing Dega to squeeze in beside him. "Go back to the second wall."

Dega grunted, backing his foe against the stonework and dispatching the man in two strokes, then sprinted through the gates on the heels of the Blue-Feather's Chieftain. The King rode up to meet them. "How do we fare?" From what he had been told the outer wall was lost, the inner one had taken substantial damage, and chaos reigned between the two. This was confirmed by both men as they hailed Halstaff from the ground.

"We need to send out our foot soldiers," said Gerharte; his chest heaved up and down, blood matted his white-blonde locks falling across his sweaty brow.

"No," said the King. "It is not the right time yet. The second wall still stands and the archers are keeping it clear. Dawn is underway and we might yet see a change in their tactics once the sky is visible."

"Sire! There is no time to wait!" The urgency in Gerharte's voice caused heads to turn. "If the second wall falls then we are lost!"

"He speaks the truth," said Dega. "If you do not release your soldiers now then you might not get the chance later."

"I will wait until dawn!" Halstaff turned his mount and cantered back to his attendants.

Another explosion rocked the city followed by cries of panic. "They are ready to break and run," said the Chieftain, and Dega nodded. If something was not done soon then it could be all over well before daybreak. "Round up your Blue-Feathers," he said. "I will ride with you."

Streaking fire raced overhead but Lockjaw did not see it, he had his hands full battling Easterlings between the walls. His axe moved up and down in a silver blur cleaving a path back to the gates. A great cry was heard and he turned his head at the sound. The gates opened and horses charged out carrying riders dressed in the garb of the Blue-Feathers. Deadly lances brought a halt to the madness and sent the enemy racing for cover.

A horn sounded far below, and Starlock leapt from her perch to the wall, then running across the top she bounded down the stairs to join the battle on the ground. A swarm of soldiers and horses pushed through the crush, forcing the enemy back outside the first wall. Rejoice went up in a resounding cheer as day broke across the sky; Halstaff let loose his foot soldiers to drive the Easterlings back down the hill. But it was the Blue-Feathers under Gerharte's command who won the day, and they sang a favorite ballad as they cut down the last of the attackers standing between the walls.

The men of Girt rested while the Easterlings retreated for a time; fires burned openly and flames had to be quelled. An uneasy truce fell upon both sides while fatalities were noted and tactics reassessed.

Dega found Starlock and they were joined by Lightfoot, Frost-Eye, and Lockjaw. The dark-haired elf grinned at the dwarf as he came near. "I thought I had lost you when you took off into the night shouting Ironfist! Ironfist!"

Lockjaw eyed his cheerful friend. "And I wondered where you had gotten to but then I heard your chatter and knew that if the mouth was working then the rest of you had to be fine."

"That is well and good and I am just as glad you did not trip over your beard while you were retreating," said Lightfoot, and he had the last laugh after all.

"It's a war we cannot win. We are sorely outnumbered," said Dega. He removed his armor (a gift from Gerharte) and undid his sword belt, tossing it on the bed. "Our only hope of defeating Sentash now lies in the hands of our allies, whether they reach us in time remains to be seen."

"You said before your second in command has likely marshaled the Ranger garrisons."

"Yes. I have every reason to believe Gareth may already be planning something."

"Then we need only keep the attackers at bay until reinforcements arrive," said Starlock.

"We could do this if the King would accept our guidance," answered Lightfoot. "But he is still distrustful and believes we are here to usurp his rule."

"Can you blame him?" Dega scowled. "Hawker's past deeds have made for a very questionable alliance. The King is threatened. And for good reason. Who knows what will happen when and if the wizard returns."

"Discord has never been Hawker's intent," said Lockjaw. He waved a finger at them. "He only wishes to help. He would see the people of Astaria live in harmony, and for that I truly stand behind him. You do not see how much he has already sacrificed to protect each and every one of you. I know this only because I have ever been by his side."

"Your loyalty is unswerving," said Dega. "And I respect that. But

I have my doubts when it comes to Hawker's intentions. It would be best if he and all the Caretakers left the world to those who must dwell in it. This whole battle reeks of meddling."

"The exploding globes," said Starlock. She too had reservations regarding Hawker's guidance. Was it just coincidence how things just happen to go wrong whenever he's involved?

"Yes." Dega sat on the bed and pulled off his boots. "The globes."

"I saw one up close and had only seconds to get rid of it. The damage they do is insurmountable to anything I have seen," said Frost-Eye.

Starlock frowned. "I saw them too, but not so close. One hit the tower I was on, doing more damage than a catapult at close range. A more fearsome weapon I cannot imagine, and I wonder if it is the work of someone else."

"What do you mean?" asked Lightfoot.

"Norii," said Dega.

"Yes. It has her signature all over it; we knew she would play a part though I wasn't sure until now how far she would extend her hand. I think she means to eradicate us all."

"The Easterling too?"

"Yes."

* * * * * * * *

"Well? What do *you* want." The sorcerer turned his head as the door to his study creaked open. The constant stream of interruptions was finally taking a toll and he glared hotly at the intruder. Bad enough that his attack on Girt was not going entirely to plan, but there was still no news of the boy. His dogs whimpered softly, tails between legs, tucking paws under bellies, and it was then he noticed the other figure that had followed the first one through the door.

"You spend too much time obsessing about the boy," Norii said, gliding into the room. The dogs whined even louder.

"And you said Girt would fall."

"I gave you the tools to overthrow Halstaff. But you have done nothing. Instead you sit in your study and use every last bit of your resources looking for one small insignificant ripple in the pool of the *Great Design*. Did I not say he would come to you. Yet you sit idly by, chasing slender threads while certain victory slips through your fingers."

"Bah! It is a setback - nothing more."

"A setback we can ill afford. Even your plans to overrun the North are failing."

"Why have you come then? Is it to aid me as was our agreement, or to criticize my methods." Norii was not to be spoken to in such a manner, but he couldn't help it; his irritation outstripped his own fear of the Caretaker. He glared at the familiar figure still standing in the shadows. "And why are you here."

But it was Norii who spoke. "To secure my investment," and she laughed in that hollow voice meant to suck the life out of the living.

XVI

The Tide Turns

Jules vaulted off his horse and sprinted into the barracks, nearly colliding with Sal and yelling at the top of his lungs for Gareth. The Lieutenant ran across the entrance hall to meet him.

"Sir!" He managed a salute. "Wildwood is no more! They are coming!"

"Who? What?" The officer shook him, but he had already guessed who and what Jules spoke of. Still, he needed to hear it with his own ears, the name said out loud so that there was no shred of doubt.

"Easterlings Sir! They are coming!"

Gareth ordered the gates barred. Archers and cavalry were sent to their units. Jules went back to his room to gather his weapons.

"Jules wait!" Sal came running after. "What happened? You look a mess. Are we really under attack?"

"Yes. We haven't much time," he said, fumbling for his sword belt. "I had a run-in with a Bounder and there are likely more out there."

Hansil came charging into the room followed by Bon, the only one not present was Caleb, still in the watchtower. "Is it true?" They said at the same time.

Jules nodded. "Look, I know it seems strange and it couldn't be happening but it is. We have to go and… " he had to choke back a lump as the words came out in a rush. "I want you all to know that if something should happen… well… you're the best friends a guy could ask for… and I just want you to know that."

"Hey," Sal held his hand out. "One for all. Right?" And the others followed, hammering their fists down on his. A trumpet blared and sent them running out of the barracks and into uncertainty.

* * * * * * * *

"Can't you stop that thing from stinking?" Tonni held her nose.

"He's scared," said Dane. "It's not like he can help it."

"Then throw him outside or something."

Dane peered at the faerie in his pocket. It looked back at him with its unblinking yellow eyes. "Can't you tone it down a little?" he asked. Buttercup shook his head; the one thing that frightened him more than an Elf apparently, was the thought of becoming a Bounder snack. "I think we're safe in this cave," he said in his most reassuring voice. "The only way they could find us is by scent and if you keep this up then we'll all end up on the menu." He stuck his hand in his pocket and fished the little critter out. "Besides, you have wings, if anyone has a chance for a getaway it's you." The smell abruptly stopped and the faerie flew up to his shoulder.

"It's about time," Tonni gasped.

"Shhh!" Chance stood at the mouth of the cave, listening to the night. "Nothing. They've likely gone back to their lairs, whether anything is left of the horses remains to be seen, but I doubt we'll find ought but bones."

"How are we supposed to get past them?" Braun sat cross-legged beside his sister.

"It'll be day soon, and if they've gone back on full bellies then perhaps sleep will be our ally." The former Ranger peered out at the pre-dawn sky. "We can't stay here much longer, we'll just have to hope this is the case."

"And if it's not?"

"You didn't have to come you know," Tonni reminded her brother.

"What? And miss ruining your day?"

Dane chuckled, and Camber tried to hold back a grin, but she caught them both and the handsign she flipped was anything but lady-like.

At daybreak they made their way up the canyon ledge. The day was cool, and a haze covered the land; wispy tendrils of fog reached beneath layers of clothing with cold clammy fingers. Damp, miserable, and grey; the landscape swathed in its dismal cloak passed its gloom onto the company. After a time they stopped for a rest and Crescent went on ahead; he came back with a grim look on his face. "Bones. Human," he said.

Chance followed him to his grisly discovery. The remains had been hastily dumped along with a few shreds of cloth. He bent down to brush away the sand, then stopped, uncovering something shiny. A button. Not just a button. He rolled it around his fingers then flipped it into his pocket.

Camber jumped as the sudden movement of bush announced the return of Crescent and Chance, but relief quickly gave way to worry when he noticed the serious frown his uncle wore. Chance kept silent and Camber didn't ask; whatever thing could trouble his uncle this much he was probably better off not knowing.

Again, they found shelter beneath the lip of rock, no cave this time but it would be protection enough from whatever the evening might bring, and most importantly, the wind could not reach them here and deliver their scent to unwelcome noses.

Night came fast, dropping down like a shadow, and with it came flashes of light, far away in the distance and growing fainter as if traveling to some predetermined destination.

"What do you make of it?" Chance growled, his voice barely audible. Crescent shook his head; his green eyes glinted like a cat's predatory glare caught unawares in the dark. "It's unnatural. Of that, I am certain."

"Yes, I was afraid of that."

"What's it mean Uncle Chance?" Camber sat close to the rock, and though he kept his voice to a whisper, it could not contain his fear.

"War has begun." His uncle went to sit beside him, and the others huddled in close.

"Then this is the doing of the Easterling King?" asked Dane.

"Yes."

"But how can he command something so far away?"

"He is very capable of that. But what worries me is he must be feeling very confident if he has already sent his armies abroad. And it's now more than ever I wish I had heard from Drake before we left. Only he would know the extent to which the Easterling's armies have been marshaled." Chance frowned, and his hand slipped inside his pocket fingering the button.

"Drake? As in Dega's father?" Dane's voice became louder with growing curiosity. His uncle put his finger to his lips and "shhh'd" him, then quietly said. "Dega's father was banished from the North so he could keep an eye on the sorcerer's armies and secretly start building an army right here in the East. This is why Hawker sent me to Shady Haven. I was to find him and bring him back to Illianther. We were almost ready to strike but... don't look so surprised... this was planned long before you were born. As I was saying, our plans were to bring the Elves and the Northern League together and use Drake's Eastern army to launch our attack. We had no idea that Sentash was prepared to this extent. Fortunately, there are still some minor kingdoms that have strength enough to withstand an attack, and I am thinking of Girt, for one. But there are others, maybe not as large or as well equipped. Let's hope they too are able to resist his assault long enough for the free people to assemble."

"Dega has already seen to that," said Camber, his eyes rolled fearfully out to the dark, afraid that any moment a Bounder might hurl itself from out of the canyon.

"Yes, Crescent has told me about the council, but it still seems like a longshot at best," and Chance looked up at the now very much faint flashes of light. "Even the Battle of N'Amorr was better planned."

The next few days went by without any more Bounder sightings, but it was the evenings that bothered Chance, and he watched the faraway lightning with an uneasiness growing in his heart. On the morning of the eighth day the end of the canyon was near. The gap narrowed as it converged upon a fast-flowing river that emptied itself down the canyon's steep walls. By evening they reached a cluster of pines and Chance signaled them to a halt. They would camp for the night, but not on the ground.

"Did you hear anything last night?" Dane climbed out of the tree, jumping the last few feet. Camber, Braun and Tonni were already on the ground, sorting through packs. "You mean Bounders?" Braun tossed an apple his way, and Dane nodded.

"Do you think they know we're here?" Tonni ran her fingers through her hair.

"Possibly," answered Camber. "It's hard to tell since they've kept their distance, but I'm sure the horses would have tipped them off that at least someone has ventured into their territory."

"But why haven't they attacked?" Braun stood beside Tonni with his arms folded; both had thick wavy hair and dark flashing eyes, but it was the full lips and a ready-set of dimples marking them brother and sister, and though they fought like cats and dogs, Camber was willing to bet that either would lay down his or her life for the other.

"They had several chances while we marched along the canyon," he continued, his sister nodded her agreement.

"Maybe they haven't figured out our location."

"Or maybe you're traveling to where they want you to go anyway," said a voice from inside Dane's coat, and the archer plucked Buttercup from his pocket. The faerie stretched his limbs, flapped his wings, then buzzed to the top of Dane's head. "It ain't rocket-science, kid."

"What's rocket-science?" asked Dane.

"Never mind that, the bug has a point," said Tonni. "What if we're walking into a trap?"

"We have no choice either way." Chance passed his waterskin to Camber as he joined the group. "If we turn back then there's a greater chance we could get caught between Bounders and Easterlings. We now have what appears to be a full-blown war to the south, and who knows what's happening elsewhere. If we continue this path we risk running into danger too. But since the whole purpose of making this trek is to recover the Winterstone, which may or may not lie beneath Tar Galleaon, depending on who you believe; then our present course seems to be the most logical one, though it seems a little too convenient. Myself, I'd rather try my hand at skirting around our present obstacle and hopefully remain undetected than run toward an army."

"A wise decision. We might yet find a way inside and possibly achieve what we're after," added Crescent. "It seems to me our coming together under such circumstances after losing the others, then locating Chance, carries too much an external influence than just pure coincidence."

"What are you saying?" asked Camber.

"The Elves believe the world has a preordained pattern that even the Caretakers know not the outcome. Over the centuries we have studied patterns and anomalies, whether random or deliberate, and have compiled all major events of the past, coordinating them with the present and matching them with what we believe will be the outcome of the future. We call it the *Threads of Destiny*."

"Threads of Destiny," repeated Camber, "is that some kind of an oracle."

"Yes and no," answered the elf. "It cannot see into the future... "

"But it gives a strong indication of what is needed in order for certain outcomes to prevail," finished Chance. "You – Camber, are part of that chain."

"Me?"

"Yes. You've been mentioned several times in the pattern, and not always by name, sometimes indirectly." Chance shaded his eyes and checked the sun's position. "I think we should be moving on. The faerie may be right afterall, if we are being herded toward the Keep then this must be how the pattern is to be woven."

At mid-day they reached the edge of the forest, daylight filtered between trees, casting away shadow under shafts of white light. A sheer rock wall rose up to greet them as they exited the trees. It was easily fifty feet straight up with no visible cracks, ledges, or crannies.

"Now what?" asked Dane. He wanted to hurl his pack at the wall, instead he threw it at the ground and plunked himself on top. It wasn't fair. All that walking to get around the stupid canyon, hiding in caves, a night in the trees, and now this... stopped by a stupid wall.

"We'll have to scale it," said Chance, "unless anyone knows another way around?"

"Go under," said Buttercup.

"What? What did you say?" Dane plucked the faerie from atop his head. For some reason the pint-sized creature thought it funny to grab his hair whenever he removed it from its lofty position. Dane held the critter up to his face. "How do we go under?"

"Why should I tell you?" Buttercup pretended to be inspecting his tiny talons.

"Because if you don't I'll snap you in half," answered Tonni; she had about as much as she could take, and Dane had to hold his hand protectively over the faerie, lest she snatch it and make good on her proposal.

"Well bug – what of it? How do we pass this thing?"

"I'll tell you if she apologizes." Buttercup folded his tiny arms across a huffed out chest.

All heads turned in Tonni's direction.

"No Way!" she snapped.

"C'mon Tonni," Braun put his arm around his sister's shoulders, guiding her to where Dane sat. "Just apologize, or do you want to stand here for the next century," and applying pressure to the back of her neck he bent her head to meet Buttercup at eye level. When she refused to utter the words he slowly added more pressure. "Okay, okay… sorry," she muttered.

"A little louder please, I'm having a problem with my ears."

"Why you little sh… " Braun's hand closed over her mouth, muffling the rest of her words.

"You have your apology, now tell us how to get past this wall." Dane glared at the faerie.

"If you follow the rock in that direction," a tiny claw pointed east, "there's a tunnel that leads directly into the fortress."

"And how do you know this?"

The green and blue faerie stared up at him. "I've been in it."

"Am I really supposed to believe you?" Dane narrowed his eyes. Was it telling the truth, or was it leading them into some kind of a trap? But Buttercup proved his loyalty back at the cabin, and seemed genuinely concerned about the archer's well-being; it was like having a miniature guardian – all of four inches tall.

"Listen Mac," Buttercup grabbed Dane's face and pulled him close. "The last thing I want in the world is to go back into that *@%&* castle. But because you and your friends over there," he pointed at the others, "are so bent on going in, then I'm going to get you in without getting caught by the sorcerer. I know this tunnel because it's the exact same one I used when I made my escape from *His Blackness* three hundred years ago."

"Well?" Dane said to his uncle.

"We don't have much of a choice since we're short on rope, and I don't see any other way around." It was true; the wall of rock seemed to stretch for miles in either direction.

Under Buttercup's guidance they followed the wall east then turned back into the forest. About halfway in they came to a stream trickling its way to a much larger water source. The faerie bade them all to stop and he flew from Dane's shoulder to the stream. A tunnel opened up along the muddy bank, large enough for a full-grown man to crawl through on hands and knees.

"Eeew… tell that bug to stop stinking." Tonni's voice trailed behind as she followed Dane up the tunnel. It was moist, and the floor was mucky, a kind of sucking mud that oozed when you placed your hand in it; the stench was overwhelming bringing tears to eyes.

"It's not me," Buttercup said, he sat on Dane's head holding his nose. "It's the tunnel."

"What?! What exactly is this tunnel used for?" asked Dane.

"Sewage," replied the bug.

* * * * * * * * *

Billowing black smoke wafted into the sky. The men of Girt were tense, wounded, and weary. At the very front they suffered from uncertainty after each strike reduced more of the wall to rubble, soon there would be nothing left, and they would be forced back to the last barrier.

During the day both sides came to a temporary truce to assess damage and tend the wounded. Skirmishes broke out but were fewer in number and less organized; all just a front until darkness, then full-scale battle waged across the walls.

"Have you seen Frost-Eye?" asked Starlock.

Lightfoot shook his head. He and the dwarf had their hands full, and he hadn't time to check on the others. The fighting was not going well for Girt. They were close to losing the front wall completely, thanks to the exploding globes.

Starlock left her companions while she forged to the front in search of Frost-Eye. On the way she passed the Captain and Gerharte organizing the Blue-Feathers for an attack.

Frost-Eye stretched his bow, marking his target. Easterlings swarmed the courtyard, breaking through gaps in the wall, fewer of Halstaff's men stood near the front, and more and more ladders scored the top without resistance. He turned in time to see Starlock charging toward him; a flash of silver left her hands, arcing through the air and slicing the naked throat of his would-be assailant. "We've lost more ground," he said. But Starlock did not need his report; it was obvious to even an untrained eye and she having more experience than the young elf. "Get back, you should not be up here by yourself."

Another explosion hit the wall; it gave a lurch, grinding rock rumbled under foot. The blast was felt on the far side, and Lockjaw stopped in mid-swing distracted by the noise. His hesitation became an advantage for the Easterling, who pressed forward, backing the dwarf up the parapet. Behind him, another foe raised his sword, ready to strike a lethal blow.

"Lockjaw! NO!" Lightfoot dropped his bow, and leaping in front of the Easterling he snatched a shield from the ground, holding it out just as the sword came down. The force of the blow rattled all the way up his arms causing his legs to buckle. Lightfoot was not a fighter, and it was all he could do to keep his feet under him as he protected Lockjaw's back.

Lockjaw turned in mid-stride as he realized what was happening. The Easterling pressing from the front gave a yell, and he suddenly found himself having to dispatch this foe at the same time Lightfoot braced for another blow.

The sword came crashing down again, splitting the shield in half. Lockjaw turned, looking over his shoulder as his friend received the next strike across his unprotected head.

"NOOOO!" The word resounded across the battlefield, carried by a rush of wind. A burst of power a hundred times the impact of a dozen exploding globes rippled the air and blew apart the Easterling that had delivered the deathblow. Lockjaw fell to his knees and pulled his friend to his arms. The sky above boiled with frightening power, the Easterlings retreated, afraid for their lives. But Lockjaw wasn't aware of anything save the stricken form of Lightfoot.

The elf opened his dark eyes, but no merry sparkle danced within. Blood spilled from the wound, running down Lockjaw's hands; the throb of life ebbing away with each retreating beat. His eyes brimmed with tears as he held his friend tenderly as if somehow only he could prevent the elf's essence from escaping.

"Dwarf – I go now." Lightfoot spoke softly. "To where I know not. And my heart grieves, for I fear we shall not meet again – unless I become a tree and you the welcoming soil." He paused, taking a gasp of air. "Come – bend your ear," and Lockjaw did as he was told and the elf beckoned him even closer. He flicked his friend on the forehead. "You dwarves are too serious." With his last breath he smiled at Lockjaw; his eyes glazed and his head turned to the side.

Tears fell from Lockjaw's eyes splashing over the now slack face of Lightfoot; he crumpled the elf to his chest, holding him tight and burying his face into that still warm body. The sky darkened, blanking out all other lights as Lockjaw wept. And he could not know, nor would he have cared, that the magic he so secretly desired had come to him at last.

"Down!" Starlock grabbed Frost-Eye by his tunic and thrust him to ground just as the wall behind them collapsed. The sky, rife with electricity, rippled with a force never before seen on this world. A

A SECRET REVEALED

BOOM rocked the night; the blast fell thick on air, raining rock down from above.

"What was that?" Frost-Eye dusted off his clothes, and Starlock shook her head. "It came from over there," she said, and they sprinted back along the yard to the inner wall.

"The sorcerer?"

"No."

They raced along the parapet, and Starlock stopped suddenly, Frost-Eye nearly running into her. Lockjaw stood in front of them, carrying Lightfoot in his arms. "How... " but she never got the words out. A beam of light lit the sky, illuminating the walls of Vintnorr.

"Look!" Frost-Eye cried, and Starlock's eyes picked out a blur circling above in the unnatural brightness. "BELIA!" she shouted with joy. A low rumble in the distance heralded the sound of an army. The falcon found its mistress and a blue-tinged ball of light exploded before their astonished eyes. No one was more surprised and more relieved than Lockjaw as he carried Lightfoot to the feet of the wizard.

"Master," he breathed, sadness framing his bearded face. "Please," he stroked Lightfoot's dark head.

"I cannot," said Hawker. "His spirit has left this world to go where I will not say." He laid a hand across the dwarf's shoulder. "You grieve. And that is good. He watches you even now, and knows you will keep his torch burning faithfully in your heart long after this war is over and the world is done with you, and you, yourself, are ready to depart." Hawker bent so that he was face to face with his apprentice. "He has given you a gift. Do you not see?" Lockjaw shook his head. "In your anguish you have found your magic. His gift to you. Do not waste it by wishing to undo the past."

"But gladly I would give it back, for the price is too great."

"He would not want you to. Mayhap it is his way of aiding the cause, and you should embrace this gift and do good with it."

Lockjaw nodded, and with head bowed low he carried his precious burden away.

"What has kept you?" asked Dega. The battle was all but over and the company now sat in the King's receiving hall. Gerharte was there, and so were a number of Blue-Feathers, Snowblind, Stonefinger, and some of the Ranger's high-ranking officers, even men from the Borderlands.

Halstaff had been mortally wounded when a last attempt to bring down the second wall had nearly succeeded. The King became separated from his personal guard and was struck down as he tried to defend his city. The Easterling who had swept Halstaff's body onto his horse in an attempt to run off with the King as a prize had been cut down by none other than Gerharte. The Chieftain regained his sovereign's body but soon found himself trapped behind enemy lines. Dega and a number of Blue-Feathers had charged into the fray with swords and lances, allowing Gerharte to escape. The Blue-Feather's Chieftain was indebted to the Captain for his bravery.

Hawker was not far from Girt when he felt the force of Lockjaw's newly acquired power and he used his magic to hasten the armies to Vintnorr.

"I came as fast as I could," he rubbed his goatee. "There was much that had to be dealt with before I could leave Atrilla and the others. When I reached Illianther, Winterleaf sent me after the Barbs, and it is only by using every resource I had that I was able to bring you their strength in time."

Dega nodded, recalling how he and Gerharte charged out Vintnorr's gates leading the Blue-Feathers into battle, and driving the Easterlings down the hill. The Barbs had reached the fighting first; a sudden onslaught of elven warriors crashing into the sorcerer's forces like a black tidal wave.

Dega used his legs to maneuver his horse between the crush, but the charger was young and spooked easily, and Dega found himself wishing for his own mount, having trained Panther from colt. The stallion, ever calm on the battlefield, knew his most subtle commands; a slight touch with rein or leg and Panther obeyed like an extension of the Captain's own body.

A spear impaled the roan, and Dega jumped, clearing the saddle and landing on his feet. Bodies pushed together, hot, sweaty. Dega whirled, finding the unprotected area under the Easterling's arm. The man was slow, and Dega struck twice, then turned to meet his next attacker.

"Dega!" Gerharte held his arm out, and the Ranger grabbed it, swinging up behind the Blue-Feather's Chieftain. Gerharte urged his bay forward, and he and Dega used boot and sword to cut a path through the mob. Stonefinger, Silvan, and the Rangers had now joined the Barbs, and with the men of Girt, beat back the sorcerer's forces.

Dega rubbed his arm; it ached from wrist to shoulder. Never had he dealt so much death.

"I fear we came too late," said Stonefinger. The Dwarven King still wore his breastplate and greaves; his axe lay propped in the corner; the edge still keen even after all the armor it had rented. "Many have died needlessly, including your own King."

"Many more might have died had you not arrived when you did," said Gerharte, on his head he wore the laurel leaves of Girt. The Blue-Feather's foremost warrior had been made the unofficial King, and though Gerharte was not happy about having such a thing thrust upon him, he took his responsibility like a man destined to make a difference and bring greatness to his people. "Halstaff died bravely, and we do not mourn for him the way the Men of the North mourn the dead, or the way dwarves carry their grief like tears of granite," he spoke quietly, his gaze resting on Lockjaw, shoulders slumped and eyes red from weeping. "Nay. Halstaff has gone to the Halls of our Ancestors, and there he will spend his days eating, drinking, and fighting."

"A fitting end for a man of his fortitude," said Hawker. "We have turned back the tide for now. But that will not stop Sentash. He has other tricks that we may yet have to evade. I fear Girt has only seen a small sampling of his power, and I wonder where he has sent all his forces. I do not believe what we have encountered thus far are truly his followers in their entirety. We must strike fast if we hope to succeed."

"What are you saying," asked Dega.

"We must bring an army to his doorstep. Only then can we be assured he will not be able to undo the advantage we have gained."

"And Camber?" The Captain leaned forward. "What of him? We cannot abandon him now. We must find him."

"And find him we shall, but we must force Sentash into using all his resources."

"The wizard is right," a growl came from Starlock's right, and an elf with smoke-colored hair gathered in a topknot measured all with his icy blue chips. This was Snowblind, general of the Janastari army, and kinsman to Starlock. His long nose - broken at the bridge, and like Starlock's, tipped down at the end, added to an already severe presence, made even more dangerous by the number of weapons he carried. "We must finish this war now. The boy is just a tool. If we find him, then so be it, but if not, then what is the life of one boy compared to the lives of many."

"The boy is under my personal care! I will not leave him for the Easterling King to find." Dega reached over and took hold of Hawker's robes. "You said before all hope lies with Camber. Have you now changed your mind?" He tugged the wizard closer. "Are you so driven by your desire to right your own wrong that you're willing to discard lives along the way?"

Hawker brushed away Dega's hand. "Camber travels in the care of others, and his thread in the fabric of fate has been woven; it will not become frayed, nor will it unravel. But I am not privileged to see how it will play out. I must trust to what feels right. And so we can only move forward. Do not despair, for we may yet cross Camber's path ere this affair is finished."

"We have to go East either way," said Starlock, her eyes found Dega's. "If we take an army so much the better. We can travel faster, and without having to hide along the way."

"We risk moving the army away from where they can be of use," argued Dega. "What if the North comes under attack. What then? How can we reach them in time?"

Gerharte laid a hand across his friend's shoulder. "What if we split the force?"

"No," said Hawker. "We must take all we can. We can leave enough men here to fortify Vintnorr but the bulk of the army must go East."

"The Barbs will go East," said Snowblind.

"So will the Dwarves," Stonefinger added.

"As do the Men of Caldorn."

"Once more your decision seems fixed," said Dega. "And you have the support of the council, and though my heart tells me one thing I see that there is no use in swaying your vote. The Rangers will go East." Hawker started to nod his approval, but Dega held up his hand. "We also look for Camber."

The council was over and Dega walked back to his apartment. Starlock and Frost-Eye stayed behind to talk with Snowblind, and Lockjaw once again took his place beside Hawker.

The young Captain strode quickly down the hall, avoiding Blue-Feathers and Rangers alike, not wishing to converse or debate with anyone for the moment, and though he accepted the decision of the council, his face clearly showed his concern. In his heart he believed this was a mistake. What if the sorcerer has already invaded the north? Perhaps Girt was just a diversion.

Someone waited in the corridor; the torchlight illuminated the shapely figure of Helena. She and the others had been released from the bunkers, and she came with her son to find Dega. "My heart is joyful that you are alive," she said, as the jingle of spurs announced his arrival.

Dega gave her a rare smile. "I see you are safe. That is well and good. But you do not have to linger in this hall. I release you, same as before."

"I know," she said. "I am now free from service. News of the King's death travels fast, and plans for a funeral pyre are underway. I came only to say good-bye. And to... to thank you."

"Thank me? For what?"

"Because you have given me hope."

Dega was about to tell her that he had only ever been himself, and any decent person would do the same, but she touched his lips with her finger and silenced his words.

"Before you came to Vintnorr I was at the end of my rope. I felt worthless. But your selfless act to save your friends at risk of your own life has given me hope. When I helped the elf escape I did it for love. *Love!* Not for myself. Not to please you. And not because I longed to leave Vintnorr. Something greater. *Something else.* You and she can have what I could not. Do you not see? It was in my power to give you this, and I did so freely, asking nothing in return. My heart is glad, Dega Darkhawk, and I thank you."

A flicker of light reflected the shine in those luminous eyes, and Dega could not look directly at them, and so he turned away. "Where will you go now?" he asked, moving his gaze to the babe sleeping soundly in his blankets.

"I go to live with Gerharte and his family. This is my son, Leif. Gerharte has promised to take him under his wing and teach him to become a great warrior like his father." She smiled brightly, and Dega couldn't help but smile back; a sudden weight had fallen from his mountain of worries, and he was genuinely glad that someone had found happiness at last.

She stood on her tiptoes, brushing her soft lips across his unshaven cheek and startling him with a kiss. "May Greatness and Goodness ever be with you." And before he could blink she was stepping lightly down the hall.

He entered the apartment and pulled off his boots. By the time Starlock and Frost-Eye had returned Dega was sound asleep.

Frost-Eye said good-night leaving Starlock to herself; she sat curled up in a chair with Belia perched behind her, nibbling gently on the strands of her hair. Snowblind had taken them to the Janastari camp just outside the walls of Vintnorr. The moment she stepped into the encampment all Barbs jumped to attention, forming straight lines and saluting her with fist to heart. She did not ask to be their sovereign and it was clear they would make her one whether she wanted it or not. Even Snowblind questioned her about returning to the White Cliffs; she had no desire to go there and she said this. Snowblind merely nodded, but Starlock knew he would not be satisfied until she resumed her rightful role.

She reached behind her and brought Belia to the front, stroking the falcon's soft feathery head. "You have ever been my friend. You never judge. You stay by my side in good times and in bad. I wish you could speak, perhaps your words would hold the answers I am seeking." But Belia only fluffed her feathers, and Starlock sighed softly.

* * * * * * * *

"Which way?" asked Dane.

"Left – No Right!"

"Tell that bug to make up its mind. If we don't get out of here soon I'm gonna be sick."

"Stop complaining," Braun's voice came from behind. "I'm the one who's trailing through everyone else's slush." He was last in line, crawling on hands and knees; his wide shoulders barely fit the breadth of the tunnel's mucky walls. Silently he agreed with his sister. If they didn't reach the end soon he just might find himself looking at his own breakfast.

The tunnel widened at the next bend and they were able to stand. Camber uncramped his arms and legs and followed his uncle to where clean water ran down the wall of the cavern. He held his hands under the spray, splashing cold water onto his clothes, cleaning away sludge. "Now what?" he asked. They seemed to be at a dead end.

"We go up." Buttercup pointed to a ledge just above their heads, and above that – an opening in the ceiling.

"Okay Camber, go." Chance cupped his hands and hoisted his nephew to where Crescent lay on his stomach, arms outstretched ready to receive the cadet. Camber grabbed the rock as he was launched up the wall and with the elf's help he hauled himself onto the ledge. Tonni was next. Then Dane.

"You go," said Braun. Chance shook his head, but Braun held up his hand. "I'm bigger, and all of you are going to have to pull me up." He pushed the former Ranger up the wall.

As Chance scrambled up the ledge, something dark bounded into the cavern.

"Aeieee!" Buttercup dug his talons into Dane's head.

A second Bounder joined the first.

"Braun!" Tonni yelled.

Braun heard the growl from behind and his neck-hair stood on end; he drew his sword. "GO!" he said, turning to face the Bounder.

"NO!" Tonni screamed; she tried to jump from the ledge but Dane grabbed her around the waist and held her. "Let me go!" She squirmed in his arms, horrified as her brother narrowly avoided the first Bounder. Chance took Dane's bow and shoved him roughly toward the exit. "Go! Get out of here." He stood on the ledge firing arrows at the two eye-less monsters.

"Noooo!" Tonni wailed; she pounded on Dane's shoulders as he carried her away from the grisly scene now unfolding in the cavern below.

One arrow left. The bow was useless against such beasts, and even if he could jump from his perch he would not be able to reach Tonni's brother in time. The former Ranger had seen a lot of horrible things in his fifty plus years, some better left forgotten. But this last thing, this carefully aimed arrow, would be by far the cruelest undertaking of his life's legacy.

"This way!" Buttercup flew to the ceiling, hovering under streaks of light filtering between slats. Crescent shoved the wooden grate aside, and hauled himself up, lowering his hand for Camber. Behind them, Braun's battle with the Bounders came to a bitter finish as his last shout ended abruptly, cut off in mid-cry. Dane pushed Tonni up through the hole, and she wailed with renewed anguish. His uncle came charging toward them, motioning Dane to go.

"Quickly!"

He barely cleared the portal before Chance was already climbing through.

"Plug it!" Chance threw the slatted cover overtop; it wobbled a few times, followed by scratching and thumping from the other side, then all went silent.

"It'll hold for now. But we have to find an exit." Chance surveyed the dimly lit cellar. "It looks like a storage area." Heaps of armor lay hidden under a layer of dirt; a dull gleam from once bright metal revealing a quality not found in the Northlands. Chance picked up a sword and examined it carefully before laying it back in its dusty bower. "Dwarven-steel; the runes are in the ancient tongue, unless my eyes deceive me."

"This place gives me the creeps," muttered Dane. "All that's missing are bones." He let go of Tonni and bent down to look at the sword his uncle had picked up. Buttercup flew back to perch atop the archer's head and flapped his iridescent wings. "Bounders... hello... Bounders just below us." He rapped a tiny claw against Dane's forehead.

"This way," said Crescent. He lifted a plank barring the exit. The door gave a grim squeal, opening on hinges that had not been used in more than a century. Chance ushered everyone through.

"Safe," said Dane. Tonni dropped to the floor.

"Not really," answered Chance. "I suspect we are directly under the Keep."

"Under the dungeons," corrected Buttercup.

"Well whatever, we can't stay here." The former Ranger followed the wall to another door and opened it.

Camber peered over his uncle's shoulder. "We need light," he said.

Chance felt his hands along the rough stone and located a brand. "Ah, so let there be light," he muttered, and taking a flint from his pocket he lit the torch.

Dane nudged Tonni with the toe of his boot. She wouldn't budge. He knelt down beside her. "We can't stay here."

"I don't care."

"Look," he said, resisting an urge to toss her over his shoulder and be done with it, but a vision of his mother, hands on hips, popped into his thoughts, and he knew he should talk to the distraught girl. "I liked your brother too, and I'm sorry for what happened. But he made his choice to save you. To save all of us." He hoped he didn't sound too wishy-washy. "Braun would want you to live, it would tear him apart, er... break his heart if he knew his sacrifice was in vain."

Tonni looked into his eyes with big dark saucers filled with tears. "For me?" she repeated. He nodded. "I never realized how much I loved my brother until now. I just never... " her words trailed off with a sob. "I never thought I would lose him. He kept on about leaving Shady Haven and taking me somewhere safe, but I wouldn't listen."

Camber stepped over and gave Dane a nudge. The archer shrugged, and Camber motioned to Tonni with his eyes then back to Dane. He nodded, and held out his hand. She grasped his fingers, (surprisingly soft), and he pulled her to her feet. "Since Braun wanted you to leave, then I promise to get you out of Shady Haven. Maybe you'd like to come with me to Hartland." Atop his head Buttercup rolled his eyes. *Whoops!* What did he just say? Too late to take it back. She nodded, swiping away her tears, and holding his hand she let him guide her out the door.

Chance led them down the passage single-file with Crescent bringing up the rear. *Ancient,* thought Camber. *It smells ancient. Like a long forgotten cemetery.* He cringed as a cobweb brushed his face and quickly brought his hand up to swipe away its invisible threads. Up ahead the soft glow of torchlight marked the location of Chance, and behind him trailed Dane, then Tonni. It was blacker than any place he had ever been; even darker than the jungti hive. *And,* it was getting stuffy. His legs labored onward, dragging ponderously along the passage. Suddenly he couldn't move!

"Snakes Alive!" Dane's voice thrummed in his ears. And behind him, Crescent cried out in elvish. The passage became bright. Bright light blinding his sensitive eyes. When he realized what was happening it was too late. Trapped! Stopped in their tracks by an unseen force. He tried to counter it, calling forth his white fire.

"No you don't." said a voice, and a figure stepped out of the light.

XVII

The Last Alliance

Thunderclouds rolled in from the east, threatening to swallow the sky. Rain came in sheets, and with it, lightning, snapping at targets with frightening accuracy. Soon the sudden onslaught of sword clashing would commence. Jules sat astride the warhorse. He waited with his squad. All young. All inexperienced. And he the only one who had come face to face with death's dumb stare.

Underneath him the charger pawed the ground; it champed its bit and threw its big black head up and down. Sergeant Weyland sat beside him, shouting at another officer, his voice rising over the wind. He hunkered into his cloak, waiting for the signal that would send them off at a gallop from the safety of the forest to collide with an army three times their strength and size.

"Do you think they have Bounders with them?" asked Hansil. He sat on Jules's left, and beside him waited Sal. Caleb was in the watchtower and Bon was holding back the Easterlings with the rest of the archers. Jules nodded. He was sure of it.

A horn ra'tahd; the warhorse gave a snort, and in two great leaps reached full gallop, surging to the forefront, and easily outdistancing his companion's cavalry mounts.

Rain slapped his face; tendrils of sandy brown hair clung to his brow; Jules gripped the haft of his sword, locking his sweaty fingers around the grooves. Down the hill his charger sped; one warhorse and one boy riding to meet death.

Arrows came whistling overhead, pinging off armor, sticking into flesh. Jules hugged the saddle; to his right, a soldier took one in the forehead; a look of surprise played across the man's face. *That could have been him.* His horse lurched sideways and he moved with his mount.

A Bounder ripped between the lines, mouth wide open. He jammed his sword down the creature's throat, thrusting in and up. A screech rattled up his arm, and he drew back his blade just as the stallion launched into the air. The warhorse was a veteran of such battles and he made up for his rider's lack of experience, rearing and using forelegs as weapons. "Thanks," Jules managed, and gave the horse a quick pat.

Sal reigned in his mount. "Hansil!" The cadet was on the ground fending off a man twice his size. He yelled again, but Hansil was pushed back and several Easterlings filled the gap between them. An arm came up, slashing at his leg. Sal answered with his sword. Another arm sprang up on his left. The cadet who had never wanted to run his family's tavern now hacked and slashed to reach his friend. To his horror, Hansil took steel. Bright blood splattered his uniform, running down his pantleg; he turned his face upward, dropped his sword, then crumbled into the mud.

Sal's horse broke free of the crush; he swept his sword across the Easterling's unprotected neck. The soldier fell and Sal leapt from his mount. "Hansil!" The body warm; the heart beating. Hansil opened his eyes. "You're safe. I won't let you go!" And wrapping his arms around his friend, he pushed him onto his charger then jumped up behind, driving his heels home.

From his lofty position, Caleb watched the surprise attack dislodge the Easterlings. Wildwood's cavalry had reached the old Ranger barracks just in time; without the help of these seasoned soldiers he doubted they would have lasted an hour, let alone a day. Somewhere over to his left, Bon stood with the archers. And out there, amid the chaos, his other friends played at soldier. "Try and stay alive. Try and stay alive," he whispered.

* * * * * * * *

The morning of the departure was dreary; winter's chill touched the very bones of the land; its slate-gray sky casting a somber mood. Lockjaw sat quietly on a sturdy pony; the brim of his hood pulled low over his face so that he appeared like a shadow inside his woolen cloak. Stonefinger sat beside him, feeding him news of the warrens, but he only half-listened. His heart was gloomy. He cared not for news.

In his mind he replayed Lightfoot's death over and over, niggling on every detail, sifting for any element that may have changed that fatal moment. "Shard." The name echoed in his ears and stirred him from his dark reverie.

"What?" he said, turning at the sound of Stonefinger's voice. The Dwarven King moved his steed closer. The bland sky did little to diminish his royal presence. Dressed in black armor, marked by the brilliant sapphires of Stone-Haven's clan and the silvery glint of his battle-axe slung behind his back, he seemed like Ironfist reborn.

"I said that Shard had asked I deliver you a message." This time he emphasized Shard's name. The amulet around Lockjaw's neck thrummed softly and he reached into his tunic to hold it. "She sent me this," he held up a scroll, "with her wish that I personally hand it to you. I nearly forgot until now. So much has happened already, and my thoughts are with the laddies who may be in need of our help. I hope we find them in time." He held out the sealed parchment and Lockjaw reached for it. "I can now rest easy," said Stonefinger. "It would have been my head on a plate had I not made good on my promise. Shard is not a dwarx easily dismissed. I daresay her slightest command must be promptly obeyed, even by a King."

But Lockjaw heard him not. He broke the seal, eagerly devouring the words on the scroll. Shard's handwriting was feather-fine and her letters perfectly formed, each one a work of art, and to Lockjaw more valuable than any treasure in the entire dwarven realm.

"*My dearest Lockjaw. How I miss you.*" He savored the words like a greedy child. "*I can only hope that you are safe. Father and Grimbeard are spending far too much time together. And Father has expressed his desire to allow Grimbeard to call on me. I cannot hold them off much longer. Know that though you fight a battle on the field, I fight another battle, and I await your safe return. My love for you shall never wilt.*" A tear came to his eye, and he reread the last bit three times before the closing line: "*If this seal is broken when you receive my letter I will hold Stonefinger personally responsible – with all my heart, Love Shard.*" He rolled up the parchment and tucked it into his tunic. *When I return it will be forever.* And it did seem to Lockjaw, the face he most desired to see appeared briefly amid the clouds, her lips formed a kiss, then vanished on a gust of wind.

"Lockjaw." The wizard's voice found his apprentice's ear. Lockjaw looked up but did not see Hawker. "*In your head, dwarf!*" The voice snapped. Lockjaw squinted, unsure, then nodded; Hawker was communicating through telepathic means. *"If you would like to join me at the front then we can be off."* He tried to say something back but only mumbled an unintelligible word. *"If you must answer. Then do so with your mouth closed and without moving your lips."* He could almost hear the note of irritation in Hawker's voice. *"Yes, Master."* Lockjaw answered, this time in unspoken words; he urged his pony to where Hawker waited, looking more annoyed than impressed by his pupil's quick study.

The column of riders rode out in front. Behind them marched the formidable Black Barbs and then came the dwarves. A parade of well-wishers stood outside in the damp gray morning; a grateful gathering for those who had delivered the fair city of Vintnorr from the Easterling King. Among the very last at the entrance to Girt's capital was Gerharte, astride his big bay. The Blue-Feather's Chieftain would be joining up later, after order was restored to the city. He lifted his lance high when Dega passed, and the Ranger's Captain turned and saluted as he rode out the gates. Out of the corner of his eye he saw Helena standing just inside the walls, and with her a tall redheaded woman. Helena waved with her free arm; the other clutched her infant son.

"I see yer over what ailed ya," an old man hailed Frost-Eye as he rode past. The elf stopped his horse. The peasant stood on the roadside holding a donkey by its lead; the old man had laden its back with too many packs and it stood dejectedly beside its master while he scratched his beard and spat at the ground. The stranger repeated his comment. "Ya look a sight better'n ya did afore."

"Do I know you?" Frost-Eye nudged his horse off the road, and Dega rode up beside him.

"Sure. But yer were t'sick to remember. Where's yer friends?"

"My friends?"

"The laddies. Them ones ya went to Shady with. I reckon ya must've found Stitches, else yer wouldn't be here. But how'd you boys git to Girt so quick? I only just got here an' I left well afore you three."

Frost-Eye exchanged a look with Dega. The officer nodded.

"Oh. We only just arrived. Did you say we met at Shady?"

"Yep. On the road to Shady Haven. Guess it weren't to yer liking then, seeing as how ya ended up here."

"Uh, yes. That's right. But my memory has failed me. Where exactly is Shady Haven?"

"Ah, I'm not surprised, givin' the fact yer were so sick. Yee, I wager the Doc had a struggle to make ya well. Shady's on the other side of the Eastlands – as far from *His Blackness* as can be fer any port city. Poor buggers'll be havin' a tough time of it, what with his war an' all. Lucky ya left when ya did."

"Thank you, good sir."

"Welcome. Best I be going. C'mon Mabel," he yanked the donkey's lead, "we got goods ta sell." He started to walk away, then turned with a toothless grin, and winked at them both. "Give my regards to the laddies."

"Thank you, I will."

The stranger doffed his hat and started up the hill to the gates.

"What was that about?" asked Starlock, reigning in beside Dega and Frost-Eye.

"I think we might have a lead to Camber's whereabouts," said Dega, and he gave his horse a kick and cantered up to the front of the procession.

The army moved quickly, and soon passed outside of Girt's borders. The Barbs and the dwarves marched on foot keeping pace with the cavalry. Elven runners were sent to scout ahead, racing back to report their findings to Snowblind. The remnants of Easterling army now blocked the Hook.

"It's bottled up tight on the Eastern side," said Snowblind. "The Barbs will take the first hit and we split the cavalry into four units." He nodded to Dega. "You bring your men in from both sides. Then Caldorn in two waves after the Barbs." He pointed to Stonefinger. "Bring your dwarves in last."

"Perhaps we should wait for Gerharte," said Stonefinger.

"No. That would take too long and we do not have the luxury of time," said Dega. He fingered the grooves of his sword as he sat in the circle with the others. The army camped not far from where he and Starlock turned back to Vintnorr. She was just as eager to push past the blockade and find Camber, Dane, and Crescent. "Is it possible for Hawker to transport us across without confrontation?" she asked.

"I cannot," answered Hawker. "I have spent too much of myself bringing the Alliance to Girt. I need to save what little strength I have, for I fear my role in this war is far from over."

"If you would but teach me how, perhaps I can help."

"No Lockjaw, you are not yet strong enough for such a thing and know not how to bend properties without revealing yourself to every other magic user. Sentash would feel your power before you even let it loose and counter with his own."

"But how am I ever to use that which was a gift?" Now that he had the means to help, he still could not.

Hawker laid a hand across his shoulder. "It takes many years to learn how to use your gift. Perhaps in time you will discover a way to channel in secret. But for now, be happy with the knowledge that you were the one responsible for shaking up his army and creating untold damage."

"Surely you can do something that will give us the edge," said Stonefinger.

"Yes," said Hawker, and he tugged at his goatee. "There is something. I can raise a barrier without drawing too much from my reserve power."

Dega nodded. A shield would be an advantage. He watched the wizard from across the campfire. Hawker had changed. And it wasn't just his outward appearance, new gray supplanting chestnut hair; or his physical form, once straight and tall, now bent and rigid. This change. This *inward* change – revealed a much more reserved Hawker, almost careful, compared to the free-spirited wizard who had accompanied them from Stone-Haven.

"Then what?" All eyes turned to Starlock. "Once we push past. What then? Are we going to look for Camber?" Her brows narrowed. "I think you have something else in mind, wizard."

Hawker held up his hand. "I know nothing more than you, except that Camber is not in any danger for the present, in fact he is in very good hands. But I will say this, Starlock," he waited until she locked her eyes with his. "Your time to reckon with the past is nigh. You will have to finish what you started long ago and take your rightful place as the Janastari's leader or you will fail." He stood up, dusting off his robes. "You know what I speak of. The Threads told you much more than you wish to believe. Winterleaf said you went to consult them before you left Illianther. Now who is keeping secrets?"

"And?" said Dega.

"And what?" she snapped.

"And what did you learn at Illianther that you have not shared with the rest of us?"

"Nothing. There is nothing to be learned from speculation."

She left the soft glow of the campfire, and Dega watched her go, running his fingers through his hair. He shook his head. The talks shifted back to the Hook, and Snowblind took center stage, a master tactician, he had already deduced every conceivable outcome, and was planning a counter-strategy for each one. It was past midnight when Dega threw his bedroll into a tent supplied by the Rangers; a bit of familiarity that reminded him of home.

The army was on the move just before dawn, and Dega rode with his former company. There was much to discuss since his unexpected departure almost a year ago, and he listened intently to the news of the other garrisons.

"And Gareth?" he asked the officer from Cambert. "How has the Lieutenant fared in my absence?"

"Ah, Lieutenant Comstock is very capable," the older man had looped his reins over the saddle while he rolled tobacco. "The last reports we had from Hartland confirmed they were ready to join Wildwood, and it was the Lieutenant who organized the summit and brought the Alliance together." He struck a flint and lit his smoke.

Dega smiled. Gareth was efficient, and he had no doubt that his company of green cadets would be fully prepared. "What news of Hartland?" More than just banter, he hoped the cavalier's conversation would take his mind off a growing unease. Why was Hawker so unconcerned with the cadets, twice now he rebuffed any such discussion regarding Camber's welfare, and with an explanation as vague as his own disappearance. When Dega had questioned the wizard about who was providing aid, he simply said, "You will learn everything, all in due time." Yet something inside refused to give up. He promised to protect them. How could he turn his back now?

The army bedded down for the evening and Dega joined the others at the campfire. The aroma of cooked meat and spices had whet his appetite, but he declined the offering. There was much on his mind and food was a distraction. Starlock came to sit beside him. *Another distraction.*

"How many ships did you say?" he asked the scout who came to report his findings to Snowblind. "Three," said the elf; he had only just returned from the Hook with news that the sorcerer's ships were anchored off the shoals.

"So where's the rest of his fleet?" mused Stonefinger. "This has all the makings of a trap." He fingered his dirk as he spoke, rolling the short blade across his palm.

"No," said Dega. The Captain from Cambert had told him that Thayneland had intercepted the Easterling fleet. "His ships have met with our own and his navy has been destroyed."

"Can you be sure?" Starlock fed bits of meat to Belia, pausing to look over at Dega.

"I have reason to believe the information is accurate."

Several Rangers quickly backed up Dega's statement, and Stonefinger held up his hand. "Ah, it was rumored that your ships have been keeping the coastal waters clear even when I struck out from Stone-Haven. But I had no news of this latest engagement. If what you say is true then perhaps these are all that remain of his warships, but I would not have thought for a minute that this war would be so easily won."

"Perhaps he has struck elsewhere," said Dega.

"And where are his Bounders?" asked Starlock.

"Yes," added Snowblind, he pointed a finger at Hawker. "Where are his Bounders, wizard? I have yet to see any and I was expecting them at Vintnorr."

Hawker tugged at his goatee. "And I too had expected to see some sign of them. It seems he is saving something for the end and mayhap we will encounter his creatures yet."

"Perhaps they hunt for Camber."

"No Lockjaw, I would know if he set them after Camber as I did before, and I have not felt their presence like I had in the Northlands. No, something else has happened; there have been changes within his inner circle. I can feel it. But I know not what it is."

"Can't you use your magic?" Dega rubbed his jaw. Starlock was right. Hawker was definitely hiding something.

"No. Something has blocked my path. It's as if Sentash has found a way to make everything around him invisible. I cannot explain, except that he has suddenly grown incredibly powerful."

"The Winterstone. He must have it, else how could he be so strong?" Lockjaw's eyes betrayed his feelings.

Dega's face darkened. With the talisman he would be unstoppable.

Hawker held up his hand. "We have no evidence that the Stone has been recovered, and I for one do not think it so. We must believe that there is yet hope."

There is yet hope. Dega lay in his bedroll; he woke just before dawn, and ordered his Rangers to clear camp. At first light the Alliance had come to the Hook. A rising trepidation played across those now gathered at the narrow land bridge that marked the edge of the eastlands. Only the Barbs were not affected, embracing death in the name of glory.

Dega too, wanted glory; he wanted glory for his comrades; heroes and defenders of freedom, whose deeds would be remembered always in songs and stories. He raised his arm, rising in his stirrups. "We came this far. We came to defeat Sentash. His armies have been affected, make no mistake." All eyes were on him, his horse danced sideways, feeling his passion. "They already doubt themselves. They are fewer, and their defeat at Vintnorr weighs heavy on their hearts. We can win this! They know it – *and they fear it.*" The world now silent, pausing in its predawn ritual to hear what the Ranger's Captain would say. "In Tar Galleaon he hides. He thinks to be invincible. But he is just a man. One man! The time of reckoning is ours!" A cheer went up from the Rangers. "I give you my word. I will storm his castle, and it will be my sword that brings vengeance down upon his neck. Who is with me?!"

The Rangers roared raising their weapons in the air, and a mighty cheer resounded across the Hook as the free people of Astaria converged upon the forces of the Easterling King.

* * * * * * * *

Gareth stared at the bodies lying on the ground. Most were covered in blankets, but they had run out of blankets a long time ago, and many more were being carried into the courtyard. The Lieutenant flipped the blanket back over the face of the cadet. How does one tell his mother, his father, that their son who had come seeking adventure would not be coming home – *ever.*

"Sir," he turned at the sound of Bonner's voice.

"What is it Corporal?" He stood, facing the officer. The battle had taken a toll on this man; a weariness had settled behind his eyes dragging his craggy features into a wretched void. *Did he look like that?* Gareth scratched his chin, wondering if this war would cause them all to lose their identities.

"The others are waiting for you."

Gareth nodded. "Tell them I'm on my way."

When he entered the boardroom a rider from Thayneland was there, wearing a mud-stained uniform and looking like he hadn't slept in days. He saluted Gareth, and the Lieutenant saluted back. "Admiral Thorson sends news concerning the battle."

"Go on," said Gareth.

"We've encountered a second fleet off the Northern coast. Our ships now engage the main host between the Narrows. We need back-up and ask that you send troops." He handed the parchment to Gareth.

"Sorry Sir." He knew there would be no aid. It would be a miracle if he could slip past the enemy a second time.

Gareth grunted. "Sorry? Don't be. But that explains why we haven't heard from Thayneland. When did you leave?"

"Six days ago, Sir."

"And did you stop along the way?"

"No. I came straight here, but took extra time to get around the enemy, Sir."

"Well, what now Lieutenant?" asked an officer from Wildwood. "We can't just sit and wait for a rescue."

"No, we can't." Gareth rubbed his thinning locks; a few more hairs managed to slip away unnoticed. "We're going to have to win this ourselves. Any suggestions?"

* * * * * * * *

The Rangers followed on the heels of Snowblind's Barbs, and Dega spurred his horse to the front. The carnage delivered by the Barbs still surprised him, though he had witnessed it first hand at Vintnorr. His horse collided with a foot soldier wielding a deadly mace. The horse reared, and the mace-wielder swung, striking it across the chest and knocking the animal off its feet. Dega jumped as the charger fell; he brought his sword across the Easterling's neck, severing the head, then turned to meet his next attacker.

The Dwarves now joined the fight and they pushed the enemy back, and now it seemed the sorcerer's warriors were hard put to test; they became unsure and their strokes fell with far less severity.

"See how the dogs run!" remarked a Ranger. "Ha! They run back to their Master, tails between their legs!" He cheered as the Easterlings withdrew, scrambling to higher ground.

Dega wasn't fooled. They still outnumbered the Alliance three to one. Big odds stacked in the sorcerer's favor. Something was not right here.

"Dega!" Starlock shouted from behind. He ducked as an arrow

whizzed overhead. More Easterlings had come up from across the Hook and were using archers to force the Alliance toward the receding host. Snowblind's Barbs answered back with a volley of arrows from elven long bows. The sorcerer's retreating force lost more ground, and was driven farther inland. Dega now stood on the blackened fields of N'Amorr where five hundred years ago to the day the *Alliance of Old* defeated the Easterling King, sending him back to the shadows.

"It's a trap!" But even as he said it the ground shook with a terrible force; the sky darkened to midnight. The earth split open and a great jet of stale air issued forth, and with it, the stench of decay. Mist swirled across the open field; a smoky veil to shroud the living. Dega felt a numbness growing in his legs, spreading rapidly through his body; only his eyes moved, and they quickly found Starlock frozen to his right; her eyes did not blink; they did not see. It was the same with the others. All but Hawker. Hawker was moving and he was speaking.

"Norii!" Hawker yelled into the mists.

A hooded figure stepped forth. "Stornoway Hawker. What a pleasant surprise." The robed figure glided across the ground to stand within a pace of the Caretaker.

Norii threw back her hood and laughed. "Still keeping your pets I see." She flipped a hand at the motionless figure of Lockjaw standing dutifully beside his Master; axe raised, ready to strike whatever evil should spring from the crevasse.

"What have you done Norii." Hawker stepped in front of his apprentice.

Green light filtered from a face that was not there, and he shook his head, recalling how she looked when they were all very new to the world. She a thing of beauty; porcelain skin, fair and delicate, it made him weep; soft silken tresses, the color of night, cascading in long thick waves down her back. But it was her eyes he longed to see – multi-hued, and ever-changing; a rainbow of dancing color, and behind their radiance, a yearning to become more than she was. "Why did you change?"

"I? I change?" The midnight void that was her face would have shown bright teeth and a dimpled smile, had it been a face. "No Jessa," she breathed. *"You* are the one who has changed. You wish to make these mortals in your own image." She turned her eyeless face to Dega. "You set them high above all else. And you forget that without usss... " she drew her breath, hissing sharply, "they would be nothing but dust and shadows. You place too much importance on your creatures. You always have. All of us: Atrilla, Shikkarri, Pel Ak A Bar, and even Defél have had to accept that we will never be able to replicate that which you have created in this world. We know this, and we do not begrudge you your power, but you go too far Jessa, you go too far. Your creatures have taken over this world and you would see them rule it."

"That has never been my intent."

"Oh? Then why are we forced to dwell in places where your precious beings cannot go? All of us have had to withdraw from this world. All of us! Atrilla in the sky. Defél and Shikkarri under the earth. Pel Ak A Bar in the ocean. And Me! Me Jessa! I must stay in the shadows where the nameless things dwell. You! Only you are free to wander this world." Norii pointed an accusing finger. "It was not meant to be so."

"Do you think this world belongs to us?" Silently he hoped Norii would back away, but he knew in his heart she would not. The stage was set for a final showdown. One for the ages. "No Norii. This world is not ours. We are here as the Caretakers, nothing more. We do not have the right to take that which was entrusted to us, and I will not let you pass your brand of judgment on a world that does not belong to you."

"You have no choice. I have Defél. And now I have your pawn. Oh don't look so surprised Jessa. I have known about the boy since before he was born. Who do you think placed the dreams in his head?"

"Let the boy go, Norii."

Dega had a clear view of both Caretakers. Though he could not hear, their body language said much, and he was able to follow the scene unfolding before his eyes. Hawker's face suddenly changed. Whatever the robed figure had said managed to shock the unflappable wizard. If he could have squeezed the pommel of his sword he would have.

"No," she whispered, and her raspy voice became louder. "But fear not. He will not be harmed. In fact I intend to use him as you, yourself, would have, had I not intervened. Even now he walks to meet his fate. I have sent him to retrieve the Stone. He is my puppet now and I control his strings." She laughed again, then stopped. "But I see you disapprove. Perhaps you were expecting a battle after all."

Dega blinked responding to Hawker's voice suddenly inside his head. *"Do not be alarmed. I know you have not been able to follow our conversation, but know the Being before you is Norii – She who governs the Dead. You must be ready for whatever happens next."*

Dega blinked rapidly. And Hawker nodded.

"Leave the boy out of it Norii. Your fight is with me. It always has been."

"Have you learned nothing over the centuries?" She drew back a pace and flung away her robes. Green light radiated from her body, spilling out her mouth, her eyes, blasting from her fingertips. Thunder boomed overhead. Now the world was dim, illuminated by a sickly green light that paled everything in its unnatural glow. Dega felt a sudden rush of warmth; his arm continued the motion of pulling his sword free, and he fell forward as life returned to his body. The ground was still shaking, it buckled, heaved, sending men and horses reeling; a network of trenches opened up, revealing more than just the earth's core.

"Behold! The Dead!" Norii waved her naked arms – two pale green limbs that dared to summon the unliving.

"Norii!!!" Hawker's shout was lost in the cries that followed. The dead rose from their resting places, still wearing armor and carrying weapons forged for the *Battle of N'Amorr.*

Horses went mad, throwing their masters as Norii's army swarmed out of the very bowels beneath their feet. Shrieks of panic reigned amid chaos as the past collided with the present.

The Barbs were the first to regroup. Snowblind led his warriors over the barren waste to repeat a battle fought five-hundred years ago. A brief display of emotion crossed his countenance when he came face to face with his first challenger – Quickbolt! The long-dead elf and his first captain nodded to Snowblind as he raised his ghostly blade.

"You cannot stop me!" Norri threw her arms in the air, lightning crackled at her fingertips. "I am stronger now Jessa! Did you not think I wouldn't take advantage of Defél's weakened state to absorb his essence?" A zigzag bolt snapped at Hawker, singing his robes.

"Did you think *We* did not foresee this? You're not the only one who calculates odds." He charged her, wrapping an arm around her waist, the other creating a barrier to contain her power.

The host of ghostly warriors were joined by the armies of Sentash, with fresh battalions coming in from all sides. Bounders raced to the front lines tearing through defenders, splitting the Alliance in half. Dega turned to face his next opponent and nearly dropped his sword!

A SECRET REVEALED

Standing in his Ranger's uniform and looking identical to the day he left was a face that caused the Captain to fall to his knees. *He's dead. It's not him.* Common sense told him what his eyes chose not to believe: it only looked like Drake Darkhawk. But Dega could only gape, as the man he had yearned to love but longed to hate, raised his sword. Here was the mentor who should have guided him to manhood, should have been there to provide fatherly advice when he needed it most.

"Why did you leave? Why?" He stretched his hand out, desperate for answers, eyes wet with tears; the boy wanting badly to touch his father.

"Dega!" Starlock screamed, but her voice was lost to the madness.

Lockjaw looked up in time to see a phantom hovering over the Captain with sword raised high. Its face could have been Dega's in about thirty years but for the vacant expression. Lockjaw couldn't reach Dega in time, but there was one thing he could do. He brought forth his staff and chanted a spell stripping away the features from Dega's ghostly attacker.

The square jaw melted, and with it the piercing blue eyes and strong straight nose, exposing a skeletal visage. It was just enough to convince Dega that this spectral figure was not his father, and as it swung its sword he rolled sideways, kicking the legs out from underneath. Dega continued to roll, snatching his sword from where it lay. He sprang to his feet, now free from the shade's hypnotic spell. One stroke smashed its hollow bones, crumbling it to dust.

Norii's army of fallen heroes seemed to grow ever larger, sweeping across the battlefield and surrounding the Alliance as more and more dead swelled the ranks.

"There's no end to this rabble." Stonefinger raised his axe, clearing a path to Dega.

Dega agreed. *Dead but not dead.* "Wait!" he shouted. "Don't kill them!"

Snowblind understood immediately. He nodded. The Barb's General gave three short whistles and one long one. Suddenly the Elves changed tactics, rendering just enough force to wound not kill. Dega yelled to Stonefinger, "If we don't kill them she can't use them against us."

The Bounders were another problem. They had to be killed. And Frost-Eye had his hands full as a Bounder wheeled on its hind legs.

Patches of sticky black blood marked its dull gray coat. Arrows bristled from its neck and Frost-Eye sent more, enraging the Bounder to an even greater degree. It lunged, sending the elf to ground. Starlock threw a star; the pinwheel sticking deep inside its maw, dropping the beast in its tracks.

"Starlock! Behind You!" Frost-Eye notched an arrow, but Starlock was Janastari, and sensing the danger she threw her dagger. It bounced off armor, giving her time to regain her feet. Frost-Eye found his mark, and the soldier made a gurgling noise, dropping his weapon and clutching the arrow with a gasp.

The plan to deplete Norii's supply of soldiers seemed to be working, but for every Easterling wounded, and some near death and not able to cross over, at least a dozen had already joined her ghostly army. Dega fought his way alongside Starlock. Blast it! Where the blue-blazes was Hawker?! The Caretakers had disappeared.

Life and Death rose to the heavens dancing a power struggle as old as the ages; two bodies pressed together like tangled vines. The boundaries of the mortal realm fell away, replaced by infinite space and endless probabilities. Then as Hawker felt his power growing, so did the cold shape of Norii. A giant serpent reared its head, dropping heavy coils in succession, bent on squeezing away his life. But even as he took his last breath, he had already begun to change. Now he was fur and sharp claws; and the mongoose had the snake at a disadvantage, sinking sharp teeth into its mottled neck. It bit air. The serpent was now a dragon, flapping leathery wings and extending its jaws to the fullest. Out of hell's bowels came a fiery blast.

Gone was the mongoose. Now Hawker took his true form. The time had come at last to reveal the real Stornoway Hawker. A figure limned in radiant blue light stepped out of the darkness. Ruggedly handsome and much younger than the world-weary Hawker of old. This Hawker donned a gleaming helm and drew a bright sword from its scabbard.

The dragon flicked its tongue, tasting the very air. It blasted flame. Hawker brought up his shield, repelling the fire and turning it back at the great beast; his sword came up in an arc of blue flame, sparking across diamond-hard scales. "You will be stopped!"

Norii roared, whipping her flat ugly head around, flapping wings and beating a gust of wind that sent him rolling backward. Then she took to the air. *She* would kill him. Be rid of this irritant once and for all. With Jessa gone, the others would fall. One by one, until only *She* was left. Life to those who revered her, and despair to all who displeased Death's Mistress.

Norii circled above, her vast wingspan and massive body blocking the stars. From the ground Dega could see a dark patch against the sky growing ever larger with each passing second. "What is that thing?" Starlock pointed at the sky. They stood beside each other, having found themselves separated from their companions.

"I don't know but it's moving fast."

Now they could see the dragon. Blue light shone brightly around its head, framing death like an aura.

"It's Hawker!" yelled Starlock. But Dega did not need this announcement, for the dragon and its rider were well within his sight. The wizard was clad in armor the like of which had never been seen on this world, but there was little time to admire the complexity of the patterns engraved on its burnished surface. Elf and Ranger were caught between a host of fallen dead and the tide of Easterlings. Off in the distance a horn rang out, announcing the arrival of the Fighting Blue-Feathers. "Gerharte!" Dega shouted, renewed hope rising in his veins.

The dragon beat its wings, fanning hot air from its smoking jowls. A jet of flame scorched the very ground where dwarves, elves, and men fought to keep Norii's forces at bay. Those who couldn't move fast enough felt a sudden blistering heat, engulfed in dragon-fire that left nothing but ash in its wake. Hawker raised his sword, plunging it deep, jamming the blade down, breaking skin and crunching bone. Blood spewed, splashing his face, slicking the scales; he slipped sideways. Norii screamed, banking left, then right. But Hawker clung to the sword, and up she went, up past the clouds.

Lockjaw saw all from the ground. Hawker, now a beam of blue light, carried higher than the stars in the eerie green twilight of Norii's world. He clutched Shard's amulet, straining his eyes, waiting with certainty for the light to drop back from the sky.

"Dega. Be ready." Hawker's voice sounded inside the Captain's head, though he could no longer see him. *"Take hold of Starlock,"* it commanded. And he grabbed the elf by her arm. *"Find Camber. Help him."* In the time it takes to blink an eye, he and Starlock were in the Keep.

XVIII

Death Match

Camber had walked this path before. He knew every inch of this cavern like the back of his hand. And he should! It was *the* cavern. The tunnel from his nightmares. His hand slid along the wall, scraping over the surface, flinching whenever it passed over something slimy.

He was at a loss to concentrate on anything for too long. Dane. *Wasn't he in the cell?* The thought fluttered away, and another thought, stronger than the rest, demanded that he keep going. He had to get to the end of this tunnel; that is what the voice in his head commanded. *He would obey.*

Wetness dripped off walls, splooshing onto rock, filling the emptiness with a steady rhythmic drip, drip, drip. He stumbled, then fell to his knees. He was tired. His head hurt. He wanted to curl up in a ball. Lie in the wetness and wait until found. *"Get Up."* the voice told him.

He turned his head, but could discern nothing in the dark. His hand found the wall a second time and he followed its sloping curve. *Here it comes.* He knew this bend. And part of him wanted to turn and flee.

* * * * * * * *

"Let go." Starlock shook away from Dega's grip. "Now let's see where we are," she grabbed a brand from the wall.

"If I had to guess I'd say Hawker placed us in the dungeon." Dega lit his torch and flashed it at the darkness, revealing rows of cells. Nowhere had the smell of rot and decay been more noticeable and more offensive than in this dank dungeon. "The battlefield wasn't this bad," he muttered.

"Hssst!" Starlock froze. Dega turned his head. Now he heard it too. *Footsteps.* Elf and Ranger hid behind a table; its worn surface covered with holes and stained with dried blood.

"He just wants the elf." Two guards came down the stairs, passing by the table.

Dega looked at Starlock and she nodded. *Crescent.*

"What's he wan' im fer?"

"Probably for one of his experiments."

"Better him than us," grunted the other, and he turned the key in the lock.

Crescent blinked. "Am I glad to see you two," he stood from where he had been sitting cross-legged on filthy straw, and stepped lightly over the guard's body.

"What took you so long?" said another voice.

"Who ya talkin' to kid?"

"Dane?" Dega followed the voice to the next cell.

"Dega!" Chance rattled the lock on his door. "Quickly! Camber's gone. If we don't stop him then who knows what will happen." Dega unlocked the former Ranger's cell. He moved to the next one. A girl sat with her legs pulled to her chest, looking up at him with big sad eyes. He was just about to ask for her name when an "Aeieee!" caught him by surprise. It was followed by a "Not now Buttercup. She's a friend. Oh for the love of….Stop Stinking!" And as Dega took his next breath he couldn't help but notice a faint odor reminiscent of old cabbage and moldy bread, wafting into sickly sweet rotting apples.

"It's not the elf," complained Buttercup, and he clawed his way through Dane's thick hair. Belia squawked and Buttercup dug his talons in deep. Dane rolled his eyes. Stupid faerie was afraid of everything.

Starlock pointed at the tiny creature. "Is that a… "

"Yes!" Dane and Tonni answered.

At last Buttercup's fear of becoming a snack subsided, and with it the incredible stench. Dane held the bug-sized critter out to Dega and Starlock. "This is Buttercup. We're stuck with him for now."

"Hey! You should be so lucky. What the kid means is I'm their guide." Buttercup huffed his chest, flapping his iridescent wings. "I made a promise and I intend to keep it. 'sides, the kid here need's a mentor."

"Well when you find one let us know," snorted Tonni, she shook the straw off her clothes.

Chance put his hand out for Dega. "Good to see you son." Dega shook his hand and gave him a nod. "Not all my doing. But where's Camber? You said he was missing."

"They took him awhile ago. He's not been brought back, and that worries me."

"Do you think Sentash has the Winterstone?" asked Starlock.

"No." Chance found his sword from a pile of confiscated weapons. "If he had then we'd all be dead by now. Sentash would have no further use for us. But – and this is my best guess – I think he knows where it is and he's sent Camber to fetch it." He tossed Dane his bow, and the archer also found his dagger.

"Which way did they take him?" asked Dega; he could see just two exits in the dim lighting, but had a hunch only one led to the Easterling King, the other was probably used to dispose whatever was left of the prisoners once the sorcerer found no more use for them.

"Wait," said Chance. "We can't all go." He pointed to the dead guards. "They came here for Crescent. If they're not back soon the King will wonder what's keeping them and will probably send more. Two of you will have to go with Crescent." He plucked Buttercup off Dane's shoulder and held him out by his wings. "Do you or do you not know where to find the Winterstone? Do not try to fool me bug. I've been patient up till now. But everything that is good in this world is about to end unless we find Camber in time. Not just for us, but for you too."

"Yes, I can take you there," squeaked the faerie.

"Dane and I will look for Camber. You three stop the sorcerer." He placed Buttercup back on Dane's shoulder.

"What am I suppose to do? Sit here and knit a sweater?" Tonni was having none of it.

"I'm sorry. But this is far too dangerous for you. You'd be much safer here."

"Forget it!" she snapped. "Where he goes. I go."

Dega hid his smile. The girl reminded him of someone else who was just as stubborn, and his eyes found Starlock dressed in the guard's uniform. "Here," he tossed the keys to Chance. "You might have need of these."

The former Ranger snatched them from the air and stuffed them into his coat. He fished in his pocket and handed Dega a button. "Your father is gone."

"I know," said Dega and he tucked the button into his pouch.

Chance clapped the young man on his shoulder. "Luck to you Dega Darkhawk," he said, and pushed Dane toward the exit.

"Should've kept the keys," muttered Starlock; she and Crescent dragged the bodies into a cell then piled straw to hide them. Dega threw the cuirass and cloak overtop his Ranger's uniform and donned the helm; it came low over his eyes, nose and cheek guards hiding his face in shadow.

Up the winding staircase and out the door at the top. The shock of brightness made Dega squint, and he waited for his eyes to adjust before stepping clear of the doorway. He scanned the hall. Nothing. But as they crossed the marble floor, a door opened on the far side.

"What's kept you? Idiots! His Highness wants that stinkin' elf now!" The guard was dressed in similar garb, but the horsehair crowning his helm was red, not black, and two gold discs on his gleaming breastplate held his cape in place. "Well?" he grunted, and walked toward the trio; his short sword swinging in its scabbard as he crossed the hall. Then noticing Crescent standing without difficulty. In fact the elf appeared quite brazen, standing straight and tall, like he had not a care in the world. Didn't the stupid creature realize in whose halls he walked? But the guard was slow to ponder the warning in his head as he came to stand within a few feet of the prisoner. "Wait a minute! Why are his hands not bound?"

"So he can do this," and tripping the guard, Crescent struck a fatal blow across his jugular. "Stuff him behind here," said Starlock; she helped Dega drag the guard behind blue velvet drapes separating an alcove from the rest of the hall. Belia poked her head out from under Starlock's cape and squawked. Starlock stood still. "What is it?" whispered Dega.

"Ache! Haeste! It cannot be!" She grabbed Crescent. "Do you feel it?!" But Crescent shook his head. The feeling disappeared, leaving Starlock to wonder whether it was just her imagination. "Let's go. I do not wish to be caught in the open." Her tone was sharp, and she meant it to be; the feeling had left her shaken. Underneath her cloak, Belia fluttered. "You felt him too, didn't you little one," she whispered.

Boots echoed across the empty hall accompanied by the quiet jingle of Dega's spurs. "Left or right?"

"Left," said Starlock. She tried the door at the end of the hallway. "Locked. Well Captain, do we knock? Or shall we just sit here and wai..." The door opened, catching the trio by surprise. And even more surprised was the guard, who unexpectedly ran himself into Starlock's dagger. He slumped over – dead. "Quick!" she said, removing her blade, and wiping it clean. She grabbed the door just as it was closing, and waited while Dega hid the body.

The stairs led to another corridor, this one had elaborate furnishings on either side. Marble statues lined the hallway, judging all who passed with vacant stares. The number of icons dedicated to his "Highness" increased dramatically at the far end.

Floor-to-ceiling doors suddenly swung open; a host of tortured souls immortalized forever on tarnished bronze gave silent warning to all who entered. Across the center, in gold gilt, the sorcerer's emblem – three fabled stars over a white staff.

"Enter," said a familiar voice, and Starlock's blood ran cold.

* * * * * * * *

"Okay bug," Dane held Buttercup out in front. "Which way?"
"Left, ummm right, no that ain't it... let's see... we took a left turn after two rights, and a....ah ha! Left!"
"Oh for Shikra's sake... he's lost."
"Am not!"
"Are too!"
"Am not!"
"Are too!"
"Stop it!"
"You stop it!"
"Both of you stop it." Dane frowned at Buttercup, then at Tonni.
"Shhh!" Chance warned. "Need I remind you that there are Bounders all over this Keep." He bent down and waved the torch at the floor. "We go left."
"See, I was right. Hey – that's no way for a lady to show her gratitude."
"Quiet Buttercup, or I'll put you back in my pocket."

* * * * * * * *

Camber slid his hand around the bend; neck-hair standing on end;

he knew what lay ahead, but could not stop, could not turn around, could not go back. Sweat dripped down his forehead; heart pounding against his chest, knowing he was going to die. He held his breath. Cold air tickled his fingertips. Blackness opened up; he teetered at the edge of endless space. And then he fell! Somewhere in a dream, half a world away, a pair of green eyes opened wide and a tear stained the satin-soft cheek of the dreamer; somewhere in a dream, half a world away, a mother kissed her son's forehead. His body whirled upside down and sideways. The necklace flew free from under his tunic, flickering like a beacon in the dark. "Noooo!" A cry of terror and a tear. Soft flesh quickly surrounded his struggling body.

* * * * * * * *

"Greetings Starlock."

"No! It can't be....your..."

"Dead?" The voice laughed. "Hardly. But how ironic that the one person who supposedly has witnessed my death – not once – but twice mind you, is the same person who keeps making that ridiculous statement."

"Traitor!" snarled Dega; his hand went for his sword. Crescent drew his bow.

"Oh I see you brought the good Captain." Warblade shook his silvery mane and stepped down from where he sat on the Easterling King's throne. "You still look like a jungti," he said, gliding up to stand in front of the Ranger.

"And you are lower than the sandworms that burrow in their lair." Dega could barely contain his hatred.

"And you Crescent," he turned his head, deliberately leaving his whole side open. "Uncock your bow." He let out a laugh, and shook the staff in his hands. "None of you truly know what I have become. None of you will even come close to understanding. I am as far above the Janastari as they are above you mortal man."

"Where's the sorcerer Warblade?" Starlock took a step back and she placed a hand inside her cloak. Belia shot out from underneath and flew to the hall's vaulted beams.

"Sentash is no more. He was weak."

"So here you are. Like a servant who has usurped his master and tries to run the empire in his stead. Now his armies take orders from you. You who couldn't even Captain the Barbs."

"Yes ME! When you left me to die like an animal at the feet of the 'hones, never did I believe I would have a second chance, and as I lay gasping my last breath, the pain so intense I could think of nothing but death and embracing it, I cursed your name, Starlock." He stepped closer and she stepped back.

"But even then I still loved you. I hated and loved you with my last breath. My world was fading and still I could think only of you. Norii came to me then. She came to claim my body, steal my spirit and take it back to the underworld. We struck a bargain. And it was *She* who nursed me back to health. And I will tell you, Starlock, not one hour of each day went by that I did not wonder why you left me. I went back to Illianther thinking to find you there."

He pointed the staff. *"But you* – you hid inside your own bitterness, uncaring, and you knew nothing of my survival, until you came to Illianther. And even then I hoped that you still loved me." He reached out to take her hand, but she took another step back. "I know now you do not feel the same. I see it in your eyes." He thrust his staff at Dega. "But this? This is who you choose in my stead. Really Starlock, you disgust me."

Her hand went for a star; it flew from her fingers but came to a stop, hovering just in front of Warblade's face, then dropped to the ground. "Your weapons are useless here," he said, and he circled like a lion preparing to pounce. "Soon the boy will have the Winterstone, and when he does he will obey *Her* command and bring it to me."

"You're mad!"

"Ahhh, my love," and he came up from behind and touched her face with his cold, cold hand. "You can speak your mind freely for the time being. But know this. I intend to have you, body, soul, and spirit. You belong to me. You always have."

"Vile worm! You will have none of it." But before she could slap his hand away Dega drew his sword and he placed the point under Warblade's chin. "Away with you. And back to your Mistress, dog."

Warblade laughed; it echoed in the great hall; a dangerous power lay beneath the pitch of his voice, and when he spoke it rumbled like the tremor of an earthquake. "Valastari you are. A son of Kings. I was there when Sentash murdered Blacker. I was there." He brushed away the blade. Now Dega found he could not move. His arms were frozen. "I had the good fortune of witnessing the whole event."

"Liar!"

Starlock and Crescent cursed in elvish.

"I watched from behind a curtain as Sentash drew his dagger. I would have stopped him too, but as Janastari I let him go. You see, I thought it was a…"

"Death-Match," finished Starlock.

"Exactly! Who am I to interfere with the laws that govern these mortals. They are here for but a fleeting moment of my eternal life."

"You! Because of you. Thousands have died, and all because of you, you who could have stopped it. Now the world stands ready to fall."

"And who do you think will rule it Captain?" he sneered. "You? I certainly hope not."

"It won't be you either."

Dega felt life return to his body. He swung his sword. But Warblade was fast. And he ducked just as the blade traveled over his head. With his free hand he swung the staff, knocking Dega's feet out from under him. Crescent lunged forward to stand over the fallen Ranger. But Warblade countered, tossing the elf backward into a wall.

"His staff!" said Starlock. "Take it!" Without the talisman, she and Warblade would be on equal footing; she whistled, and Belia dove at his face; Dega went for the hand that held the staff. Warblade was not so easily taken. He rebuffed their combined attack, and sent them sprawling in all directions.

"Shall I finish him Starlock?" He pointed his staff at the Ranger's Captain, raising Dega off his feet and up the wall.

"NO!" she raged. "Unhand him!"

"Ah, so you do harbor feelings for this mortal." He shook his staff, twisting his rival so that he arched crazily backward. Dega cried out, dropping his sword.

"Stop! Let him go."

"For what price, my love – for you?"

"Death-Match!"

* * * * * * * *

Camber stopped squirming. He called forth the power; it came crashing over like the waves of the Barrier. He laughed! He stopped. The creature said something. It told him its name. It told him why it needed him. And, it told him where it hid the Winterstone.

* * * * * * * *

A sudden blast shook the earth, raining rock from the top of the cavern.

"What was that?!" Dane yelled.

"An explosion!" Chance sprinted down the tunnel.

The air was dank and heavy; a whisper of mist made running difficult, tripping and slipping over wet rocks. Dane raced up the tunnel after his uncle; he did not want to end up lost in this wretched cave, though he suspected there was probably only one exit. Up ahead, Chance disappeared as he rounded a bend, then came back into view as Dane and Tonni caught up. He collided with the former Ranger and both of them slipped in the wetness. Dane touched air, and his uncle pulled him back by his shirt.

A shaft of bright light shot up from the blackness. Dane covered his eyes from the glare. "Snakes and Spirits!" From his pocket he heard *@%&*!

"Stand back," said Chance, and he shoved Tonni and Dane out of the way.

"What is it?" asked Tonni. Bright stars swirled within the beam of light, filling the void and illuminating the cavern with a soft glow.

"CAMBER!" Dane pointed at a figure twirling amid the stars. He cried out again as his cousin spun slowly past the portal; a blank expression on his face, staring off into space. "He can't see us! CAMBER!!!"

"He can't hear us either," said Chance, and he took a moment to ponder this new predicament. "Dane, try throwing something. But don't hurt him."

Dane reached for his sling. For some reason the guards had overlooked it. Well, it didn't really look like a weapon. He picked a smallish stone off the ground. Not too big, but big enough to knock some sense into his cousin's head.

* * * * * * * *

A wonderful feeling made him shout. The World filled his head; it sang of the past, the present, and the future. He knew what Hawker knew. The Stone gave up its power, and Camber greedily added it to his own. And to think Defél gave it to him willingly. Hooo!!! Heee!!!

* * * * * * * *

"I've Won!!!" shrieked Norii. Hawker's blade pushed through dark green scales as she changed back to her true form; the sword materialized between her breast. "Jessa! What have you done!" Her eyes shifted color, staring at the hand that held the blade, and for a moment her face was clear, now free of the hate that held it in thrall for far too many centuries.

Hawker let go of the sword. Norii's midnight locks wafted in the air. Life and Death came face to face, two opposing ancients held up in more than just the ethereal realm. "What have I done!!!" he screamed.

The wind blew strong. It grew in pitch, reaching a wild velocity. "You have taken a Life," said a voice. Out of a swirling mass of clouds stepped Atrilla. She lifted Norii's wilted form, stroking the long dark hair cascading over her arms. "It is not over yet," she said. "The boy still needs to make his choice."

"Ah! I am lost. I cannot help now. I have taken a Life. Something I swore never to do."

"Norii had to be stopped. You cannot undo what you have already done, do not trouble your heart with regret. You have to go on Jessa. You must see it to the end. Good or Bad."

An eye opened, and it shut quickly, small and cruel, and filled with ghostly green light. He blinked, and Norii's face appeared as it had a moment ago. "Then what? If he makes the wrong choice then all is for naught. Ah, woe, what does it matter?" He lifted his head, and his soft hazel eyes misted as he looked up at Atrilla's face, whiter than the mantle of clouds that framed it. "Why were we sent here Atrilla?"

"I cannot answer that for you Jessa. Each of us has our own belief as to why we are here; it is as individual as our personalities. If you do not know by now then you may never know." The wind gathered strength as she made ready to depart. "Go Jessa. See it to the end."

"Atrillaaaa...."

Hawker felt himself falling. He landed gently on his feet, as if a giant hand had placed him carefully on a chessboard.

"Master!" Lockjaw ran up to meet him, cutting a swath through the melee. Frost-Eye had joined them; on his arm a nasty cut, hastily bound with cloth. "The dead are departing," he said, and even as he finished saying it, they had all but disappeared; and with the last of the shades slipping back into the crevices the armies of the Easterling King broke rank and fled for their lives.

"It's over," breathed Lockjaw. His axe was notched and his armor dented where it had withstood the mightiest of blows.

"Not quite," answered Hawker.

* * * * * * * *

"Death-Match?" Warblade sneered as only he could. "Do you seriously think you can take me down? You were lucky the last time. I was trying not to hurt you. Oh, don't give me that face. I knew you were upset because of Night-Raker. I thought to let you spend your energy, maybe you would listen once you wore yourself out."

"I won fair."

"Fine. Then I accept your challenge. Let's see if the blood of Night-Raker runs true, Janastari."

"No Starlock." Crescent pulled himself off the ground. "He'll kill you. He's too strong."

"He's right. It wouldn't be a fair match," and he concentrated more of the staff's power at Dega, who bit his lip to avoid a shameful scream. Blood flowed from his mouth as Warblade squeezed out more of the life within.

"No weapons."

"Ah, Dar-Ginne. The ancient dance of our ancestors."

"Yes!"

"Alright. I will humor you. But if you lose… "

"To the Death, Warblade. There will be no bargaining."

"Just to be sure we are not interrupted," he waved the staff and Dega found himself standing on his feet alongside Crescent; they could speak but they could not move. "And," Belia dropped down from overhead and alighted on the back of a chair. Warblade checked his spell then carefully placed his staff beside the throne. He vaulted to the floor, and Starlock lunged at him with a flying kick. He dodged it, recovering just in time to duck from her follow-up blow. "Very good," he sneered. "I see you've been practicing."

"Too bad for you," she blocked a volley of punches. But the punches only served to distract, and she received a blow across her mid-section, knocking her off balance and having to take another hit while flipping backward to land on her correct stride.

The fight seemed to go either way, both elves using every combination of kicks, twists, and punches, and though Dega appeared to be calmly waiting for the outcome, inside he squirmed as hard as he could, every fiber trying to shirk off the invisible bonds that held him tight. Finally! He could move a toe. Then a finger. It wasn't much, but it seemed to increase with each blow Warblade took from Starlock. "Crescent," he whispered. The elf raised an eyebrow. Dega had assumed correctly, Crescent's bonds were also weakening.

Another severe kick to his body. Warblade felt a twinge of pain. A broken rib. He tried to hide it by taunting Starlock. "Is that the best you can do? I thought you were Janastari."

"And I thought you had honor." She caught him again in the ribs, and this time his grimace did not go unnoticed.

Dega found he could now move both his arms.

Warblade doubled-over. Starlock moved in for the kill. Up came his fist, sending Night-Raker's daughter flying backward. Blood gushed from her nose; a metallic taste on her tongue. She shook her head to stop the ringing. Warblade was at her side, and he grabbed her by the throat. "You think I'm going to honor you with a clean death?" He hauled her to her knees. "You're going to beg for one by the time I'm done with you. Ha! To think I wanted you as my Queen. But you chose this mortal dog over me! Over ME!"

"You could live and die a hundred times and still you would never be his equal."

He tightened his grip and her eyes rolled to the back of her head.

An explosion rocked the foundations of the fortress; tiles fell from the ceiling, shattering on impact. Warblade turned just in time to see Dega charging from across the room; he rolled with the Ranger across the floor.

Dega smashed his fist into Warblade's ribs. But the elf was a warrior, and he knew how to take the pain, sucking it up and using it as an outlet for his rage; he pushed away the Captain, giving himself room to move. The entire Keep was now shaking, and Warblade's staff fell off the dais; it bounced across the floor.

Dega stretched his arm, fingers brushing the rod just as the shaking brought it that much closer. Warblade snatched a piece of tile, slicing his rival, then scrambled over the Captain to grab the staff.

"HA!" A triumphant shout as his hand wrapped around the talisman. The room pitched and sent him back toward Dega. The Captain took hold of a leg and yanked as hard as he could.

A glint of metal flew straight and true, embedding itself between Warblade's eyes. Wild-eyed and desperate he tried one more time to call forth the power. Then fell to his knees. A stunned look played across his face. Starlock stood before him. "Death-Match," she said.

* * * * * * * *

Power! Sweet, delicious. MASTER OF ALL THINGS. From the tiniest insect to the great beasts in the sea. Now HE Camber Bloodstone would rule the world. And he would start by wiping away those who would oppose him. The Easterling King was no more. He knew that. But his armies were still intact. And so were the Southlanders. And the jungti. So many to crush between his fingers.

The voice in his head again. It begged to be released. "No." he said, and he meant it. "I will not trade you my life." It argued. It told him he couldn't do this. A cage created by his thoughts opened its door, and he pushed Defél inside, slamming it shut. There would be no more Caretakers.

Defél was dying. He knew it. Camber knew it. Norii had bleached him dry. The Mistress of Death had taken his life threads, but Defél held just enough in reserve to keep away her cold dead fingers, enough to keep the Winterstone safe. Only Norii knew that his body housed Astaria's most powerful weapon, but she had not the power to claim it.

The Winterstone was not meant to be used as such; it was his gift to the world; a thing of beauty, treasure like nothing else above or below Astaria. But there were many who wanted its power for themselves, and so Defél took it back, placing it in the one spot where he was assured it would never be found. And there it stayed, becoming a thing of legend; a myth only spoken of in bed-time stories, drifting out of memory, thought, and time, passing away like dry leaves on an Autumn breeze.

Until now. Defél had given it to the boy. The one whose destiny was interwoven with his own. But the boy would not bend, he would not commit to the future, and without his sacrifice Defél was lost.

The pulse of power made Camber shout. Anything was possible. He merely had to think it. His mother's face formed among the stars, floating just out of reach. She cast her eyes toward the sky, looking up with sadness. A desire to see her happy tore at his heart; he would see her smile, this he would do, call forth his father, and make his family whole.

"No," she said. "You must not change the past; what is done must remain."

"Why?" More than anything he wanted to be held in the arms of his mother and father. "I can do this now. We can all be together."

"No Camber," she said, and her voice held back tears. "It is wrong. Great is your gift, do not use it for your own design."

"I don't want to die. I want to live! Help me mother."

"Gladly, I would trade places. But this path is yours, and yours alone. Know that I love you. I have and always will."

* * * * * * * * *

"Throw it now Dane!" Chance yelled; a storm had been brewing since the explosions. The wind was fierce, knocking them backward with its fury. Dane gripped the sling. Whatever it was that Camber was doing, it was definitely gaining momentum. Maybe he should've picked a bigger rock. He let the stone fly just as the back of Camber's head spun into view.

* * * * * * * * *

Something hit the back of his head. Camber blinked. What was he doing? He turned. Dane? Chance! Strange. They were yelling. Tonni was there too, holding tightly to Dane's arm. Then he remembered. Caught between time and space. Caught like a rabbit in a snare. *Your Life for Mine.* NO! The power rose again filling his eyes, ears, and mouth.

* * * * * * * * *

"What's he doing?" yelled Tonni. There was not enough room for the three of them at the opening in the wall and she feared they might fall or be sucked in if they got too close.

"I don't know," answered Dane over the roar of the wind.

"Throw another rock," said a voice from his pocket.

"Wait!" Chance cautioned his nephew. "We need to try something else."

"Dane." Camber stretched his arm toward his cousin; his fingers hit something like glass. Trapped! *Not trapped – Protected,* corrected Defél. He spun slowly, coming right up to the portal. A symbol he instantly recognized - because he wore it around his neck on a fine silver chain – glowed like a ghostly imprint across the glass. He took hold of his necklace and saw that it was indeed one and the same. "Dane. Help me."

Dane tried to grab Camber's arm but a glass barrier blocked his way. He smashed at it. "We can't get him out!"

"He is not allowed to leave." They turned at the sound of a familiar voice.

Tonni dropped Dane's arm; she backed away. "Where'd you come from?" She clutched her cloak with one hand, the other scrambled to catch hold of a rock; the wind now so strong it threatened to carry her away.

"Hawker." Chance looked relieved. "Thank the stars!"

"Camber's destiny is tied to something far greater. He must stay where he is."

"I'm not leaving my nephew! He is a son to me!"

"You must go," Hawker said. "This is no place for you."

Chance drew his sword, and he snarled at the Caretaker. "If you aren't here to help then leave us be." The sword came up, but Lockjaw stepped in front. "Stay your hand," he warned.

"Listen to me," Hawker shouted above the wind. "I was not expecting Camber's fate to be woven with the Caretakers' fabric. But it is. Camber must stay where he is and give himself over to Defél, who is dying. Only with Camber's life can we avoid that which will be the undoing of the world if Defél disappears. Six of us are tied to this world, bound by shackles far older than the stars in the sky. Defél is the core of Astaria. Without his spirit, mountains would crumble, valleys and pastures would disappear. I must preserve Life, but I must also look to the future. Camber is the future. Without him there won't be one."

"I can't leave him," repeated Chance; he touched the portal and a heavy sob fell from his heart. "I won't leave him."

"It is not your place to stay. And at last I understand my purpose on this world." He placed a hand on his shoulder. "Will it comfort you in some small way to know Camber's life will not be completely extinguished; his spirit will live on through Defél, and they will be one and the same. It will be as if Camber has been reborn; a new Caretaker, who will govern both Earth and Underworld." As he said these words the ground shook. "It has begun." He placed his hands upon the glass, and the faint markings of a symbol etched in eldritch light suddenly appeared. "You must get them out of here! Go. Lead them to safety and leave Camber to his destiny."

Chance gritted his teeth. This was beyond anything in his power to stop. "Bitter and cruel is the hand that guides our hearts. And mine has had its share of hardships as of late. But this day will be remembered always as the day I lost faith in those who say they protect and preserve us." The ground erupted, shaking with an incredible force, and the cavern gave a mighty groan.

Dane pressed himself up to the portal. His face hit the glass, and he watched as Camber spun slowly in circles. His orbit brought him alongside the window; Dane put his hand up and Camber touched it from the other side. For a mere moment they were two best friends racing up to Eagle Reach, raiding orchards, and swimming in the cool waters of the Whitewash. Side by side they lay on the banks of the river, basking in the golden warmth of summer. "I'll miss you," he said. And Dane smiled. "I know. I'll come visit."

The moment dissolved, and Dane found himself staring through glass. A tear ran down his cheek as his cousin and best friend floated past the portal and across the starlit void.

His uncle's hand squeezed his shoulder, gently guiding Dane away from the portal. Tonni slipped her hand in his. "Come," she said. "He would want you to live." Chance pushed them both down the tunnel. The ground rumbled beneath their feet.

Lockjaw stood dutifully beside Hawker. "Go with them," he said to his apprentice.

"I stay with you. As always," answered the dwarf.

"Not this time." Hawker bent so he was face to face with his pupil. "You have gained your magic, and you have learned how precious your gift is by your own loss. I believe you will make your decisions carefully and not carelessly."

"But Sir," Lockjaw protested, and Hawker brought up his hand.

"I release you from your commitment."

"But... "

"Go Lockjaw. I need you by my side no longer."

These last words hurt far greater than Hawker had intended. But the dwarf had to leave of his own volition. It was high time he looked to his own future, and perhaps he would use his knowledge and new found power to continue Hawker's work in the world.

The ground rumbled again, louder and with greater ferocity than before. Lockjaw hurried up the tunnel after the others. He took one last look at his mentor, but Hawker turned his back to him, and the dwarf choked a sigh and sprinted up the cavern. Behind him the sound of falling rock signaled the collapse of the tunnel.

* * * * * * * * *

"The place is coming down!" Dega yelled. Tile rained down upon their heads, they scrambled for the exit, but not before Starlock took the staff from Warblade's hand. It was still warm, and she nearly dropped it in disgust, but dared not; it was far too powerful to be left behind. It would be returned to Illianther, where it had been taken by Sentash long ago.

"Look out!"

The ceiling gave way, crashing down in front of the great bronze doors; timber and stone filled the hall. "We can't get around it," cried Crescent.

"Here. This way!" Dega smashed a window with a chunk of marble, clearing away shards of glass. He let Starlock go first, then Crescent, and joined them on the shelf.

"The ledge is giving away! Quickly the banner, we'll use the rope to swing down." He pointed to a flag wrapped around a pole; the cord tying it in place was firmly anchored to the wall by a metal ring. They ran along the narrow ledge, and Dega held Starlock by one arm as she carefully retrieved the rope. "Good riddance," she muttered, cutting the cord and sending the sorcerer's standard into the wind.

Down the wall she went, followed by Crescent, then Dega. The castle shook with force, and the block securing the ring suddenly gave way. The elves dropped onto the parapet, but Dega sailed past. His hand caught the edge, stopping his freefall, and Crescent pulled him to safety.

They sprinted along the length of wall and down the stairs, racing across the courtyard, and reaching the iron gate. The force of the quakes had knocked it off the pins and Starlock kicked at it until it opened just wide enough for all three to squeeze between. Behind them, the Keep groaned, as it unwillingly gave up its supports, crumbling into its foundations. Rock and debris flew past even as they fled across the field. And when Dega looked back, the fortress of the once mighty Easterling King was no more.

XIX

Time and Tide

The mood of the camp was high-spirited despite the many loss of lives. With the fall of the Easterling King and the defeat of his army the defenders of Astaria had much to celebrate. Dega sat with Crescent and Frost-Eye; now reunited after spending several months apart. They spoke excitedly about their adventures, and drew comparisons between their separate journeys. "Ah, I see your face bears the scars of your numerous exploits," remarked Frost-Eye noticing his brother's head wound.

"But even with this reminder, which I think adds a degree of distinction, I am still much fairer than thou," Crescent laughed, and he hugged his twin fiercely. "It would be a bleak world for me if you were no longer in it, and I'm glad we are both here today."

Dega stood and excused himself, not wanting to hear anymore; he had enough war to last a lifetime. He left the twins and went to seek some privacy beneath the forest's silent canopy. As he walked he let his mind wander back to yesterday when he, Starlock, and Crescent were found by none other than Snowblind. Frost-Eye was with the search party and he led them by the mental link he shared with his twin, and Belia had circled above, guiding the party to where the trio waited. He was relieved to learn Chance, Dane, and the girl were already at the camp, and so was Lockjaw, but choked back a bitter lump when he had learned of Camber's fate. Somehow he had always imagined that Camber would come out unscathed, given the extraordinary amount of luck he seemed to carry. Memories of youth came rushing back from the past; he frowned at how he had treated Camber and Dane during those troubled times. The night sky was clear, and he stared up at the stars peeking through treetops. "I'm sorry," he said. "Sorry for everything."

"Apology accepted."

He turned at the sound of Starlock's voice. The branches above his head shook and she landed in front of him.

"Please," he waved his hand. "I wish to be alone."

"Alone?" Her eyes found his; pain and sorrow mirrored in pools of blue. "Why alone?"

"I swore to protect him."

She placed her hand gently on his shoulder and moved closer, a little too close. "Do not condemn yourself to a fate worse than Camber's. I know you feel responsible for what happened, and I know you hurt. All of us are saddened by this loss. But you have done what no other has been able to do. Because of you Sentash has been defeated."

"Not me. Warblade," he corrected.

"You were the one who put everything in motion. Some might argue it was Hawker. But if you hadn't looked after the boy from the moment you set out from Hartland and until we parted ways at the jungti hive he would never have been able to play his part." She stroked his chin and ran her finger over his lips. "Shhh. I know what you would say. But were you not the man I saw on the walls of Vintnorr, or the same who faced down his father's shade, then I would not be standing here right now."

"I don't understand," he said; his face grew warm. His heart beat rapidly between his ears. "I did as any Ranger. I fought for freedom."

"And they fought for you. As did I."

"You?"

"Yes. I see your greatness. You cannot hide it any longer. You shine greater than any hero ever known; your brightness is ten times the sun that eclipses the stars. All are drawn to your presence whether they realize it or not." She pressed her lips to his. And in that moment Dega felt a sudden urge to grab her and not let go. He kissed her hard. In the dark corners of his mind, where all emotion lay conveniently stored, a bottle came unstopped, and with it everything.

Suddenly he tore himself loose. "No. I cannot do this."

"I cannot," he repeated. "I have but one heart to give."

"Then give it to me, and I will keep it safe."

"Then you must keep it safe forever."

She kissed him again, and he laid her gently in the grass, they stayed wrapped in each other's arms all through the night with only the stars as their witness. But the stars were the eyes of Atrilla and she smiled upon the lovers and waved the sun away so that the night lasted twice its natural spell. She listened as they talked; he spoke so softly to her, reminding Atrilla of the Hunter and his lost love, and she wept for their happiness. Pel Ak A Bar gathered her tears and gave them to Shikkarri, who heated them in the sacred fire, then took her prize to Defél; he fused the tears with metal and shaped two solid bands. In the centre of each he set a piece of the Winterstone. He handed the rings to Camber who blessed them with his love. Then Hawker took the rings, and came to stand before Dega and Starlock. They sat up, startled by his sudden appearance.

"Hawker! It cannot be. Does this mean that you have returned with Camber?" asked Dega. Hawker held up his hand. "No," he said. "Camber is with us now; he and Defél are a part of each other. My coming to you at this time is to give you these." He held the rings out in the palm of his hand, and they each took one.

"With these rings you shall be neither mortal or immortal. But you will wear them for as long as you live, growing old and aging not. Together you will choose the hour that you weary of this world, and only by removing the rings from each other's finger shall you leave this world to be transported to the realm of the Caretakers; here you will sit on the left and right side of Atrilla as the *Hand of Justice* and the *Sword of Truth* for all eternity."

Dega placed the ring on Starlock's finger, and she in turn placed the other on his. The Winterstone blazed a brilliant white, sealing the promise of Valastari and Janastari.

Dega woke with the sun shining on his face. Starlock was curled under his arm, hot skin warming his bare chest. He touched her gently on the nose. She opened her eyes and they sparkled mischievously as she ran her hand along the rough stubble on his chin. He smiled, and pulled her close for a kiss.

"Your beard tickles," she laughed.

"Maybe I should shave."

"No don't. I like it. It makes you appear less..."

"Younger?"

"I was going to say naïve."

They returned to camp around mid-day, and Gerharte appeared before them with a ready smile on his face. "My friends," he said, and placed his hands on Dega's shoulders. "I almost gave up looking for you. I was told you were found along with the others ere yesterday, but had not seen your faces. Yet here you both be, alive and well." Dega gladly clasped the arm of Gerharte, and he shook his hand with great force. "I am heartened that you and your Blue-Feathers survived," he said. "And from what Frost-Eye has told me, your timely arrival saved many lives."

"Ah, the war was nearly over when we got here. All that remained was to finish off the great beasts and their masters. Now then, come sit with me and share a drink so that I might hear how it was with you. Too many rumors have spread already about your showdown with this Warblade, and some say his power, even greater than the Easterling King's, had no effect on you. But I would have the truth."

"All in good time my friend. I wish to find someone." He clapped his hand across the warrior's shoulder. "Save me a seat at your fire and I will gladly tell you all I know."

Gerharte nodded to them both. "I will see you later then."

Starlock also took her leave to look for Snowblind, and Dega wandered through the encampment in search of Dane. He was recognized by many and greeted by name almost everywhere he went. Rangers, Elves, Dwarves, all paused to congratulate him, and he, every bit as puzzled as to why so many held him in such high esteem. Anyone would have done the same in his place. At last he found the cadet sitting cross-legged with the girl and Lockjaw, throwing dice into an eager group of gamblers.

"C'mon, c'mon." Dane shook the dice and let them fall.

"Catch," Dega threw a leather pouch at the cadet.

"What's this?" asked Dane; he peered at the coins inside.

"It's yours," answered Dega. All the coins he had taken from Dane since the journey began. Now it seemed like a hundred years ago.

"Thanks," he said, not entirely sure it wasn't some kind of a test. Dega nodded, leaving him to his sport.

"Wow! There's enough here to buy a small castle," said Tonni. "What are you gonna do with it?"

"He's gonna double it," said Buttercup; he sat atop Dane's head watching the action.

"No he's not," said Dane, suddenly he didn't feel much like gambling. He paid out his loss and picked up his dice. "Nope. I think he's going to save it."

Tonni followed him as he strolled past tents, horses, and cook-fires.

"I don't understand," she said, doubling her pace to keep up with his long stride. "Why not turn it over. You could've won big."

"I'm gonna need this once I get back to Hartland."

"Why?" she asked.

"For a house."

"A house?"

"Do you want to camp outdoors all year long?"

She stopped dead in her tracks. Dane turned when he realized she wasn't following. Now what?! He could live a hundred life times and still never understand women. "Well?" he said, walking back to where she stood.

"Well what? Am I suppose to suddenly jump up and down because your taking me back to your homeland as some kind of a prize?"

Buttercup rolled his eyes. "Listen kid. This has all the makings of a trap. If I were you I'd turn around right now. Just keep walking."

"What's that suppose to mean?" he asked, completely ignoring the faerie pulling at his hair. He marched over and stuck his finger in her face. She turned her nose up in the other direction and crossed her arms. "I'm not some harlot you picked up in your travels, Dane Strongbow."

"I never said you were." Now he was completely baffled.

"Oh for the love of... I can't listen to this." Buttercup plugged his ears.

"Did you or did you not say you wanted to leave Shady Haven?"

"My parents brought me up with morals. And even after they died my brothers made sure I stayed that way."

"So what does that have to do with living in Hartland?"

"Here it comes...." Buttercup flew down to his ear. "If you're wise you best be turning around now."

"I will not live with a man unless I'm married first."

"Mmm... mm... arried?" he could hardly get the word out.

Buttercup slapped his forehead. "Hoo boy! I told ya kiddo."

Dane pulled Buttercup off his shoulder and held him out by his wings. "Mind your own business." He shoved the faerie into his pocket. "Married?" he said again. "To you?"

Tonni glared hotly, then dropped her head and a big tear welled up in her eye. Dane suddenly found himself holding her while she sobbed into his shoulder. Years later he would swear an invisible hand had shoved him.

The celebrations lasted nearly a month, and during this time Starlock and Dega found any excuse to slip away. But their disappearances did not go unnoticed by Tonni, who remarked how funny it was that she missed seeing them at the evening meals, or never missed an opportunity to voice her concern that they spent far too much time 'tending the horses' than partaking in the evening's entertainment. This last observation was also mimicked by Dane, now seeming to enjoy less time gambling and more time in the company of Tonni.

Scavengers and trophy-seekers took what they could from the crumbled ruins of the sorcerer's fortress. The pickings were slim, but some still managed to carry away a piece of stone or a shard of metal to cherish as a keepsake. Dega too, found something of interest: a broken sword; the design decorating the haft was one he instantly recognized, a hawk in full wingspan, and when he polished it clean he could clearly see back to back double D's. He smiled to himself, and tucked his treasure with his belongings on the back of his horse.

The day finally came for the long journey home. Dane rode between his uncle and Tonni. Buttercup sat on his finger, and he held the faerie up to his face. "I'm going to miss you."

"Why? Where ya going kid?" The bug-sized creature scrunched his face into a frown.

"Me? I'm not going anywhere. You are. You did your part and now I release you." He shook his finger to give the faerie a proper send off. Then shook it harder as Buttercup stayed in place. Frustrated, he held his hand upside-down and shook with great force. The faerie had firmly wrapped his talons around Dane's finger. "Get off! I release you!"

"No thanks. I think I'll hang out with you and your girl for awhile," he inspected one of his toenails as he spoke.

"Ummm, I thought you wanted your freedom."

"Nah! I think I'll hitch a ride to this place you keep talking about. What's it called? Oh yeah... Hartland."

"Why?"

Buttercup stopped filing his nail and took hold of Dane's face with his tiny hands. "Because if the rest of the townsfolk are anything like you I'll have a field day!"

Crossing back over the Hook took far less time with no foes to block the way; an endless column of cavalry and infantry, made up of Elves, Dwarves, and Men. *The Last Alliance.* The war had rebuilt relations between the races; King Stonefinger was eager to start trading with Snowblind, who coveted dwarven-steel above all else. In return,

Snowblind promised to open communications between Winterleaf and Willowsnap's people. Dega also agreed to help the Dwarven King bring his trade to Hartland, and from there it would spread across the Northlands to the most remote locations. Even Gerharte swore to upkeep peaceful relations with his newly formed allies. He said his good-byes to Dega. "You will always be welcome in my Halls, and I not only salute you as both friend and honorary Blue-Feather, but I bow my head in your presence and recognize your lineage as King of the Valastari and thereby Girt bends her knee."

Dega held up his hand. "Never have I wanted the crown. Had I known my heritage from the beginning I would still choose not to pursue it." He reached over and shook the warrior's hand. "Call me friend, and I will gladly accept your invitation. But do not call me liege for I dismiss the title as quick as I would that of tyrant."

"Your spirit is ancient and your tam is powerful. You, Dega Darkhawk, are a leader of Men whether you like it or not," and he spurred his horse toward the rolling plains of Girt, taking his Fighting Blue-Feathers with him.

* * * * * * * *

Lockjaw could hardly contain his excitement as he led the Ironfist army home. It seemed strange, returning without Hawker; the wizard and he had traveled side-by-side for two and a half centuries, now he traveled alone. But Shard was waiting.

The pace quickened as the dwarves drew ever nearer to their warren. Smoke curled into the bright blue afternoon sky; Lockjaw's face changed from joy to panic, and was reflected on the faces of his brethren as every pair of eyes scanned the landscape. The grass was charred. Trees that had stood for thousands of years offering shade to the inhabitants of Ironfist were twisted and black, many still smoldering. Carrion fed on the dead, heaped in piles to either side of the secret entrance.

The entrance! Lockjaw raced to where the rock had been forced open, and beat his breast. "NOOOOO!!!" Words could not express his anguish. Something tingled under his tunic and he pulled loose the amulet. The rubble blocking the porch was quickly cleared away; he entered the passage clutching Shard's charm. A dwarf came running up the tunnel with axe in hand. As soon as he saw Lockjaw he dropped to his knee and bowed his head. Soon the passage was filled as the returning army climbed into the South porch, and more and more dwarves came to see what new threat entered their realm.

"What has happened here?! Where is my brother! Where is Grimbeard?"

Not one dwarf who knelt before him dared to utter a word.

"Where is Grimbeard?! I wish to speak with him." Lockjaw repeated. His voice grew angry. Why wouldn't they answer? "Is there one among you with a tongue in his head!"

"Grimbeard is dead." The voice belonged to Shard. Lockjaw dropped his pack. Lovely was that face, but for the grief betraying its ugly torment. "Oh Lockjaw," she wrapped her arms around him.

"Shard. Shard." He held her out at arm's length. "What happened?"

"The K'Ahtars."

"Hail Lockjaw. Hail the King." Shard was abruptly cut off by the army of dwarves chanting Lockjaw's name. It was picked up by the survivors of Ironfist and grew to a fever pitch. When he entered the Atrium he barely saw the wreckage, for every single dwarf and dwarx left alive filled the emerald dome, cheering his return.

* * * * * * * *

Today marked one year to the day that Lockjaw had buried his brother; a burial fit for a King, done in the ancient and unchanging custom of the dwarves. Atop the cairn was a simple marker that stated Grimbeard's lineage and date of death. Lockjaw planned to commission a marble likeness and place it in the Atrium. But not today. Today was his wedding day. And he came only to ask his brother for forgiveness. "Wish me well," and taking a rose he laid it across the tomb.

Many guests had journeyed far from home, and many more were still arriving for the wedding feast that would last seven days and seven nights. Among those held in highest awe were King Stonefinger of Stone-Haven, the Lord and Lady of Girt and their household, Winterleaf and Dovetail of Illianther, and several other notable elvish folk. Only Snowblind had declined the invitation, but he sent a fine gift with Willowsnap for the new Ironfist King and his Queen.

But it was the arrival of his former companions that caused Lockjaw's face to light up. He embraced them each, and introduced them to Shard, she happily recalled the Captain and his cadet whom she had seen briefly on their first visit to the warren.

"My heart is glad to finally meet you," she said to Dega. "Lockjaw has told me how you used your wits to save them from the tambril, and many other stories of your selfless deeds." Dega kissed her tiny hand, and thanked her for such kind words. She turned to Starlock. "The dwarxen of Ironfist welcome she who is a great warrior in her own right. Know that it was us who saved our home and chased away the K'Ahtars. I hope one day we will find ourselves as equals, but your valor exceeds our reach until such a time."

Starlock smiled at the dwarx, such a diminutive lady with a heart of a lion, and she handed Shard one of her daggers; all the dwarves, including Lockjaw, gasped at such an inappropriate gift for a Queen who was likened to Shale, Mother of all Dwarves. "A gift for you then," she said. "A strong warrior needs a good sword."

Shard took the dagger; it was truly a sword fit for a lady of her miniature stature. "I will cherish this gift always, and practice with it as often as I can. I thank you." She placed the dagger in the hands of Sparkle, who held it out as though it were a serpent, handing it quickly to the nearest dwarf.

The twins bowed gracefully, and Shard laughed. "I cannot tell you apart."

"I'm the handsome one," said Crescent, and placed a kiss on her delicate hand.

Lastly, she spoke to Dane. "You are the one responsible for teaching Lockjaw that game. It has infested our warren like a colony of ants. Everywhere I turn I see dwarves playing with those ivory stones. I do not understand this new diversion but I hope that while you're here you will find the time to teach me."

"Shard!" Lockjaw turned red with embarrassment. "First a sword and now dice. I do not believe my beard!"

"It is my opinion that the dwarxen have been kept in the dark far too long. I plan to make some changes, and very soon." She shook her finger at Lockjaw, but he only smiled. "You already have. Is it not enough that you have regulated for dwarxen to wander freely through the warren? Do you not know the havoc you have now created?"

Dovetail raised her eyebrows, and turned to Winterleaf. "So it begins."

They sat at the head table dressed in royal finery, and it was like Khollinther during the height of her golden glory. The days that followed found Lockjaw in the company of Dane and Dega as much as possible. They talked of Camber and of Hawker. It was then that Dega showed him the ring given by Hawker. The dwarf inspected the piece of Winterstone set like white fire on his finger. "It has a radiance like none other. I can feel its potency." He dropped his head. "I wonder if Hawker will ever come back? I would like for him to see with his own eyes what the student has learned." With the magic that was bestowed upon him he had rebuilt the warren. Outside, the trees again grew tall and the grass flushed brilliant green; the only traces of devastation now remained in the memory of the dwarves.

"You are too hard on yourself," said Dega. "It's time to let go of the past and embrace the future."

Lockjaw sighed. "I know."

"Why don't we visit the forges?" Dane was eager to see Shikkarri's gift one more time. Buttercup flew from his pocket to the top of his head; he too, was eager to see this eternal flame, especially since he might find some way to create another mishap.

A smile appeared on Lockjaw's face, and he shook his finger at Dane, cadet no longer but still with the same youthful exuberance that he exhibited on his first visit. "As long as you keep your hands to yourself."

"You'd be surprised where he puts his hands," said the faerie. Dane pulled him off his head and stuffed him back into his pocket, fastening the button.

On the last evening of celebration Lockjaw and Shard handed each person a gift. To Winterleaf and Dovetail they gave two leather-bound tomes belonging to the legendary Ironfist, upon their yellowed pages was the history of the Dwarves in the King's own words. "This is too great a gift," said Winterleaf as he accepted the books.

"We are writing a new history now," answered Lockjaw, "and I will sleep better at night knowing they will be forever safe in Illianther's archives."

"Then we shall honor them in a special place, and you may view them whenever you wish."

To Crescent and Frost-Eye he gave a pair of matching rings, each with a stunning emerald in the center. "These belonged to my brother and I," said Lockjaw. "It would gladden my heart to see them on the hands of brothers once more."

"And we shall never remove them," answered Crescent; he and Frost-Eye took the rings, placing them on their fingers.

To Gerharte and the Lords of his household he gave swords of dwarven-steel, the craftsmanship exquisitely fine. The King of Girt brandished his with a flourish. "Never then have I seen such a weapon, so light but so powerful. I thank you." To Gretchen and her Ladies, the King and Queen gave bracelets of gold, each trinket worked with a rainbow of gems.

"I have no gift for you," he said to Stonefinger. "For your warren is by far the largest and the most grand of any of its time, and I would be ashamed to give you something that would be inferior for the Halls of Stone-Haven."

Stonefinger laughed, and he slapped Lockjaw on his back. "I already have your gift," he said. And Lockjaw looked at Shard, not sure of his meaning. "It is a gift just to see how happy you have made my niece." He kissed the lovely hand of Shard. "And, I might add, that I'm determined to see the dwarxen of Stone-Haven enjoy the same liberties as they do in Ironfist. Mayhap this change will encourage a new generation of dwarves and increase our importance in this world."

"Thank you," she said. "It's truly a dream to be realized."

From the top of Dane's head, Buttercup clasped his tiny hands, mimicking Shard, "It's truly a dream."

Lockjaw handed Chance an ivory carving, no bigger than his hand, but the artist who rendered the piece had captured the features of Camber perfectly, and Chance nearly wept as he took the treasure. "This is by far the greatest gift I shall ever receive," he said. "Know that I will look upon it daily, though I'm afraid I might wear down its delicate craftsmanship."

"Then if you happen to do so, come visit, and I shall see you leave with it made perfect and whole as this day." Lockjaw gave Chance a friendly shake, before taking Dega by the hand. "I'm glad you told me of Hawker, and though my heart grieves it was not me he spent his last hour with I am greatly relieved he has not departed this world, and this gives me hope."

"There is no doubt in my mind that someday he will return," answered Dega.

"Until that day then," said Lockjaw.

Shard passed him something wrapped carefully in silks. "I wanted your gift to have great importance," he passed the bundle to Dega who quickly unwrapped it, revealing a diary.

"Where'd you get this," he said, flipping open the pages. He immediately recognized the meticulous handwriting of his father. Lockjaw's face flushed, whether from pride at having given his friend the ultimate present or from embarrassment at having to come clean and tell how he obtained the journal. But he stared at the ground instead of the Captain's fearless blue eyes. "I had some help," he said.

Dega frowned. "Oh? From where?"

"From Starlock."

Now more surprised than ever he turned and faced the elf. "When did you get this?"

"It was in my library," she said. "I completely forgot about it until I came across it by accident. I seem to recall it turned up around the same time Hawker had sent me on his fountain quest. I glanced at it once and shoved it on the shelf; it has sat in the same spot since."

He carefully wrapped it back in the silks and tucked it inside his coat. "Thank you. I never imagined such a thing existed."

"Ah!" Shard came forward. "I would be pleased if Starlock would now accept my gift." She handed the elf an arrow. It looked oddly familiar. The shaft was bent and the point dulled.

"This is one of mine."

"Yes it is," agreed Shard. "It's the same arrow you shot at Hawker when he coaxed you into joining the company. Lockjaw has kept it all this time."

She twirled it around her fingers, and chuckled.

Dega raised his eyebrow. "What's so funny?"

"To think I nearly shot it through his head."

"I doubt it would have stopped his meddling," said Lockjaw. He left Dane's gift for last. Now he clapped his hands, and two dwarves stepped forward carrying a crystal container. A brilliant flame shimmered inside, soft orange bouncing off the crystal's facets, sparkling like a million tiny suns. "Shikkarri's sacred flame," he said. "And it has never gone out."

* * * * * * * * *

Dane rode alongside his uncle, down the road that led to Hartland's sprawling farmlands. When they crossed the bridge, they turned their horses toward home. In his pack he carried letters from Dega addressed to certain high-ranking officers in Hartland's Rangers.

One was for Gareth, who was now the Captain in Dega's place and from what Dane had learned was widely recognized as the key player responsible for keeping the Easterlings at bay. Gareth had a big hand in bringing the Alliance together, and with the help of Dane and Dega he was able to maintain those carefully managed relations. The officer and his cadet had been decorated with the highest honors and officially discharged from the cavalry. Now they worked "unofficially" as ambassadors of good faith.

"So how is the Mrs.?" asked Chance.

His nephew shrugged. "It's like living with a different person everyday. Sometimes it's best if I never get within ten feet of the house, and lately it's been especially bad since she found out her brothers are coming for a visit."

"I told ya to run kid." Buttercup sat atop his head.

"Pregnancy will do that to women," said Chance. "You should have seen your mother when she was pregnant with you. I felt sorry for your father. He spent more nights at my place than he did at home. That's how I got the spare room."

"Why didn't you mention this before?" complained Dane. He could barely make out his uncle in the dark as they rode beneath the tree-lined lane that led to the Strongbow household. He and Tonni had moved in with his parents until their house was finished. But the way Tonni had been snapping lately three walls and no roof was sounding pretty darn good.

"If I told you, you wouldn't have listened anyway."

"That's because she's got him wrapped around her finger," chortled the faerie. He began to recite a less than wholesome poem about a young girl with a curl, and Dane noted that most of the words would have sent his mother running for a bar of soap. Funny how she had taken to Tonni. The two of them never seemed to run out of things for him to do, and when he did find time to himself they thought him idle. He took to hiding in the woodshed with his father.

"How come you never married Uncle Chance?" Dane asked; they stopped in front of the cottage. A cozy glow emanated from every window; a miniature haven in the hand of night. Dane dismounted. The front door opened, spilling light onto the porch, and two figures, one very much pregnant, stepped out into the cool evening air.

"Well son, I've never been one for fetters."

* * * * * * * *

Life in Hartland, and especially around the old Ranger's barracks was slowly returning to normal. Sure there was the odd happening now and then, and visits from strange folk, sometimes an elf or a dwarf was enough to create a stir, throwing the townsfolk into a frenzy of gossip and tall tales, but for the most part, the people of Hartland had quickly gone back to their peaceful rural lives, seeming to slough off the horrors of war, shedding it like an old skin.

Jules walked alongside Sergeant Weyland, leading his horse back to the stables after finishing up with a group of green cadets in the exercise ring. He and the Sergeant had become good friends, and Jules was as much a permanent fixture around the stables as Weyland. He had cause to celebrate too – he had just been promoted to Corporal.

"Congratulations Son." Weyland grinned and gave him a mighty slap across his back. Three years ago he would have fallen over from the force of the blow. But Jules was not that same Jules who had at one time been all but afraid of his own shadow. Three years had changed him. He had seen death – stared it down from the end of a sword point. *And*, he had grown - in mind and in body. The sun beat down upon them both; the day had been a hot one, and as Jules walked, the shadow he cast was every bit as broad and muscular as the stable sergeant's. Yes, he had changed.

"Come, come, why so pensive?" asked Weyland. The young man he had come to know like a son was strangely quiet.

"Why didn't you take the Lieutenant's post?" he asked, sliding his saddle off the stallion. It had been offered to Weyland after Gareth was made Captain in Dega's stead. He and Dane were now ambassadors of some sort. Jules still didn't quite understand it all, even when Hansil tried unsuccessfully to explain it.

"How could I leave all this open space for four walls and a desk," said Weyland; he threw hay into the stallion's stall.

Jules grinned. He knew exactly how the Sergeant felt. Horses were like people, each with their own personality. And when he felt the need to reflect, it was to the stables he went, seeking comfort in the quiet presence of his equine friends. He even slept in the loft. It was where he had first laid his head after learning of Camber's fate.

"Don't be sad," Dane had tried to reassure him. "Be happy. Camber is all around us now. He's part of this world instead of in it." But Jules cried. He didn't care, and was not ashamed of his tears.

Yes. He was the only one left. Even Dega was gone. He came back for his mother and took her away west. Now Dane lived with his wife and children on the Darkhawk's old farmstead. A gift from Dega no less! Jules chuckled softly to himself. Dane married. And to some foreign girl he met in his travels! And Dega now living among the elves. His sister had a fit when she heard that the Captain had lost his heart to an elvish maiden.

Yep. Out of three of them, only he remained in the service of Hartland's Rangers. He tucked away his grooming kit and he and the Sergeant walked back to the barracks. The sun slowly sunk below the horizon and lit the sky like crimson fire.

"Have you thought of a name for him yet?" asked Weyland. The big black was now tame as a kitten, and if Jules had let him, he would've followed him right into the barracks.

"Yeah," he said. "Freedom."

XX

Epilogue

A weathered traveler climbed the grassy summit of a small rounded hillock. In his hand he carried a staff. It was not a walking staff. The traveler needed no such aid. His legs were sturdy, though his back was bent from too many turns of the seasons. He had seen more than his share. And it showed in the creases of his face, and in the snowy white of his beard. At last he toiled to the top, and when he got there he contemplated sitting down to catch his breath. No. He would not. He came here to do something. And placing his hand where he thought the exact center must be, he thrust his staff deep into the hilltop, plunging it more than a third of the way up the shaft.

"You said to me once that Dwarves lack a sense of humor. And I do not doubt this – for I know it is true enough. But I come here today to prove to you at least one Dwarf can match your wit." He pointed his finger at the base of his staff and began to chant. The staff shimmered blue, and thickened into the trunk of a tree. Limbs sprouted strong, and green leaves grew thick, ripening with yellow fruit. The tree grew heavy from its bounty; the branches spreading like the span of the ancient oak in the courtyard of Illianther. It sagged with the weight of its fruit, and Lockjaw picked one from a nearby limb.

"These are lemons my friend," and he chuckled softly. "Now when people come to visit Lightfoot they will partake of his fruit, and you will witness how they pucker. Lemons are sour to taste, but they leave a lasting impression – like you did on my soul." And he walked away, knowing that the last of the magic he once desired had been used to repay an old debt. He would never do magic again.

ISBN 1425135668